THE ANCHOR BOOK OF

NEW AMERICAN
SHORT STORIES

THE ANCHOR BOOK OF
NEW AMERICAN
SHORT STORIES

edited by
BEN MARCUS

ANCHOR BOOKS
A Division of Random House, Inc.
New York

AN ANCHOR BOOKS ORIGINAL, AUGUST 2004

Copyright © 2004 by Ben Marcus

All rights reserved under International and Pan-American Copyright Conventions. Published in the United States by Anchor Books, a division of Random House, Inc., New York, and simultaneously in Canada by Random House of Canada Limited, Toronto.

Anchor Books and colophon are registered trademarks of Random House, Inc.

Permissions can be found at the end of the book.

Library of Congress Cataloging-in-Publication Data
The Anchor book of new American short stories / edited by Ben Marcus.
p.   cm.
ISBN 1-4000-3482-5 (pbk.)
1. Short stories, American. 2. United States—Social life and customs—
Fiction. 3. American fiction—20th century. 4. American fiction—21st
century. I. Marcus, Ben, 1967–
PS648.S5A57 2004
813'.010805—dc22   2003070896

Book design by Johanna S. Roebas

www.anchorbooks.com

Printed in the United States of America
10 9 8 7 6

CONTENTS

CONTENTS *vii*

Introduction

This was back when houses were bigger than people, and people ate food, and air was what birds flew through. If you were me, you pretended to be asleep when story hour ended, when the person obligated to read to you closed the book and announced your bedtime. You faked sleep not because you particularly cared for being carried upstairs and tucked into bed. Being carried can hurt, slung over someone's massive back, stomach crushed into a shoulder, a bigger person's bones grinding into your own. Being carried is something we are supposed to want but that I always found wanting—it requires more exertion than skipping upstairs under one's own power. No, faking sleep after a story ended was the only way to have private time, an afterlude of silence so the story could bloom inside you, and not get ruined by explanations and claims and arguments. When you stayed asleep, the subject could not change and the story could not be defeated by the trivia of aftermath that seeks to noise up the room.

What did you think?

What was it about?

How do you feel?

These are not bad questions. Some people get paid to ask or answer them. They reveal us yearning to be interesting in the fashion of our interesting stories, trying to live up to the energy we have just so greedily devoured. We might be at our best when we pursue such questions, thinking out loud in the electrified periphery a story creates. But I wanted instead, during those times, to keep my eyes closed and hear nothing more. The story was sufficient and it would echo on after it finished. I was suspicious of discussion because I suspected that magic was at work, the kind that asked for silence. The best stories were stun guns that held my attention completely, leaving me paralyzed on the outside, but very nearly spasming within.

It is this place, "within," where all stories take place, despite their ruse to the contrary. We talk about the world of a story, or its setting, but stories are only set inside us. We keep making up other names for our interior. Setting is a myth, like all properties of a story. When it succeeds, we insist it is not a myth. We call this believability. The words *real* or *realistic* are curious, because stories are not real whatsoever. Other misnomers abound. A voice in a short story is, in fact, not something you hear but something you see. This is a strange attribute of writing—its silence. A literary voice is silence that we decorate—we spray a private noise into it. We, the readers, are the true speakers of the stories we read. Yes, storytelling was oral from the beginning, and we've all sat through public readings and books-on-tape. But the very probable fact is that no one is reading this to you but yourself, and you are most likely not even moving your lips. Yet it comes to you in a kind of sound that only your eye enables. If you are hearing the words in your head, that is your business. If I were to watch you read this, I would hear nothing but your own fidgets. I would not know your thoughts. One of our last privacies is to plot this way, while reading.

The question I wanted to ask, as I read the stories that would fill this book, was not: *What is the plot,* but rather, *What is the story plotting for?* Not: *What is it about,* but *How is it going about its business,* whatever its business might be? What is the story's tactic of mattering, its strategy to last inside a reader? How is it scheming to be something I might care about?

Plot, in fiction, usually refers to "the series of events consisting of an outline of the action of a narrative." But it seems hard to ignore those other, better meanings of plot, such as: small piece of ground. In this sense, plot would refer to setting, the space in which a story occurs. The question we would ask about a story would be not: *What is the plot,* but *What plot does it occur on?* The plot would be what we bring, as readers, to a story. A place for the story to come to life inside us. Plot would be another name for our bodies, carved hollow to receive something amazing.

When we plot for something, we devise secretly, we conspire. It is in this sense that plot might best concern fiction, when it suggests mystery, unrevealed conditions driving the characters or language through a story. If a story has a plot in this sense, then, it is what the story is withholding, not what it tells. Plot is the hidden machinery that animates a story. When plots are revealed they cease being plots. They are uncovered, as tedious as a fully nude person. Good fiction is busy keeping secrets, protecting its plots. The story, then, is what the story is hiding, and the hide is indeed a piece of skin, whose effect is to *conceal the body.*

How it does this is what we might call style—the focus of this book. As various as the methods of storytelling are here, what unites these stories, what might be called their shared business, is a relentless drive to matter, to mean something, to make feeling where there was none. My idea was to read hundreds of stories, in as many styles as I could find. I wanted to align contemporary American story writers who might have radically different ways of getting to a similar place. In each case as I sat down to read, I had to be turned from a somewhat dull, unpromising person into one enlivened, antagonized, buttressed, awed, stunned by what he was reading. I required to be transformed, however little I believed that it could happen. I was asking for something I no doubt did not deserve, but these stories were more than capable of demanding my attention. In twenty-nine separate but ingenious ways, these stories seek permanent residence within a reader. They strive to become an emotional or intellectual cargo that might accompany us wherever, or however, we go. Stories conspire not to be forgotten; they scheme to outlast their moment. That they each do it with entirely different methods, from separate but thriving literary traditions, attests that the current practice of the short story has ample methods of matterfulness and that it might be shortsighted of us to believe that only one tradition of fiction might succeed.

If we are made by what we read, if language truly builds people into what they are, how they think, the depth with which they feel, then these stories are, to me, premium material for that construction project. You could build a civilization with them. They are toolkits for the future. They could be projected by megaphone onto an empty field and people would grow there. These stories prove that many stylistic literary traditions, from brainy to simple, plain to complex, coldly immoral to forgiving, lyrical to terse, easy to difficult, weird to mundane, realist to experimental, long to short, sad to happy, bitter to accepting, circuitous to direct, and cruel to kind, can produce colossal feeling and manage to be true, deep, memorable, and brilliant.

There are allegedly two stories to tell: a stranger comes to town, or a person goes on a trip. If you think you know another story, it is supposedly toiling in the powerful shadow of one of these. This was an idea I paid to hear. It came packaged with my college education. Like many provocative ideas, it is grossly untrue in ways we needn't bother revealing, and will no doubt continue to make people angry for years to come. But the error of this arrogant claim, like any good mistake, provides some genuine provocation: that we have very little to say to ourselves, in our stories, but many ways of saying it, like the fabled one-word language with thousands of pronunciations. To communicate something new, members of this society need only pronounce the single word differently. The mouth becomes the sole agent of originality.

Stories keep mattering by reimagining their own methods, manners, and techniques. A writer has to believe, and prove, that there are, if not new stories, then new ways of telling the old ones. A stylist is an artist of diction, a grammarist, a shaper of sentences, who recognizes language as the sole technology at work in a story. A stylist seeks to master that technology, to not let it lead or dictate terms, but to control it and make it produce whatever effects the stylist desires.

If any story must concern us, then, it is the *way* our very few stories are told, and I hope that is the story this anthology tells. As long as we keep looking and reading, we'll discover that the English language has endless ways of making our stories matter. This resource will not be exhausted. In other words, it is asking to be stylized in a delirious number of ways.

This anthology presents twenty-nine of those ways, and it readily admits that these ways are not really new, in the literal sense, arising from nowhere, with no precedents or contexts. Calling them new, other than indicating that they are recent, is a way of noticing how they have soaked up the styles and techniques of the literary habits—well-known and otherwise—before them. It is a way of saying that the writers are laboring in an entirely new stylistic moment, and these are the voices they have carved out for their stories. This is their guess at what literary styles will puncture our inattention and qualify as relevancies. The writers here have absorbed the fiction methods of the past and added their own hunches, instincts, desires, fears, cravings, and artfulness to command a reader's attention in compelling ways.

I tried to include a single vigorous practitioner of each thriving literary style I could identify, which doesn't mean I was trying to label everyone I read, but rather that some voices sounded louder, purer, more forceful, and lasted longer in my head, while other stories seemed to be sharing a single voice. It is hard, when reading deeply into the current American short story, to ignore certain collective passions, techniques, or beliefs of what a story should be and how it should operate. There are movements and schools, camps and gangs. I did my best to read their best work: the realists, the metafictionists, the lyricists of the south, the brainy storyless writers who obsess over information, the writers using nonfiction forms for fiction's purposes, the child-voiced writers who eschew all forms of knowingness, the patient, detail-oriented slice-of-life writers, the domestic minimalists, and the fabulist maximalists (yes, there are other groups, and no, I don't really subscribe to these labels). In doing this reading and research, in asking for lists of writers from everyone I knew, I often discovered that my favorite writers from the various camps were all awkward members of any one group, not comfortably situated in a single rigid aesthetic, but rather embracing or originalizing several styles at once. In short, they helped make these subcategories meaningless.

What I found in my reading was an amazing range of styles, beliefs, methods, ideologies, and instincts. Writers are reaffirming tradition, ignoring it, or subverting it. Where once we could have observed a divide between the kind of fiction we call realist and that which we might call innovative or experimental—anthologies themselves have often reinforced these divisions, seeking ever-more specific stylistic subcategories—now there are writers synthesizing the heartfelt and cerebral approaches, the traditional with the innovative impulse, with astonishing results. But let's admit right now that these categories can have a crushing effect: they are first of all inexact, they reduce the aim of the writer, they can have derogatory overtones, and they can unfortunately shape a reader's impression of the work before even one word has been read. This is true not just of terms like postmodern, or realist, but also lyrical, southern, gothic, minimalist, metafictional, academic, or naive.

So then, without using classifiers, a note about the various traditions of the short story represented in this book: some seem easy to read, some seem hard, some don't seem like stories at all. Some seem to read themselves, while others must nearly be studied like a book of codes, evading understanding. Some we can escape into, others we feel we must very nearly escape from. The stories are written simply, intricately, with declared or concealed feeling, with sentences freighted with adjectives and modifiers of every sort, or in partial sentences with made-up words. The usage, diction, and grammar might be familiar, the kind we all use every day, or it might be exceedingly strange, stylized, in the shape of sentences we've never seen before. The voice could be that of a child or of a jaded professor, hauntingly naive or disturbingly knowing. Some stories want you aware of their technique, others seek to hide it. Some admit to being fictional, others would not do so even at gunpoint. In other words, to each style is a counterpoint, not in argument against it, but to complement it. I see the cohabitation of these stories as proof that style's burden is being met.

The terrible secret about short stories is that they are made of language. Entirely. Nothing else goes into them. They might be plausible or implausible, but they are always invented actions created for our interior. Yet we are still more comfortable discussing a story's *imagery.* Discussions of language can render us mute. Stories are language-made hallucinations, fabrications that persuade us to believe in them for their duration. They happen on the inside and we can keep them secret. But the word language, used in relation to writing, seems to convey something heavy, cerebral, forbidding, a promise of readerly labor. It is frequently omitted during discussions of our finer stories. Its citation in relation to a writer can often indicate what a reader might call unreadability or difficulty.

But character is, after all, a piece of language slapped to life by a writer. So is plot. And setting. And conflict. These are acts of language rubbed over the air to make people appear. We could list all the traits of fiction we care for and find that none of them would exist if it weren't for language, one word after another, constructing a world we believe in.

We should not forget that to be a fine story writer is to be an artist of language, someone who uses sentences to produce feeling. However simple this sounds, there is something extraordinary about it to me, given how few sentences that we encounter in our daily lives can manage to make us feel anything, to stir us toward revelation. The sentence, as a technology, is used for so many rote exchanges, so many basic communication requirements, that to rescue it from these necessary mundanities, to turn it into feeling, is to do something strenuous and heroic. But language is also the way we communicate privately to ourselves, the true code of our inner lives, and to be a story writer is to know this, to tap into and reveal those ways of personal address we reserve for the private, necessary messages we send ourselves, when we think no one is listening.

Ben Marcus

THE ANCHOR BOOK OF

NEW AMERICAN
SHORT STORIES

SEA OAK

GEORGE SAUNDERS

At six Mr. Frendt comes on the PA and shouts, "Welcome to Joysticks!" Then he announces Shirts Off. We take off our flight jackets and fold them up. We take off our shirts and fold them up. Our scarves we leave on. Thomas Kirster's our beautiful boy. He's got long muscles and bright-blue eyes. The minute his shirt comes off two fat ladies hustle up the aisle and stick some money in his pants and ask will he be their Pilot. He says sure. He brings their salads. He brings their soups. My phone rings and the caller tells me to come see her in the Spitfire mock-up. Does she want me to be her Pilot? I'm hoping. Inside the Spitfire is Margie, who says she's been diagnosed with Chronic Shyness Syndrome, then hands me an Instamatic and offers me ten bucks for a close-up of Thomas's tush.

Do I do it? Yes I do.

It could be worse. It is worse for Lloyd Betts. Lately he's put on weight and his hair's gone thin. He doesn't get a call all shift and waits zero tables and winds up sitting on the P-51 wing, playing solitaire in a hunched-over position that gives him big gut rolls.

I Pilot six tables and make forty dollars in tips plus five an hour in salary.

After closing we sit on the floor for Debriefing. "There are times," Mr. Frendt says, "when one must move gracefully to the next station in life, like for example certain women in Africa or Brazil, I forget which, who either color their faces or don some kind of distinctive headdress upon achieving menopause. Are you with me? One of our ranks must now leave us. No one is an island in terms of being thought cute forever, and so today we must say good-bye to our friend Lloyd. Lloyd, stand up so we can say good-bye to you. I'm sorry. We are all so very sorry."

"Oh God," says Lloyd. "Let this not be true."

But it's true. Lloyd's finished. We give him a round of applause, and Frendt gives him a Farewell Pen and the contents of his locker in a trash bag and out he goes. Poor Lloyd. He's got a wife and two kids and a sad little duplex on Self-Storage Parkway.

"It's been a pleasure!" he shouts desperately from the doorway, trying not to burn any bridges.

What a stressful workplace. The minute your Cute Rating drops you're a goner. Guests rank us as Knockout, Honeypie, Adequate, or Stinker. Not that I'm complaining. At least I'm working. At least I'm not a Stinker like Lloyd.

I'm a solid Honeypie/Adequate, heading home with forty bucks cash.

At Sea Oak there's no sea and no oak, just a hundred subsidized apartments and a rear view of FedEx. Min and Jade are feeding their babies while watching *How My Child Died Violently*. Min's my sister. Jade's our cousin. *How My Child Died Violently* is hosted by Matt Merton, a six-foot-five blond who's always giving the parents shoulder rubs and telling them they've been sainted by pain. Today's show features a ten-year-old who killed a five-year-old for refusing to join his gang. The ten-year-old strangled the five-year-old with a jump rope, filled his mouth with baseball cards, then locked himself in the bathroom and wouldn't come out until his parents agreed to take him to FunTimeZone, where he confessed, then dove screaming into a mesh cage full of plastic balls. The audience is shrieking threats at the parents of the killer while the parents of the victim urge restraint and forgiveness to such an extent that finally the audience starts shrieking threats at them too. Then it's a commercial. Min and Jade put down the babies and light cigarettes and pace the room while studying aloud for their GEDs. It doesn't look good. Jade says "regicide" is a virus. Min locates Biafra one planet from Saturn. I offer to help and they start yelling at me for condescending.

"You're lucky, man!" my sister says. "You did high school. You got your frigging diploma. We don't. That's why we have to do this GED shit. If we had our diplomas we could just watch TV and not be all distracted."

"Really," says Jade. "Now shut it, chick! We got to study. Show's almost on."

They debate how many sides a triangle has. They agree that Churchill was in opera. Matt Merton comes back and explains that last week's show on suicide, in which the parents watched a reenactment of their son's suicide, was a healing process for the parents, then shows a video of the parents admitting it was a healing process.

My sister's baby is Troy. Jade's baby is Mac. They crawl off into the kitchen and Troy gets his finger caught in the heat vent. Min rushes over and starts pulling.

"Jesus freaking Christ!" screams Jade. "Watch it! Stop yanking on him and get the freaking Vaseline. You're going to give him a really long arm, man!"

Troy starts crying. Mac starts crying. I go over and free Troy no problem. Meanwhile Jade and Min get in a slap fight and nearly knock over the TV.

"Yo, chick!" Min shouts at the top of her lungs. "I'm sure you're slapping me? And then you knock over the freaking TV? Don't you care?"

"I care!" Jade shouts back. "You're the slut who nearly pulled off her own kid's finger for no freaking reason, man!"

Just then Aunt Bernie comes in from DrugTown in her Drug-Town cap and hobbles over and picks up Troy and everything calms way down.

"No need to fuss, little man," she says. "Everything's fine. Everything's just hunky-dory."

"Hunky-dory," says Min, and gives Jade one last pinch.

Aunt Bernie's a peacemaker. She doesn't like trouble. Once this guy backed over her foot at FoodKing and she walked home with ten broken bones. She never got married, because Grandpa needed her to keep house after Grandma died. Then he died and left all his money to a woman none of us had ever heard of, and Aunt Bernie started in at DrugTown. But she's not bitter. Some-times she's so nonbitter it gets on my nerves. When I say Sea Oak's a pit she says she's just glad to have a roof over her head. When I say I'm tired of being broke she says Grandpa once gave her pen-cils for Christmas and she was so thrilled she sat around sketching horses all day on the backs of used envelopes. Once I asked was she sorry she never had kids and she said no, not at all, and besides, weren't we her kids?

And I said yes we were.

But of course we're not.

For dinner it's beanie-wienies. For dessert it's ice cream with freezer burn.

"What a nice day we've had," Aunt Bernie says once we've got the babies in bed.

"Man, what an optometrist," says Jade.

Next day is Thursday, which means a visit from Ed Anders from the Board of Health. He's in charge of ensuring that our penises never show. Also that we don't kiss anyone. None of us ever kisses anyone or shows his penis except Sonny Vance, who does both, because he's saving up to buy a FaxIt franchise. As for our Penile Simulators, yes, we can show them, we can let them stick out of the top of our pants, we can even periodically dampen our tight pants with spray bottles so our Simulators really contour, but our real penises, no, those have to stay inside our hot uncomfortable oversized Simulators.

"Sorry fellas, hi fellas," Anders says as he comes wearily in. "Please know I don't like this any better than you do. I went to school to learn how to inspect meat, but this certainly wasn't what I had in mind. Ha ha!"

He orders a Lindbergh Enchilada and eats it cautiously, as if it's alive and he's afraid of waking it. Sonny Vance is serving soup to a table of hairstylists on a bender and for a twenty shoots them a quick look at his unit.

Just then Anders glances up from his Lindbergh.

"Oh for crying out loud," he says, and writes up a Shutdown and we all get sent home early. Which is bad. Every dollar counts. Lately I've been sneaking toilet paper home in my briefcase. I can fit three rolls in. By the time I get home they're usually flat and don't work so great on the roller but still it saves a few bucks.

I clock out and cut through the strip of forest behind FedEx. Very pretty. A raccoon scurries over a fallen oak and starts nibbling at a rusty bike. As I come out of the woods I hear a shot. At least I think it's a shot. It could be a backfire. But no, it's a shot, because then there's another one, and some kids sprint across the courtyard yelling that Big Scary Dawgz rule.

I run home. Min and Jade and Aunt Bernie and the babies are huddled behind the couch. Apparently they had the babies outside when the shooting started. Troy's walker got hit. Luckily he wasn't in it. It's supposed to look like a duck but now the beak's missing.

"Man, fuck this shit!" Min shouts.

"Freak this crap you mean," says Jade. "You want them growing up with shit-mouths like us? Crap-mouths I mean?"

"I just want them growing up, period," says Min.

"Boo-hoo, Miss Dramatic," says Jade.

"Fuck off, Miss Ho," shouts Min.

"I mean it, jagoff, I'm not kidding," shouts Jade, and punches
Min in the arm.

"Girls, for crying out loud!" says Aunt Bernie. "We should be
thankful. At least we got a home. And at least none of them bullets actually hit nobody."

"No offense, Bernie?" says Min. "But you call this a freaking
home?"

Sea Oak's not safe. There's an ad hoc crack house in the laundry room and last week Min found some brass knuckles in the kid-
die pool. If I had my way I'd move everybody up to Canada. It's
nice there. Very polite. We went for a weekend last fall and got a
flat tire and these two farmers with bright-red faces insisted on fix-
ing it, then springing for dinner, then starting a college fund for
the babies. They sent us the stock certificates a week later, along
with a photo of all of us eating cobbler at a diner. But moving to
Canada takes bucks. Dad's dead and left us nada and Ma now lives
with Freddie, who doesn't like us, plus he's not exactly rich himself. He does phone polls. This month he's asking divorced women
how often they backslide and sleep with their exes. He gets ten
bucks for every completed poll.

So not lucrative, and Canada's a moot point.

I go out and find the beak of Troy's duck and fix it with
Elmer's.

"Actually you know what?" says Aunt Bernie. "I think that
looks even more like a real duck now. Because sometimes their
beaks are cracked? I seen one like that downtown."

"Oh my God," says Min. "The kid's duck gets shot in the face
and she says we're lucky."

"Well, we are lucky," says Bernie.

"Somebody's beak is cracked," says Jade.

"You know what I do if something bad happens?" Bernie says. "I don't think about it. Don't take it so serious. It ain't the end of the world. That's what I do. That's what I've always done. That's how I got where I am."

My feeling is, Bernie, I love you, but where are you? You work at DrugTown for minimum. You're sixty and own nothing. You were basically a slave to your father and never had a date in your life.

"I mean, complain if you want," she says. "But I think we're doing pretty darn good for ourselves."

"Oh, we're doing great," says Min, and pulls Troy out from behind the couch and brushes some duck shards off his sleeper.

Joysticks reopens on Friday. It's a madhouse. They've got the fog on. A bridge club offers me fifteen bucks to oil-wrestle Mel Turner. So I oil-wrestle Mel Turner. They offer me twenty bucks to feed them chicken wings from my hand. So I feed them chicken wings from my hand. The afternoon flies by. Then the evening. At nine the bridge club leaves and I get a sorority. They sing intelligent nasty songs and grope my Simulator and say they'll never be able to look their boyfriends' meager genitalia in the eye again. Then Mr. Frendt comes over and says phone. It's Min. She sounds crazy. Four times in a row she shrieks get home. When I tell her calm down, she hangs up. I call back and no one answers. No biggie. Min's prone to panic. Probably one of the babies is puky. Luckily I'm on FlexTime.

"I'll be back," I say to Mr. Frendt.

"I look forward to it," he says.

I jog across the marsh and through FedEx. Up on the hill there's a light from the last remaining farm. Sometimes we take the boys to the adjacent car wash to look at the cow. Tonight however the cow is elsewhere.

At home Min and Jade are hopping up and down in front of Aunt Bernie, who's sitting very very still at one end of the couch.

"Keep the babies out!" shrieks Min. "I don't want them seeing something dead!"

"Shut up, man!" shrieks Jade. "Don't call her something dead!" She squats down and pinches Aunt Bernie's cheek.

"Aunt Bernie?" she shrieks. "Fuck!"

"We already tried that like twice, chick!" shrieks Min. "Why are you doing that shit again? Touch her neck and see if you can feel that beating thing!"

"Shit shit shit!" shrieks Jade.

I call 911 and the paramedics come out and work hard for twenty minutes, then give up and say they're sorry and it looks like she's been dead most of the afternoon. The apartment's a mess. Her money drawer's empty and her family photos are in the bathtub.

"Not a mark on her," says a cop.

"I suspect she died of fright," says another. "Fright of the intruder?"

"My guess is yes," says a paramedic.

"Oh God," says Jade. "God, God, God."

I sit down beside Bernie. I think: I am sorry. I'm sorry I wasn't here when it happened and sorry you never had any fun in your life and sorry I wasn't rich enough to move you somewhere safe. I remember when she was young and wore pink stretch pants and made us paper chains out of DrugTown receipts while singing "Froggie Went A-Courting." All her life she worked hard. She never hurt anybody. And now this.

Scared to death in a crappy apartment.

Min puts the babies in the kitchen but they keep crawling out. Aunt Bernie's in a shroud on this sort of dolly and on the couch are a bunch of forms to sign.

We call Ma and Freddie. We get their machine.

"Ma, pick up!" says Min. "Something bad happened! Ma, please freaking pick up!"

But nobody picks up.

So we leave a message.

Lobton's Funeral Parlor is just a regular house on a regular street. Inside there's a rack of brochures with titles like "Why Does My Loved One Appear Somewhat Larger?" Lobton looks healthy. Maybe too healthy. He's wearing a yellow golf shirt and his biceps keep involuntarily flexing. Every now and then he touches his delts as if to confirm they're still big as softballs.

"Such a sad thing," he says.

"How much?" asks Jade. "I mean, like for basic. Not super-fancy."

"But not crappy either," says Min. "Our aunt was the best."

"What price range were you considering?" says Lobton, cracking his knuckles. We tell him and his eyebrows go up and he leads us to something that looks like a moving box.

"Prior to usage we'll moisture-proof this with a spray lacquer," he says. "Makes it look quite woodlike."

"That's all we can get?" says Jade. "Cardboard?"

"I'm actually offering you a slight break already," he says, and does a kind of push-up against the wall. "On account of the tragic circumstances. This is Sierra Sunset. Not exactly cardboard. More of a fiberboard."

"I don't know," says Min. "Seems pretty gyppy."

"Can we think about it?" says Ma.

"Absolutely," says Lobton. "Last time I checked this was still America."

I step over and take a closer look. There are staples where Aunt Bernie's spine would be. Down at the foot there's writing about Folding Tab A into Slot B.

"No freaking way," says Jade. "Work your whole life and end up in a Mayflower box? I doubt it."

We've got zip in savings. We sit at a desk and Lobton does what he calls a Credit Calc. If we pay it out monthly for seven years we can afford the Amber Mist, which includes a double-thick balsa box and two coats of lacquer and a one-hour wake.

"But seven years, jeez," says Ma.

"We got to get her the good one," says Min. "She never had anything nice in her life."

So Amber Mist it is.

We bury her at St. Leo's, on the hill up near BastCo. Her part of the graveyard's pretty plain. No angels, no little rock houses, no flowers, just a bunch of flat stones like parking bumpers and here and there a Styrofoam cup. Father Brian says a prayer and then one of us is supposed to talk. But what's there to say? She never had a life. Never married, no kids, work work work. Did she ever go on a cruise? All her life it was buses. Buses buses buses. Once she went with Ma on a bus to Quigley, Kansas, to gamble and shop at an outlet mall. Someone broke into her room and stole her clothes and took a dump in her suitcase while they were at the Roy Clark show. That was it. That was the extent of her tourism. After that it was DrugTown, night and day. After fifteen years as Cashier she got demoted to Greeter. People would ask where the cold reme-dies were and she'd point to some big letters on the wall that said COLD REMEDIES.

Freddie, Ma's boyfriend, steps up and says he didn't know her very long but she was an awful nice lady and left behind a lot of love, etc. etc. blah blah blah. While it's true she didn't do much in her life, still she was very dear to those of us who knew her and never made a stink about anything but was always content with whatever happened to her, etc. etc. blah blah blah.

Then it's over and we're supposed to go away.

"We gotta come out here like every week," says Jade.

"I know I will," says Min.

"What, like I won't?" says Jade. "She was so freaking nice."

"I'm sure you swear at a grave," says Min.

"Since when is freak a swear, chick?" says Jade.

"Girls," says Ma.

"I hope I did okay in what I said about her," says Freddie in his full-of-crap way, smelling bad of English Navy. "Actually I sort of surprised myself."

"Bye-bye, Aunt Bernie," says Min.

"Bye-bye, Bern," says Jade.

"Oh my dear sister," says Ma.

I scrunch my eyes tight and try to picture her happy, laughing, poking me in the ribs. But all I can see is her terrified on the couch. It's awful. Out there, somewhere, is whoever did it. Someone came in our house, scared her to death, watched her die, went through our stuff, stole her money. Someone who's still living, someone who right now might be having a piece of pie or running an errand or scratching his ass, someone who, if he wanted to, could drive west for three days or whatever and sit in the sun by the ocean.

We stand a few minutes with heads down and hands folded.

Afterward Freddie takes us to Trabanti's for lunch. Last year Trabanti died and three Vietnamese families went in together and bought the place, and it still serves pasta and pizza and the big oil of Trabanti is still on the wall but now from the kitchen comes this very pretty Vietnamese music and the food is somehow better.

Freddie proposes a toast. Min says remember how Bernie always called lunch dinner and dinner supper? Jade says remember how when her jaw clicked she'd say she needed oil?

"She was a excellent lady," says Freddie.

"I already miss her so bad," says Ma.

"I'd like to kill that fuck that killed her," says Min.

"How about let's don't say fuck at lunch," says Ma.

"It's just a word, Ma, right?" says Min. "Like pluck is just a word? You don't mind if I say pluck? Pluck pluck pluck?"

"Well, shit's just a word too," says Freddie. "But we don't say it at lunch."

"Same with puke," says Ma.

"Shit puke, shit puke," says Min.

The waiter clears his throat. Ma glares at Min.

"I love you girls' manners," Ma says.

"Especially at a funeral," says Freddie.

"This ain't a funeral," says Min.

"The question in my mind is what you kids are gonna do now," says Freddie. "Because I consider this whole thing a wake-up call, meaning it's time for you to pull yourselfs up by the bootstraps like I done and get out of that dangerous craphole you're living at."

"Mr. Phone Poll speaks," says Min.

"Anyways it ain't that dangerous," says Jade.

"A woman gets killed and it ain't that dangerous?" says Freddie.

"All's we need is a dead bolt and a eyehole," says Min.

"What's a bootstrap?" says Jade.

"It's like a strap on a boot, you doof," says Min.

"Plus where we gonna go?" says Min. "Can we move in with you guys?"

"I personally would love that and you know that," says Freddie. "But who would not love that is our landlord."

"I think what Freddie's saying is it's time for you girls to get jobs," says Ma.

"Yeah right, Ma," says Min. "After what happened last time?"

When I first moved in, Jade and Min were working the info booth at HardwareNiche. Then one day we picked the babies up at day care and found Troy sitting naked on top of the washer and Mac in the yard being nipped by a Pekingese and the day-care lady sloshed and playing KillerBirds on Nintendo.

So that was that. No more HardwareNiche.

"Maybe one could work, one could babysit?" says Ma.

"I don't see why I should have to work so she can stay home with her baby," says Min.

"And I don't see why I should have to work so she can stay home with her baby," says Jade.

"It's like a freaking veece versa," says Min.

"Let me tell you something," says Freddie. "Something about this country. Anybody can do anything. But first they gotta try. And you guys ain't. Two don't work and one strips naked? I don't consider that trying. You kids make squat. And therefore you live in a dangerous craphole. And what happens in a dangerous craphole? Bad tragic shit. It's the freaking American way—you start out in a dangerous craphole and work hard so you can someday move up to a somewhat less dangerous craphole. And finally maybe you get a mansion. But at this rate you ain't even gonna make it to the somewhat less dangerous craphole."

"Like you live in a mansion," says Jade.

"I do not claim to live in no mansion," says Freddie. "But then again I do not live in no slum. The other thing I also do not do is strip naked."

"Thank God for small favors," says Min.

"Anyways he's never actually naked," says Jade.

Which is true. I always have on at least a T-back.

"No wonder we never take these kids out to a nice lunch," says Freddie.

"I do not even consider this a nice lunch," says Min.

For dinner Jade microwaves some Stars-n-Flags. They're addictive. They put sugar in the sauce and sugar in the meat nuggets. I think also caffeine. Someone told me the brown streaks in the Flags are caffeine. We have like five bowls each.

After dinner the babies get fussy and Min puts a mush of ice cream and Hershey's syrup in their bottles and we watch *The Worst*

That Could Happen, a half-hour of computer simulations of tragedies that have never actually occurred but theoretically could. A kid gets hit by a train and flies into a zoo, where he's eaten by wolves. A man cuts his hand off chopping wood and while wandering around screaming for help is picked up by a tornado and dropped on a preschool during recess and lands on a pregnant teacher.

"I miss Bernie so bad," says Min.

"Me too," Jade says sadly.

The babies start howling for more ice cream.

"That is so cute," says Jade. "They're like, *Give it the fuck up!*"

"We'll give it the fuck up, sweeties, don't worry," says Min. "We didn't forget about you."

Then the phone rings. It's Father Brian. He sounds weird. He says he's sorry to bother us so late. But something strange has happened. Something bad. Something sort of, you know, unspeakable. Am I sitting? I'm not but I say I am.

Apparently someone has defaced Bernie's grave.

My first thought is there's no stone. It's just grass. How do you deface grass? What did they do, pee on the grass on the grave? But Father's nearly in tears.

So I call Ma and Freddie and tell them to meet us, and we get the babies up and load them into the K-car.

"Deface," says Jade on the way over. "What does that mean, deface?"

"It means like fucked it up," says Min.

"But how?" says Jade. "I mean, like what did they do?"

"We don't know, dumbass," says Min. "That's why we're going there."

"And why?" says Jade. "Why would someone do that?"

"Check out Miss Shreelock Holmes," says Min. "Someone done that because someone is a asshole."

"Someone is a big-time asshole," says Jade.

Father Brian meets us at the gate with a flashlight and a golf cart.

"When I saw this," he says, "I literally sat down in astonishment. Nothing like this has ever happened here. I am so sorry. You seem like nice people."

We're too heavy and the wheels spin as we climb the hill, so I get out and jog alongside.

"Okay, folks, brace yourselves," Father says, and shuts off the engine.

Where the grave used to be is just a hole. Inside the hole is the Amber Mist, with the top missing. Inside the Amber Mist is nothing. No Aunt Bernie.

"What the hell," says Jade. "Where's Bernie?"

"Somebody stole Bernie?" says Min.

"At least you folks have retained your feet," says Father Brian. "I'm telling you I literally sat right down. I sat right down on that pile of dirt. I dropped as if shot. See that mark? That's where I sat."

On the pile of grave dirt is a butt-shaped mark.

The cops show up and one climbs down in the hole with a tape measure and a camera. After three or four flashes he climbs out and hands Ma a pair of blue pumps.

"Her little shoes," says Ma. "Oh my God."

"Are those them?" says Jade.

"Those are them," says Min.

"I am freaking out," says Jade.

"I am totally freaking out," says Min.

"I'm gonna sit," says Ma, and drops into the golf cart.

"What I don't get is who'd want her?" says Min.

"She was just this lady," says Jade.

"Typically it's teens?" one cop says. "Typically we find the loved one nearby? Once we found the loved one nearby with, you know, a cigarette between its lips, wearing a sombrero? These kids today got a lot more nerve than we ever did. I never would've dreamed of digging up a dead corpse when I was a teen. You might tip over a stone, sure, you might spray-paint something on a crypt, you might, you know, give a wino a hotfoot."

"But this, jeez," says Freddie. "This is a entirely different ball game."

"Boy howdy," says the cop, and we all look down at the shoes in Ma's hands.

Next day I go back to work. I don't feel like it but we need the money. The grass is wet and it's hard getting across the ravine in my dress shoes. The soles are slick. Plus they're too tight. Several times I fall forward on my briefcase. Inside my briefcase are my T-backs and a thing of mousse.

Right off the bat I get a tableful of MediBen women under a banner saying BEST OF LUCK, BEATRICE, NO HARD FEELINGS. I take off my shirt and serve their salads. I take off my flight pants and serve their soups. One drops a dollar on the floor and tells me feel free to pick it up.

I pick it up.

"Not like that, not like that," she says. "Face the other way, so when you bend we can see your crack."

I've done this about a million times, but somehow I can't do it now.

I look at her. She looks at me.

"What?" she says. "I'm not allowed to say that? I thought that was the whole point."

"That is the whole point, Phyllis," says another lady. "You stand your ground."

"Look," Phyllis says. "Either bend how I say or give back the dollar. I think that's fair."

"You go, girl," says her friend.

I give back the dollar. I return to the Locker Area and sit awhile. For the first time ever, I'm voted Stinker. There are thirteen women at the MediBen table and they all vote me Stinker. Do the MediBen women know my situation? Would they vote me Stinker if they did? But what am I supposed to do, go out and say, Please ladies, my aunt just died, plus her body's missing?

Mr. Frendt pulls me aside.

"Perhaps you need to go home," he says. "I'm sorry for your loss. But I'd like to encourage you not to behave like one of those Comanche ladies who bite off their index fingers when a loved one dies. Grief is good, grief is fine, but too much grief, as we all know, is excessive. If your aunt's death has filled your mouth with too many bitten-off fingers, for crying out loud, take a week off, only don't take it out on our Guests, they didn't kill your dang aunt."

But I can't afford to take a week off. I can't even afford to take a few days off.

"We really need the money," I say.

"Is that my problem?" he says. "Am I supposed to let you dance without vigor just because you need the money? Why don't I put an ad in the paper for all sad people who need money? All the town's sad could come here and strip. Good-bye. Come back when you feel halfway normal."

From the pay phone I call home to see if they need anything from the FoodSoQuik.

"Just come home," Min says stiffly. "Just come straight home."

"What is it?" I say.

"Come home," she says.

Maybe someone's found the body. I imagine Bernie naked, Bernie chopped in two, Bernie posed on a bus bench. I hope and pray that something only mildly bad's been done to her, something we can live with.

At home the door's wide open. Min and Jade are sitting very still on the couch, babies in their laps, staring at the rocking chair, and in the rocking chair is Bernie. Bernie's body.

Same perm, same glasses, same blue dress we buried her in.

What's it doing here? Who could be so cruel? And what are we supposed to do with it?

Then she turns her head and looks at me.

"Sit the fuck down," she says.

In life she never swore.

I sit. Min squeezes and releases my hand, squeezes and releases, squeezes and releases.

"You, mister," Bernie says to me, "are going to start showing your cock. You'll show it and show it. You go up to a lady, if she wants to see it, if she'll pay to see it, I'll make a thumbprint on the forehead. You see the thumbprint, you ask. I'll try to get you five a day, at twenty bucks a pop. So a hundred bucks a day. Seven hundred a week. And that's cash, so no taxes. No withholding. See? That's the beauty of it."

She's got dirt in her hair and dirt in her teeth and her hair is a mess and her tongue when it darts out to lick her lips is black.

"You, Jade," she says. "Tomorrow you start work. Andersen Labels, Fifth and Rivera. Dress up when you go. Wear something nice. Show a little leg. And don't chomp gum. Ask for Len. At the end of the month, we take the money you made and the cock money and get a new place. Somewhere safe. That's part one of Phase One. You, Min. You babysit. Plus you quit smoking. Plus you learn how to cook. No more food out of cans. We gotta eat right to look our best. Because I am getting me so many lovers. Maybe you kids don't know this but I died a freaking virgin. No babies, no lovers. Nothing went in, nothing came out. Ha ha! Dry as a bone, completely wasted, this pretty little thing God gave me between my legs. Well I am going to have lovers now, you fucks! Like in the movies, big shoulders and all, and a summer house, and nice trips, and in the morning in my room a big vase of flowers, and I'm going to get my nipples hard standing in the breeze from the ocean, eating shrimp from a cup, you sons of bitches, while my lover watches me from the veranda, his big shoulders shining, all hard for me, that's one damn thing I will guarantee you kids! Ha ha! You think I'm joking? I ain't freaking joking. I never got nothing! My life was shit! I was never even up in a freaking plane. But that was that life and this is this life. My new life. Cover me up now! With a blanket. I need my beauty rest. Tell anyone I'm here, you all die. Plus they die. Who-ever you tell, they die. I kill them with my mind. I can do that. I am very freaking strong now. I got powers! So no visitors. I don't exactly look my best. You got it? You all got it?"

We nod. I go for a blanket. Her hands and feet are shaking and she's grinding her teeth and one falls out.

"Put it over me, you fuck, all the way over!" she screams, and I put it over her.

We sneak off with the babies and whisper in the kitchen.

"It looks like her," says Min.

"It is her," I say.

"It is and it ain't," says Jade.

"We better do what she says," Min says.

"No shit," Jade says.

All night she sits in the rocker under the blanket, shaking and swearing.

All night we sit in Min's bed, fully dressed, holding hands.

"See how strong I am!" she shouts around midnight, and there's a cracking sound, and when I go out the door's been torn off the microwave but she's still sitting in the chair.

In the morning she's still there, shaking and swearing.

"Take the blanket off!" she screams. "It's time to get this show on the road."

I take the blanket off. The smell is not good. One ear is now in her lap. She keeps absentmindedly sticking it back on her head.

"You, Jade!" she shouts. "Get dressed. Go get that job. When you meet Len, bend forward a little. Let him see down your top.

Give him some hope. He's a sicko, but we need him. You, Min! Make breakfast. Something homemade. Like biscuits."

"Why don't you make it with your powers?" says Min.

"Don't be a smartass!" screams Bernie. "You see what I did to that microwave?"

"I don't know how to make freaking biscuits," Min wails.

"You know how to read, right?" Bernie shouts. "You ever heard of a recipe? You ever been in the grave? It sucks so bad! You regret all the things you never did. You little bitches are gonna have a very bad time in the grave unless you get on the stick, believe me! Turn down the thermostat! Make it cold. I like cold. Something's off with my body. I don't feel right."

I turn down the thermostat. She looks at me.

"Go show your cock!" she shouts. "That is the first part of Phase One. After we get the new place, that's the end of the first part of Phase Two. You'll still show your cock, but only three days a week. Because you'll start community college. Pre-law. Pre-law is best. You'll be a whiz. You ain't dumb. And Jade'll work weekends to make up for the decrease in cock money. See? See how that works? Now get out of here. What are you gonna do?"

"Show my cock?" I say.

"Show your cock, that's right," she says, and brushes back her hair with her hand, and a huge wad comes out, leaving her almost bald on one side.

"Oh God," says Min. "You know what? No way me and the babies are staying here alone."

"You ain't alone," says Bernie. "I'm here."

"Please don't go," Min says to me.

"Oh, stop it," Bernie says, and the door flies open and I feel a sort of invisible fist punching me in the back.

Outside it's sunny. A regular day. A guy's changing his oil. The clouds are regular clouds and the sun's the regular sun and the only nonregular thing is that my clothes smell like Bernie, a combo of wet cellar and rotten bacon.

Work goes well. I manage to keep smiling and hide my shaking hands, and my midshift rating is Honeypie. After lunch this older woman comes up and says I look so much like a real Pilot she can hardly stand it.

On her head is a thumbprint. Like Ash Wednesday, only sort of glowing.

I don't know what to do. Do I just come out and ask if she wants to see my cock? What if she says no? What if I get caught? What if I show her and she doesn't think it's worth twenty bucks?

Then she asks if I'll surprise her best friend with a birthday table dance. She points out her friend. A pretty girl, no thumbprint. Looks somehow familiar.

We start over and at about twenty feet I realize it's Angela.

Angela Silveri.

We dated senior year. Then Dad died and Ma had to take a job at Patty-Melt Depot. From all the grease Ma got a bad rash and could barely wear a blouse. Plus Min was running wild. So Angela would come over and there'd be Min getting high under a tarp on the carport and Ma sitting in her bra on a kitchen stool with a fan pointed at her gut. Angela had dreams. She had plans. In her notebook she pasted a picture of an office from the J. C. Penney catalog and under it wrote, *My (someday?) office*. Once we saw this black Porsche and she said very nice but make hers red. The last straw was Ed Edwards, a big drunk, one of Dad's cousins. Things got so bad Ma rented him the utility room. One night Angela and I were making out on the couch late when Ed came in soused and started peeing in the dishwasher.

What could I say? He's only barely related to me? He hardly ever does that?

Angela's eyes were like these little pies.

I walked her home, got no kiss, came back, cleaned up the dishwasher as best I could. A few days later I got my class ring in the mail and a copy of the *The Prophet*.

You will always be my first love, she'd written inside. *But now my*

*path converges to a higher ground. Be well always. Walk in joy. Please
don't think me cruel, it's just that I want so much in terms of accomplish-
ment, plus I couldn't believe that guy peed right on your dishes.*

No way am I table dancing for Angela Silveri. No way am I
asking Angela Silveri's friend if she wants to see my cock. No way
am I hanging around here so Angela can see me in my flight jacket
and T-backs and wonder to herself how I went so wrong etc. etc.

I hide in the kitchen until my shift is done, then walk home
very, very slowly because I'm afraid of what Bernie's going to do to
me when I get there.

Min meets me at the door. She's got flour all over her blouse and it
looks like she's been crying.

"I can't take any more of this," she says. "She's like falling
apart. I mean shit's falling off her. Plus she made me bake a freaking pie."

On the table is a very lumpy pie. One of Bernie's arms is now
disconnected and lying across her lap.

"What are you thinking of?" she shouts. "You didn't show
your cock even once? You think it's easy making those thumbprints? You try it, smartass! Do you or do you not know the plan?
You gotta get us out of here! And to get us out, you gotta use
what you got. And you ain't got much. A nice face. And a decent
unit. Not huge, but shaped nice."

"Bernie, God," says Min.

"What, Miss Priss?" shouts Bernie, and slams the severed arm
down hard on her lap, and her other ear falls off.

"I'm sorry, but this is too fucking sickening," says Min. "I'm
going out."

"What's sickening?" says Bernie. "Are you saying that I'm
sickening? Well, I think you're sickening. So many wonderful
things in life and where's your mind? You think with your lazy
ass. Whatever life hands you, you take. You're not going anywhere. You're staying home and studying."

"I'm what?" says Min. "Studying what? I ain't studying. Chick comes into my house and starts ordering me to study? I freaking doubt it."

"You don't know nothing!" Bernie says. "What fun is life when you don't know nothing? You can't find your own town on the map. You can't name a single president. When we go to Rome you won't know nothing about the history. You're going to study the *World Book*. Do we still have those *World Book*s?"

"Yeah right," says Min. "We're going to Rome."

"We'll go to Rome when he's a lawyer," says Bernie.

"Dream on, chick," says Min. "And we'll go to Mars when I'm a stockbreaker."

"Don't you dare make fun of me!" Bernie shouts, and our only vase goes flying across the room and nearly nails Min in the head.

"She's been like this all day," says Min.

"Like what?" shouts Bernie. "We had a perfectly nice day."

"She made me help her try on my bras," says Min.

"I never had a nice sexy bra," says Bernie.

"And now mine are all ruined," says Min. "They got this sort of goo on them."

"You ungrateful shit!" shouts Bernie. "Do you know what I'm doing for you? I'm saving your boy. And you got the nerve to say I made goo on your bras! Troy's gonna get caught in a cross fire in the courtyard. In September. September eighteenth. He's gonna get thrown off his little trike. With one leg twisted under him and blood pouring out of his ear. It's a freaking prophecy. You know that word? It means prediction. You know that word? You think I'm bullshitting? Well I ain't bullshitting. I got the power. Watch this: All day Jade sat licking labels at a desk by a window. Her boss bought everybody subs for lunch. She's bringing some home in a green bag."

"That ain't true about Troy, is it?" says Min. "Is it? I don't believe it."

"Turn on the TV!" Bernie shouts. "Give me the changer."

I turn on the TV. I give her the changer. She puts on *Nathan's Body Shop*. Nathan says washboard abs drive the women wild. Then there's a close-up of his washboard abs.

"Oh yes," says Bernie. "Them are for me. I'd like to give those a lick. A lick and a pinch. I'd like to sort of straddle those things."

Just then Jade comes through the door with a big green bag.

"Oh God," says Min.

"Told you so!" says Bernie, and pokes Min in the ribs. "Ha ha! I really got the power!"

"I don't get it," Min says, all desperate. "What happens? Please. What happens to him? You better freaking tell me."

"I already told you," Bernie says. "He'll fly about fifteen feet and live about three minutes."

"Bernie, God," Min says, and starts to cry. "You used to be so nice."

"I'm still so nice," says Bernie, and bites into a sub and takes off the tip of her finger and starts chewing it up.

Just after dawn she shouts out my name.

"Take the blanket off," she says. "I ain't feeling so good."

I take the blanket off. She's basically just this pile of parts: both arms in her lap, head on the arms, heel of one foot touching the heel of the other, all of it sort of wrapped up in her dress.

"Get me a washcloth," she says. "Do I got a fever? I feel like I got a fever. Oh, I knew it was too good to be true. But okay. New plan. New plan. I'm changing the first part of Phase One. If you see two thumbprints, that means the lady'll screw you for cash. We're in a fix here. We gotta speed this up. There ain't gonna be nothing left of me. Who's gonna be my lover now?"

The doorbell rings.

"Son of a bitch," Bernie snarls.

It's Father Brian with a box of doughnuts. I step out quick and close the door behind me. He says he's just checking in. Perhaps we'd like to talk? Perhaps we're feeling some residual anger about Bernie's situation? Which would of course be completely understandable. Once when he was a young priest someone broke in and drew a mustache on the Virgin Mary with a permanent marker, and for weeks he was tortured by visions of bending back the finger of the vandal until he or she burst into tears of apology.

"I knew that wasn't appropriate," he says. "I knew that by indulging in that fantasy I was honoring violence. And yet it gave me pleasure. I also thought of catching them in the act and boinking them in the head with a rock. I also thought of jumping up and down on their backs until something in their spinal column cracked. Actually I had about a million ideas. But you know what I did instead? I scrubbed and scrubbed our Holy Mother, and soon she was as good as new. Her statue, I mean. She herself of course is always good as new."

From inside comes the sound of breaking glass. Breaking glass and then something heavy falling, and Jade yelling and Min yelling and the babies crying.

"Oops, I guess?" he says. "I've come at a bad time? Look, all I'm trying to do is urge you, if at all possible, to forgive the perpetrators, as I forgave the perpetrator that drew on my Virgin Mary. The thing lost, after all, is only your aunt's body, and what is essential, I assure you, is elsewhere, being well taken care of."

I nod. I smile. I say thanks for stopping by. I take the doughnuts and go back inside.

The TV's broke and the refrigerator's tipped over and Bernie's parts are strewn across the living room like she's been shot out of a cannon.

"She tried to get up," says Jade.

"I don't know where the hell she thought she was going," says Min.

"Come here," the head says to me, and I squat down. "That's it for me. I'm fucked. As per usual. Always the bridesmaid, never the bride. Although come to think of it I was never even the freaking bridesmaid. Look, show your cock. It's the shortest line between two points. The world ain't giving away nice lives. You got a trust fund? You a genius? Show your cock. It's what you got. And remember: Troy in September. On his trike. One leg twisted. Don't forget. And also. Don't remember me like this. Remember me like how I was the night we all went to Red Lobster and I had that new perm. Ah Christ. At least buy me a stone."

I rub her shoulder, which is next to her foot.

"We loved you," I say.

"Why do some people get everything and I got nothing?" she says. "Why? Why was that?"

"I don't know," I say.

"Show your cock," she says, and dies again.

We stand there looking down at the pile of parts. Mac crawls toward it and Min moves him back with her foot.

"This is too freaking much," says Jade, and starts crying.

"What do we do now?" says Min.

"Call the cops," Jade says.

"And say what?" says Min.

We think about this awhile.

I get a Hefty bag. I get my winter gloves.

"I ain't watching," says Jade.

"I ain't watching either," says Min, and they take the babies into the bedroom.

I close my eyes and wrap Bernie up in the Hefty bag and twistie-tie the bag shut and lug it out to the trunk of the K-car. I throw in a shovel. I drive up to St. Leo's. I lower the bag into the hole using a bungee cord, then fill the hole back in.

Down in the city are the nice houses and the so-so houses and the lovers making out in the dark yards and the babies crying for their moms, and I wonder if, other than Jesus, this has ever happened before. Maybe it happens all the time. Maybe there's angry dead all over, hiding in rooms, covered with blankets, bossing around their scared, embarrassed relatives. Because how would we know?

I for sure don't plan on broadcasting this.

I smooth over the dirt and say a quick prayer: If it was wrong for her to come back, forgive her, she never got beans in this life, plus she was trying to help us.

At the car I think of an additional prayer: But please don't let her come back again.

When I get home the babies are asleep and Jade and Min are watching a phone-sex infomercial, three girls in leather jumpsuits eating bananas in slo-mo while across the screen runs a constant disclaimer: "Not Necessarily the Girls Who Man the Phones! Not Necessarily the Girls Who Man the Phones!"

"Them chicks seem to really be enjoying those bananas," says Min in a thin little voice.

"I like them jumpsuits though," says Jade.

"Yeah them jumpsuits look decent," says Min.

Then they look up at me. I've never seen them so sad and beat and sick.

"It's done," I say.

Then we hug and cry and promise never to forget Bernie the way she really was, and I use some Resolve on the rug and they go do some reading in their *World Books*.

Next day I go in early. I don't see a single thumbprint. But it doesn't matter. I get with Sonny Vance and he tells me how to do it. First you ask the woman would she like a private tour. Then you show her the fake P-40, the Gallery of Historical Aces, the shower stall where we get oiled up, etc. etc. and then in the hall near the restroom you ask if there's anything else she'd like to see. It's sleazy. It's gross. But when I do it I think of September. September and Troy in the cross fire, his little leg bent under him etc. etc.

Most say no but quite a few say yes.

I've got a place picked out at a complex called Swan's Glen. They've never had a shooting or a knifing and the public school is great and every Saturday they have a nature walk for kids behind the clubhouse.

For every hundred bucks I make, I set aside five for Bernie's stone.

What do you write on something like that? LIFE PASSED HER BY? DIED DISAPPOINTED? CAME BACK TO LIFE BUT FELL APART? All true, but too sad, and no way I'm writing any of those.

BERNIE KOWALSKI, it's going to say: BELOVED AUNT.

Sometimes she comes to me in dreams. She never looks good. Sometimes she's wearing a dirty smock. Once she had on handcuffs. Once she was naked and dirty and this mean cat was clawing its way up her front. But every time it's the same thing.

"Some people get everything and I got nothing," she says. "Why? Why did that happen?"

Every time I say I don't know.

And I don't.

EVERYTHING RAVAGED, EVERYTHING BURNED

WELLS TOWER

Just as we were all getting back into the mainland domestic groove, somebody started in with dragons and crop blights from across the North Sea. We all knew who it was. A turncoat Norwegian monk named Naddod had been big medicine on the dragon-and-blight circuit for the last decade or so, and was known to bring heavy ordnance for whoever could lay out some silver. Scuttlebutt had it that Naddod was operating out of a monastery on Lindisfarne, whose people we'd troubled on a pillage-and-consternation junket in Northumbria after Corn Harvesting Month last fall. Now bitter winds were screaming in from the west, searing the land and ripping the grass from the soil. Salmon were turning up spattered with sores, and grasshoppers clung to the wheat in rapacious buzzing bunches.

I tried to put these things out of my mind. We'd been away three long months harrying the Hibernian shores, and now I was back with Pila, my common-law, and thinking that home was very close to paradise in these endless golden summer days. We'd built our house together, Pila and I. It was a fine little wattle-and-daub cabin on a pretty bit of plain where a wide blue fjord stabbed into the land. On summer evenings my young wife and I would sit out front, high on potato wine, and watch the sun stitch a brilliant orange skirt across the horizon. At times such as these, you get a big feeling, like the gods made this place, this moment, first, and concocted you as an afterthought just to be there to enjoy it.

I was doing a lot of enjoying and relishing and a lot of lying around the rack with Pila, though I knew what it meant when I heard those flint-edged winds howling past the house. Sons of bitches three weeks' boat ride off were fucking up our summer and were probably going to need their asses whipped.

Of course, Djarf Fairhair had his stinger out even before his wife spotted those dragons winging it inland from the coast. He was boss on our ship and a fool for warfare. His appetite for action was so terrifying and infectious, he'd once riled up a gang of Frankish slaves and led them south to afflict and maim their own country-men. He'd gotten in four days of decent sacking when the slaves began to see the situation for what it was and underwent a sudden change of attitude. Djarf had been fighting his way up the Rhine Valley, making steady progress through a half-assed citizens' militia of children and farmers, when the slaves closed in behind him. People who were there say he turned absolutely feral and began berserking with a pair of broadaxes, chewing through the lines like corn kernels on a cob, and that when the axes broke, he cut loose with a dismembered human head, so horrifying those gentle provincials that they fell back and gave him wide berth to the ship.

Djarf was from Hedeby-Slesvig up the Slie fjord, a fairly foul and rocky locality whose people take a worrisome pleasure in the gruesome sides of life. They have a habit down there if they don't like a child's looks when he slides from the womb. They pitch him into the deep waters and wait for the next one. Djarf himself was supposedly a colicky, peaked baby, and it was only the beneficence of the tides and his own vicious tenacity that got him to the far shore when his father grew tired of his caterwauling and tried to wash him from the world.

He'd been campaigning for payback ever since. I was with him on a search-and-destroy tour against Louis the Pious, and with my own eyes watched him climb up over the soldiers' backs and stride like a saint across men's heads, golf-stroking skulls as he went. On that same trip, we ran low on food, and it was Djarf who decided to throw our own dead on the fire and have at last night's mutton when their stomachs burst. He'd been the only one of us to dig in, apart from a crazy Arab along as a spellbuster. He reached right in there, scooping out chewed-up victuals with a shank of pine bark. "Faggot greenhorns," he called us, the firelight twitching on his face. "Food's food. If these guys hadn't gotten their threads snipped, they'd tell you the same thing."

So Djarf, whose wife was a rotten, carp-mouthed thing and little argument for staying home, was agitating to hop back in the ship and go straighten things out in Northumbria. My buddy Gnut, who lived just over the stony moraine our wheat field backed up on, came down the hill one day and admitted that he too was giving it some thought. Like me, he wasn't big on warrioring. He was just crazy for boat. We used to joke and say Gnut would ride a boat from his shack to his shithouse if somebody would invent one whose prow could cut sod. Gnut's wife had passed years ago, dead from bad milk, and now that she was gone, the part of him that felt peaceful in a place that didn't move beneath him had sickened and died as well.

Pila saw him coming down the hill and frowned at me. "Don't need to guess what he'll be wanting," she said. She scowled and headed back indoors. Gnut ambled down over the hummocky earth and stopped at the pair of stump chairs Pila and I had put up on the hill where the view was so fine. From there, the fjord shone like poured silver, and sometimes you could spot a seal poking his head up through the waves.

Gnut's wool coat was stiff with filth and his long hair so heavy and unclean that even the wind keening up from the shore was having a hard time getting it to move. He had a good crust of snot going in his mustache, not a pleasant thing to look at, but then he had no one around to find it disagreeable. He tore a sprig of heather from the ground and chewed at its sweet roots.

"Djarf get at you yet?" he asked.

"No, not yet, but I'm not worried he'll forget."

He took the sprig from his teeth and briefly jammed it into his ear before tossing it away. "You gonna go?"

"Not until I hear the particulars, I won't."

"You can bet I'm going. A hydra flew in last night and ran off Rolf Hierdal's sheep. We can't be putting up with this shit. It comes down to pride, is what it comes down to."

"Shit, Gnut, when'd you get to be such a gung ho mother-fucker? I don't recall you being so proud and thin-skinned before Astrud went off to her good place. Anyway, Lindisfarne is probably sacked out already. If you don't remember, we just about pillaged the living shit out of those people on the last swing through, and I doubt they've come up with much in the meantime to justify a trip."

I wished Gnut would go ahead and own up to the fact that his life out here was making him lonely and miserable instead of laying on with this warrior-man routine. I could tell just to look at him that most days he was thinking of walking into the water and not bothering to turn back. He wanted back on the boat among company.

Not that I was all that averse myself, speaking in the abstract, but I was needing more sweet time with Pila. I loved that girl even more than she probably knew, and I wanted to get in some thorough lovemaking before the Haymaking Month was under way and see if I couldn't make us a little monkey.

But the days wore on and the weather worsened. Pila watched

it sharply, and a sort of hysterical sadness welled up in her, as it often did when I'd be leaving. She cussed me on some days, and others she'd hold me to her and weep. And late one evening, far toward dawn, the hail started. It came suddenly, with the hard, terrifying scraping sound a ship makes when its hull hits stone. We hunkered down in the sheepskins, and I whispered soothing things to Pila, trying to drown out the clatter.

The sun was not yet full up in the sky when Djarf came and knocked. I rose and stepped across the floor, damp with cool morning dew. Djarf stood in the doorway wearing a mail jacket and shield and breathing like he'd jogged the whole way over. He chucked a handful of hail at my feet. He had a wild grin on his face. "Today's the day," he said. "We got to get it on."

Sure, I could have told him thanks anyway, but once you back down from one job, you're lucky if they'll even let you put in for a flat-fee trade escort. I had to think long term, me and Pila, and any little jits we might produce. Still, she didn't like to hear it. When I got back in bed, she tucked the covers over her face, hoping I'd think she was angry instead of crying.

The clouds were spilling out low across the sky when we shoved off. Thirty of us on board, Gnut rowing with me at the bow and behind us a lot of other men I'd been in some shit with before. Some, like Ørl Stender, were men with families and cried when the boat left the shore. Ørl fucked up the cadence waving to his son, who stood on the beach waving back. He was a tiny one, not four or five, standing there with no pants on, holding a baby pig on a hide leash, sweetly ignorant of the business his father was heading off into.

Most of the others on board were young men, brash and violent children, so innocent about the world, they would just as soon stick a knife in you as shake your hand.

Gnut was overjoyed. He laughed and sang and put a lot of

muscle into the oar, me just holding my hands on it to keep up appearances. I was limp with grief and missing Pila already. The hills humping up behind the beach were a shrill green hue, vivid and outrageous, an angry answer to all of that gray water that lay before them. I watched the beach for Pila and her bright white hair. She hadn't come down to see me off, too mad and sad about me leaving to get up out of bed. But I looked for her anyway, the land scooting away from me with every jerk of the oars.

If Gnut knew I was hurting, he didn't say so. He nudged me and joked, and maintained a steady patter of inanities, as though this whole thing was a private vacation the two of us had cooked up together. "If you had to live on the ship, but you got to have a magic basket full of your favorite food, but only one favorite food, what would it be? I'd have black pudding. Black pudding and plums. So all right, you get two foods." Or: "If someone put a curse on you, and you had to have horns like a goat, and shit little shits like a goat, would you rather have that, or a seven-foot dick that you had to have hanging out of your pants at all times?" And so on.

Djarf stood at his spot in the bow, all full of vinegar and righteous enthusiasm at being back on the sea. Slesvigers, as you know, will bust into song with no provocation whatsoever, their affinity for music roughly on a par with the wretchedness of their singing. Djarf screamed out the cadence in a sickening, wobbly melody that buzzed into the ears and stung you on the brain. His gang of young hockchoppers acted like it was the best thing they'd ever heard, and they piped up too, howling like spaniels whose nuts hadn't dropped yet.

Three days out, the sun punched through the dirty clouds and put a steely shimmer on the sea. It cooked the brine out of our clothes and got everybody dry and happy. I couldn't help but think that if Naddod were really as serious as we were all sure he was, this crossing would have been a fine opportunity to call up a typhoon and hold a massacre. But the weather held, and the seas stayed drowsy and low.

We had less light in the evenings out here than at home, and it was a little easier sleeping in the open boat without a midnight sun. Gnut and I slept where we rowed, working around each other to get comfy on the bench. I woke up once in the middle of the night and found Gnut dead asleep, muttering and slobbering and holding me in a rough embrace. I tried to peel him off, but he was a big man, and his hard arms stayed on me sure as if they'd grown there. I poked him and jabbered at him, but the dude would not be roused, so I just tried to work up a little slack to where he wasn't hurting my ribs, and I drifted back to sleep.

Later, I told him what had happened. "That's a lot of horse-shit," he said, his broad, loose cheeks going red.

"I wish it were," I said. "But I've got bruises I could show you. Hey, if I ever come around asking to be your sweetheart, do me a favor and remind me about this."

He was all upset. "Fuck you, Harald. You're not funny. Nobody thinks you're funny."

"I'm sorry," I said. "Guess you haven't had a whole lot of practice lately having a body beside you at night."

He got quiet and rested on the oar a second. "That's right," he said, turning his face away. "I haven't."

Thanks to an easy wind blowing from the east, we crossed fast and sighted the island six days early. One of the hockchoppers spotted it first, and when he did, he let everyone know it by cutting loose with a battle howl he'd probably been practicing in his father's pigyard. He drew his sword and swung it in figure eights above his head, causing the men around him to scatter under the gun-wales. This boy was a nasty item, a face like a shoat hog and a vibrant beard of acne ravaging his cheeks. I'd seen him around at home. He had three blackened, chopped-off fingers reefed to his belt.

Haakon Gokstad looked up from his seat in the stern and shot the boy a baleful look. Haakon had been on more raids and runs than the bunch of us put together. He was old and creaky and worked the rudder, partly because he could read the tides by how the blood moved through his hands, and also (though you'd never say it when he could hear) because those old arms were poor for pulling oars. "Put your ass on that bench, young man," Haakon said to the boy. "We got twelve hours' work between here and there."

The boy colored. He let his sword arm hang. He looked at his friends to see if he'd been humiliated in front of them, and if he had, what he needed to do about it. The whole boat was looking over at him. Even Djarf paused in his song. The other kid on his bench whispered something and scooted over. The boy quickly sat and grabbed the oar, head bowed. The rowing and the chatter started up again.

You could say that those people on Lindisfarne were fools, living out there on a tiny island without high cliffs or decent natural defenses, and so close to us and also the Swedes and the Norwegians—how we saw it, we couldn't afford *not* to come by and sack every now and again. But when we came into the bright little bay, a quiet fell over all of us. Even the hockchoppers quit grabassing and looked. The place was wild with fields of purple thistle, and when the wind blew, it twitched and rolled, like the hide of some fantastic critter shrugging in its sleep. Red wildflowers spurted on the hills in gorgeous, indecent gouts. Apple trees lined the shore, and there was something sorrowful in how they hung so low with fruit. We could see a man making his way toward a clump of white-walled cottages, his donkey loping along behind him with a load. On the far hill, I could make out the silhouette of the monastery. They hadn't got the roof back on from when we'd burned it last, and with orphaned roof joists jutting up, it looked like a giant bird's nest whose occupant had left for distant shores. It was such a lovely place, and I hoped there would still be something left to enjoy after we got off the ship and wrecked everything up.

We gathered on the beach, and already Djarf was in a lather. He did a few deep knee bends. He got down on the beach in front of all of us and ran through some poses, cracking his bones and drawing out the knots in his muscles. Then he closed his eyes and said a silent prayer. His eyes were still closed when a man in a long robe appeared, picking his way down through the thistle.

Haakon Gokstad had a finger stuck in his mouth where one of his teeth had fallen out. He removed the finger and spit through the hole. He nodded up the hill at the figure heading our way. "My, that sumbitch has got some brass," he said. Then he put the finger back.

The man walked straight to Djarf. He stood before him and removed his hood. His hair lay thin on his scalp and had probably been blond before it went white. He was old, with lines on his face that could have been drawn with a dagger point.

"Naddod," Djarf said, dipping his head slightly. "S'pose you've been expecting us."

"I certainly have not," Naddod said. He brought his hand up to the rude wooden cross that hung from his neck. "And I won't sport with you and pretend the surprise is entirely a pleasant one. Frankly, there isn't much left here worth pirating, so, yes, it's a bit of a puzzle."

"Uh-huh," said Djarf. "Can't tell us anything about a hailstorm, or locusts and shit, or a bunch of damn dragons coming around and scaring the piss out of everybody's wife. You don't know nothing about any of that."

Naddod held his palms up and smiled piteously. "No, I'm very sorry, I don't. We did send a monkeypox down to the Spanish garrison at Much Wenlock, but honestly, nothing your way."

Djarf's tone changed, and his voice got loud and amiable. "Huh. Well, that's something." He turned to us and held up his hands. "Hey, boys, hate to break it to you, but it sounds like somebody fucked something up here. Old Naddod says it wasn't him, and as soon as he tells me just who in the motherfuck it was behind the inconveniences we been having, we'll get back under way."

"Right." Naddod was uneasy, and I could see a chill run through him. "If you're passing through Mercia, I know they've just gotten hold of this man Ethelred. Supposed to be a very tough customer. You know, that was his leprosy outbreak last year in—"

Djarf was grinning and nodding, but Naddod looked stricken.

Djarf kept a small knife in his belt, and in the way other men smoked a pipe or chewed seeds, Djarf stropped that little knife. It was sharpened down to a little fingernail of blade. You could shave a fairy's ass with that thing.

And while Naddod was talking, Djarf had pulled out his little knife and unzipped the man. At the sight of blood washing over the white seashells, everybody pressed forward, hollering and whipping their swords around. Djarf was overcome with a sort of crazed elation, and he hopped up and down, yelling for everybody to be quiet and watch him.

Naddod was not dead. His insides had pretty much spilled out, but he was still breathing. Not crying out or anything, though, which you had to give him credit for. Djarf hunkered and flipped Naddod onto his stomach and rested a foot in the small of his back.

Gnut was right beside me. He sighed and put his hand over his eyes. "Ah, shit, is he doing a blood eagle?"

"Yeah," I said. "Looks that way."

Haakon spit again. "He don't need to mess with that. Damn tedious waste of time."

Djarf held up his hand to quiet the crowd. "Now I know most of the old-timers have seen one of these before, but it might be a new one on some of you young men." The hockchoppers elbowed each other, giddy with anticipation. "This thing is what we call a 'blood eagle,' and if you'll just sit tight a second you can see—well, it's a pretty wild effect."

The men stepped back to give Djarf room to work. Djarf placed the point of his sword to one side of Naddod's spine. He leaned into it, and worked the sword in gingerly, as though he were doing elaborate embroidery on a piece of rare silk. He went at it slowly, delicately crunching through one rib at a time until he'd made an incision about a foot long. He paused to wipe sweat from his brow, and made a parallel cut on the other side of the backbone. Then he knelt and put his hands into the cuts. He fumbled around in there a second, and then drew Naddod's lungs through the slits. As Naddod huffed and gasped, the lungs flapped, looking sort of like a pair of wings. I had to turn away myself. It was very grisly stuff.

The young men roared, and Djarf stood there, flushed with pride, conducting the applause. Then, at his command, they all broke out their sieging tackle and swarmed up the hill.

Only Gnut and Haakon and Ørl Stender and I didn't go. Ørl watched the others flock up toward the monastery, and when he was sure no one was looking back, he went to where Naddod lay dying, and struck him hard on the skull with the back of a hatchet. We were all relieved to see those lungs stop quivering. Ørl sighed and crossed himself. He said a funerary prayer, the gist of which was that he didn't know what this man's god was all about, but he was sorry that this humble servant had gotten sent up early, and on a bullshit pretext too. He said he didn't know the man but that he seemed nice enough, and he probably deserved something better the next time around.

"Hell of a rigged-up-ass excuse for a raid," Haakon grumbled.

Gnut smiled and squinted up at the sky. "Have you ever seen a day like this? This is a heck of a fine day. Let's go up the hill and see if we can't scratch up something for a picnic."

It was all the same to him, a month away from home for neither moral purpose nor riches. He did not have a wife waiting on him who was pissed already and would require extravagant palliating with Northumbrian booty.

We hiked up to the little settlement on the top of the hill. Some ways over, where the monastery was, the young men were on a spree, shouting and setting the trees on fire, dragging out the monks and pulling blood eagles.

Our hands were sore from the row over, and we paused at a well in the center of the village to wet our palms and have a drink. We were surprised to see the young hockchopper from the boat bust forth from a stand of ash trees, yanking some poor half-dead citizen along behind him. He walked over to where we were standing and let his victim collapse on the dusty boulevard.

"This is a hell of a sight," he said to us. "You'd make good chieftains, standing around like this, watching other people work."

"Why, you little turd," Haakon said. He took his hand off his hip and backhanded the boy across the mouth. The fellow lying there in the dust looked up and chuckled. The boy squealed with rage, plucked a dagger from his hip scabbard, and stabbed Haakon in the stomach. There was a still moment. Haakon gazed down at the ruby stain spreading across his tunic. He looked greatly irritated.

A sweet, angelic expression of overmastering anxiety crept across the young man's face as he realized what he'd done. He was still looking that way when Haakon cleaved his head across the eyebrows with a single, graceful stroke.

Haakon cleaned his sword and looked again at his stomach. "Sumbitch," he said, probing the wound with his pinky. "It's deep. I believe I'm in a fix."

"Nonsense," said Gnut. "Just need to lay you down and stitch you up."

Ørl, who was softhearted, went over to the man the youngster had left. He propped him up against the well and gave him the bucket to sip at.

Across the road, an old dried-up farmer had come out of his house. He stared off at the smoke from the monastery rolling down across the bay. He nodded at us. We walked his way.

"Hullo," he said. He looked hard at my face. "Hm. I might recognize you."

"Could be," I said. "I was through here last fall."

"Uh-huh," he said. "Now that was a hot one. Don't know why you'd want to come back. You got everything that was worth a shit on the last going-over."

"Yeah, well, we're having a hard time figuring it ourselves. Just supposed to be an ad hominem deal on your man Naddod. Wrong guy, as it turns out, but he got gotten anyway, sorry to say."

The man sighed. "Doesn't harelip me any. We all had to tithe in to cover his retainer. Do just as well without him, I expect. So what are you doing, any looting?"

"Why?" I said. "You got anything to loot?"

"Me? Oh, no. Got a decent cookstove, but I can't see you toting that back on the ship."

"Don't suppose you've got a coin hoard or anything buried out back?"

"Ah, a coin hoard. Jeezum crow, I wish I did have a coin hoard. Coin hoard, I'd really turn things around for myself."

"Yeah, well, I don't suppose you'd own up if you did have."

He laughed. "You got that right, my friend. But I guess you got to kill me or believe me, and either way, no hoard." He pointed at Haakon, who was leaning on Gnut and looking pretty spent. "Looks like your friend's got a problem. Unless you'd like to watch him die, why don't you bring him inside? Got a daughter who's hell's own seamstress."

The man, who was called Bruce, had a cozy little place. We all filed in. His daughter was standing by the stove, and she gave a nervous "pip" when we came through the door. She was a small thing and looked neither young nor old. She had a head full of thick black hair, and a thin face, pale as sugar. She was a pretty girl. So pretty, in fact, that it took a second to notice she was missing an arm. We all balked and had a look at her. Haakon took his hand off his stomach and gave a boyish wave. Ørl farted anxiously. But Gnut, you could tell, was truly smitten. The way he looked, blanched and wide-eyed, he could have been facing a wild dog instead of a good-looking woman. He rucked his hands through his ropy hair and tried to lick the crust off his lips. Then he nodded to her and uttered a solemn "hullo."

"Mary," Bruce said. "This man has developed a hole in his stomach. I said we'd help fix him up."

Mary looked at Haakon. "Aha," she said. She lifted his tunic and surveyed the wound. "Water," she said to Ørl, who was looking on. Gnut eyed him jealously as he left for the well. Then Gnut cleared his throat. "I'd like to pitch in," he said. Mary directed him to a little sack of onions in the corner, and told him to chop. Bruce got a fire going in the stove. Mary set the water on and shook in some dry porridge. Haakon, who had grown rather waxen, crawled up on the table and lay still. "I don't feel like no porridge," he said.

"Don't worry about that," Bruce said. "The porridge is just for the onions to ride in on."

Gnut kept an eye on Mary as he bent over a small table and overdid it on the onions. He chopped and chopped, and when he'd chopped all they had, he started chopping the chopped-up ones over again. Finally, Mary looked over and told him, "That's fine, thank you," and Gnut laid the knife down.

When the porridge was cooked, Mary threw in a few handfuls of onion and took the concoction over to Haakon. He regarded her warily, but when she held the wooden spoon out toward him, he opened his mouth like a baby bird. He chewed and swallowed. "That doesn't taste very good," he said, but he kept eating anyway.

A minute passed, and then a peculiar thing occurred. Mary lifted Haakon's tunic again, put her face to the wound, and sniffed at it. She paused a second and then did it again.

"What in the world is this?" I asked.

"Gotta do this with a wound like that," Bruce said. "See if he's got the porridge illness."

"He doesn't have any porridge illness," I said. "At least he didn't before now. What he's got is a stab hole in his stomach. Now stitch the man up."

"Won't do any good if you smell onions coming out of that hole. Means he's got the porridge illness and he's done for."

Haakon looked up. "Oh, you're talking about a pierced bowel."

"Yes," said Bruce. "Pierced bowels, the porridge illness."

Mary had another sniff. The wound, evidently, did not smell like onions. It only smelled like a wound. She cleaned him with hot water and was able to stitch the hole to a tight pucker, after telling Gnut about fifty times, thanks very much, she could manage without his help.

Haakon fingered the stitches, and, satisfied, passed out. The five of us stood around, and no one could think of anything to say.

"So," Gnut said in an offhand way. "Were you born like that?"

"Like what?" Mary said.

"Without both arms, I mean. Is that how you came out?"

"Sir, that is a hell of a thing to ask my daughter," Bruce said. "It was your people that did it to her."

Gnut said, "Oh." And then he said it again: "Oh." And then really no one could think of anything to say. Finally, Gnut stepped around the table and quietly let himself out. Then we heard him out in the yard, cussing and kicking things. He did that for a minute or two, but he was calm when he came back in, and silent again.

Then Mary spoke. "It wasn't you who did it," she said. "But the man who did, I think I'd like to kill him."

Gnut told her that if she would please let him know who it was, he'd consider it a favor if she'd let him intervene on her behalf.

She thanked him and Gnut nodded and grunted.

I said, "I would like a drink. Ørl, what have you got in that wineskin?"

"Hmph," Ørl said. The skin hung from his shoulder, and he put his hands on it protectively.

"I asked what have you got to drink."

"I've got some carrot brandy, for your damned information. But it's got to last me the way back. I can't be damp and not have something to take the chill off."

Gnut was glad to have something to raise his voice about. "Ørl, you're a son of a bitch. This man's daughter got her arm chopped off on our account, Haakon is maybe gonna die, and you can't even see your way to splash a little booze around. Now, that is the worst, the lowest, thing I've ever heard."

So Ørl opened up his wineskin, and we all had a dose. It was sweet and potent and we drank and laughed and carried on. Haakon came to, and in the mawkish way of someone who has almost died and sees the world through new eyes, he made a sentimental toast to what a splendid day it was. Bruce and Mary got loosened up and we all talked like old friends. Mary told a funny story about a filthy-minded apothecary who lived down the road. She was having a good time, and did not seem to mind how Gnut was getting all up in her personal space. No one looking in on us would have known we were the reason this girl was missing an arm, and also the reason, probably, that nobody asked where Bruce's wife had gone.

It was not long before we heard Djarf causing a commotion at the well. Me and Gnut and Ørl stepped outside. He had stripped to his waist, and his face and arms and pants looked about how you'd figure. He was hauling up buckets of cold water, dumping it over his head, and shrieking with delight. The blood ran off him pink and watery. He saw us and came over.

"Hoo," he said, shaking water from his hair. He jogged in place for a minute, shivered and then straightened up. "Mercy, that was a spree. Not much loot to speak of, but, damn, a hell of a goddamn spree." He did another deep knee bend, massaged his thighs and spat a few times. Then he said, "So, you do much killing?"

"Nah," I said. "Haakon killed that little what's-his-name lying over there, but no, we've just been sort of taking it easy."

"Hm. What about in there?" he asked, indicating Bruce's cottage. "Who lives there? You kill them?"

"No, we didn't," Ørl said. "They helped put Haakon back together and everything. They seem like very nice people."

"Nobody's killing them," Gnut said darkly.

"So everybody's back at the monastery, then?" I asked.

"Well, most of them. Those young men had a disagreement over some damn thing or other and fell to killing one another. Gonna make for a tough row out of here. Pray for wind, I guess."

Brown smoke was heavy in the sky, and I could hear dim sounds of people screaming.

"So here's the deal," Djarf said. "We bivouac here tonight, and if the weather holds, we shoot down to Mercia tomorrow and see if we can't sort things out with this fucker Ethelred."

"I don't know," Ørl said.

"Fuck that," I said. "This shit was a damn goose chase as it is. I got a wife at home and wheatstraw to bale. I'll be fucked if I'll row your ass to Mercia."

Djarf clenched his jaw. He looked at Gnut. "You too?"

Gnut nodded.

Djarf yelled. "Aaaaah! You motherfuckers are mutinizing me? You sons of bitches are mutinizing my fucking operation?"

"Look, Djarf," I said. "Nobody's doing anything to anybody. We just need to head on back."

"Motherfuck!" Djarf yelled. He drew his sword and leaped around the yard, striking at the earth and chunking up his gobs of sod. Then he snorted and ran at us with the sword raised high, and Gnut had to slip behind him quickly and put a bear hug on him. I went over and clamped one hand over Djarf's mouth and pinched his nose shut with the other, and after a while he started to cool out.

We let him go. He stood there huffing and eyeing us, and we kept our knives and things out, and finally he put the sword back and composed himself.

"Okay, sure, I read you," he said. "Fair enough. Okay, we go back. Oh, I should have told you, Olaffsen found a stash of beef shells somewhere. He's gonna cook those up for everybody who's left. Ought to be tasty." He turned and humped it back toward the bay.

Gnut didn't come down to the feast. He said he needed to stay at Bruce and Mary's to look after Haakon. Bullshit, of course, seeing as Haakon made it down the hill by himself and crammed his tender stomach with about nine tough steaks. When the dusk started turning black and still no Gnut, I legged it back up to Bruce's to see about him. Gnut was sitting on a hollow log outside the cottage, flicking gravel into the weeds.

"She's coming back with me," he said.

"Mary?"

He nodded gravely. "I'm taking her home with me to be my wife. She's in there talking it over with Bruce."

"This a voluntary thing, or an abduction-type deal?"

Gnut looked off toward the bay as though he hadn't heard the question. "She's coming with me."

I mulled it over. "You sure this is such a hot idea, bringing her back to live among our people, you know, all things considering?"

Gnut's voice grew quiet. "Any man that touches her, or says anything unkind, it will really be something different, the sort of shit I'll do to him."

We sat a minute and watched the sparks rising from the bonfire on the beach. The warm evening wind carried smells of blossoms and wood smoke, and I was overcome with a feeling of deep satisfaction. It had been such a pleasant day.

We walked into Bruce's where only a single candle was going. Mary stood by the window with her one arm across her chest. Bruce, we could see, was having a fit of anxiety, and when we came in he moved to block the door. "Get back out of my house," he said. "You just can't take her, with what little I've got."

Gnut did not look happy, but he shouldered past and knocked Bruce on his ass. I went and put a hand on the old farmer. His whole body had gone tight with grief and fury.

Mary did not hold her hand out to Gnut, but she did not cry when Gnut put his arm around her and moved her toward the door. The look she gave her father was a wretched thing to see, but still she went easy, because with just one arm like that, what could she do? What other man would have her?

Their backs were to us when Bruce grabbed up an awl from the table and made for Gnut. I stepped in front of him and broke a chair on his face, but still he kept coming, scrabbling at my sword, trying to snatch up something he could use to keep his daughter from going away. I had to hold him steady and run my knife into his cheek. I held it there like a horse's bit, and then he didn't want to move. When I got up off him he was crying quietly. As I was leaving, he threw something at me and knocked the candle out.

And you might think it was a good thing, that Gnut had found a woman who would let him love her, and if she didn't exactly love him back, at least she would, in time, get to feeling something for him that wasn't so far from it. But what would you say about that ride back when the winds went slack and it was five long weeks before we finally fetched up home? Gnut didn't hardly say a word to anybody, just held Mary close to him, trying to keep her soothed and safe from all of us, his friends. He wouldn't look me in the face, stricken as he was with the awful fear that comes with getting hold of something you can't afford to lose.

Things got different then and they stayed like that. Not long after we got home, Djarf had a worm crawl up a hole in his foot and had to give up raiding. Gnut and Mary turned to home-steading full-time, and it got to where we just stopped talking because those times we did get together he would laugh and chat a little bit, but you could see he had his mind on other things.

Where had the good times gone? I didn't know, but when Pila and me had our little twins and we put a family together, I got an understanding of how terrible love can be. You wish you hated those people, your wife and children, because you know what awful things the world will do to them, because you have done some of those things yourself. It's crazy-making, but you cling to them with everything and close your eyes against the rest of it. But still you wake up late at night and lie there listening for the creak and splash of oars, the clank of steel, the sounds of men row-ing toward your home.

DO NOT DISTURB

A. M. HOMES

My wife, the doctor, is not well. In the end she could be dead. It started suddenly, on a country weekend, a movie with friends, a pizza, and then pain. "I liked the part where he lunged at the woman with a knife," Eric says.

"She deserved it," Enid says.

"Excuse me," my wife says, getting up from the table.

A few minutes later I find her doubled over on the sidewalk. "Something is ripping me from the inside out."

"Should I get the check?" She looks at me like I am an idiot.

"My wife is not well," I announce, returning to the table. "We have to go."

"What do you mean—is she all right?"

Eric and Enid hurry out while I wait for the check. They drive us home. As I open the front door, my wife pushes past me and goes running for the bathroom. Eric, Enid, and I stand in the living room, waiting.

"Are you all right in there?" I call out.

"No," she says.

"Maybe she should go to the hospital," Enid says.

"Doctors don't go to the hospital," I say.

She lies on the bathroom floor, her cheek against the white tile. "I keep thinking it will pass."

"Call us if you need us," Eric and Enid say, leaving.

I tuck the bath mat under her head and sneak away. From the kitchen I call a doctor friend. I stand in the dark, whispering, "She's just lying there on the floor, what do I do?"

"Don't do anything," the doctor says, half-insulted by the thought that there is something to do. "Observe her. Either it will go away, or something more will happen. You watch and you wait."

Watch and wait. I am thinking about our relationship. We haven't been getting along. The situation has become oxygenless and addictive, a suffocating annihilation, each staying to see how far it will go.

I sit on the edge of the tub, looking at her. "I'm worried."

"Don't worry," she says. "And don't just sit there staring."

Earlier in the afternoon we were fighting, I don't remember about what. I only know—I called her a bitch.

"I was a bitch before I met you and I'll be a bitch long after you're gone. Surprise me," she said. "Tell me something new."

I wanted to say, I'm leaving. I wanted to say, I know you think I never will and that's why you treat me like you do. But I'm going. I wanted to get in the car, drive off, and call it a day.

The fight ended with the clock. She glanced at it. "It's six-thirty, we're meeting Eric and Enid at seven; put on a clean shirt."

She is lying on the bathroom floor, the print of the bath mat making an impression on her cheek. "Are you comfortable?" I ask.

She looks surprised, as though she's just realized she's on the floor.

"Help me," she says, struggling to get up.

Her lips are white and thin.

"Bring me a trash can, a plastic bag, a thermometer, some Tylenol, and a glass of water."

"Are you going to throw up?"

"I want to be prepared," she says.

We are always prepared. We have flare guns and fire extinguishers, walkie-talkies, a rubber raft, a hundred batteries in assorted shapes and sizes, a thousand bucks in dollar bills, enough toilet paper and bottled water to get us through six months. When we travel we have smoke hoods in our carry-on bags, protein bars, water purification tablets, and a king-sized bag of M&Ms. We are ready and waiting.

She slips the digital thermometer under her tongue; the numbers move up the scale—each beep is a tenth of a degree.

"A hundred and one point four," I announce.

"I have a fever?" she says in disbelief.

"I wish things between us weren't so bad."

"It's not as bad as you think," she says. "Expect less and you won't be disappointed."

We try to sleep; she is hot, she is cold, she is mumbling something about having "a surgical belly," something about "guarding and rebound." I don't know if she's talking about herself or the NBA.

"This is incredible." She sits bolt upright and folds over again, writhing. "Something is struggling inside me. It's like one of those alien movies, like I'm going to burst open and something's going to spew out, like I'm erupting." She pauses, takes a breath. "And then it stops. Who would ever have thought this would happen to me—and on a Saturday night?"

"Is it your appendix?"

"That's the one thought I have, but I'm not sure. I don't have the classic symptoms. I don't have anorexia or diarrhea. When I was eating that pizza, I was hungry."

"Is it an ovary? Women have lots of ovaries."

"Women have two ovaries," she says. "It did occur to me that it could be *Mittelschmertz*."

"*Mittelschmertz?*"

"The launching of the egg, the middle of the cycle."

At five in the morning her temperature is 103. She is alternately sweating and shivering.

"Should I drive you back to the city or to the hospital out here?"

"I don't want to be the doctor who goes to the ER with gas."

"Fine."

I am dressing myself, packing, thinking of what I will need in the waiting room: cell phone, notebook, pen, something to read, something to eat, my wallet, her insurance card.

We are in the car, hurrying. There is an urgency to the situation, the unmistakable sense that something bad is happening. I am driving seventy miles an hour.

She is not a doctor now. She is lost, inside herself.

"I think I'm dying," she says.

I pull up to the emergency entrance and half-carry her in, leaving the car doors open, the engine running; I have the impulse to drop her off and walk away.

The emergency room is empty. There is a bell on the check-in desk. I ring it twice.

A woman appears. "Can I help you?"

"My wife is not well," I say. "She is a doctor."

The woman sits at her computer. She takes my wife's name. She takes her insurance card and then she takes her temperature and blood pressure. "Are you in a lot of pain?"

"Yes," my wife says.

Within minutes a doctor is there, pressing on my wife. "It's got to come out," he says.

"What?" I ask.

"Appendix. Do you want some Demerol?"

She shakes her head. "I'm working tomorrow and I'm on call."

In the cubicle next to her, someone vomits.

The nurse comes to take blood. "They called Barry Manilow—he's a very good surgeon." She ties off my wife's arm. "We call him Barry Manilow because he looks like Barry Manilow."

"I want to do right by you," Barry Manilow says, as he's feeling my wife's belly. "I'm not sure it's your appendix, not sure it's your gall bladder either. I'm going to call the radiologist and have him scan it. How's that sound?" She nods.

I take the surgeon aside. "Should she be staying here? Is this the place to do this?"

"It's not a kidney transplant," he says.

The nurse brings me a cold drink. She offers me a chair. I sit close to the gurney where my wife lies. "Do you want me to get you out of here? I could hire a car and have us driven to the city. I could have you medevaced home."

"I don't want to go anywhere," she says. She is on the wrong side of it now.

Back in the cubicle, Barry Manilow is talking to her. "It's not your appendix. It's your ovary. It's a hemorrhagic cyst; you're bleeding and your hematocrit is falling. We have to operate. I've called a gynecologist and the anesthesiologist—I'm just waiting for them to arrive. We're going to take you upstairs very soon."

"Just do it," she says.

I stop Barry Manilow in the hall. "Can you try and save the ovary, she very much wants to have children. It's just something she hasn't gotten around to yet—first she had her career, then me, and now this."

"We'll do everything we can," he says, disappearing through the door marked "Authorized Personnel Only."

I am the only one in the surgical waiting room, flipping through copies of *Field and Stream, Highlights for Children,* a pamphlet on colon cancer. Less than an hour later, Barry Manilow comes to find me. "We saved the ovary. We took out something the size of a lemon."

"The size of a lemon?"

He makes a fist and holds it up—"A lemon," he says. "It looked a little funny. We sent it to Pathology." He shrugs.

A lemon, a bleeding lemon, like a blood orange, a lemon souring in her. Why is fruit used as the universal medical measurement?

"She should be upstairs in about an hour."

When I get to her room she is asleep. A tube poking out from under the covers drains urine into a bag. She is hooked up to oxygen and an IV.

I put my hand on her forehead. Her eyes open.

"A little fresh air," she says, pulling at the oxygen tube. "I always wondered what all this felt like."

She has a morphine drip, the kind she can control herself. She keeps the clicker in her hand. She never pushes the button.

I feed her ice chips and climb into the bed next to her. In the middle of the night I go home. In the morning she calls, waking me up.

"Flowers have been arriving like crazy," she says, "from the hospital, from the ER, from the clinic."

Doctors are like firemen. When one of their own is down they go crazy.

"They took the catheter out, I'm sitting up in a chair. I already had some juice and took myself to the bathroom," she says proudly. "They couldn't be nicer. But, of course, I'm a very good patient."

I interrupt her. "Do you want anything from the house?"

"Clean socks, a pair of sweatpants, my hairbrush, some toothpaste, my face soap, a radio, maybe a can of Diet Coke."

"You're only going to be there a couple of days."

"You asked if I needed anything. Don't forget to feed the dog."

Five minutes later she calls back, crying. "I have ovarian cancer."

I run out the door. When I get there the room is empty. I'm expecting a big romantic scene, expecting her to cling to me, to tell me how much she loves me, how she's sorry we've been having such a hard time, how much she needs me, wants me, now more than ever. The bed is empty. For a moment I think she's died, jumped out the window, escaped. Her absence is terrifying.

In the bathroom, the toilet flushes. "I want to go home," she says, stepping out, fully dressed.

"Do you want to take the flowers?"

"They're mine, aren't they? Do you think all the nurses know I have cancer? I don't want anyone to know."

The nurse comes with a wheelchair; she takes us down to the lobby. "Good luck," she says, loading the flowers into the car.

"She knows," my wife says.

We are on the Long Island Expressway. I am dialing and driving. I call my wife's doctor in New York.

"She has to see Kibbowitz immediately," the doctor says.

"Do you think I'll lose my ovary?"

She will lose everything—instinctively I know that.

We are home. She is on the bed with the dog on her lap. She peeks beneath the gauze; her incision is crooked, the lack of precision an incredible insult. "Do you think they can fix it?"

In the morning we go to Kibbowitz. She is again on a table, her feet in stirrups, in launch position, waiting. Before the doctor arrives she is interviewed and examined by seven medical students. I hate them. I hate them for talking to her, for touching her, for wasting her time. I hate Kibbowitz for keeping her on the table for more than an hour, waiting.

And she is angry with me for being annoyed. "They're just doing their job."

Kibbowitz arrives. He is enormous, like a hockey player, a brute and a bully. It is hard to understand how a man gets gynecologic oncology as his calling. I can tell immediately that she likes him. She will do anything he says.

"Scootch down a little closer to me," he says, settling himself on a stool between her legs. She lifts her ass and slides down. He examines her. He looks under the gauze—"Crooked," he says. "Get dressed and meet me in my office."

"I want a number," she says. "A survival rate."

"I don't deal in numbers," he says.

"I need a number."

He shrugs. "How's seventy percent?"

"Seventy percent what?"

"Seventy percent live five years."

"And then what?" I ask.

"And then some don't," he says.

"What has to come out?" she asks.

"What do you want to keep?"

"I wanted to have a child."

This is a delicate negotiation; they talk parts. "I could take just the one ovary," he says. "And then after the chemo you could try and get pregnant and then after you had a child we could go in and get the rest."

"Can you really get pregnant after chemo?" I ask.

The doctor shrugs. "Miracles happen all the time," he says. "The problem is you can't raise a child if you're dead. You don't have to decide now, let me know in a day or two. Meanwhile I'll book the operating room for Friday morning. Nice meeting you," he says, shaking my hand.

"I want to have a baby," she says.

"I want to have you," I say.

Beyond that I say nothing. Whatever I say she will do the opposite. We are at that point—spite, blame, and fault. I don't want to be held responsible. She opens the door of the consulting room. "Doctor," she shouts, hurrying down the hall after him, clutching her belly, her incision, her wound. "Take it," she screams. "Take it all the hell out."

He is standing outside another examination room, chart in hand.

He nods. "We'll take it through your vagina. We'll take the ovaries, the uterus, cervix, omentum, and your appendix, if they didn't already get it in Southampton. And then we'll put a port in your chest and sign you up for chemotherapy—eight rounds should do it."

She nods.

"See you Friday."

We leave. I am holding her hand, holding her pocketbook on my shoulder, trying to be as good as anyone can be.

"Why don't they just say 'eviscerate'? Why don't they just come out and say, on Friday at nine we're going to eviscerate you—be ready."

"Do you want a little lunch? Some soup? There's a lovely restaurant near here."

She looks flushed. I put my hand to her forehead. She's burning up. "You have a fever. Did you mention that to the doctor?"

"It's not relevant."

Later, when we are at home, I ask, "Do you remember our third date? Do you remember asking—how would you kill yourself if you had to do it with bare hands? I said I would break my nose and shove it up into my brain, and you said you would reach up with your bare hands and rip your uterus out through your vagina and throw it across the room."

"What's your point?"

"No point—I just suddenly remembered it. Isn't Kibbowitz taking your uterus out through your vagina?"

"I doubt he's going to throw it across the room," she says. There is a pause. "You don't have to stay with me now that I have cancer. I don't need you. I don't need anyone. I don't need anything."

"If I left, I wouldn't be leaving because you have cancer. But I would look like an ass, everyone would think I couldn't take it."

"I would make sure they knew it was me, that I was a monster, a cold steely monster, that I drove you away."

"They wouldn't believe you."

She suddenly farts and runs, embarrassed, into the bathroom—as though this is the first time she's farted in her life. "My life is ruined," she yells, slamming the door.

"Farting is the least of it."

When she comes out she is calmer, she crawls into bed next to me, wrung out, shivering.

I hold her. "Do you want to make love?"

"You mean one last time before I'm not a woman, before I'm a dried old husk?"

Instead of fucking we fight. It's the same sort of thing, dramatic, draining. When we're done, I roll over and sleep in a tight knot on my side of the bed.

"Surgical menopause," she says. "That sounds so final." I turn toward her. She runs her hand over her pubic hair. "Do you think they'll shave me?"

I am not going to be able to leave the woman with cancer. I am not the kind of person who leaves the woman with cancer, but I don't know what you do when the woman with cancer is a bitch. Do you hope that the cancer prompts the woman to reevaluate herself, to take it as an opportunity, a signal for change? As far as she's concerned there is no such thing as the mind-body connection; there is science and there is law. There is fact and everything else is bullshit.

Friday morning, while she is in the hospital registration area waiting for her number to be called, she makes another list out loud: "My will is in the top left drawer of the dresser. If anything goes wrong, pull the plug. No heroic measures. I want to be cremated. Donate my organs. Give it away, all of it, every last drop." She stops. "I guess no one will want me now that I'm contaminated." She says the word "contaminated" filled with disgust, disappointment, as though she has failed, soiled herself.

It is nearly 8:00 P.M. when Kibbowitz comes out to tell me he's done. "Everything was stuck together like macaroni and cheese. It took longer than I expected. I found some in the fallopian tube and some on the wall of her abdomen. We cleaned everything out."

She is wheeled back to her room, sad, agitated, angry.

"Why didn't you come and see me?" she asks accusatorily.

"I was right there the whole time, on the other side of the door, waiting for word."

She acts as though she doesn't believe me, as though I screwed with a secretary from the patient services office while she was on the table.

"How're you feeling?"

"Like I've taken a trip to another country and my suitcases are lost."

She is writhing. I adjust her pillow, the position of the bed.

"What hurts?"

"What doesn't hurt? Everything hurts. Breathing hurts."

Because she is a doctor, because she did her residency at this hospital, they give me a small folding cot to set up in the corner of the room. Bending to unfold it, something happens in my back, a hot searing pain spreads across and down. I lower myself to the floor, grabbing the blanket as I go.

Luckily she is sleeping.

The nurse who comes to check her vital signs sees me. "Are you in trouble?"

"It's happened before," I say. "I'll just lie here and see where it goes."

She brings me a pillow and covers me with the blanket.

Eric and Enid arrive. My wife is asleep and I am still on the floor. Eric stands over me.

"We're sorry," Eric whispers. "We didn't get your message until today. We were at Enid's parents'—upstate."

"It's shocking, it's sudden, it's so out of the blue." Enid moves to look at my wife. "She looks like she's in a really bad mood, her brow is furrowed. Is she in pain?"

"I assume so."

"If there's anything we can do, let us know," Eric says.

"Actually, could you walk the dog?" I pull the keys out of my pocket and hold them in the air. "He's been home alone all day."

"Walk the dog—I think we can do that," Eric says, looking at Enid for confirmation.

"We'll check on you in the morning," Enid says.

"Before you go; there's a bottle of Percocet in her purse—give me two."

During the night she wakes up. "Where are you?" she asks.

"I'm right here."

She is sufficiently drugged that she doesn't ask for details. At around six she opens her eyes and sees me on the floor.

"Your back?"

"Yep."

"Cancer beats back," she says and falls back to sleep.

When the cleaning man comes with the damp mop, I pry myself off the floor. I'm fine as long as I'm standing.

"You're walking like you have a rod up your ass," my wife says.

"Is there anything I can do for you?" I ask, trying to be solicitous.

"Can you have cancer for me?"

The pain management team arrives to check on my wife's level of comfort.

"On a scale of one to ten, how do you feel?" the pain fellow asks.

"Five," my wife says.

"She lies," I say.

"Are you lying?"

"How can you tell?"

The specialist arrives. "I know you," he says, seeing my wife in the bed. "We went to school together."

My wife tries to smile.

"You were the smartest one in the class and now look," he reads my wife's chart. "Ovarian cancer and you, that's horrible."

My wife is sitting up high in her hospital bed, puking her

guts into a metal bucket, like a poisoned pet monkey. She is throwing up bright green like an alien. Ted, her boss, stares at her, mesmerized.

The room is filled with people—people I don't know, medical people, people she went to school with, people she did her residency with, a man whose fingers she sewed back on, relatives I've not met. I don't understand why they don't excuse themselves, why they don't step out of the room. I don't understand why there is no privacy. They're all watching her like they've never seen anyone throw up before—riveted.

She is not sleeping. She is not eating. She is not getting up and walking around. She is afraid to leave her bed, afraid to leave her bucket.

I make a sign for the door. I borrow a black Magic Marker from the charge nurse and print in large black letters, DO NOT DISTURB.

They push the door open. They come bearing gifts, flowers, food, books. "I saw the sign, I assumed it was for someone else."

I am wiping green spittle from her lips.

"Do you want me to get rid of everyone?" I ask.

I want to get rid of everyone. The idea that these people have some claim to her, some right to entertain, distract, bother her more than I, drives me up the wall. "Should I tell them to go?"

She shakes her head. "Just the flowers, the flowers nauseate me."

An hour later, I empty the bucket again. The room remains overcrowded. I am on my knees by the side of her hospital bed, whispering, "I'm leaving."

"Are you coming back?" she whispers.

"No."

She looks at me strangely. "Where are you going?"

"Away."

"Bring me a Diet Coke."

She has missed the point.

It is heartbreaking seeing her in a stained gown, in the middle of a bed, unable to tell everyone to go home, unable to turn it off. Her pager is clipped to her hospital gown, several times it goes off. She returns the calls. She always returns the calls. I imagine her saying, What the hell are you bothering me for—I'm busy, I'm having cancer.

Later, I am on the edge of the bed, looking at her. She is increasingly beautiful, more vulnerable, female.

"Honey?"

"What?" Her intonation is like a pissy caged bird—*cawww.* "What? What are you looking at? What do you want?" *Cawww.*

"Nothing."

I am washing her with a cool washcloth.

"You're tickling me," she complains.

"Make sure you tell her you still find her attractive," a man in the hall tells me. "Husbands of women who have mastectomies need to keep reminding their wives that they are beautiful."

"She had a hysterectomy," I say.

"Same thing."

Two days later, they remove the packing. I am in the room when the resident comes with a long tweezers like tongs and pulls yards of material from her vagina, wads of cotton, and gauze, stained battlefield red. It's like a magic trick gone awry, one of those jokes about how many people you can fit in a telephone booth, more and more keeps coming out.

"Is there anything left in there?" she asks.

The resident shakes his head. "Your vagina now just comes to a stop, it's a stump, an unconnected sleeve. Don't be surprised if you bleed, if you pop a stitch or two." He checks her chart and signs her out. "Kibbowitz has you on pelvic rest for six weeks."

"Pelvic rest?" I ask.

"No fucking," she says.

Not a problem.

Home. She watches forty-eight hours of Holocaust films on cable TV. Although she claims to compartmentalize everything, suddenly she identifies with the bald, starving prisoners of war. She sees herself as a victim. She points to the naked corpse of a woman. "That's me," she says. "That's exactly how I feel."

"She's dead," I say.

"Exactly."

Her notorious vigilance is gone. As I'm fluffing her pillows, her billy club rolls out from under the bed. "Put it in the closet," she says.

"Why?" I ask, rolling it back under the bed.

"Why sleep with a billy club under the bed? Why do anything when you have cancer?"

During a break between *Shoah* and *The Sorrow and the Pity,* she taps me. "I'm missing my parts," she says. "Maybe one of those lost eggs was someone special, someone who would have cured something, someone who would have invented something wonderful. You never know who was in there. They are my lost children."

"I'm sorry."

"For what?" She looks at me accusingly.

"Everything."

"Thirty-eight-year-olds don't get cancer, they get Lyme disease, maybe they have appendicitis, on rare occasions in some other parts of the world they have Siamese twins, but that's it."

In the middle of the night she wakes up, she throws the covers off. "I can't breathe, I'm burning up. Open the window, I'm hot, I'm so hot."

"Do you know what's happening to you?"

"What are you talking about?"

"You're having hot flashes."

"I am not," she says, as though I've insulted her. "They don't start so soon."

They do.

"Get away from me, get away," she yells. "Just being near you makes me uncomfortable, it makes my temperature unstable."

On Monday she starts chemotherapy.

"Will I go bald?" she asks the nurse.

I cannot imagine my wife bald.

"Most women buy a wig before it happens," the nurse says, plugging her into the magic potion.

One of the other women, her head wrapped in a red turban, leans over and whispers, "My husband says I look like a porno star." She winks. She has no eyebrows, no eyelashes, nothing.

We shop for a wig. She tries on every style, every shape and color. She looks like a man in drag, like she's wearing a bad Halloween costume, like it's all a horrible joke.

"Maybe my hair won't fall out?" she says.

"It's okay," the woman in the wig shop says. "Insurance covers it. Ask your doctor to write a prescription for a cranial prosthesis."

"I'm a doctor," my wife says.

The wig woman looks confused. "It's okay," she says, putting another wig on my wife's head.

She buys a wig. I never see it. She brings it home and immediately puts it in the closet. "It looks like Linda Evans, like someone on *Dynasty*. I just can't do it," she says.

Her scalp begins to tingle. Her hair hurts. "It's as though someone grabbed my hair and is pulling as hard as they can."

"It's getting ready to go," I say. "It's like a time bomb. It ticks and then it blows."

"What are you, a doctor? Suddenly you know everything about cancer, about menopause, about everything?"

In the morning her hair is falling out. It is all over the pillow, all over the shower floor.

"Your hair's not really falling out," Enid says when we meet them for dinner. Enid reaches and touches her hair, sweeps her hand through it, as if to be comforting. She ends up with a handful of hair; she has pulled my wife's hair out. She tries to put it back, she furiously pats it back in place.

"Forget that I was worried about them shaving my pubic hair, how 'bout it all just went down the drain."

She looks like a rat, like something that's been chewed on and spit out, like something that someone tried to electrocute and failed. In four days she is 80 percent bald.

She stands before me naked. "Document me."

I take pictures. I take the film to one of those special stores that has a sign in the window—we don't censor.

I give her a baseball cap to wear to work. Every day she goes to work, she will not miss a day, no matter what.

I, on the other hand, can't work. Since this happened, my work has been nonexistent. I spend my day as the holder of the feelings, the keeper of sensation.

"It's not my fault," she says. "What the hell do you do all day while I'm at the hospital?"

Recuperate.

She wears the baseball cap for a week and then takes a razor, shaves the few scraggly hairs that remain, and goes to work bald, without a hat, without a wig—starkers.

There's something admirable and aggressive about her baldness, as if she's saying to everyone—I have cancer and you have to deal with it.

"How do you feel?" I ask at night when she comes home from the hospital.

"I feel nothing."

"How can you feel nothing?"

"I am made of steel and wood," she says happily.

As we're falling asleep she tells me a story. "It's true, it happened as I was walking to the hospital. I accidentally bumped into someone on the sidewalk. Excuse me, I said and continued on. He ran after me, 'Excuse me, boy. Excuse me, boy. You knocked my comb out of my hand and I want you to go back and pick it up.' I turned around—we bumped into each other, I said excuse me, and that will have to suffice. 'You knocked it out of my hand on purpose, white boy.' I said, I am not a boy. 'Then what are you—Cancer Man? Or are you just a bitch? A bald fucking bitch.' I wheeled around and chased him. You fucking crazy ass, I screamed. You fucking crazy ass. I screamed it about four times. He's lucky I didn't fucking kill him," she says.

I am thinking she's lost her mind. I'm thinking she's lucky he didn't kill her.

She stands up on the bed—naked. She strikes a pose like a bodybuilder. "Cancer Man," she says, flexing her muscles, creating a new superhero. "Cancer Man!"

Luckily she has good insurance. The bill for the surgery comes—it's itemized. They charge per part removed. Ovary $7,000, appendix $5,000, the total is $72,000. "It's all in a day's work," she says.

We are lying in bed. I am lying next to her, reading the paper.

"I want to go to a desert island, alone. I don't want to come back until this is finished," she says.

"You are on a desert island, but unfortunately you have taken me with you."

She looks at me. "It will never be finished—do you know that? I'm not going to have children and I'm going to die."

"Do you really think you're going to die?"

"Yes."

I reach for her.

"Don't," she says. "Don't go looking for trouble."

"I wasn't. I was trying to be loving."

"I don't feel loving," she says. "I don't feel physically bonded to anyone right now, including myself."

"You're pushing me away."

"I'm recovering," she says.

"It's been eighteen weeks."

Her blood counts are low. Every night for five nights, I inject her with Nupagen to increase the white blood cells. She teaches me how to prepare the injection, how to push the needle into the muscle of her leg. Every time I inject her, I apologize.

"For what?" she asks.

"Hurting you."

"Forget it," she says, disposing of the needle.

"Could I have a hug?" I ask.

She glares at me. "Why do you persist? Why do you keep asking me for things I can't do, things I can't give?"

"A hug?"

"I can't give you one."

"Anyone can give a hug. I can get a hug from the doorman."

"Then do," she says. "I need to be married to someone who is like a potted plant, someone who needs nothing."

"Water?"

"Very little, someone who is like a cactus or an orchid."

"It's like you're refusing to be human," I tell her.

"I have no interest in being human."

This is information I should be paying attention to. She is telling me something and I'm not listening. I don't believe what she is saying.

I go to dinner with Eric and Enid alone.

"It's strange," they say. "You'd think the cancer would soften her, make her more appreciative. You'd think it would make her stop and think about what she wants to do with the rest of her life. When you ask her, what does she say?" Eric and Enid want to know.

"Nothing. She says she wants nothing. She has no needs or desires. She says she has nothing to give."

Eric and Enid shake their heads. "What are you going to do?"

I shrug. None of this is new, none of this is just because she has cancer—that's important to keep in mind, this is exactly the way she always was, only more so.

A few days later a woman calls; she and her husband are people we see occasionally.

"Hi, how are you, how's Tom?" I ask.

"He's a fucking asshole," she says. "Haven't you heard? He left me."

"When?"

"About two weeks ago. I thought you would have known."

"I'm a little out of it."

"Anyway, I'm calling to see if you'd like to have lunch."

"Lunch, sure. Lunch would be good."

At lunch she is a little flirty, which is fine, it's nice actually, it's been a long time since someone flirted with me. In the end, when we're having coffee, she spills the beans. "So I guess you're wondering why I called you?"

"I guess," I say, although I'm perfectly pleased to be having lunch, to be listening to someone else's troubles.

"I heard your wife was sick, I figured you're not getting a lot of sex, and I thought we could have an affair."

I don't know which part is worse, the complete lack of seduction, the fact that she mentions my wife not being well, the idea that my wife's illness would make me want to sleep with her, her stun-gun bluntness—it's all too much.

"What do you think? Am I repulsive? Thoroughly disgusting? Is it the craziest thing you ever heard?"

"I'm very busy," I say, not knowing what to say, not wanting to be offensive, or seem to have taken offense. "I'm just very busy."

My wife comes home from work. "Someone came in today— he reminded me of you."

"What was his problem?"

"He jumped out of the window."

"Dead?"

"Yes," she says, washing her hands in the kitchen sink.

"Was he dead when he got to you?" There's something in her tone that makes me wonder, did she kill him?

"Pretty much."

"What part reminded you of me?"

"He was having an argument with his wife," she says. "Imagine her standing in the living room, in the middle of a sentence, and out the window he goes. Imagine her not having a chance to finish her thought?"

"Yes, imagine, not being able to have the last word. Did she try to stop him?" I ask.

"I don't know," my wife says. "I didn't get to read the police report. I just thought you'd find it interesting."

"What do you want for dinner?"

"Nothing," she says. "I'm not hungry."

"You have to eat something."

"Why? I have cancer. I can do whatever I want."

Something has to happen.

I buy tickets to Paris. "We have to go." I invoke the magic word, "It's an *emergency.*"

"It's not like I get a day off. It's not like I come home at the end of the day and I don't have cancer. It goes everywhere with me. It doesn't matter where I am, it's still me—it's me with cancer. In Paris I'll have cancer."

I dig out the maps, the guidebooks, everything we did on our last trip is marked with fluorescent highlighter. I am acting as though I believe that if we retrace our steps, if we return to a place where things were good, there will be an automatic correction, a psychic chiropractic event, which will put everything into alignment.

I gather provisions for the plane, fresh fruit, water, magazines, the smoke hoods. It's a little-known fact, smoke inhalation is a major cause of death on airplanes.

"What's the point," she says, throwing a few things into a suitcase. "You can do everything and think you're prepared, but you don't know what's going to happen. You don't see what's coming until it hits you in the face."

She points at someone outside. "See that idiot crossing the street in front of the truck—why doesn't he have cancer?"

She lifts her suitcase—too heavy. She takes things out. She leaves her smoke hood on the bed. "If the plane fills with smoke, I'm going to be so happy," she says. "I'm going to breathe deeply, I'm going to be the first to die."

I stuff the smoke hood into my suitcase, along with her rain-coat, her extra shoes, and vitamin C drops. I lift the suitcases, I feel like a pack animal, a Sherpa.

In France, the customs people are not used to seeing bald women. They call her "sir."

"Sir, you're next, sir. Sir, please step over here, sir."

My wife is my husband. She loves it. She smiles. She catches my eye and strikes a subdued version of the superhero/bodybuilder pose, flexing. "Cancer Man," she says.

"And what is the purpose of your visit to France?" the inspector asks. "Business or pleasure?"

"Reconciliation," I say, watching her—Cancer Man.

"Business or pleasure?"

"Pleasure."

Paris is my fantasy, my last-ditch effort to reclaim my marriage, myself, my wife.

As we are checking into the hotel, I remind her of our previous visit—the chef cut himself, his finger was severed, she saved it, and they were able to reattach it. "You made medical history. Remember the beautiful dinner they threw in your honor."

"It was supposed to be a vacation," she says.

The bellman takes us to our room—there's a big basket of fruit, bottles of Champagne and Evian with a note from the concierge welcoming us.

"It's not as nice as it used to be," she says, already disappointed. She opens the Evian and drinks. Her lips curl. "Even the water tastes bad."

"Maybe it's you. Maybe the water is fine. Is it possible you're wrong?"

"We see things differently," she says, meaning she's right, I'm wrong.

"Are you in an especially bad mood, or is it just the cancer?" I ask.

"Maybe it's you?" she says.

We walk, across the river and down by the Louvre. There could be nothing better, nothing more perfect, and yet I am suddenly hating Paris—the beauty, the fineness of it is dwarfed by her foul humor. I realize there will be no saving it, no moment of reconciliation, redemption. Everything is irredeemably awful and getting worse.

"If you're so unhappy, why don't you leave?" I ask her.

"I keep thinking you'll change."

"If I changed any more I can't imagine who I'd be."

"Well, if I'm such a bitch, why do you stay?"

"It's my job, it's my calling to stay with you, to soften you."

"I absolutely do not want to be softer, I don't want to give another inch."

She trips on a cobblestone, I reach for her elbow, to steady her, and instead unbalance myself. She fails to catch me. I fall and recover quickly.

"Imagine how I feel," she says. "I am a doctor and I can't fix it. I can't fix me, I can't fix you—what a lousy doctor."

"I'm losing you," I say.

"I've lost myself. Look at me—do I look like me?"

"You act like yourself."

"I act like myself because I have to, because people are counting on me."

"I'm counting on you."

"Stop counting."

All along the Tuileries there are Ferris wheels—the world's largest Ferris wheel is set up in the middle.

"Let's go," I say, taking her hand and pulling her toward them.

"I don't like rides."

"It's not much of a ride. It's like a carousel, only vertical. Live a little."

She gets on. There are no seat belts, no safety bars. I say nothing. I am hoping she won't notice.

"How is it going to end?" I ask while we're waiting for the wheel to spin.

"I die in the end."

The ride takes off, climbing, pulling us up and over. We are flying, soaring; the city unfolds. It is breathtaking and higher than I thought. And faster. There is always a moment on any ride when you think it is too fast, too high, too far, too wide, and that you will not survive. And then there is the exhilaration of surviving, the thrill of having lived through it, and immediately you want to go around again.

"I have never been so unhappy in my life," my wife says when we're near the top. "It's not just the cancer, I was unhappy before the cancer. We were having a very hard time. We don't get along, we're a bad match. Do you agree?"

"Yes," I say. "We're a really bad match, but we're such a good bad match it seems impossible to let it go."

"We're stuck," she says.

"You bet," I say.

"No. I mean the ride, the ride isn't moving."

"It's not stuck, it's just stopped. It stops along the way."

She begins to cry. "It's all your fault. I hate you. And I still have to deal with you. Every day I have to look at you."

"No, you don't. You don't have to deal with me if you don't want to."

She stops crying and looks at me. "What are you going to do, jump?"

"The rest of your life, or my life, however long or short, should not be miserable. It can't go on this way."

"We could both kill ourselves," she says.

"How about we separate?"

I am being more grown-up than I am capable of being. I am terrified of being without her, but either way, it's death.

The ride lurches forward.

I came to Paris wanting to pull things together and suddenly I am desperate to be away from her. If this doesn't stop now, it will never stop, it will go on forever. She will be dying of her cancer and we will still be fighting. I begin to panic, to feel I can't breathe. I am suffocating; I have to get away.

"Where does it end?"

"How about we say good-bye?"

"And then what? We have opera tickets."

I cannot tell her I am going. I have to sneak away, to tiptoe out backwards. I have to make my own arrangements.

We stop talking. We're hanging in midair, suspended. We have run out of things to say. When the ride circles down, the silence becomes more definitive.

I begin to make my plan. In truth, I have no idea what I am doing. All afternoon, everywhere we go, I cash traveler's checks, I get cash advances, I have about five thousand dollars' worth of francs stuffed in my pocket. I want to be able to leave without a trace, I want to be able to buy myself out of whatever trouble I get into. I am hysterical and giddy all at once.

We are having an early dinner on our way to the opera.

I time my break for just after the coffee comes. "Oops," I say, feeling my pockets. "I forgot my opera glasses."

"Really?" she says. "I thought you had them when we went out."

"They must be at the hotel. You go on ahead, I'll run back. You know I hate not being able to see."

She takes her ticket. "Hurry," she says. "I hate it when you're late."

This is the bravest thing I have ever done. I go back to the hotel and pack my bag. I am going to get out. I am going to fly away. I may never come back. I will begin again, as someone else—unrecognizable.

I move to lift the bag off the bed, I pull it up and my knee goes out. I start to fall but catch myself. I pull at the bag and take a step—too heavy. I will have to go without it. I will have to leave everything behind. I drop the bag, but still I am falling, folding, collapsing. There is pain, searing, spreading, pouring, hot and cold, like water down my back, down my legs.

I am lying on the floor, thinking that if I stay calm, if I can just find my breath, and follow my breath, it will pass. I lie there waiting for the paralysis to recede.

I am afraid of it being over and yet she has given me no choice, she has systematically withdrawn life support: sex and conversation. The problem is that, despite this, she is the one I want.

There is a knock at the door. I know it is not her, it is too soon for it to be her.

"*Entrez,*" I call out.

The maid opens the door, she holds the DO NOT DISTURB sign in her hand. "Ooooff," she says, seeing me on the floor. "Do you need the doctor?"

I am not sure if she means my wife or a doctor other than my wife.

"No."

She takes a towel from her cart and props it under my head. She takes a spare blanket from the closet and covers me with it. She opens the Champagne and pours me a glass, tilting my head up so I can sip. She goes to her cart and gets a stack of night chocolates and sits beside me, feeding me Champagne and chocolate, stroking my forehead.

The phone in the room rings, we ignore it. She refills my glass. She takes my socks off and rubs my feet. She unbuttons my shirt and rubs my chest. I am getting a little drunk. I am just beginning to relax and then there is another knock, a knock my body recognizes before I am fully awake. Everything tightens. My back pulls tighter still, any sensation below my knees drops off.

"I thought something horrible happened to you, I've been calling and calling the room, why haven't you answered? I thought you'd killed yourself."

The maid excuses herself. She goes into the bathroom and gets me a cool washcloth.

"What are you doing?" my wife asks.

There is nothing I can say.

"Knock off the mummy routine. What exactly are you doing? Were you trying to run away and then you chickened out? Say something."

To talk would be to continue; for the moment I am silenced. I am a potted plant, and still that is not good enough for her.

"He is paralyzed," the maid says.

"He is not paralyzed. I am his wife, I am a doctor. I would know if there was something really wrong."

GENTLEMAN'S AGREEMENT

MARK RICHARD

The child had been warned. His father said he would nail that rock-throwing hand to the shed wall, saying it would be hard to break windshields and people's windows with a hand nailed to the shed wall. Wouldn't it? said his father, home for a few hours from the forest he could not extinguish. Goddamn it, didn't the child know what windshields costed? His father held the child up by his ear to better see the spiderweb burst of windshield glass. All the clawing child could better see were the rivets holding his father's smoke-smelling pants together.

Even the child could not understand how the windshield had happened, the child that morning playing splay-legged in the dusty rough driveway, dripping seed-size gravel from a tiny hourglass of fist, flipping a fake stone kernel to a crow come flying down to watch, and the crow not fooled, flapping back away, taking flight when the child rained sand, the child splashing around in the dirt like a seaside idiot, rock droplets up in the air, into the smoky sky that was white like broken melon rind and smelled like the old man's beard and breath.

A playmate had sprung up from the ground near the gully where the good rocks grew, and they began gauging themselves against themselves again, lessons of arc and trajectory, the specific nature of things spinning farther today than yesterday in that white-rind sky, until one rock left the child's fingers while his mind was on something else, this rock on a course that even the playmate ceased fire to regard.

Time slowed for them, the rock arcing toward the friendly family car parked pleasantly in the pecan tree shade. Time slowed and slowed. If time had not slowed, the rock would have sailed over the car, over the pecan tree, over the rented house, and over the town and the burning forests beyond. But the world was enormous that morning, its gravity immense. To arc and trajectory add the lessons of apogee and descent, the rock descending into a broken-glass poke in the eye for the friendly family car, the playmate suddenly skipping away dropping stones, skipping away to slither, laughing, along the gully home.

All afternoon the rind sky lowered and smelled of burning woods.

Goddamn it! Didn't the child know what windshields costed? His father in his dirty, roughed-up denim, of all days to come home, mud and ash, machete on the hip and the snake pistol, timber boots laced with wire that wouldn't burn, the blackened shanks of ankles, the boot soles cracked by heat and desperate shoveling, his father footprinting crazy mazes of topography across the clean wooden floors.

Goddamn it, what was in that head his father shook in his hands like a snow globe? Nothing, said the child, and in his heart the words of the covenant: Never, ever throw another rock ever again. Ever.

In those days the fire went south and the old man was gone again, sleeping in woods and fields the flames had not yet found. The child posted himself at the top of the rough driveway and waited for his father's truck, pious with an unbroken covenant in his heart, no stone had touched his fingers, no rock had he held. He knew his mother was watching him wait for his father from the front window of the rented house. He had heard her wonder if her husband would ever come home again.

On a Saturday afternoon when it did not seem like his father was ever coming home, the child stood at the top of the rough driveway, watching a mule pull a wagon full of black men past the rented house into town. A black man sitting on the tailgate of the wagon extended a middle finger toward the child and the child waved back. The wind was keeping the smoke out of town that day and the child decided to go lie in the gully and pretend he was dead in a battlefield trench.

The child walked down the washed-out driveway, shirtless, Indian-brown, and barefoot, scuffing along until a baby-headed tomahawk stone revealed itself in the dust. The child stopped and poked at the stone with his toe. The child poked at the stone and worried the stone with his toe until the stone was free in the drive-way dirt. The child searched the covenant in his heart and discovered nothing about just *kicking* a stone, so the child kicked the baby-headed tomahawk stone to the end of the driveway where the grass was tall and dense, uncut by his absent father. There was nothing in the covenant, nothing in the agreement the child had in his heart with his father about just *picking up a stone over grass,* that's all it was, so the child just picked up the stone to carry it over the grass to the gully where he could look at it while pretending to be dead in a battlefield trench.

But just picking up the stone from its place in the common earth seemed to signify the stone somehow, and it would probably be best to put it in a special place. Not to throw, never to throw, because that would break the agreement in the heart with the father, but just to put the stone away somewhere to consider it later, maybe even as a test to never, ever throw another rock ever again. So the child carried the stone to the tin-roofed shed. There was nothing in the covenant about just *carrying a stone into a shed as an example of the child's goodness.* There was a box in the shed where the child could hide the stone. To study later. And when he grew up and was older than the old man, he could even shake the thing up to the old man's face and say, *See? Here* is a rock I *didn't* throw!

In the tin-roofed shed was the lawn mower his father used to cut the ragged yard. There were broken fire tools the father brought home to fix. On a nail hung a drip of steel helmet melted by a mad-dog fire that had chased the father hatless across three firebreaks, had chased him into a steaming river, had run him through an orange-and-red ravine where his father dove into the ragged mouth of a cave, and his father crawled as deep as he could crawl into that worst-smelling place until he crawled on top of a bear trying to crawl as deep as it could crawl away from the mad-dog fire that was barking at the mouth of the cave to come in. His father and the bear crawled to the fartherest corner of the cave and curled up together, the bear hugging his father and calling out and crying the worst you've ever heard, said his father, because she had left her cub out in the orange-and-red ravine where the mad-dog fire was barking and where the world was coming to an end.

And in the tin-roofed shed the child saw where the Goat should have been parked—the Goat, the big, yellow fire bike, the marble-size knobs on the tire treads, the homemade steel-mesh cages the old man had welded around the chain and spokes against brush and branches, his father riding the Goat's back in wild reconnaissance of the fire's forward lines, and on Sundays when the world was not on fire the old man and his disciples drank beer in the backyard and rode the Goat down the washed-out driveway fast enough to leap the gully, doing drunken doughnuts and wheelies in the cornfield until somebody's wife went home mad or until somebody broke his arm and thought it was funny.

Considering the spot where the Goat should have been parked warmed the baby-headed tomahawk stone in the child's hand until there was no comfortable way to hold it.

It was much easier to hold the stone behind the tin-roofed shed where there was nothing of his father's to see, nothing to see at all except oceans of corn you would need a ship to cross. Behind the tin-roofed shed was the pile of rocks from the time the landlord tore down the old well house, and the child was never to go near where the old well house had been, he and his father had a handshake agreement about that, he was never to go near the place in the ground that was covered with thick planks; there were snakes down there and the hole was bottomless and even the child knew how bottomless it was by all the sticks and tree limbs he had shoved down between the planks trying to stir the snakes up to the surface.

The child had to decide how to hide the stone to distinguish it from all these other common well-house rocks piled behind the tin-roofed shed. The rotten lean of the place put the edge of the tin roof within the child's reach if he stood on the pile of common rocks, so he did, he climbed the rock pile and reaching up he could almost hide his stone on the roof if he could just toss it up there, not throw it, that was not what he was going to do, but to just toss the stone up on the roof to distinguish it from the other common rock-pile rocks, putting the stone in a special place, keeping it for later.

It was a cheap gunshot noise the child made when he tossed the stone up on the tin-roofed shed, not artillery or anything apocalyptic yet, just a nice, good, gunfight-starting shot, and immediately the common rocks in the rock pile the child was standing on were jealous, he could feel them jealous under his feet. They wanted to be not rocks but rockets, rockets and artillery, and the child said, Okay, just a couple, tossing a couple of rocks is not like throwing a couple of rocks where windshields and people's windows break. He was just being nice to the common well-house rocks.

So the child began to heave the rocks from the rock pile he was standing on up onto the tin roof of the shed. It was a gunfight and a battle and a war, the way they bounced and blew up on the roof, bouncing and clattering around, he worked his way through the pistols and the rifles, bending and tossing, bending and tossing, not waiting until the din had dimmed, but keeping rocks in the air, bouncing and banging. Rockets! the child tossed, Hangernades! until the large keystone of the well house was uncovered and the child said, Adam bomb! and the child had to heave the heavy rock with both hands with all of that day's strength, and in his strength his foot slipped on the loose rocks and the child slipped off the rock pile. The doomsday rock failed to clear the edge of the roof. Down it came square on top of the fallen child's crew-cut head.

The best white doctor in town was the abortionist up the wooden steps across from the courthouse. It was sticky hot, and the doctor slept stuck to the dirty exam-table paper. Flawless liftoffs from Florida tarmac, warm pulpy orange juice, the cool white spread of oscillating fan across the naked backs of Nurse Bedpan's legs, these the morphine dreams of an ex–flight surgeon, grounded, a rough shuddering landing from his sleep when the friendly green family car jumps the sidewalk curb just outside and crushes in the corner of the doctor's wooden building, so difficult to see to drive when the windshield is shattered in bright and opaque pieces, the mother's head out the window to see to steer, one hand on the steering wheel and the other keeping constant pressure on the pretty pink ruined towel turban-wrapped around the child's head, driving a shift, too, more balls than all of us, the old man would say about her, her driving, her springing young black men from their places on the sidewalk where they have come by mule wagon and on foot to loiter and to spit, black bucks jumping back from the kneecap-crushing fender-leveled friendly green family car, the front end rattling the doctor from where he had bid sweet Morpheus take him to his beloved Nurse Bedpan, the fender rattling the old building and the old building's rainspout and gutters where the nightwings hid, the bats behind there, bats hanging by the hundreds and thousands over Main Street all day long if you really looked for them, gone at night flitting for the ton or two of mosquitoes the ballpark ditches and third-base mud hole yielded in the evenings, but back during the day and you could see them if you really looked for them, a tiny wing here and there folded over a bent rain gutter, that long line of black tar caulking the roof beams, not really caulking at all, just the tops of thousands of tiny bat heads hanging upside down along the eaves and roofline, at least one shaken awake by the crash that woke the doctor, awake now and cotton-mouthed, a fleeting face in the ceiling corner of his favorite flyboy, the one endowed with extraterrestrial hand-eye and an irritating venereal drip.

Creatures were stirred, creatures were stirring, and en route to the doctor's, through a gap in the wrapping of the turban towel, the child had studied the tiny pebbles stuck in the green rubber floor mat of the family car, excruciating corduroy design was all he could see, was all that was his focus, those tiny pebbles stuck in the long green rubber lines. He had felt the collision of friendly car and drain spout, had felt himself being pulled across the seat, and then he could see his blood-mottled dusty feet down through the slit in his towel wrap, he saw his feet take a step up a curb. There was a splattering of tobacco chew beside his mother's foot, the pressure of her hand tightened on the towel over the spot where his head had broken open. He felt her pressure on the towel on his head and her other hand leading him to a wooden step leading to another wooden step leading up, and then suddenly he heard her scream, and he heard men laughing, and he felt the towel fall away because she was not holding it any longer and he felt the towel fall like a mantle onto his shoulders, and the light was white to his turbaned eyes as he squinted, and just after he felt the wet towel fall to his shoulders something else fell, and it fell flapping against his neck where the blood ticked dripping from his broken-open head and the thing that fell against his neck felt like tickling fingers, and still blinded he shrugged it off and it fell at his feet, and it flapped around and shrieked at his toes and his eyes focused on the thing and he heard his mother screaming and he heard men laughing and someone caught him and lifted him up the wooden stairs before he went into a different kind of sleep that day.

The child was sitting in cold bathwater worrying about bats falling out of his head again when they finally brought his father home. The large sanitary napkin the doctor had taped to the top of the child's head was now dirty and ragged, the doctor saying not to wash his hair for two weeks until the stitches came out, and now it had been two weeks and the stitches itched to come out, or at least something felt like it was scratching its little black claws in the child's scalp to come out. The child did not trust the stitches to hold against the bats and was hoping they would not break while his mother was around because he was sure it would frighten her to see things falling out of his head again, and what if they didn't just fall out but flew around the house getting into the curtains? The doctor had been eager to get back to his dreaming and even the child knew he had done a hurry-up job on his head, the mother saying later that the doctor's sewing was better suited for patching a Mexican blanket, the doctor even forgetting to be paid until the mother insisted on a bill and the doctor wrote some numbers on a piece of yellow paper and then locked the door behind them so he could needle himself back to that place with the white patio, him in his white uniform, the nurse with the white breasts he loved so much, that white place, the white sand, those white waves.

When they brought his father into the hallway, the child did not recognize him at first. His father was missing his hair on his head and his eyebrows were gone and his beard had melted into little black knots on his skin. He had been the only one left, they said. They told his mother in the hall that it was as if the father had refused to burn when everyone else they found had turned into short, black, shriveled roasts of people. The child's father was wearing just a ladies' raincoat that was clear plastic and wouldn't stick to the burns you could see that were red and raw and black on the father's back and arms. The father's hands were packed in grease and wrapped in gauze and the child wondered if those hands would even be able to hold a hammer to nail a rock-throwing hand to the shed wall. The child stood over his parents' bed for a long time, watching his father sleep in the room that smelled like a curing barn.

On Sunday on their way to the shed the father gathered his tools and showed the child his reckoning, his little column of figures, his carryovers, his paperwork. The white papers were windows and windshield. The yellow paper was the doctor. The little green stub was what they paid the father for keeping the fire from coming into town. By the father's figuring, he didn't think he could afford to keep the child, could not keep him in glass at least. It had been two weeks, but there were to be no more trips to Doctor Duck, the Quack, he called him. The rock-throwing hand had finally costed the father more than he had earned.

Sorry, said the father.

At the shed the father opened his toolbox and told the child it would be all right to holler if it hurt, that the child's hollering probably wouldn't bother anybody. It was Sunday and the mother had gone to church. The father rattled the tools around in his toolbox, poking around with his clawed fingers. The child had closed his eyes and when he smelled his father standing beside him, he lifted up his rock-throwing hand.

Here we go, said the father, and with his shears and his pliers the father set to work on the child's head, snipping and tugging at the black silky thread that had bound together the torn flesh of his only son.

THE GIRL IN THE FLAMMABLE SKIRT

AIMEE BENDER

When I came home from school for lunch my father was wearing a backpack made of stone.

Take that off, I told him, that's far too heavy for you.

So he gave it to me.

It was solid rock. And dense, pushed out to its limit, gray and cold to the touch. Even the little zipper handle was made of stone and weighed a ton. I hunched over the bulk and couldn't sit down because it didn't work with chairs very well so I stood, bent, in a corner, while my father whistled, wheeling about the house, relaxed and light and lovely now.

What's in this? I said, but he didn't hear me, he was changing channels.

I went into the TV room.

What's in this? I asked. This is so heavy. Why is it stone? Where did you get it?

He looked up at me. It's this thing I own, he said.

Can't we just put it down somewhere, I asked, can't we just sit it in the corner?

No, he said, the backpack must be worn. That's the law.

I squatted on the floor to even out the weight. What law? I asked. I never heard of this law before.

Trust me, he said, I know what I'm talking about. He did a few shoulder rolls and turned to look at me. Aren't you supposed to be in school? he asked.

I slogged back to school with it on and smushed myself and the backpack into a desk and the teacher sat down beside me while the other kids were doing their math.

It's so heavy, I said, everything feels very heavy right now.

She brought me a Kleenex.

I'm not crying, I told her.

I know, she said, touching my wrist. I just wanted to show you something light.

Here's something I picked up:

Two rats are hanging out in a labyrinth.

One rat is holding his belly. Man, he says, I am in so much pain. I ate all those sweet little sugar piles they gave us and now I have a bump on my stomach the size of my head. He turns on his side and shows the other rat the bulge.

The other rat nods sympathetically. Ow, she says.

The first rat cocks his head and squints a little. Hey, he says, did you eat that sweet stuff too?

The second rat nods.

The first rat twitches his nose. I don't get it, he says, look at you. You look robust and aglow, you don't look sick at all, you look bump-free and gorgeous, you look swinging and sleek. You look plain great! And you say you ate it too?

The second rat nods again.

Then how did you stay so fine? asks the first rat, touching his distended belly with a tiny claw.

I didn't, says the second rat. I'm the dog.

*   *   *

My hands were sweating. I wiped them flat on my thighs.

Then, ahem, I cleared my throat in front of my father. He looked up from his salad. I love you more than salt, I said.

He seemed touched, but he was a heart attack man and had given up salt two years before. It didn't mean *that* much to him, this ranking of mine. In fact, "Bland is a state of mind" was a favorite motto of his these days. Maybe you should give it up too, he said. No more french fries.

But I didn't have the heart attack, I said. Remember? That was you.

In addition to his weak heart my father also has weak legs so he uses a wheelchair to get around. He asked me to sit in a chair with him once, to try it out for a day.

But my chair doesn't have wheels, I told him. My chair just sits here.

That's true, he said, doing wheelies around the living room, that makes me feel really swift.

I sat in the chair for an entire afternoon. I started to get jittery. I started to do that thing I do with my hands, that knocking-on-wood thing. I was knocking against the chair leg for at least an hour, protecting the world that way, superhero me, saving the world from all my horrible and dangerous thoughts when my dad glared at me.

Stop that knocking! he said. That is really annoying.

I have to go to the bathroom, I said, glued to my seat.

Go right ahead, he said, what's keeping you. He rolled forward and turned on the TV.

I stood up. My knees felt shaky. The bathroom smelled very clean and the tile sparkled and I considered making it into my new bedroom. There is nothing soft in the bathroom. Everything in the bathroom is hard. It's shiny and new; it's scrubbed down and whited out; it's a palace of bleach and all you need is one fierce sponge and you can rub all the dirt away.

I washed my hands with a little duck soap and peered out the bathroom window. We live in a high-rise apartment building and I often wonder what would happen if there was a fire, no elevator allowed, and we had to evacuate. Who would carry him? Would I? Once I imagined taking him to the turning stairway and just dropping him down the middle chute, my mother at the bottom with her arms spread wide to catch his whistling body. Hey, I'd yell, catch Dad! Then I'd trip down the stairs like a little pony and find them both splayed out like car-accident victims at the bottom and that's where the fantasy ends and usually where my knocking-on-wood hand starts to act up.

Paul's parents are alcoholics and drunk all the time so they don't notice that he's never home. Perhaps they conjure him up, visions of Paul, through their bleary whiskey eyes. But Paul is with me. I have locked Paul in my closet. Paul is my loverboy, sweet Paul is my olive.

I open the closet door a crack and pass him food. He slips the dirty plates from the last meal back to me and I stack them on the floor next to my T-shirts. Crouched outside the closet, I listen to him crunch and swallow.

How is it? I ask. What do you think of the salt-free meatball?

Paul says he loves sitting in the dark. He says my house is so quiet and smells so sober. The reason it's so quiet is because my father feels awful and is resting in his bedroom. Tiptoe, tiptoe round the sick papa. The reason it smells sober is because it is *so* sober. I haven't made a joke in this house in ten years at least. Ten years ago, I tried a Helen Keller joke on my parents and they sent me to my room for my terrible insensitivity to suffering.

I imagine in Paul's house everyone is running around in their underwear, and the air is so thick with bourbon your skin tans from it. He says no; he says the truth is his house is quiet also. But it's a more pointy silence, he says. A lighter one with sharper pricks. I nod and listen. He says too that in his house there are moisture rings making Olympian patterns on every possible wooden surface.

Once instead of food I pass my hand through the crack. He holds it for at least a half hour, brushing his fingers over my fingers and tracing the lines in my palm.

You have a long lifeline, he says.

Shut up, I tell him, I do not.

He doesn't let go of my hand, even then. Any dessert?

I produce a cookie out of my front shirt pocket.

He pulls my hand closer. My shoulder crashes against the closet frame.

Come inside, he says, come join me.

I can't, I say, I need to stay out here.

Why? He is kissing my hand now. His lips are very soft and a little bit crumby.

I just do, I say, in case of emergency. I think: because now I've learned my lesson and I'm terribly sensitive to suffering. Poor poor Helen K, blind-and-deaf-and-dumb. Because now I'm so sensitive I can hardly move.

Paul puts down his plate and brings his face up close to mine. He is looking right at me and I'm rustling inside. I don't look away. I want to cut off my head.

It is hard to kiss. As soon as I turn my head to kiss deeper, the closet door gets in the way.

After a minute Paul shoves the door open and pulls me inside with him. He closes the door back and now it is pitch black. I can feel his breath near mine, I can feel the air thickening between us.

I start shaking all over.

It's okay, he says, kissing my neck and my shoulder and my chin and more. He lets me out when I start to cry.

My father is in the hospital on his deathbed.

Darling, he says, you are my only child, my only heir.

To what? I ask. Is there a secret fortune?

No, he says, but you will carry on my genes.

I imagine several bedridden, wheelchaired children. I imagine throwing all my children in the garbage can because they don't work. I imagine a few more bad things and then I'm knocking on his nightstand and he's annoyed again.

Stop that noise, he says, I'm a dying man.

He grimaces in agony. He doesn't die though. This has happened a few times before and he never dies. The whole deathbed scene gets a little confusing when you play it out more than twice. It gets a bit hard to be sincere. At the hospital, I pray a lot, each time I pray with gusto, but my prayers are getting very strained; lately I have to grit my teeth. I picture his smiling face when I pray. I push that face into my head. Three times now when I picture this smiling face it explodes. Then I have to pray twice as hard. In the little hospital church I am the only one praying with my jaw clenched and my hands in fists knocking on the pew. Maybe they think I'm knocking on God's door, tap tap tap. Maybe I am.

When I'm done, I go out a side door into the day. The sky is very hot and the hospital looks dingy in the sunlight and there is an outdoor janitorial supply closet with a hole in the bottom, and two rats are poking out of the hole and all I can see are their moving noses and I want to kick them but they're tucked behind the door. I think of bubonic plague. I think about rabies. I have half a bagel in my pocket from the hospital cafeteria and the rats can probably smell it; their little noses keep moving up and down frantically; I can tell they're hungry. I put my hand in my pocket and bring out the bagel but I just hold it there, in the air. It's cinnamon raisin. It smells like pocket lint. The rats don't come forward. They are trying to be polite. No one is around and I'm by the side of the hospital and it's late afternoon and I'm scot-free and young in the world. I am as breezy and light as a wing made from tissue paper. I don't know what to do with myself so I keep holding on tight to the bagel and sit down by the closet door. Where is my father already? I want him to come rolling out and hand over that knapsack of his; my back is breaking without it.

I think of that girl I read about in the paper—the one with the flammable skirt. She'd bought a rayon chiffon skirt, purple with wavy lines all over it. She wore it to a party and was dancing, too close to the vanilla-smelling candles, and suddenly she lit up like a pine needle torch. When the boy dancing next to her felt the heat and smelled the plasticky smell, he screamed and rolled the burning girl up in the carpet. She got third-degree burns up and down her thighs. But what I keep wondering about is this: That first second when she felt her skirt burning, what did she think? Before she knew it was the candles, did she think she'd done it herself? With the amazing turns of her hips, and the warmth of the music inside her, did she believe, for even one glorious second, that her passion had arrived?

THE CARETAKER

ANTHONY DOERR

For his first thirty-five years, Joseph Saleeby's mother makes his bed and each of his meals; each morning she makes him read a column of the English dictionary, selected at random, before he is allowed to set foot outside. They live in a small collapsing house in the hills outside Monrovia in Liberia, West Africa. Joseph is tall and quiet and often sick; beneath the lenses of his oversized eyeglasses, the whites of his eyes are a pale yellow. His mother is tiny and vigorous; twice a week she stacks two baskets of vegetables on her head and hikes six miles to sell them in her stall at the market in Mazien Town. When the neighbors come to compliment her garden, she smiles and offers them Coca-Cola. "Joseph is resting," she tells them, and they sip their Cokes, and gaze over her shoulder at the dark shuttered windows of the house, behind which, they imagine, the boy lies sweating and delirious on his cot.

Joseph clerks for the Liberian National Cement Company, transcribing invoices and purchase orders into a thick leather-bound ledger. Every few months he pays one more invoice than he should, and writes the check to himself. He tells his mother the extra money is part of his salary, a lie he grows comfortable making. She stops by the office every noon to bring him rice—the cayenne she heaps onto it will keep illness at bay, she reminds him, and watches him eat at his desk. "You're doing so well," she says. "You're helping make Liberia strong."

In 1989 Liberia descends into a civil war that will last seven years. The cement plant is sabotaged, then transformed into a guerrilla armory, and Joseph finds himself out of a job. He begins to traffic in goods—sneakers, radios, calculators, calendars—stolen from downtown businesses. It is harmless, he tells himself, everybody is looting. We need the money. He keeps it in the cellar, tells his mother he's storing boxes for a friend. While his mother is at the market, a truck comes and carries the merchandise away. At night he pays a pair of boys to roam the townships, bending window bars, unhinging doors, depositing what they steal in the yard behind Joseph's house.

He spends most of his time squatting on the front step watching his mother tend her garden. Her fingers pry weeds from the soil or cull spent vines or harvest snap beans, the beans plunking regularly into a metal bowl, and he listens to her diatribes on the hardships of war, the importance of maintaining a structured lifestyle. "We cannot stop living because of conflict, Joseph," she says. "We must persevere."

Spurts of gunfire flash on the hills; airplanes roar over the roof of the house. The neighbors stop coming by; the hills are bombed, and bombed again. Trees burn in the night like warnings of worse evil to come. Policemen splash past the house in stolen vans, the barrels of their guns resting on the sills, their eyes hidden behind mirrored sunglasses. Come and get me, Joseph wants to yell at them, at their tinted windows and chrome tailpipes. Just you try. But he does not; he keeps his head down and pretends to busy himself among the rosebushes.

In October of 1994 Joseph's mother goes to the market in the morning with three baskets of sweet potatoes and does not return. He paces the rows of her garden, listening to the far-off thump-

thump of artillery, the keening of sirens, the interminable silences between. When finally the last hem of light drops behind the hills, he goes to the neighbors. They peer at him through the rape gate across the doorway to their bedroom and issue warnings: "The police have been killed. Taylor's guerrillas will be here any minute."

"My mother . . ."

"Save yourself," they say and slam the door. Joseph hears chains clatter, a bolt slide home. He leaves their house and stands in the dusty street. At the horizon columns of smoke rise into a red sky. After a moment he walks to the end of the paved road and turns up a muddy track, the way to Mazien Town, the way his mother traveled that morning. At the market he sees what he expected: fires, a smoldering truck, crates hacked open, teenagers plundering stalls. On a cart he finds three corpses; none is his mother's, none is familiar.

No one he sees will speak to him. When he collars a girl running past, cassettes spill from her pockets; she looks away and will not answer his questions. Where his mother's stall stood there is only a pile of charred plywood, neatly stacked, as if someone had already begun to rebuild. It is light before he returns home.

The next night—his mother does not return—he goes out again. He sifts through remains of market stalls; he shouts his mother's name down the abandoned aisles. In a place where the market sign once hung between two iron posts, a man has been suspended upside down. His insides, torn out of him, swing beneath his arms like black infernal ropes, marionette strings cut free.

In the days to come Joseph wanders farther. He sees men leading girls by chains; he stands aside so a dump truck heaped with corpses can pass. Twenty times he is stopped and harassed; at makeshift checkpoints soldiers press the muzzles of rifles into his chest and ask if he is Liberian, if he is a Krahn, why he is not helping them fight the Krahns. Before they let him go they spit on his shirt. He hears that a band of guerrillas wearing Donald Duck masks has begun eating the organs of its enemies; he hears about terrorists in football cleats trampling the bellies of pregnant women.

Nowhere does anyone claim to know his mother's whereabouts. From the front step he watches the neighbors raid the garden. The boys he paid to loot stores no longer come by. On the radio a soldier named Charles Taylor brags of killing fifty Nigerian peacekeepers with forty-two bullets. "They die so easily," he boasts. "It is like sprinkling salt onto the backs of slugs."

After a month, with no more information about his mother than he had the night she disappeared, Joseph takes her dictionary under his arm, stuffs his shirt, pants and shoes with money, locks the cellar—stocked with stolen notepads, cold medicine, boom boxes, an air compressor—and leaves the house for good. He travels awhile with four Christians fleeing to the Ivory Coast; he falls in with a band of machete-toting kids roving from village to village. The things he sees—decapitated children, drugged boys tearing open a pregnant girl, a man hung over a balcony with his severed hands in his mouth—do not bear elaboration. He sees enough in three weeks to provide ten lifetimes of nightmares. In Liberia, in that war, everything is left unburied, and anything once buried is now dredged up: corpses lie in stacks in pit latrines, wailing children drag the bodies of their parents through the streets. Krahns kill Manos; Gios kill Mandingoes; half the travelers on the highway are armed; half the crossroads smell of death.

Joseph sleeps where he can: in leaves, under bushes, on the floorboards of abandoned houses. A pain blooms inside his skull. Every seventy-two hours he is rocked with fever—he burns, then freezes. On the days when he is not feverish, it hurts to breathe; it takes all his energy to continue walking.

Eventually he comes to a checkpoint where a pair of jaundiced soldiers will not let him pass. He recites his story as well as he can—the disappearance of his mother, his attempts to gather information about her whereabouts. He is not a Krahn or a Mandingo, he tells them; he shows them the dictionary, which they confiscate. His head throbs steadily; he wonders if they plan to kill him. "I have money," he says. He unbuttons his collar, shows them the bills in his shirt.

One of the soldiers talks on a radio for a few minutes, then returns. He orders Joseph into the back of a Toyota and takes him up a long, gated drive. Rubber trees run out in seemingly endless rows beneath a plantation house with a tiled roof. The soldier leads him behind the house and through a gate onto a tennis court. On it are a dozen boys, perhaps sixteen years old, lounging on lawn furniture with assault rifles in their laps. White sunlight reflects off the concrete. They sit, and Joseph stands, and the sun bears down upon them. No one speaks.

After several minutes, a sweating captain hauls a man from the back door of the house, down the breezeway to the tennis court, and throws him onto the center line. The man wears a blue beret; his hands are tied behind his back. When they turn him over, Joseph sees his cheekbones have been broken; the face sags inward. "This parasite," the captain says, toeing the man's ribs, "piloted an airplane which bombed towns east of Monrovia for a month."

The man tries to sit up. His eyes drift obscenely in their sockets. "I am a cook," he says. "I am traveling from Yekepa. They tell me to go by road to Monrovia. So I try to go. But then I am arrested. Please. I cook steaks. I have bombed nobody."

The boys in the lawn furniture groan. The captain takes the beret from the man's head and flings it over the fence. The pain in Joseph's head sharpens; he wants to crumple; he wants to lie down in the shade and go to sleep.

"You are a killer," the captain says to the prisoner. "Why not come clean? Why not own up to what you have done? There are dead mothers, dead girls, in those towns. You think you had no hand in their deaths?"

"Please! I am a cook! I grill steaks in the Stillwater Restaurant in Yekepa! I have been traveling to see my fiancée!"

"You have been bombing the countryside."

The man tries to say more but the captain presses his sneaker over his mouth. There is a faraway grinding sound, like pebbles knocking together inside a rag. "You," the captain says, pointing at Joseph. "You are the one whose mother has been killed?"

Joseph blinks. "She sold vegetables in the market at Mazien Town," he says. "I have not seen her for three months."

The captain takes the gun from the holster on his hip and holds it out to Joseph. "This parasite has killed probably one thousand people," the captain says. "Mothers and daughters. It makes me sick to look at him." The captain's hands are on Joseph's hips; he draws Joseph forward as if they are dancing. The light reflecting off the tennis court is dazzling. The boys in the chairs watch, whisper. The soldier who brought Joseph leans against the fence and lights a cigarette.

The captain's lips are in Joseph's ear. "You do your mother a favor," he murmurs. "You do the whole country a favor."

The gun is in Joseph's hand—its handle is warm and slick with sweat. The pain in his head quickens. Everything before him—the dusty and still rows of trees, the captain breathing in his ear, the man on the asphalt, crawling now, feebly, like a sick child—stretches and blurs; it is as though the lenses of his glasses have liquefied. He thinks of his mother making that final walk to the market, the sun and shadow of the long trail, the wind muscling through the leaves. He should have been with her; he should have gone in her stead. He should be the one who felt the ground open beneath him, the one who disappeared. They bombed her into vapor, Joseph thinks. They bombed her into smoke. Because she thought we needed the money.

"He is not worth the blood in his body," the captain whispers. "He is not worth the air in his lungs."

Joseph lifts the pistol and shoots the prisoner through the head. The sound of the shot is quickly swallowed, dissipated by the thick air, the heavy trees. Joseph slumps to his knees; glittering rockets of light detonate behind his eyes. Everything reels in white. He collapses onto his chest, and faints.

He wakes on the floor inside the plantation house. The ceiling is bare and cracked and a fly buzzes against it. He stumbles from the room and finds himself in a hallway with no doors at either end and columns of rubber trees below stretching out nearly to the horizon. His clothes are damp; his money—even the bills beneath the soles of his boots—is gone.

At the doorway two boys loll in lounge chairs. Behind them, through the fence of the tennis court, Joseph can see the body of the man he has killed, unburied, slumped on the asphalt. He descends through the long rows of trees. None of the soldiers he sees pays him any mind. After an hour or so of walking he reaches a road; he waves to the first car that passes and they give him water to drink and a ride to the port city of Buchanan.

Buchanan is at peace—no tribes of gun-toting boys patrol the streets; no planes roar overhead. He sits by the sea and watches the dirty water wash back and forth along the pilings. There is a new kind of pain in his head, dull and trembling, no longer sharp; it is the pain of absence. He wants to cry; he wants to throw himself into the bay and drown himself. It would be impossible, he thinks, to get far enough away from Liberia.

He boards a chemical tanker and begs work washing pans in the galley. He scrubs the pans carefully enough, the hot spray washing over him as the tanker bucks its way across the Atlantic, into the Gulf of Mexico and through the Panama Canal. In the bunkroom he studies his shipmates and wonders if they can tell he is a murderer, if he wears it like a mark on his forehead. At night he leans over the bow rail and watches the hull as it cleaves the darkness. Everything feels empty and ragged; he feels as if he has left behind a thousand unfinished tasks, a thousand miscalculated ledgers. The waves continue on their anonymous journeys. The tanker churns north up the Pacific Coast.

He disembarks in Astoria, Oregon; the immigration police tell him he is a refugee of war and issue him a visa. Some days later, in the hostel where he stays, he is shown an ad in a newspaper: *Handy person needed for winter season to tend Ocean Meadows, a ninety-acre estate, orchard and home. We're desperate!*

Joseph washes his clothes in the bathroom sink and studies himself in a mirror—his beard is long and knotted; through the lenses of his glasses, his eyes look warped and yellow. He remembers the definition from his mother's dictionary: *Desperate: beyond hope of recovery, at one's last extreme.*

He takes a bus to Bandon, then thirty miles down 101, and walks the last two miles down an unmarked dirt road. Ocean Meadows: a bankrupted cranberry farm turned summer playground, the original house demolished to make way for a three-story mansion. He picks his way past the shrapnel of broken wine bottles on the porch.

"I am Joseph Saleeby, from Liberia," he tells the owner, a stout man in cowboy boots called Mr. Twyman. "I am thirty-six years old, my country is at war, I seek only peace. I can fix your shingles, your deck. Anything." His hands shake as he says this. Twyman and his wife retreat, shout at each other behind the kitchen doors. Their gaunt and taciturn daughter drags a bowl of cereal to the dining table, eats quietly, leaves. The clock on the wall chimes once, twice.

Eventually Twyman returns and hires him. They have advertised for two months, he says, and Joseph is the only applicant. "Your lucky day," he says, and eyes Joseph's boots warily.

*   *   *

They give him a pair of old coveralls and the apartment above the garage. During his first month the estate bulges with guests: children, babies, young men on the deck shouting into cell phones, a parade of smiling women. They are millionaires from something to do with computers; when they get out of their cars they inspect the doors for scratches; if they find one they lick their thumbs and try to buff it out. Half-finished vodka tonics on the railings, guitar music from loudspeakers dragged onto the porch, the whine of yellow jackets around half-cleaned plates, plump trash bags piling up in the shed: these are their leavings, these are Joseph's chores. He fixes a burner on the stove, sweeps sand out of the hallways, scrubs salmon off the walls after a food fight. When he isn't working he sits on the edge of the tub in his apartment and stares at his hands.

In September Twyman comes to him with a list of winter duties: install storm windows, aerate the lawns, clear ice from the roof and walkways, make sure no one comes to rob the house. "Can you handle that?" Twyman asks. He leaves keys to the caretaker's pickup and a phone number. The next morning everybody is gone. Silence floods the place. The trees swing in the wind as if shaking off a spell. Three white geese crawl out from under the shed and amble across the lawn. Joseph wanders the main house, the living room with its massive stone fireplace, the glass atrium, the huge closets. He lugs a television halfway down the stairs but cannot summon the will to steal it. Where would he take it? What would he do with it?

Each morning the day ranges before him, vast and empty. He walks the beach, fingering up stones and scanning them for uniqueness—an embedded fossil, the imprint of a shell, a glittering vein of mineral. It is rare that he doesn't pocket the stone; they are all unique, all beautiful. He brings them to his apartment and sets them on the sills—a room lined with rows of pebbles like small, unfinished battlements, fortifications against tiny invaders.

For two months he speaks to no one, sees no one. There is only the slow, steady tracking of headlights along 101, two miles away, or the contrails of a jet as it hurtles overhead, the sound of it lost somewhere in the space between sky and earth.

Rape, murder, an infant kicked against a wall, a boy with a clutch of dried ears suspended from his neck: in nightmares Joseph replays the worst things men do to each other. He sweats through his blankets and wakes throttling his pillow. His mother, his money, his neat, ordered life: all are gone—not finished, but vanished, as if some madman kidnapped each element of his life and dragged it to the bottom of a dungeon. He wants terribly to do something good with himself; he wants to do something right.

In November five sperm whales strand on the beach a half mile from the estate. The largest—slumped on the sand a few hundred yards north of the others—is over fifty feet long and is half the size of the garage where Joseph lives. Joseph is not the first to discover them: already a dozen Jeeps are parked in the dunes; men run back and forth between the animals, lugging buckets of seawater, brandishing needles.

Several women in neon anoraks have lashed a rope around the flukes of the smallest whale and are trying to tow it off the sand with a motorized skiff. The skiff churns and skates over the breaking waves; the rope tightens, slips and bites into the whale's fluke; the flesh parts and shows white. Blood wells up. The whale does not budge.

Joseph approaches a circle of onlookers: a man with a fishing pole, three girls with plastic baskets half full of clams. A woman in a blood-smeared lab coat is explaining that there is little hope of rescuing the whales: already they are overheating, hemorrhaging, organs pulping, vital tubes conceding to the weight. Even if the whales could be towed off the beach, she says, they would probably turn and swim back onto shore. She has seen this happen before. "But," she adds, "it is a great opportunity to learn. Everything must be handled carefully."

The whales are written over with scars; their backs are mottled with pocks and craters and plates of barnacles. Joseph presses his palm to the side of one and the skin around the scar trembles beneath his touch. Another whale slaps its flukes against the beach and emits clicks that seem to originate from the center of it. Its brown bloodshot eye rolls forward, then back.

For Joseph it is as if some portal from his nightmares has opened and the horrors crouched there, breathing at the door, have come galloping through. On the half-mile trail back to Ocean Meadows, he falters in his step and has to kneel, his body quaking, the ragged clouds coursing overhead. Tears pour from his eyes. His flight has been futile; everything remains unburied, floating just at the surface, a breeze away from being dredged back up. And why? Save yourself, the neighbors had told him. Save yourself. Joseph wonders if he is beyond saving, if the only kind of man who can be saved is the man who never needed saving in the first place.

He lies in the trail until it is dark. Pain rolls behind his forehead. He watches the stars blazing in their lightless tracts, their twisting and writhing, their relentless burning, and wonders what the woman meant, what he should be learning from this.

By morning four of the five whales have died. From the dunes they look like a flotilla of black submarines run aground. Yellow tape has been strung around them on stakes and the crowds have swelled further: there are new, more civilian spectators—a dozen Girl Scouts, a mail carrier, a man in wing tips posing for a photo.

The bodies of the whales have distended with gas; their sides sag like the skin of withered balloons. In death the white crosshatchings of scars on their backs look like ghastly lightning strokes, nets the whales have snared themselves in. Already the first and largest of them—the cow that stranded several hundred yards north of the others—has been beheaded, its jaw turned up at the sky, bits of beach sand stuck to the fist-sized teeth. Using chain saws and long-handled knives, men in lab coats strip blubber from its flanks. Joseph watches them haul out steaming purple sacs that must be organs. Onlookers mill around; some, he sees, have taken souvenirs, peeling off thin membranes of skin and rolling them up in their fists like gray parchment.

The researchers in lab coats labor between the ribs of the largest whale, finally manage to extract what must be the heart—a massive lump of striated muscle, bunched with valves at one end. It takes four of them to roll it onto the sand. Joseph cannot believe the size of it; maybe this whale had a large heart or maybe all whales have hearts this big, but the heart is the size of a riding mower. The tubes running into it are large enough to stick his head into. One of the researchers jabs it with a needle, draws some tissue and deposits it in a jar. His colleagues are already back in the whale; there is the sound of a saw starting up. The researcher with the needle joins the others. The heart steams lightly in the sand.

Joseph finds a forest-service cop eating a sandwich in the dunes.

"Is that the heart?" he asks. "That they've left there?"

She nods. "They're after the lungs, I think. To see if they're diseased."

"What will they do with the hearts?"

"Burn them, I'd guess. They'll burn everything. Because of the smell."

All day he digs. He chooses a plot on a hill, concealed by the forest, overlooking the western edge of the main house and a slice of lawn. Through the trunks behind him he can just see the ocean shimmer between the treetops. He digs until well after dusk, setting out a lantern and digging in its white circle of light. The earth is wet and sandy, rife with stones and roots, and the going is rough. His chest feels like it has cracks running through it. When he sets down the shovel, his fingers refuse to straighten. Soon the hole is deeper than Joseph is tall; he throws dirt over the rim.

Hours after midnight he has a tarp, a shovel, a tree saw and an alloy-cased hand winch in the bed of the estate's truck, the load rattling softly as he eases over the back lawn of the house and down the narrow lane to the beach. Tribes of white birch stand bunched and storm-broken in the headlights like bundles of shattered bones; their branches scrape the sides of the truck.

Twin campfires smolder by the four whales to the south but nobody is near the cow to the north, and he has no trouble driving past the hanks of kelp at tideline to the dark, beheaded hulk lying at the foot of the dunes like the caved-in hull of a wrecked ship.

Viscera and blubber are everywhere. Intestines lie unfurled across the beach like parade streamers. He holds a flashlight in his teeth and, through the giant slats of its ribs, studies the interior of the whale: everything is wet and shadowed and run-together. A few yards away the heart sits in the sand like a boulder. Crabs tear plugs from its sides; gulls squabble in the shadows.

He lays the tarp over the beach, anchors the hand winch to a crossbar at the head of the bed of the truck and hooks the bow-shackle through the grommets on the corners of the tarp. With great difficulty he rolls the heart onto the plastic; then it is merely a matter of winching the entire gory bundle into the bed. He turns the crank, the gears ratcheting loudly; the winch tackle growls; the corners of the tarp come up. The heart inches toward him, plowing through the sand, and soon the truck takes its weight.

The first pale streaks of light show in the sky as he parks the pickup beside the hole he has made above the property. He lowers the tailgate and lays the tarp flat. The heart, stuck all over with sand, lies in the bed like a slain beast. Joseph wedges his body between it and the cab, and pushes. It rolls out easily enough, sliding heavily over the slick tarp, and bounces into the hole with a wet, heavy thump.

He kicks out the extra pieces of flesh and muscle and gore still in the flatbed and drives slowly, in a daze, down the hill and back onto the beach where the other four whales lie in various stages of decomposition.

Three men stand over the dregs of a campfire, soaked in gore, drinking coffee from Styrofoam cups. The heads of two of the whales are missing; all the teeth from the remaining heads have been taken away. Sand fleas jump from the carcasses. There is a sixth whale lying in the sand, Joseph sees, a near-term fetus hauled from the body of its mother. He gets out, steps over the yellow tape and walks to them.

"I'll take the hearts," he says. "If you're done with them."

They stare. He takes the tree saw from the back of the truck bed and goes to the first whale, lifting the flap of skin and stepping inside the great tree of its ribs.

A man seizes Joseph's arm. "We're supposed to burn them. Save what we can and burn the rest."

"I'll bury the hearts." He does not look at the man but keeps his eyes away, on the horizon. "It will be less work for you."

"You can't . . ." But he has released Joseph, who is already back in the whale, sawing at tissue. With the tree saw as his flensing knife he hacks through three ribs, then a thick, dense tube that could be an artery. Blood spurts onto his hands: congealed and black and slightly warm. The cavern inside the whale smells, already, like rot, and twice Joseph has to step back and breathe deeply, the front of his coveralls soaked from mucus and blubber and seawater.

He had told himself it would be like cleaning a fish, but it is completely different—it's more like eviscerating a giant. The plumbing of the whale is on a massive scale; house cats could gallop through its veins. He parts a final layer of blubber and lays a hand on what he decides must be the heart. It is still a bit damp, and warm, and very dark. He thinks: I did not make the hole large enough for five of these.

It takes ten minutes to saw through three remaining veins; when he does the heart comes loose easily enough, sliding toward him and settling muscularly against his ankles and knees. He has to tug his feet free. A man appears, thrusts a syringe into the heart and draws up some matter. "Okay," the man says. "Take it."

Joseph tows it into the truck. He does this all morning and all afternoon, hacking out the hearts and depositing them in the hole on the hill. None of the hearts were as big as the first whale's but they are huge, the size of the range in Twyman's kitchen or the engine in the truck. Even the fetus's heart is extraordinary: as big as a man's torso, and as heavy. He cannot hold it in his arms.

By the time Joseph is pushing the last heart into the hole on the hill, his body has begun to fail him. Purple halos spin at the fringes of his vision; his back and arms are rigid and he has to walk slightly bent over. He fills the hole, and as he leaves it, a mound of earth and muscle, stark amid a thicket of salmonberry with the trunks of spruce falling back all around it, high above the property in the late evening, he feels removed from himself, as though his body were a clumsy tool needed only a little longer. He parks in the yard and falls into bed, gore-soaked and unwashed, the door to the apartment open, the hearts of all six whales wrapped in earth, slowly cooling. He thinks: I have never been so tired. He thinks: at least I have buried something.

During the following days he does not have the energy or will to climb out of bed. He tortures himself with questions: Why doesn't he feel any better, any more healed? What is revenge? Redemption? The hearts are still there, sitting just beneath the earth, waiting. What good does burying something really do? In nightmares it always manages to dig itself out. Here was a word from his mother's dictionary: *Inconsolable: not to be consoled, spiritless, hopeless, brokenhearted.*

An ocean between himself and Liberia and still he will not be saved. The wind brings curtains of yellow-black smoke over the trees and past his windows. It smells of oil, like bad meat frying. He buries his face in the pillow to avoid inhaling it.

Winter. Sleet sings through the branches. The ground freezes, thaws, freezes again into something like sludge, immovably thick. Joseph has never seen snow; he turns his face to the sky and lets it fall on his glasses. He watches the flakes melt, their spiked struts and delicate vaulting, the crystals softening to water like a thousand microscopic lights blinking out.

He forgets his job. From the window he notices he has left the mower in the yard but the will to return it to the garage does not come. He knows he ought to flush the pipes in the main house, sweep the deck, install storm windows, switch on the cables to melt ice from the shingles. But he does not do any of it. He tells himself he is exhausted from burying the whale hearts and not from a greater fatigue, from the weight of memory all around him.

Some mornings, when the air feels warmer, he determines to go out; he throws off the covers and pulls on his trousers. Walking the muddy lane down from the main house, cresting the dunes, the sea laid out under the sky like molten silver, the low forested islands and gulls wheeling above them, a cold rain slashing through the trees, the sight of the world—the utter terror of being out in it—is too much for him, and he feels something splitting apart, a wedge falling through the center of him. He clenches his temples and turns, and has to go sit in the toolshed, among the axes and shovels, in the dark, trying to find his breath, waiting for the fear to pass.

Twyman had said the coast didn't get much snow but now the snow comes heavily. It falls for ten days straight and because Joseph does not switch on the deicing cables, the weight of it collapses a section of the roof. In the master bedroom warped sheets of plywood and insulation sag onto the bed like ramps to the heavens. Joseph splays on the floor and watches the big clusters of flakes fall through the gap and gather on his body. The snow melts, runs down his sides, freezes again on the floor in smooth, clear sheets.

He finds jars of preserves in the basement and eats them with his fingers at the huge dining-room table. He cuts a hole in a wool blanket, pulls it over his head and wears it like a cloak. Fevers come and go like wildfires; they force him to his knees and he must wait, wrapped in the blanket, until the shivers pass.

In a sprawling marble bathroom he studies his reflection. His body has thinned considerably; tendons stand out along his forearms; the slats of his ribs make drastic arcs across his sides. A yellow like the color of chicken broth floats in his eyes. He runs his hand over his hair, feels the hard surface of skull just beneath the scalp. Somewhere, he thinks, there is a piece of ground waiting for me.

He sleeps, and sleeps, and dreams of whales inside the earth, swimming through soil like they would through water, the tremors of their passage quaking the leaves. They breach up through the grass, turning over in a spray of roots and pebbles, then fall back, disappearing through the ground which stitches itself over them, whole again.

Warblers in the fog, ladybugs traversing the windows, fiddleheads nosing their way up through the forest floor—spring. He crosses the yard with the blanket over his shoulders and examines the first pale sleeves of crocuses rising from the lawn. Swatches of dirty slush lie melting in the shade. A memory rises unbidden: every April in his home, in the hills outside Monrovia, a wind blew down from the Sahara and piled red dust inches deep against the walls of the house. Dust in his ears, dust on his tongue. His mother fought back with brooms and whisks, enlisted him in the defense. Why? he would ask. Why sweep the steps when tomorrow they'll be covered again? She would look at him, fierce and disappointed, and say nothing.

He thinks of the dust, blowing now through the gaps in the shutters, piling up against the walls. It hurts him to imagine it: their house, empty, soundless, dust on the chairs and tables, the garden plundered and grown over. Stolen goods still stacked in the cellar. He hopes someone has crammed the place with explosives and bombed it into splinters; he hopes the dust will close over the roof and bury the house forever.

Soon—who is to say how many days had passed?—there is the sound of a truck grinding up the drive. It is Twyman; Joseph is discovered. He retreats to the apartment, crouches behind the windowsill and his neatly stacked rows of pebbles. He takes one, rolls it in his palm. There is shouting in the main house. He watches Twyman stride across the lawn.

Cowboy boots thud upon the stairs. Already Twyman is bellowing.

"The roof! The floors are flooded! The walls are buckling! The mower's rusted to hell!"

Joseph wipes his glasses with his fingers. "I know," he says. "It is not good."

"Not good?! Damn! Damn! Damn! Damn!" Twyman's throat is turning red; the words clog on their way out. "My God!" he manages to spit. "You fucker!"

"It is okay. I understand."

Twyman turns, studies the pebbles along the sills. "Fucker! Fucker!"

Twyman's wife drives him north in a sleek, silent truck, the wipers slipping smoothly over the windshield. She keeps one hand in her purse, clenched around what Joseph guesses to be Mace or perhaps a gun. She thinks I am an idiot, thinks Joseph. To her I am a barbarian from Africa who knows nothing about work, nothing about caretaking. I am disrespectful, I am a nigger.

They stop at a red light in Bandon and Joseph says, "I will get out here."

"Here?" Mrs. Twyman glances around as if seeing the town for the first time. Joseph climbs out. She keeps her hand in the purse. "*Duty*," she says. "It's an issue of duty." Her voice tremors; inside, he can see, she is raging. "I told him not to hire you. I told him what good is it hiring someone who runs from his country at the first sign of trouble? He won't know duty, responsibility. He won't be able to understand it. And now look."

Joseph stands, his hand on the door. "I never want to see you again," she says. "Close the fucking door."

For three days he lies on a bench in a Laundromat. He studies cracks in the ceiling tiles; he watches colors drift across the undersides of eyelids. Clothes turn loops behind portholes in the dryers. *Duty: behavior required by moral obligation.* Twyman's wife was right; what does he understand about that? He thinks of the hearts lumped into the earth, ground bacteria chewing microscopic labyrinths through the centers. Hadn't burying those hearts been the right thing, the decent thing to do? Save yourself, they said. Save yourself. There were things he had been learning at Ocean Meadows, things yet unfinished.

Hungry but not conscious of his hunger, he walks south down the road, loping through the sogged, muddy grass on the shoulder. All around him the trees stir. When he hears a car or truck approaching, tires hissing over the wet pavement, he retreats into the woods, draws his blanket around him and waits for it to pass.

Before dawn he is back on Twyman's property, high above the main house, hiking through dense growth. The rain has stopped, and the sky has brightened, and Joseph's limbs feel light. He climbs to the small clearing between the trunks where he buried the whale hearts and lays down armfuls of dead spruce boughs for a bed and lies among them on top of the buried hearts, half buried himself, and watches the stars wheel overhead.

I will become invisible, he thinks. I will work only at night. I will be so careful they will never suspect me; I will be like the swallows on their gutter, the insects in their lawn, concealed, a scavenger, part of the scenery. When the trees shift in the wind, so I will shift, and when rain falls I will fall too. It will be a kind of disappearing.

This is my home now, he thinks, looking around him. This is what things have come to.

In the morning he parts the brambles and peers down at the house where two vans are on the lawn, ladders propped against the siding, the small figure of a man kneeling on the roof. Other men cart boxes or planking into the house. There is the industrious sound of banging.

On the shady hillside below his plot of ground Joseph finds mushrooms standing among the leaves. They taste like silt and make his stomach hurt but he swallows them all, forcing them down.

He waits until dusk, squatting, watching a slow fog collect in the trees. When it is finally night he goes down the hill to the tool-shed beside the garage and takes a hoe from the wall and fumbles in the shadows around the seed box. In a paper pouch he can feel seeds—this he tucks into the pocket of his trousers and retreats, back through the clubfoot and fern, onto the wet, needled floor of the forest, to the ring of trunks and his small plot. In the dim, silvery light he opens the packet. There are maybe two palmfuls of seeds, some thin and black like thistle, some wide and white, some fat and tan. He stows them in his pocket. Then he stands, lifts the hoe, and drives it into the earth. A smell comes up: sweet, wealthy.

All through the smallest hours he turns earth. There is no sign of whale hearts; the soil is black and airy. Earthworms come up flailing, shining in the night. By dawn he is asleep again. Mosquitoes whine around his neck. He does not dream.

The next night he uses his index finger to make rows of tiny holes, and drops one seed like a tiny bomb into each hole. He is so weak from hunger that he must stop often to rest; if he stands quickly his vision floods away and the sky rushes into the horizon, and for a moment it feels like he will dissolve. He eats several of the seeds and imagines them sprouting in his gut, vines pushing up his throat, roots twisting from the soles of his shoes. Blood drips from one of his nostrils; it tastes like copper.

In the ruins of a cranberry press he finds a rusted five-gallon drum. There is a small, vigorous brook that threads between boulders by the beach and he fills the drum with the water and carts it, sloshing and spilling, up the hill to his garden.

He eats kelp, salmonberries, hazelnuts, ghost shrimp, a dead sculpin washed up by the tide. He tears mussels from rocks and boils them in the salvaged drum. One midnight he creeps down to the lawn and gathers dandelions. They taste bitter; his stomach cramps.

The workmen finish rebuilding the roof. The tide of people builds. Mrs. Twyman arrives one afternoon with a flourish of activity; she whirls across the deck in a business suit, a young man at her heels taking notes in a pad. Her daughter takes long, lonesome hikes across the dunes. The evening parties begin, paper lanterns hung from the eaves, a swing band blowing horns in the gazebo, laughter drifting on the wind.

With the hoe and several hours of persistence Joseph manages to knock a chickadee from a low bough and kill it. In the dead of night he roasts it over a tiny fire; he cannot believe how little meat there is on it; it is all bone and feather. It tastes of nothing. Now, he thinks, I really am a savage, killing tiny birds and tearing the tendons from their bones with my teeth. If Mrs. Twyman saw me she would not be surprised.

* * *

Besides daily carting water up the hill and splashing it over the rows of seeds, there is little to do but sit. The scents of the forest run like rivers between the trunks: growing, rotting. Questions come in bevies: Is the soil warm enough? Didn't his mother start plants in small pots before setting them in the ground? How much sun do seeds need? And how much water? What if these seeds were wrapped in paper because they were sterile, or old? He worries the rust from his watering drum will foul the garden; he scrapes it as clean as he can with a wedge of slate.

Memories, too, volunteer themselves up: three charred corpses in the smoking wreck of a Mercedes, a black beetle crossing the back of a broken hand. The head of a boy kicked open and lying in red dust, Joseph's own mother pushing a barrow of compost, the muscles in her legs straining as she crosses the yard. For thirty-five years Joseph had envisioned a quiet, safe thread running through his life—a thread made for him, incontrovertible, assured. Trips to the market, trips to work, rice with cayenne for lunch, trim columns of numbers in his ledger: these were life, as regular and probable as the sun's rising. But in the end that thread turned out to be illusion—there was no rope, no guide, no truth to bind Joseph's life. He was a criminal; his mother was a gardener. Both of them turned out to be as mortal as anything else, the roses in her garden, whales in the sea.

Now, finally, he is remaking an order, a structure to his hours. It feels good, tending the soil, hauling water. It feels healthy.

In June the first green noses of his seedlings begin to show above the soil. When he wakes in the evening and sees them in the paling light, he feels his heart might burst. Within days the entire plot of ground, an unbroken black a week ago, is populated with small dashes of green. It is the greatest of miracles. He becomes convinced that some of the shoots—a dozen or so proud thumbs pointed at the sky—are zucchini plants. On his hands and knees he examines them through the scratched lenses of his glasses: the stalks are already separating into distinct blades, tiny platters of leaves poised to unfold. Are there zucchinis in there? Big shining vegetables carried somehow in the shoots? It doesn't seem possible.

He agonizes over what to do next. Should he water more, or less? Should he prune, mulch, heel in, make cuttings? Should he limb the surrounding trees, clear some of the bramble away to provide more light? He tries to remember what his mother had done, the mechanics of her gardening, but can only recall the way she stood, a fistful of weeds trailing from her fist, looking down at her plants as if they were children, gathered at her feet.

He finds a nest of fishing tackle washed up on the rocks, untangles the monofilament and coils it around a block of driftwood. Around the dull and rusty hook he sheaths an earthworm; he weights the line and lowers it into the sea from a ledge. Some nights he manages to hook a salmon, grab it around the tail and knock its head against a rock. In the moonlight he lays it on a flat stone and eviscerates it with a piece of oyster shell. The meat he roasts over a tiny fire and eats thoughtlessly, chewing as he scuttles back up the rocks, into the woods. He does not think of taste; he goes about eating in the same manner he might go about digging a hole: it is a job, vaguely troubling, hardly satisfying.

The mansion, like the garden, swings into life. Every night there are the sounds of parties: music, the clink of silver against china, laughter. He can smell their cigarettes, their fried potatoes, the gasoline of landscapers' Weed Eaters and tractors. Cars rotate through the driveway. One afternoon Twyman appears on the deck and begins firing a shotgun into the trees. He is dressed in shorts and dark socks and stumbles across the planks of the deck. He reloads the gun, shoulders it, fires. Joseph crouches against a trunk. Does he know? Has Twyman seen him out there? The shot tears through the leaves.

*   *   *

By mid-June the stems of his plants are inches high. When he sticks his face close he can see that several of the buds have separated into delicate flowers; what looked like a solid green shoot was actually a tightly folded blossom. He feels like shouting with joy. Because of their pale, toothed leaflets, he decides some of the seedlings might be tomatoes, so he tries to construct small trellises with sticks and vine, as his mother used to do with wire and string, upon which the plants might climb. When he finishes he picks his way down the hillside to the sea and kicks a depression in the dunes and sleeps.

An hour later he wakes to see a sneaker shuffle past, hardly ten yards away. Adrenaline rockets to the tips of his fingers. His heart riots inside his chest. The sneaker is small, clean, white. Its mate moves past him, dragging through the sand, moving toward the sea.

He could run. Or he could ambush the person, claw him to death or drown him or fill his throat with sand. He could rise screaming and improvise from there. But there is no time for anything—on his stomach he flattens himself as much as possible and hopes his shape in the darkness resembles driftwood, or a tangled mess of kelp.

But the sneakers do not slow. Their owner labors down the front of the dunes, stooped and straining, lugging in the basket of its arms what looks to Joseph like a pair of cinder blocks. When it crosses the tideline Joseph raises his head and makes out features: curly, unbound hair, small shoulders, thin ankles. A girl. There is something wrong with the way she carries her head, the way it lolls on her neck, the way her shoulders ride so low—she looks defeated, overcome. She stops often to rest; her legs strain beneath her as she muscles her load forward. Joseph lowers his eyes, feels the cool sand against his chin, and tries to calm his heartbeat. Above him the clouds have blown away, and the spray of stars sends a frail light onto the sea.

When he looks again the girl is a hundred feet away. In the surf she squats with what looks like a bight of rope and runs it through the holes in the cinder block—she seems to be lashing her wrist to it. As he watches she fastens one wrist to one block, the other to the other. Then she struggles to her feet, dragging the blocks and staggering into the water. Waves clap against her chest. The blocks drop into the water with heavy splashes. She goes to her knees, then to her back, and floats, arms pulled behind and under her, still affixed to the cinder blocks. The flux of water bears her up, then closes over her chin and she is gone.

Joseph understands: the cinder blocks will hold her down and she will drown.

He lets his forehead back down against the sand. There is only the sound of waves collapsing against the shore and that starlight, faint and clean, reflecting off the mica in the sand. It is the same all over the world, Joseph thinks, in the smallest hours of the night. He wonders what would have happened if he had decided to sleep elsewhere, if he had spent one more hour framing trellises in the garden, if his seedlings had failed to shoot. If he had never seen an ad in a newspaper. If his mother had not gone to market that day. Order, chance, fate: it does not matter what brought him here. The stars burn in their constellations. Beneath the surface of the ocean countless lives are being lived out every minute.

He runs down the dunes and dives into the water. She floats just below the waves, her eyes closed; her hair washed out in a fan. Her shoelaces, untied, drift in the current. Her arms disappear beneath her into the murk.

She is, Joseph realizes, Twyman's daughter.

He dives under and lifts one of the cinder blocks from the sand and frees her wrist. With his arms beneath her body, dragging the other block, he hauls her onto the sand. "Everything is okay," he tries to say, but his voice is unused and it cracks and the words do not come. For a long moment nothing happens. Goose pimples stand up on her throat and arms. Then she coughs and her eyes fly open. She scrambles up, one arm still tied to its anchor, and flails her feet. "Wait," Joseph says. "Wait." He reaches down and lifts the block and frees her wrist. She pulls back, terrified. Her lips tremble; her arms shake. He can see how young she is— maybe fifteen years old, small pearls in her earlobes, big eyes above pink, unmarked cheeks. Water pours from her jeans. Her shoelaces trail in the sand.

"Please," he says. "Don't." But she is already gone, running hard and fast over the slope of the dunes, in the direction of the house.

Joseph shivers; the ragged blanket he still wears over his shoulders drips. If she tells someone, he considers, there will be searches. Twyman will comb the woods with his shotgun; his guests will make a game of capturing the trespasser in the woods. He must not let them find the garden. He must find a new place to sleep, acres away from the house, a damp depression in a thicket or—better still—a hole in the ground. And he will stop making fires; he will eat only those things he is willing to eat cold. He will visit the garden only every third night, only in the darkest, deepest hours, carrying water to his plants, being careful to cover his tracks. . . .

Out on the sea the reflected stars quiver and shake. The crest of each wave is limned with light, a thousand white rivers running together—it is beautiful. It is, he thinks, the most beautiful thing he has ever seen. He watches, shivering, until the sun begins to color the sky behind him, then trots down the beach, into the forest.

Four nights later: jazz, a woman on the porch making slow turns in the twilight, her skirt flaring out. Softly he creeps into his garden to weed, to yank out intruders. The music washes through the trees, piano, a saxophone. He strains to see the shoots standing up from the dirt. Blight—tiny bull's-eyes of rot—stains many of the leaves. A slug is chewing another shoot and a few of the plants have been cropped off at the ground. Over half the seedlings are dead or dying. He knows he should fence off the garden, spray the plants with something to protect them. He ought to construct a blind and stake out whatever is grazing the garden, scare it off or bludgeon it with the hoe. But he cannot—he can hardly afford the luxury of weed pulling. Everything must be done softly, must be made to look untended.

No longer does he go down to the shore or cross the lawns of the estate—they make him feel exposed, naked. He prefers the cover of the woods, the towering firs, the patches of giant clover and groves of maples; here he is just one of many, here he is small.

With a flashlight she begins searching the woods at night. He knows it is she because he has hidden in a hollowed nurse log and waited for her to pass; first the light swinging frantically through the ferns, then her pinched, scared face, eyes unblinking. She moves noisily, snapping twigs, breathing hard on the hills. But she is determined; her light prowls the woods, ranges over the dunes, hurries across the lawn. Every night for a week he watches the light drifting across the property like a displaced star.

Once, in a moment of courage, he calls hello, but she doesn't hear. She continues on, stepping down through the dark shapes of the trees, the noise of her passage and the beam of the light growing fainter until they finally disappear.

On a stump not a hundred yards from his garden she begins leaving food: a tuna sandwich, a bag of carrots, a napkin full of chips. He eats them but feels slightly guilty about it, as if he's cheating, as if it's unfair that she's making it easier for him.

After another week of midnights, watching her blunder through the forest, he cannot stand it anymore and places himself in the field of her light. She stops. Her eyes, already wide, widen.

She switches off her flashlight and sets it in the leaves. A pale fog hovers in the branches. They have a sort of standoff. The girl does not seem threatened although she keeps her hands just off her hips like a gunfighter.

Then she begins to move her arms in a short, intricate dance, striking the palm of one hand with the edge of the other, circling her fingers through the air, touching her right ear, finally pointing both index fingers at Joseph.

He does not know what to make of it. Her fingers repeat the dance: her hands draw a circle; the palms turn up; the fingers lock. Her lips move but no sound comes out. There is a large silver watch on her wrist which rides up and down her forearm as she gesticulates.

"I don't understand." His voice cracks from disuse. He waves toward the house. "Go away. I'm sorry. You must not come through here anymore. Someone will come looking for you." But the girl is running through the routine a third time, rolling her hand, tapping her chest, moving her lips in silence.

And then Joseph sees; he places his hands over his ears. The girl nods.

"You cannot hear?" She shakes her head. "But you know what I say? You understand?" She nods again. She points to her lips, then opens her hands like a book: lipreading.

She pulls a notebook from her shirt and opens it. With a pencil hung around her neck, she scribbles. She holds the page out. In the dimness he reads: *How do you live?*

"I eat what I can. I sleep in the leaves. I have all I need. Please go home, miss. Go to bed."

I won't tell, she writes.

When she leaves he watches the light bob and sweep until it becomes just a spark, a firefly spiraling through the gloom. He is surprised when he realizes it makes him lonely, watching the light fade, as if, although he told her to go, he had hoped she would stay.

*　　*　　*

Two nights later, full moon, her light is back, wobbling through the forest. He knows he should leave; he should start walking north and not stop until he is a hundred miles into Canada. Instead he paces through the leaves, finally goes to her. She is wearing jeans, a hooded sweatshirt, a knapsack over her shoulders. She switches off the light as before. Moonlight spills over the boughs, sends a patchwork of shadows shifting over their shoulders. He leads her through the bramble, past the verbena, to a ledge overlooking the sea. At the horizon a lone freighter blinks its tiny light.

"I almost did it too," he says. "The thing you tried to do." She holds her hands before her like two thin and pale birds. "I was leaning over the bow of a tanker, looking down at the waves a hundred feet below. We were in the middle of the ocean. All I needed to do was push with my feet and I would have gone over."

She writes in her pad. *I thought you were an angel. I thought you had come to take me to heaven.*

"No," Joseph says. "No." She looks at him, looks away. *Why did you come back?* she writes. *After you got fired?*

The light of the ship begins to fade. "Because it's beautiful here," he says. "Because I had nowhere else to go."

A night later they again face each other in the dimness. Her hands flutter in front of her, rolling in loops, rising to her neck, her eyes. She touches an elbow, points at him.

"I'm going for water," he says. "You can come if you like."

She follows him down through the forest until they reach the stream. He leans over a lichened rock, finds his rusty drum and fills it. They climb back through the ferns and moss and deadfall to the top of the hill. He pulls aside some cut boughs of spruce.

"This is my garden," he says, and steps in among the plants, tendrils clinging greenly to their trellises, creepers running out over the bare soil. In the air there is the fragrance of earth and leaf and sea. "This is why I came back. I needed to do this. It's why I stay."

In the nights to come she visits the garden and they crouch among the plants. She brings him a blanket and a baguette he reluctantly chews. She brings him a book of sign language—several thousand cartoon drawings of hands, each with a word beneath. There are hands above *tree*, hands above *bicycle*, hands above *house*. He studies the pages, wonders how anyone could ever learn all the signs. Her name is Belle, he learns: he practices making it in the air with his long, clumsy fingers.

He teaches her to find pests—slugs, iridescent beetles, aphids, tiny red spider mites—and crush them between her fingers. Some of the vines have grown knee-high; they range across the soil; rain pops against the leaves. "What is it like?" he asks her. "Is it very quiet? Is it silent?" She doesn't see him speak or else chooses not to answer. She sits and stares down at the house.

She brings a plant food that they mix with creek water and pour over the rows. Each time she leaves he finds himself watching her go, her body moving down through the trees, finally appearing down on the lawn, a dim silhouette slipping back into the house.

Some nights, sitting among ferns far from the garden, watching headlights creep down 101 in the distance, he clamps his palms over his ears and tries to imagine what it must be like. He shuts his eyes, tries to quiet himself. For a moment he thinks he has it; a kind of void, a nothingness, an oblivion. But it doesn't—it cannot—last; there is always noise, the flux and murmur of his body's machinery, a hum in his head. His heart beats and flexes in its cage. His body, in those moments, sounds to him like an orchestra, a rock band, an entire prison of inmates crowded into one cell. What must it be like to not hear that? To never know even the whisper of your own pulse?

*   *   *

The garden explodes into life; Joseph gets the impression it would grow even if the world was plunged into permanent darkness. Each night there are changes; clusters of green spheres materialize and swell on the tomato stems; yellow flowers emerge from the vines like burning lamps. He begins to wonder if the large, bushy creepers are zucchini after all—maybe they are squash, some kind of gourd.

But they are melons. Days later he and Belle find six pale spheres sitting in the soil under the broad leaves. Each night they seem to grow larger, drawing more mass from the earth. They nearly glow in the midnight. He cakes their flanks with mud, patting them down, hiding them. He coats the tomatoes, too—it seems to him that their pale yellows and reds must shine like beacons, easily visible from the lawns of the estate, too outrageous to miss.

She is in the garden, sitting and staring down at the house, and he leaves the cover of the forest to join her. He taps her shoulder and makes the sign for night, and the sign for how are you. Her face brightens; her fingers flash a response.

"Slow down, slow down," laughs Joseph. "Good night was as far as I got."

She smiles, stands, brushes off her knees. She's written something on her pad: *Something to show you*. From her knapsack she takes a map and unfolds it over the dirt. It is worn along its creases and very soft. When he takes the whole thing in, he can see that it is a map of the entire Pacific Coast of the Americas, beginning with Alaska and ending at Tierra del Fuego.

Belle points at herself, then the map. She draws her finger down a series of highways, all north–south, that she has highlighted in color. Then she places her hands on an imaginary steering wheel and mimes driving a car.

"You want to drive this? You are going to drive this far?"

Yes, she nods. Yes. She leans forward and with her pencil, writes, *When I turn sixteen I get a Volkswagen. From my father.*

"Can you even drive?"

She shakes her head, holds up ten fingers, then six. *When I'm sixteen.*

He studies the map awhile. "Why? I don't get it."

She looks away. She makes a series of signs he does not know. On the paper she writes, *I want to leave,* and underlines it furiously. The tip of the pencil breaks.

"Belle," Joseph says. "No one could drive that far. There probably aren't even roads the whole way." She is looking at him; her mouth hangs open.

"You are, what, fifteen years old? You cannot drive to South America. You would be kidnapped. You would run out of petrol." He laughs, then, and puts his hand over his mouth. After a moment he begins to work, his fingers prying a leaf miner from the underside of a melon. Belle studies her map in the paling light.

When he looks up she is gone, her light moving quickly down the hillside, disappearing. He watches the thin shape of her hurry across the lawn.

She stops coming into the woods. As far as he can tell, she stops going outside altogether. Maybe she uses the front door, he thinks. He wonders how long she'd harbored that strange dream—to drive from Oregon to Tierra del Fuego, alone, a deaf girl.

A week passes and Joseph finds himself crouching beside the trail to the beach, sleeping on the fringes of the dunes, waking several times in the afternoon and wandering in a circle, his heart quick-beating. After dawn he studies the sign-language book, working his fingers into knots, his hands aching, admiring in his memory the precision of Belle's signing, the abrupt dips, the way her hands pour together like liquid, then stop, then worry and gnash like the teeth of gears grinding. He never imagined the body could be so eloquent.

But he is learning. It is as if he is learning all over again how to put the world into words. A tree is an open hand shaken twice by your right ear; whale is three fingers dipped through a sea made by the opposite forearm. The sky is two hands touched above the head, then swept apart, as though a rift has formed in the clouds and you are swimming through them, into heaven.

Thunder over the ocean, ravens screaming in the high branches. A little longer, Joseph thinks. The tomatoes will be ready. It begins to rain—cold, earnest drops fly through the boughs. He has not seen Belle in two weeks when he finds her in the garden, wearing a blue raincoat, stooped among the rows of plants, yanking weeds from the ground and hurling them into the brambles. The drops pop off her shoulders. He watches for a moment. Lightning strobes the sky. Rain runs off the end of her nose.

He steps in among the plants, the tomatoes weighing dreamily on their stems, the melons a pale green against the gray mud on their flanks. He pulls a thin weed and shakes the mud from its roots. "Last year," he says, "whales died here. On the beach. Six of them. Whales have their own language, clicks and creaks and clinking like bottles being smashed together. On the beach they talked to each other as they died. Like old ladies."

She shakes her head. Her eyes are red. I'm sorry, he signs. Please. He says, "I was stupid. Your idea is not any more strange than probably every idea I have ever had."

After a moment he adds, "I buried the hearts from the whales in the forest." He makes the sign for heart over his chest.

She looks at him, canting her head. Her face softens. What? she signs.

"I buried them here." He wants to say more, wants to tell her the whales' story. But does he even know it? Does he even know why they came ashore, what they do when they don't come ashore? What happens to the bodies of whales which do not strand—do they wash up, rolling in the surf one day, rotten and bloated? Do they sink? Are their bodies mulled over at the bottom of the oceans where some strange, deepwater garden can grow up through their bones?

She studies him, her hands spread in the dirt. It's her attention, he thinks. The way she fixes me with her eyes. The way I feel like she's listening all the time, enwombed in that impenetrable silence. Her pale fingers browse among the stems, a raindrop slips down the curve of a green tomato, he has a sudden need to tell her everything. All his petty crimes, the way his mother left for the market in the morning while he *slept*—a hundred confessions surge through him. He has been waiting too long; the words have been building behind a dyke and now the dyke is breached and the river is slipping its banks. He wants to tell her what he has learned about the miracles of light, the way a day's light fluxes in tides: pale and gleaming at dawn, the glare of noon, the gold of evening, the promise of twilight—every second of every day has its own magic. He wants to tell her that when things vanish they become something else, in death we rise again in the blades of grass, the splitting bodies of seeds. But his past is flooding out: the dictionary, the ledger, his mother, the horrors he has seen.

"I had a mother," he says. "She disappeared." He cannot tell if Belle is reading his lips; she is looking away, lifting a tomato and scraping some mud from its underside, letting it back down. Joseph squats in front of her. The storm stirs the trees.

"She had a garden. Like this but nicer. More . . . orderly."

He realizes he does not know how to talk about his mother; he has no words for it. "For years I stole money," he says. He is not sure she understands. Rain pours over his glasses. "And I killed a man." She looks over the top of his head and makes no sign.

"I did not even know who he was or if he was the man they said he was. But I killed him."

Now Belle looks at him with her forehead creased as if in fear and Joseph cannot bear the look but he cannot stop either. There are so many things to give words to: how beached whales smother themselves with the black cannons of their own bodies, the songs of the forest, starlight limning the crests of waves, the way his mother bent in furrows to scatter seeds. He wants to use hand signs that will remake them; he wants her to see his poor, sordid histories reassembled out of the darkness. Every corpse he passed and left unburied; the body of the man slumped on the tennis court; the stolen junk locked even now in the cellar of his mother's house.

Instead he speaks of the whales. "One of the whales," he says, "lived longer than the others. People were tearing skin and fat from the dead one beside it. It watched them do it with its big brown eye and in the end it beat the beach with its flippers, slapping the sand. I was as far away as the house is from us right now and I could feel the ground shaking."

Belle is looking at him, a dirty tomato in her palm. Joseph is on his knees. Tears are flooding his eyes.

A ripening: one last warm day, a half-dozen tanagers poised on a branch like golden flowers, a leaning of tomatoes to the sun. The silk of the melon flowers seems infused with light; any moment they could burst into flame. Joseph watches Belle fight on the lawn with her mother—they are returning from the beach. Belle slashes the air with her hands. Her mother flings down her beach chair, signs something back. Does the girl, Joseph wonders, carry her secrets deep within her? Or do they sit on the edges of her fingertips, ready to fly into language, ready to sign to her mother? *The African you fired lives in the woods. He embezzled money and killed a man.* Do secrets boil inside her like steam in a kettle? Or do they settle like seeds, waiting to open until the time is right? No, Joseph thinks, Belle understands. She has kept her secrets far better than I've kept mine.

He smells the sweet fruit of a tomato, pink now with a swatch of yellow on one side, and the aroma is almost too much to bear.

But in the morning he is discovered. It is just dawn and he is tearing mussels from the rocks and placing them in his rusted drum when a figure appears atop the dunes. Bars of light break through the trees and then—as if the sun conspired to give him away—a single ray fixes him against the water. Behind the figure appear several others; they tumble down the dunes, wading in the loose sand, laughing toward him.

They are carrying drinks and their voices sound drunken and he considers dumping his drum and turning and swimming out to sea to be swept away in some current and dashed forever against the rocks of a faraway place. When they get close to him they stop. Twyman's wife is with them and she walks right to him—her face flushed and twitching—and throws her drink against his chest and screams.

He does not think to get rid of the book of hand signs and when they see it tucked inside the waistband of his trousers things become more serious. Mrs. Twyman turns the book over in her hands and shakes her head and seems unable to speak. "Where did he get that?" the others say. Two men move to flank him, their faces quivering, their fists clenched.

They take him over the dunes, up the trail and across the lawn, past the garage where he lived, the shed he raided for his hoe and seeds. There is no sign of Belle. Mr. Twyman charges out of the house shirtless, hitching up his sweatpants. The words tangle inside him. "The nerve," he spits. "The *nerve*."

There is the sound of sirens, far off. From the lawn Joseph tries to make out the spot atop the hill where the garden is, a small break in a bulwark of spruce, but there is only a smear of green, and soon they are pushing him forward into the house and there is nothing at all to see, only the massive dining table strewn with dishes and half-empty drinks and the faces all around him, spitting questions.

They drive him, handcuffed, to Bandon and place him in an office with antique sirens and plastic softball trophies along the shelves. Two policemen sit on the edge of a desk and take turns repeating questions. They ask what he did with the girl, why, where they went. Twyman rages somewhere in the building: Joseph cannot hear the words but only the cracking of Twyman's voice as it reaches its limits. The policemen on the desk are blank-faced, leaning in.

"What did you eat? Did you eat anything? You don't look like you've eaten at all." "How much time did you spend with the girl? Where did you take her?" "Why don't you speak to us? We can make it easier for you." They ask for the fiftieth time how he got the book of sign language. I'm a gardener, he wants to tell them. Leave me be. But he says nothing.

They lock him in a cell where the texture has been painted off of everything—the cinder-block walls, the floor, the frame of the cot, the bars in the window, all rounded over with coats of paint. Only the sink and toilet are unpainted, the curling design of a thousand scrubbings worked into the steel. The window looks onto a brick wall fifteen or so feet away. A naked bulb hangs from the ceiling, too high to reach. Even at night it burns, a tiny, unnatural sun.

He sits on the floor and imagines weeds overwhelming the garden, their blades hauling down the tomato plants, their interloping roots curling through whatever is left of the whales' hearts. He imagines the tomatoes blooming into full ripeness, drooping from the vines, black spots opening like burns on their sides, finally falling, eaten hollow by flies. The melons turning over and crumpling. Platoons of ants tunneling through rinds, bearing off shining chunks of fruit. In a year the garden will be nothing but salmonberry and nettle, no different than anywhere else, nothing to tell its story.

He wonders where Belle is. He hopes she is far away and tries to picture her behind the wheel of a Volkswagen, a forearm on the sill, some southern highway unrolling before her, the wide fields of the sea coming into view as she rounds a bend.

He does not eat the peanut-butter sandwiches they slide under the bars. After two days the marshal stands at the bars and asks if he wants something else. Joseph shakes his head.

"A body has to eat," the marshal declares. He slides a pack of crackers through. "Eat these. You'll feel better."

Joseph does not. It is not protest or sickness, as the policemen seem to think. It is merely the idea of eating that makes him queasy, the idea of mashing food in his teeth and forcing lumps of it down his throat. He sets the crackers beside the sandwiches, on the rim of the sink.

The marshal watches him a full minute before turning to go. "You know," he says, "I'll put you in the hospital and you can die there."

A lawyer tries to coerce a story out of him. "What did you do in Liberia? These people think you're dangerous—they're saying you're retarded. Are you? Why won't you speak?" There is no fight in Joseph, no anger, no outrage at injustice. He is not guilty of their crimes but he is guilty of so many others. There has never been a man guilty of so much, he thinks, a man more deserving of penalty. "Guilty!" he wants to scream. "I have been guilty all my life." But he has no energy. He shifts and feels his bones settling against the floor. The lawyer, exasperated, departs.

There are no more gates within him, no more divisions. It is as if everything he has done in his life has pooled together inside him and slops dully against his edges. His mother, the man he has killed, the languishing garden—he will never be able to live it down, never live through it, never live enough to compensate for all the things he has stolen.

Two more days without food and he is taken to a hospital—they carry him like his skin is a bag inside which his bones knock together. He can remember only the dull pain of knuckles on his sternum. He wakes in a room, propped on a bed, with tubes plugged into his arms.

In half-dreams he sees terrible visions: the limbless bodies of men materialized on the bureau or the corner chair; the floor lined with corpses in the unnatural poses of death, flies on their eyes, dried blood in their ears. Sometimes when he wakes he sees the man he has killed kneeling on the foot of the bed, his blue beret in his lap, his arms still tied behind his back. The wound in his forehead is fresh, a drill hole rimmed in black, his eyes open. "I have never even *been* in an airplane," he says. Any minute now a nurse will come into the room and see the dead man kneeling on the foot of the bed and that will be it. Finally, Joseph thinks, I must pay for it.

There are other visitors: Mrs. Twyman in the corner chair, her thin arms crossed over her chest. Her eyes are on his; purple stains like bruises throb beneath her eye sockets. "What?" she screams. "What?" And Belle comes, or what might have been Belle—Joseph wakes and remembers her sliding open the window, pointing at gulls on the Dumpsters. But he does not know if he dreamed it, if she is on her way to Argentina, if she even thinks of him. His window is closed, the curtains drawn. When the nurse opens it he can see there are no Dumpsters, just lawn, a parking lot.

Another week or so and a lawyer comes, a clean-shaven pink man with acne around his collar. He reads to Joseph from a newspaper article that says Liberia has held democratic elections; Charles Taylor is the new president, the war is over, refugees are flooding back. "You are to be deported, Mr. Saleeby," he says. "It's very very good for you. The tools you stole and the trespassing—the court will drop these things. Negligence and the accusations of abuse are dropped too. You're absolved, Mr. Saleeby. Free."

Joseph leans back in his bed and realizes that he does not care.

A nurse announces a visitor. She has to help him from the bed and when he stands black spots fill his vision. She folds him into a wheelchair and carts him down the hall and out a side door into a small fenced courtyard.

It is so bright Joseph feels as if his head might crack open. She wheels him to a picnic table in the center of the lawn, fringed by a fence, with cars parked in a lot behind it, and returns the way she came. Joseph strains his eyes toward the sky; it is dazzling, a seething bowl of clouds. A bank of trees beyond the lot tosses in the wind—half the leaves are down and the branches swing together. It is autumn, he realizes. He imagines the blackened, withered roots of his garden, the shriveled tomatoes and wrinkled leaves, a frost paralyzing everything. He wonders if this is where they'll leave him, finally, to die. The nurse will return in a few days, empty him from the chair and bury what's left, the leather of his skin pulling back, the black seed of his heart giving way, the bones settling into the earth.

A door opens into the courtyard and from the doorway steps Belle. She has her knapsack over her shoulders and she walks toward Joseph with a shy smile and seats herself at the picnic table. Beneath the collar of her windbreaker he can see the strap of her shirt, a pale collarbone, a trio of freckles above it. The wind lifts strands of her hair and sets them back down.

He holds his head in his hands and studies her and she studies him. She makes the sign for how are you and Joseph tries to make it back. They smile and sit. Sun winks off the cars in the lot. "Is this real?" Joseph asks. Belle cocks her head. "Are you real? Am I awake?" She squints and nods as if to say, of course. She points over her shoulder, at the parking lot. I drove here, she signs. Joseph says nothing but smiles and props his head in his hands because his neck will not hold it up.

Then she seems to remember why she has come and takes the knapsack from her shoulder and produces two melons, which she sets on the table between them. Joseph looks at her with his eyes wide. "Are those . . . ?" he asks. She nods. He takes one of the melons in his hands. It is heavy and cool; he raps his knuckles against it.

Belle takes a penknife from the pocket of her windbreaker and stabs the other melon, cutting in an arc across its diameter, and when, with a tiny sound of yielding, the melon splits into two hemispheres, a sweet smell washes up. In the wet, stringy cup within are dozens of seeds.

Joseph scoops them out and spreads them over the wood of the table, each white and marbled with pulp and perfect. They shine in the sun. The girl saws a wedge from one of the halves. The flesh is wet and shining and Joseph cannot believe the color—it is as if the melon carried light within it. They each lift a chunk of it to their lips and eat. It seems to him that he can taste the forest, the trees, the storms of the winter and the size of the whales, the stars and the wind. A tiny gob of melon slides down Belle's chin. Her eyes are closed. When they open she sees him and her mouth splits into a smile.

They eat and eat and Joseph feels the wet pulp of the melon slipping down his throat. His hands and lips are sticky. Joy mounts in his chest; any moment his whole body could dissolve into light.

They eat the second melon too, again taking the seeds from the core and spreading them over the table to dry. When they are done they divide the seeds and the girl wraps each half in a piece of notebook paper and they put the damp packets of seeds in their pockets.

Joseph sits and feels the sun come down on his skin. His head feels weightless, as though it would float away if not for his neck. He thinks: If I had to do it over again, I'd bury the whole whales. I'd sow the ground with bucketfuls of seeds—not just tomatoes and melons, but pumpkins and beans and potatoes and broccoli and maize. I'd fill the beds of a hundred dump trucks with seeds. Huge gardens would come up. I'd make a garden so huge and colorful everyone would see it; I'd let the weeds grow and the ivy, everything would grow, everything would get its chance.

Belle is crying. He takes her hands and holds her thin, articulate fingers against his own. He wonders if the dust has piled up against the walls of the house in the hills outside Monrovia. He wonders if hummingbirds still flit between the cups of the flowers, if by some miracle his mother could be there, kneeling in the soil, if they could work together cleaning away the dust, sweeping, brooming it up, carrying it out the door and pitching it into the yard, watching it unfurl in great rust-colored clouds, to be taken up by the wind and scattered somewhere else.

"Thank you," he says, but cannot be sure if he says it aloud. The clouds split and the sky brims over with light—it pours onto them, glazing the surface of the picnic table, the backs of their hands, the wet, carved bowls of the melon rinds. Everything feels very tenuous, just then, and terribly beautiful, as if he is straddling two worlds, the one he came from and the one he is going to. He wonders if this is what it was like for his mother, in the moments before she died, if she saw the same kind of light, if she felt like anything was possible.

Belle has reclaimed her hands and is pointing somewhere far off, somewhere over the horizon. Home, she signs. You are going home.

I'M SLAVERING

SAM LIPSYTE

Everybody wanted everything to be gleaming again, or maybe they just wanted their evening back. Everybody was from everywhere, had gathered here to hide from the daylight. Some of these people sat around a marble table with straws in their hands. It looked like they were waiting for lemonade. They were trying to get my friend Gary on the phone to get more lemonade. It was early, late, lockjaw hour.

"Is it like this in Geneva?" I said to a man at the table. I was new here, recommended to the straw people by Gary. I felt like the pupil of a great instructor out alone in the dead city.

"Is what like what?" he said.

"Is this like this?"

"I'm from Scarsdale," he said. "All I can tell you about is Zurich."

About then the woman with the telephone called out the terrible news.

"Gary's not anywhere," she said.

There were moans, whispers, ruminations on fate, hard words

for God. People started to shuffle out of the room. A few fell on the coat pile in the corner.

"This is why I hate America," said the man from Scarsdale. "This brand of bullshit. Where the hell is Gary?"

"He told me he'd be over later," I said.

"That's exactly what I'm talking about," said the man. "And here comes the fucking sun."

The man bent his straw into a periscope, poked it over the windowsill.

"The sun, the sun," he said. "You fiery whore."

"Maybe I can find Gary," I said.

"You flame-blown bitch," he said.

"I think I know where Gary is," I said.

The man from Scarsdale spun his periscope.

"That's a good story," he said. "Work with that story."

I walked around the ruined sectors of the city and worked with that story.

It was really my story and it went like this: shaky, steady, shaky, steady. I was in shaky right now. I tended to waste a lot of time looking for Gary. It's difficult to stay the course to steadiness when you've got to find Gary all the time. It's difficult to do anything at all. Sometimes, when I needed money, I stole my girl-friend Molly's stuff, but the quality goods were running low. To top it off, I was pretty certain I was suffering from that deficit thing. That disorder. Everything flickered a lot, and I never knew which story I was working with.

Take the story of Gary's thumb. Many years ago, on the eve of manhood, Gary sawed it off with his father's Black & Decker table saw. Gave it to his mother on an olive dish, or maybe it was a cookie plate.

"You should have seen the look on my mother's face," said Gary, back from emergency.

The truth was, you could still see it on her a few days later, there in the bar mitzvah ballroom. That kind of look, it doesn't disappear, even with all that disco-nagila going, and Gary bouncing high in the chair. Gary's uncles, men with great bony mouths, slid Gary from his throne into my arms. I held him there, the bandaged hand between us, and under the din of Hebrew synths, I asked him why he did the sawing.

"They wouldn't let me watch TV," he said. "The late movie. Now I watch all hours. Anything I want."

That's the story of how Gary left his thumb and his youth behind, though they did sew the dead thumb back on.

We had years as strangers before I saw him again, but somehow I've always been following Gary. What he did to his thumb made him, I believe, a wisdom-giver.

Me, I was never bar mitzvah'd. According to the tenets of my faith, I'm nothing close to a man, though I have a hairy neck and look older.

Walking around now I thought of all the times I used to walk around and see Gary on the streets of this city. It's funny to see someone down here from your town. You think everyone will stay behind and do everything you did all over again, forever. You picture old geezers in jean jackets doing whip-its behind the Plaza.

But I got out and Gary got out. Everybody gets out. Getting out is not the problem.

You can picture what the problem is.

For instance, Gary tried to be a rock star, even trained his bad thumb to squeeze on a guitar pick, but rock was dead.

"Somebody should have mentioned something," he said.

Next thing, I see him loitering near trust-fund bistros, looking smug and hunted.

"I'm in goods and services," he said. "It's the only uncompromised medium left."

That was when I decided to buy his services, his goods. I was in a steady phase, but Molly was tired of my clarity. It's hard to fuck your girlfriend when she's fucked up and you're not. It's harder than the Skee-Ball they used to have at the Plaza arcade, all that agony over a fuzzy prize.

Now the sun was clearing the rooftops, the water towers. I thought of the man with the periscope. I looked for Gary in all of the Gary places, but I was too early. These places were all haunted by the future of Gary.

I wanted to score for the straw people, maybe make Gary proud.

I wanted to have friends from all over the world in the way of a man who has no friends. Maybe some of them were still heaped on the coats.

I went home when I knew Molly would be at work and started to pull her music off the shelves. This was what I called a mercy burgle, all those bands overmuch with faux hope for the world and untricky beats. I unloaded a stack of them on a British guy with a store down the block. He got by selling crap at a markup to club kids—used-up ideas, pants unpopular in their own time.

"I just staple a tag on and they buy it," he told me. "It helps that I'm a Limey."

The Brit's eyes had this pucker of awful witness. He'd been everywhere just as everything got ugly: art, philosophy, rugby, love. Maybe what he'd seen had made his teeth fall out, too.

I asked him if he knew where I could get what the straw people needed.

"I don't travel that road anymore," he said. "It's clogged with idiots like you. Now sod off."

He held a mug of tea and I noticed a sliver of cellophane floating on top. Was that the new dead style?

I went down to the park and watched the sparrows peck things off the blacktop. Those animal kingdom shows I always watched with Molly made like there were animal societies, but these birds just hopped around unbidden. I picked one sparrow to be the hero. He proved himself the moocher of the flock.

There was a man in Lycra on a nearby bench, breathing hard, a paper sign pinned to his chest.

RACE FOR THE CURE, the sign said.

I went over to another bench and waited for a feel in the air that would mean the coming of Gary.

"I'm resting," said the racer. "I'm going to get up. Just give me a damn minute."

People always said that what Gary did to his thumb was due to a disturbance, but I figured it happened in a moment of calm. Once he sawed off his thumb and gave it to his mother on a breakfast tray, he was in the free and clear. Who would ever bother a boy like that again? Who would tell him when to go to bed?

This is what I mean by wisdom.

The death of rock was just bad luck.

But Gary was getting it together. Meanwhile, he was mentoring me. The last time I'd seen him he came over with his knapsack, dumped out pills, powders and plant kingdoms on the kitchen table. Molly was gone and I looked around for something of hers to give Gary.

"Hey, are you sure you can handle all this stuff?" he said, pinched a razor blade between his living finger and his dead thumb. "Look at you, you're slavering."

I asked Gary for some girlfriend advice.

"Do you love her?" said Gary.

"That's what I'm asking you," I told him. "Do I?"

He kept propping his thumb up against the side of the razor.

"Why don't you use the other hand?" I said.

"Give a man a fish," said Gary.

"You want fish?" I said.

*   *   *

Now Molly was home with her mortar, her pestle. She liked to crush things for wellness when enough was enough.

"You're home," I said.

I smelled fennel.

"I had a headache."

"I'm sorry," I said.

"So sorry you went and took more of my stuff? Don't tell me, you just need it for a little while."

"I need to find Gary," I said.

"You need a better embalmer," she said. "Look at you."

"Look at these," I said, spread out my hands for her, my thumbs. "These are all that separate us from the beasts of the field."

"What beasts?" said Molly.

"The ones of the field. In the field."

"Actually," said Molly, "that's a myth."

"Actually," I said.

"I mean," said Molly, "factually."

"If Gary calls," I said, "tell him I love you."

"Get the hell out of here," said Molly.

"Just give me a damn minute," I said.

I went to get some coffee, to think hard about where Gary might be. But then I started to think hard about what Gary said about fish. Give a man one why?

There was a straw dispenser on the counter next to my coffee cup. You pushed a little lever and the straw jerked out.

I had a flitter, a flicker.

I saw Gary bouncing high in his ballroom chair. I saw him carried in it across the city, waving to crowds with his bandaged hand. His tusked uncles bore him across wide avenues full of birds. They took him into all of the Gary places, the parks, the bars, bodegas. Gary's mother and the Brit danced around the chair with feathered parasols. I was running to keep up. I had a message to deliver, memorized on some prior occasion. The message went: "I am running to keep up."

A hand poked out of the crowd and hooked my arm.

"Pay extra to nod on my counter," the coffee man said.

"I wasn't nodding," I said. "I was passing out. You want to work in this town you should learn the difference."

I paid for the coffee and headed off to the straw party. I pictured the man from Scarsdale watching me arrive through his periscope.

There were only a few coats left on the hallway floor when I got back. Through a doorway I saw some of the women on a bed. One slept with her tongue out in the other one. A phone glowed open in her hand.

I heard Gary in the next room, laughing with the man from Scarsdale. They looked to be lords of something fallen. There were white dunes and straws on the marble, pills and cash on the floor.

"This guy," said the man from Scarsdale, pointing. "He was here before. Who is he?"

"He's a rising young angler," said Gary.

"Come again?"

"Give a man a fish," said Gary.

"Ah, yes," said the man from Scarsdale. "Many applications to that little homily. Gary here has not yet taught me how to fish, so it's a good thing he finally came over. I was starting to do lint off the carpet again. Are you familiar with the fable of the dropped rock?"

"He knows all about it," said Gary, chopping, sifting.

"Hey," the man said to Gary, "what happened to your thumb? Did you break it?"

"Childhood accident," I called from the couch.

"Yeah," said Gary, "my mother misjudged me."

"Listen," I said, "I just saw this guy with a sign on his shirt. RACE FOR THE CURE, it said."

"Sucker," said the man from Scarsdale, stood.

"Where are you going?" said Gary.

"Me?" said the man from Scarsdale. "I'm going into the bedroom. I'm going to put some of this shit on my cock and slip it in those dyke asses before they know what hit them. Then I'm going to take some valium and fall into a deep, beautiful sleep filled with dreams of Geneva."

The man from Scarsdale winked at me, walked out of the room.

"Jesus," said Gary.

"Christ," I said.

"I mean, what is that?" said Gary. "What are we supposed to do with that?"

He stared into the mirror. His razor hand shook.

"Tell me what I'm supposed to do with that?" said Gary.

"It's okay," I said. "He's just some guy."

"I'm tired," said Gary. "I'm so tired."

"Everything's fine," I said. "You're here. I'm here. Everything's fine."

"Fuck here," said Gary. "We were from a town. A little town. Do you remember?"

"What a question," I said.

"There were people there," said Gary. "There were cars. Carports. You knew where to park."

"Dog hatches in the doors," I said. "Dog doors. Nearmont Avenue. The trestles on Main."

"Spartakill Road," said Gary. "Venus Drive. The Hobby Shop, the Pitch-n-Putt, Big Vin's Pizza, the Plaza."

"Behind the Plaza," I said.

"Exactly," said Gary. "Behind it."

We were quiet for a while.

"Evil's not one thing," said Gary. "They didn't teach us the gradients. We could have stayed."

"Blown our brains out in our cars," I said.

"Not me," said Gary. "What did he mean, Geneva?"

I got up, took the man from Scarsdale's seat, pressed Gary's dead thumb in my hand.

"Are you sorry you did it?" I said.

"Get the hell off me."

I stroked his thumb, brushed it, tenderly, the way you would a blind, tiny thing fresh-pulled from a hole.

"Just tell me if you're sorry," I said. "Because here we are. Because, me, I've been following you. Do you understand that? I've been following you all along. So, just tell me, are you sorry?"

"Hell, no," said Gary. "I wanted to watch TV. Anyway, what's done is done."

"Done and gone," I said.

"Don't fucking wallow," said Gary, and pulled his thumb away. "Never fucking wallow. You wallow, you're pretending you were something else in the first place. I know who I am. I'm Gary. I go down into the street, I'm Gary. I've never stopped being Gary. There's no cure for it. There's no race. It's not a race, okay? It's a contest. Do you get what I'm saying?"

"Yes," I said. "I'm with you."

He walked over to the window, a vista of sky, brick.

"Don't be with me," said Gary.

THE OLD DICTIONARY

LYDIA DAVIS

I have an old dictionary, about 120 years old, that I need to use for
a particular piece of work I'm doing this year. Its pages are brown-
ish in the margins and brittle, and very large. I risk tearing them
when I turn them. When I open the dictionary I also risk tearing
the spine, which is already split more than halfway up. I have to
decide, each time I think of consulting it, whether it is worth
damaging the book further in order to look up a particular word.
Since I need to use it for this work, I know I will damage it, if not
today, then tomorrow, and that by the time I am done with this
work it will be in poorer condition than it was when I started, if
not completely ruined. When I took it off the shelf today, though,
I realized that I treat it with a good deal more care than I treat my
young son. Each time I handle it, I take the greatest care not to
harm it: my primary concern is not to harm it. What struck me
today was that even though my son should be more important to
me than my old dictionary, I can't say that each time I deal with
my son, my primary concern is not to harm him. My primary concern is almost always something else, for instance to find out what

his homework is, or to get supper on the table, or to finish a phone conversation. If he gets harmed in the process, that doesn't seem to matter to me as much as getting the thing done, whatever it is. Why don't I treat my son at least as well as the old dictionary? Maybe it is because the dictionary is obviously fragile. When a corner of a page snaps off, it is unmistakable. My son does not look fragile, bending over a game or manhandling the dog. Certainly his body is strong and flexible, and is not easily harmed by me. I have bruised his body and then it has healed. Sometimes it is obvious to me when I have hurt his feelings, but it is harder to see how badly they have been hurt, and they seem to mend. It is hard to see if they mend completely or are forever slightly damaged. When the dictionary is hurt, it can't be mended. Maybe I treat the dictionary better because it makes no demands on me, and doesn't fight back. Maybe I am kinder to things that don't seem to react to me. But in fact my houseplants do not seem to react much and yet I don't treat them very well. The plants make one or two demands. Their demand for light has already been satisfied by where I put them. Their second demand is for water. I water them but not regularly. Some of them don't grow very well because of that and some of them die. Most of them are strange-looking rather than nice-looking. Some of them were nice-looking when I bought them but are strange-looking now because I haven't taken very good care of them. Most of them are in pots that are the same ugly plastic pots they came in. I don't actually like them very much. Is there any other reason to like a houseplant, if it is not nice-looking? Am I kinder to something that is nice-looking? But I could treat a plant well even if I didn't like its looks. I should be able to treat my son well when he is not looking good and even when he is not acting very nice. I treat the dog better than the plants, even though he is more active and more demanding. It is simple to give him food and water. I take him for walks, though not often enough. I have also sometimes slapped his nose, though the vet told me never to hit him anywhere near the head, or maybe he said anywhere at all. I am only sure I am not neglecting the dog when he is asleep. Maybe I am kinder to things that are not alive. Or rather if they are not alive there is no question of kindness. It does not hurt them if I don't pay attention to them, and that is a great relief. It is such a relief it is even a pleasure. The only change they show is that they gather dust. The dust won't really hurt them. I can even get someone else to dust them. My son gets dirty, and I can't clean him, and I can't pay someone to clean him. It is hard to keep him clean, and even complicated trying to feed him. He doesn't sleep enough, partly because I try so hard to get him to sleep. The plants need two things, or maybe three. The dog needs five or six things. It is very clear how many things I am giving him and how many I am not, therefore how well I'm taking care of him. My son needs many other things besides what he needs for his physical care, and these things multiply or change constantly. They can change right in the middle of a sentence. Though I often know, I do not always know just what he needs. Even when I know, I am not always able to give it to him. Many times each day I do not give him what he needs. Some of what I do for the old dictionary, though not all, I could do for my son. For instance, I handle it slowly, deliberately, and gently. I consider its age. I treat it with respect. I stop and think before I use it. I know its limitations. I do not encourage it to go farther than it can go (for instance to lie open flat on the table). I leave it alone a good deal of the time.

THE FATHER'S BLESSING

MARY CAPONEGRO

Allow me, if you would, to tell you of a wedding, which took place not long ago, a wedding no different from any other—not objectively—in which I played my role to everyone's satisfaction, at least initially. For all I know, the bride might have been already with child when I performed the rite, but I would never be so crude as to count months upon my fingers, when I hear of joyous news, for these very fingers may be called upon to cradle the wailing infant's tender head at christening time, to give him support as he enters new terrain, unaware of the security, solace, and spiritual wealth that define it. To him, at that moment, I must seem merely a stranger offering unfamiliar, disturbing sensations. But later in his life he will realize the value of my gesture, and our bond.

The parents of this hypothetical child are perhaps another matter: the couple I recently wed, for instance; they were, in my opinion, naive. They did not realize the contract they were making—with me, that is—when they asked if I would sanctify their union. They assumed they could bid me good riddance, I expect, once the vows were exchanged, as if the rite were mere formality.

How strangely they regarded me when—after I had played my role to the satisfaction of all, from the solemnity of the vows to the levity of the reception, chatting pleasantly, even wittily, with the parents, both sets, commenting in passing on the beauty of the bride, lest they think me at too great a remove from human experience— when there was a lull in the receiving line, I took the couple aside (who would question my doing it?) and asked if they would have me perform the last rites.

Without affectation or cynicism, I announced, "I live, as you know, in the rectory far away, and there is always the chance— though etiquette prohibits our acknowledging—that should you summon me at the last minute, I would be unable to reach you in time. There are so few of us, exiguously placed, and the parishes likewise scarce. The road to the rectory is seldom plowed in winter, and in spring the potholes impede smooth travel. When it rains, the roads turn almost instantly to clay, so that only in a skillful driver's hands at high speeds can they be traversed successfully. If I were to administer the sacrament to one of you now, think of the time and anxiety we all might be spared, and the law of averages indicates that the partner to receive this prophylactic blessing would likely be that party to require it later on. I realize it is hard to think ahead in the bloom of youth. . . . "

The bride, aghast, clutched the arm of the man who only hours ago had been made, under my aegis, her husband, and challenged him by her fear to confront me, which he, I must admit, quite eloquently did; no doubt a heroic effort to match my own eloquence and to impress her by trying to rhyme with my authority. "Father," he scolded, "what can be your intent? This is a time of rejoicing. You yourself pronounced the words, 'till death do us part.' Would you part us so soon then?"

Realizing that I had been misunderstood, I, who am an accommodating man—I do not proselytize, do not force myself— desisted (my objectives were unlikely to be understood within that public context—for heads were beginning to turn; those who had passed through the line were beginning to gravitate toward it again) and promptly took my leave, against the parents' puzzled protests: "Do visit us again soon, Father." And I had the sense, even as I gracefully accepted defeat, that I would see them all again soon enough.

Walking in town to collect myself, I realized there was another related visit I could make, to clarify what had been muddled. And so I sought out an acquaintance, or might one say, a colleague: the owner, as it happens, of a funeral home. Indeed, the bride and groom appeared surprised when I returned, accompanied, much later in the evening, to the family's house, where the wedding had taken place—the reception had been elsewhere, as is the custom. Little could they appreciate my willingness, my eagerness, to initiate them into a yet-deeper mystery than the one upon which they had already, by laws of convention, embarked, allegedly for the first time. I even brought my friend the undertaker with me—he required considerable persuasion—to reinforce what might otherwise seem mere words, and to balance the awkwardness of a third party lest they misinterpret my intentions. The undertaker and I allowed no ambiguity in our presentation; we were straightforward, precise.

"I've come," he said, just as I instructed him, barely glancing at the two individuals he addressed, "to take the measurements for the casket. Would you be so kind as to lie apart, upon your backs, hands folded so, and I'll be through in no time." They seemed in shock, paralyzed, in their melded state, until the undertaker brought forward his implement to measure the bridegroom's member.

"All parts are parts of the whole," was his speech; "all shall come to dust." Meanwhile the groom hid himself the more deeply inside his bride, as if this would render the whole of him invisible. The bride's cry I could not pretend to interpret; perhaps she was pleased to offer him haven, or startled by his urgency; yet I would have thought the volume appropriate to an instance of assault. The ruler may as well have been a dagger: such was her alarm. Or did she fear that to which she had been newly joined would be, by the former's measure, reduced? Who can possibly surmise the unbridled musings of the young in unfamiliar circumstances in a world relentlessly novel? I suppose in some ways the equanimity of a man of the cloth is an enviable thing.

Because I am a sincere man I must tell you that there is indeed advantage to the closet called confessional: one can be so close, intimate; only a thin screen separates oneself from the sinner, one's own sagacious voice from the whispers which reveal the deepest secrets. That is our special privilege; one might say power: that no one can justify surprise or suspicion when I appear on the other side of, by extension, any partition. There is, with me, potentially greater intimacy than that between a man and wife: one bound to breed resentment, foster ambivalence; for people are uncomfortable robbed of accusations: meddler, eavesdropper, peeping tom, spy; no one of these terms applies to a man of my vocation.

Father is the name by which all know me, the term by which I'm ceaselessly addressed. But was that the sound that echoed in mythic Daedalus's ears long after he'd watched the flesh of his flesh falling inexorably from air into water: Father? Father? I am the man who must give answers; thus expectation begets my ingenuity, for I want them prepared, as one does one's children. And I, like any parent, will never learn my sermon's lesson: that they must have their own experience; one cannot spare them. The more you try the more they will reject, be repelled—and thereby eject themselves from the sky. Seldom are they equipped to receive the truth, though one wants to believe sheer force of one's sincerity will smooth the roughest road, quarry hardest stone. Yet one must exercise caution, for sincerity is a dangerous thing.

It was caution that dictated I depart, with my accomplice, allowing the other two to sort through their admittedly challenging instruction. A man in my profession must be bold, as He whom I revere was bold, but never reckless. The long journey back to the rectory is always an ideal opportunity for reflection.

As I might have guessed, no sooner had the season changed— or so it seemed; perhaps it had changed more than once—than I received a summons: I was needed. It must, I thought, be time for the baptism now. As my sense of direction is acute, my memory guided me accurately to the town, the tree-lined avenue, the stately Victorian house which was the Callahan residence and inside it, the very chamber from which I had once been banished. I was unable to persuade the undertaker to accompany me this time; from his point of view the prior experience had bred only humiliation. His profession has not taught him, as mine has, the value, the necessity, of perseverance. I would represent him, as I represented so many already. I had my vial of holy water and prayer book in hand as I entered the house of the bride's parents, the same in which the ceremony had occurred. I assumed I would lead the family to the church after exchanging pleasantries, becoming reacquainted. Perhaps I would hold the child once we arrived, so that my hand upon him would not feel strange when the ritual was enacted.

But when I arrived, the cries I heard were not an infant's, but those of a mature woman, and that is how I came to grace the threshold of their chamber, for I ascended the staircase to investigate with the intention of assisting. As I squinted through the crack in the door, I saw the mother-to-be perspiring, panting, writhing, from time to time moaning in effort of that singular process of which I can perforce have no inkling, called *labor,* derived from Eve's seduction by a serpent. Even a husband, it is said, cannot soothe a woman during this arduous period; but I who as a priest possess potentially greater intimacy, thought to humbly offer solace.

"I am here," I said, through the crack which gave me witness.

"No," she screamed, I assumed to the source of her pain.

And when she repeated it over and over, I questioned whether contractions could be so frequent. I realized I possessed not even clinical knowledge regarding this miraculous yet commonplace event. I felt something akin to shame, before her next and more explicit statement jarred me from the sentiment: "It's that horrid priest again!" Her husband rushed to the door and said diplomatically, "There must be some mistake, Father; we sent for the midwife, to assist delivery. It was planned that we have a home birth."

I replied that I found it odd they had chosen this alternative with a hospital down the street.

"Father," the groom was losing his studied patience, "medicine—am I correct?—is not your area of expertise, and our affairs are not your"—he used His name in vain—"business. Besides, isn't it obvious that my wife is in no condition to travel, even a short distance, at this stage? On the other hand, there is nothing to hold you here. If priests are in as scarce supply as you report, then I would not want it on my conscience that we had monopolized you."

As the groom spoke, admittedly with cleverness, I realized that the suggestion that served his convenience was not without substance, for if it was the case that the couple had not summoned me, then some miscommunication must have occurred through the secretary at the rectory, and some other couple required my ministrations in some fashion. But before I could take action, the most searing cry of all pierced the air, and the woman, to whom the groom turned again to face, and who had previously appeared distorted only in the distention of her abdomen, now manifested a most peculiar symmetry, for she possessed two heads, one at each end. We stood transfixed by this sight, suspended in time, in awe, until the bride herself corrected this anomaly as she pushed out—with disconcertingly audible discomfort, through that chamber that will ever be a secret to me—a diminutive whole human being.

The completed act restored us to our senses and he dismissed me, saying, "Father, you must not distract me any longer. I have neglected my wife at her most critical hour. She must have no disturbance now. If you want to make yourself useful, you might go find the midwife for us." Then with his foot he closed the slender aperture that had been my access to the two, now three.

Although for reasons other than those the groom believed, it was, I felt, my duty to explore elsewhere. The hospital was my destination for there was very likely another couple, another newborn, with whom I had business, a family more receptive to that business. I recalled the pleasant and devout man and woman I had married quite some time ago, who had wanted nothing in the world as much as children, but the pregnancies had been in every case problematic; I knew not the details of the matter.

When I arrived at the hospital, after quietly exiting the house, I walked immediately to the front desk and offered the name of this prior couple. The nurse recognized my attire, and directed me to the room where the wife had recently given birth. The couple received me gratefully, but they were not alone. A doctor was with them, as well as several others I presumed to be medical students, peering at a Polaroid photograph. My presence did not distract them from their concentration, nor their discussion, the focal point of which seemed to be the ascription of blame, and which became increasingly agitated. I was, I eventually realized, too late, although I blessed the recently departed child, gone to God no sooner had he exited the womb, strangled by the very cord which bound him to his mother's nurture, in the act of being born. Ah, to witness life and death in such proximity; what more profound instruction could one receive? Although I was too late in one sense, the gift of this lesson was not denied me, and my duty was to offer it to those who could most profit from it. I granted myself permission to borrow documentation.

I hastened from the room to the corridor to the elevator and so on, until I was once again at the Callahans' residence. As I was the last to leave, the door had not been latched, so I let myself in; then, like a child, I took the steps two at a time until I stood before the door of the bride and groom. I knocked before entering and addressed them by their Christian names.

"Kathleen," I cried, "David. There is something I must show you. Something you must see."

"Where's the midwife, Father?" the groom asked with little animation, concentrating on the pulsating cord that sustained mother and child as unity, clamped at two sites with paper clips, above which he held a small blunt scissors, moving them between two different sites only inches apart, unable to decide, it seemed, where to sever the bond, or simply unable to bring himself to make the cut. The thing which eluded him seemed to me some dense but slender fish, perhaps an eel, caught between sea and land, its respiration intact despite its dislocation. Through the power of grace, it had not been an infelicitous agent in this instance.

"Here in my hand," I replied, "in my very hand." I held the picture to the light. "Kathleen," I whispered tenderly to her weary form, her sweat-drenched face. I knelt beside her, conscious of, yet not repelled by, the odor of sweat and flesh that pervaded the room, the sight of the bright white linen stained with blood. "This is for you."

She squinted at the image I held before her, then gazed at me incredulously before releasing a sound whose frequency seemed almost too high for human ears. Hurriedly, I veiled the truth again, covering what had been for a moment visible. Moments of the truth are all we can bear. And in the next, the midwife arrived. (I heard the bride's mother answer the bell, explaining that she refused to get involved; her participation had not been invited, and could anyone imagine how difficult it must be to listen to a daughter's cries and feel so impotent?)

The newest guest appeared before us, and promptly took charge. Regarding the bride's glazed eyes and distorted expression (and no doubt informed by the shriek preceding her entry), she said, "What happened here?" The groom motioned toward me, using the scissors as a teacher might a pointer, but spoke no words. "Father, it would be better if you left me alone with her." Then she addressed the groom. "I'm sorry I was delayed. A breech birth at the hospital involved unforeseen complications and I was called in to help." After a pause, she added, "Unfortunately to no avail." She gently released the rounded handles of the implement from his grip, then laid her hand on Kathleen's forehead, and I was struck by how similar to a sacramental gesture was this contact. "David, you should accompany the Reverend, since Kathleen will need complete rest to recover from the trauma. I doubt she'll be able to nurse."

After performing with expediency the maneuver the groom had been unable to execute, the midwife lifted the tiny form, wrapped it carefully in a blanket she had brought, and handed it to me, then quickly corrected herself, offering it to the groom. Once the bundle was dispensed with, she took the bride's wrist between her thumb and fingers, feeling for a rhythm I suspected she feared absent. "If only I could have gotten here on time," she said to herself, no longer communicating with the groom and myself, shaking her head with concern at the bride's vacant face. Then she repeated it, like a dirge.

Remembering our presence, she gave instruction and bade us depart, promising to send word when things stabilized. Who were we to doubt her? "It makes most sense for the baby to be cared for in maternity at the hospital, until Kathleen revives," she clarified, gazing at the infant in its father's arms, then whispered, "Such a lovely little boy." The groom followed me, reluctant but obedient, out the door, while she set about with her humble instruments, wiping, sponging, disinfecting. We heard her strained but authoritative voice behind us: "And buy some formula, in the hospital pharmacy, in case we need it later."

My second trip to the hospital, then, was a simple twofold errand. David, as soon as we reached the building, adopted a rapid pace; I assumed that his strategy was to divide our errands for the sake of maximum efficiency. After clearing the front desk with a nod from the receptionist, I rode the elevator to the room where I had first been inspired by the photograph. Having been unprepared for Kathleen's strong reaction to it, I now wondered whether I needed to protect the stillborn's mother from the reminder of what she had seen, as it were, in the flesh; of her flesh. Probably she too should not be disturbed, regardless of how welcoming the two appeared.

Discreetly I slipped the Polaroid under their door, facedown, and rode the elevator back to street level to find the pharmacy. It was clearly marked and a woman from behind the counter offered me assistance.

"I have been instructed," I began, but could not manage to complete the sentence; it seemed awkward.

"There is a woman," I began anew.

She raised her eyes. "Yes, Father?"

"A mother."

She lowered them again.

"Her milk . . ."

"I understand perfectly, Father. There is no need to continue." And she turned her back to me to search the shelves behind her, before handing me a box approximately ten inches high. I felt inside my cassock for my billfold, but she placed her own hand over mine to stop me.

"Please, Father," she said. "We know about the tragedy. The hospital staff is very concerned, and supportive. Some of us feel the word"—she whispered it—"ashamed"—"is not too strong. In any case, do let this be our contribution."

"But, miss," I protested, fearful of appearing ungrateful or obtuse. "I am not certain I have made myself clear, or if I myself am clear, regarding the equipment that is . . . needed."

"I am a woman, Father," she said, with gravity and unflinching gaze. "I know things you cannot know. Trust me."

I had no response to her authority and conviction. I could only go back to the Callahans', perhaps not correctly but at least not empty-handed. David may have been required to remain with the child, and it was best for one of us to be available.

This time, however, I did not venture upstairs, but remained in the lower portion of the house, seeking refuge in a room, to the rear of the staircase—a room immaculate and austere, containing a long oak table and eight matching straight-backed chairs with brocade seats, upon one of which I sat. I slid the package to the far end of the polished table, then laid my head in my hands, resting this weight on the smooth wooden surface. After some time I lifted up my head, taking several deep breaths, the last exhalation interrupted by the appearance of Mrs. Callahan, mother of the bride.

"Father Faraday, what a lovely surprise! Have you come to say Mass at St. Agnes?"

"No, Mrs. Callahan," I said, regaining my composure—a man who must attend, through the vehicle of a single sense, to a sequence of stories, of lives, of sins whose range spans from the barely worth mentioning to the most debased; a man who must juxtapose the only confession in the life of an evil practitioner; such a man has evolved the skill of flexibility, of quick recovery; to use the colloquial metaphor of our automobile-dependent culture, the ability to switch gears—"no, another appointment"—there was no need to be specific—"now completed." Talking was easier than I'd anticipated, even reassuring.

"All the better, Father; you can join us then, for our Sunday meal," she said, unfolding an embroidered white cloth and spreading it over the table, letting it billow out as one might a bedsheet. "I'm sure the children will be delighted."

"I wouldn't assume anything, Mrs. Callahan." I thought she had not heard me; she was already through the door, then back again, the first of numerous trips to heap the Lord's bounty onto the table: steaming platters, casseroles, a roast ready to be carved.

"You must excuse the children," she said, as if there had been no interruption to our conversation, and as she continued to lay out the meal, concluding with, as afterthought, a bottle of fine red wine, and another Waterford glass. "They are not beholden to tradition, as our generation was." She smiled at me, pausing in her activity. "They will appear when it suits them."

"Shall I begin carving?" I asked, as she began to light the candles in the candelabra, no trace of concern marring her flawless countenance as the flame drew nearer and nearer her slender fingers. I was fatigued and felt less in command of my expressions. I feared Mrs. Callahan might have thought me greedy rather than eager to offer a gesture of assistance; I was ashamed of how much effort she had expended while I sat immobile in my temporary stupor.

"The one favor I would ask of you, Father Faraday, is to say grace for us, if it wouldn't be too much of an imposition—not until everyone arrives, of course." She sighed, and seemed to raise her voice slightly when she added wistfully, "If we could just for once all be together at the table." She sighed again.

"Mrs. Callahan," I sought to console her, "I would urge you to consider that your daughter and son-in-law may be occupied with matters of some significance, and their absence is not necessarily an expression of indifference or hostility. Or, for that matter, ingratitude."

"No, indeed, Father," she replied, and with dignity continued, "but you, as a man of the cloth, are unlikely to be acquainted with that wrenching feeling, that torture of wanting to intervene, wanting to make available the wisdom of maturity, but knowing you must not surrender to it, for if you do, every strategy will go awry before your eyes."

Mrs. Callahan was visibly moved by what she shared, as was I to be receiving her words—more than she knew—and she permitted herself to digress: "Everything today is natural. But would the

Lord have allowed man the mind to evolve technology if he meant him to be left to only natural devices? You are obviously the expert here, Father, excuse my . . . trespassing." She half-smiled. "I asked them, what is wrong with a good old-fashioned hospital? Now, I was a nurse, Father Faraday, before the Lord blessed our marriage with a child, and I know a bit about these matters, but we left to doctors the work of doctors and did not monkey around, if you'll excuse the expression, with life and death. There are risks, are there not, in every natural process?"

"You are a thoughtful woman, Mrs. Callahan."

"I suppose you might as well begin the carving," she said, resigned; "otherwise we may be waiting here until everything is cold." As I could infer the tenderness of the meat from its succulent aroma, I was more than willing to comply. "It is nice to have a man about, to lend a hand. My husband, you see, he's been . . . unwell."

"I'm very sorry to hear that." My memory of Mr. Callahan at the wedding—robust, energetic—was difficult to reconcile with these words—unless I confused him with the father of the groom; I did not think this was the case. And yet, our world fluctuates before us daily; appearances ever-unreliable indices of truth.

"The Lord works in mysterious ways; isn't that right, Father Faraday?"—as if she'd read my mind. I could not decipher her tone: conspiratorial, mocking, perhaps even . . . flirtatious? Fortunately, the moment of intense ambiguity passed.

"So much in life is confusing, isn't it? Nothing more so than being a parent in this day and age—I'm sure you've heard the stories, Father. In fact, I wonder if I might be so bold as to impose upon you for an even larger favor—since we may not get to grace, at this rate." She made an enigmatic gesture with her mouth, that seemed half sinister, half coquettish, or perhaps neither, some neutral expression colored by my fatigue? My job—I thank the Lord—is not to judge, outside a certain circumscribed, sacred enclosure. "My daughter, I'm convinced, is in need of guidance," she said, "guidance beyond my capacity. I thought marriage would make a difference, but I'm afraid that in some ways, it's only made things worse, and I wondered——I thought, perhaps, if you went up, and spoke with her . . ."

"I would like to very much, Mrs. Callahan," I said sincerely, "very much indeed; but there are times when no one, not even a man of God, can take the place of a mother." As I said the last word I rose to procure the package that had remained undisturbed (but for Mrs. Callahan's occasional furtive glances)——then returned to the seat, placing on the table its contents: a box which I began to push toward her slowly.

"What can it be?" she asked, staring at the thing as if it would speak its name.

I continued to push with my fingers the device I had procured at the hospital pharmacy. Both of us regarded its incremental progress as a child might a caterpillar's. It whispered across the tablecloth: my fingers its gentle engine. When the box had achieved sufficient distance to be within close range, I drew back my hand and remained silent while she studied the labeling. Mrs. Callahan blushed, giggled, and then rose, smoothing the front of her blouse, and I was reminded, for some reason, of the expression *blushing bride*.

"You are admirably down-to-earth, Father Faraday, and yet so . . . discreet. Please do help yourself while I have a brief chat with my daughter." She grasped the box, tentatively at first, but then walked decisively out of the room, to the stairs. Would Kathleen be conscious? Would her mother's presence rouse her if not, and stimulate her healing? I hoped it would be so, but my own hunger distracted me from this concern.

In truth, I could not remember the last time I had eaten. Had I even had breakfast? I carved a few slices of beef——it should certainly not go to waste, this bounty——and there was no point in serving Mrs. Callahan's portion only to watch it grow cold. I passed myself the green beans, the roast potatoes. With the first bite, I realized I was ravenous. What a relief it was to nourish myself without the burden of conversation, to leave the world, for just a few moments, to its own devices.

I ate much more rapidly than was salubrious. Perhaps this was the source of my indigestion, although I suspect it had more to do with the bride's raised voice, followed by the shattering of glass. I laid down my fork, went back to the living room, and leaned against the banister, wincing at the words toward which I could not keep myself from straining.

"You're positively medieval, Mother." At least the bride possessed the energy to raise her voice. The midwife had either cured her—one of the innumerable daily miracles we take for granted—or misapprehended the situation from the start. Perhaps the former was now with David and the child, and all would return shortly.

"Darling, that is very discourteous. The breast pump was a gift from Father Faraday."

"The priest! Mother, you must be kidding. That man is very peculiar."

"He's not a man exactly, is he—a priest? But I think he's quite nice, dear, and you were rude to him."

"No, Mother, he was .... cruel to me; you can't imagine."

"I'm sure you exaggerate, Kathleen; he performed the ceremony so beautifully. He keeps in touch, and you can tell he cares. I sense he's very . . . trustworthy."

I slowly climbed the stairs, no more rapidly than I had pushed the problematic box, now discarded. I climbed almost against my will. Certain projects seem to have no end in sight, before we gain the profit of perspective. Yet we must never cease to strive, to hope. It seemed that the voices grew muted as I drew near.

"Mother, I feel nervous when I know he's around, and I'm feeling weak as it is. We need a quiet place to talk. There's just too much going on here, and he is a man after all, no matter what any of you say."

"Well of course, dear, technically, that's true. But a priest is a special kind of man, and if you can't trust a priest, whom can you trust? It isn't as if he were Episcopalian; they have wives and worse. Father Faraday is a good old-fashioned Catholic priest. And insofar as he's a man, what's wrong with having a man around the house?"

I was right against the door now, squatting to make my eye level with the keyhole. There was a long pause in their conversation.

"Mother," the bride said suddenly—with urgency and a noticeable maturity—no longer whining, "if I asked you to follow me somewhere, would you?"

"That depends, Kathleen. What I mean is, of course I would, if it seemed reasonable, but don't you think you'd be better off resting for a few days?—here where there are people to look after you, a familiar environment, the comforts of home. . . ."

"No, I don't mean to go away from here, to travel, but you have to promise not to ask any questions, just to go with me."

I was curious myself as to the destination the bride had in mind, although slightly distracted by the pain in my knees, a sensation with which I am well-acquainted, and have, over the years, developed the stamina to endure.

"You are being very mysterious, young lady, but your mother will go along."

"Thank you, oh thank you, Mother, because I discovered just the perfect place while I was having my contractions, and I was afraid it might . . . disappear—I mean I might forget it—just like when you have a dream sometimes that's so vivid and powerful but then you can't remember anything specific the next day, or even an hour later."

I watched the bride splay her legs; she spread them as far, it seemed, as legs could separate, and farther still—perhaps she had as an adolescent performed the acrobatic maneuver called a split; she might have been a cheerleader—it seemed it must be terribly uncomfortable but this time she uttered no cries, not a sound, as they, adopting what appeared an exaggerated yoga position, crept inside, one after the other, to be embraced by those contours which are, even in the imagination, forbidden to the man who inhabits, as vocation, a chamber of secrets. I heard them twice removed now, as if underwater.

"I must admit I feel a bit uneasy here, Kathleen; would you do me the favor of telling me where we are?"

"Well, it's hard to say exactly where, but I can tell you how I found it. In the excruciating and terribly lonely pain of labor, when all of me was opened up, I felt almost delirious, and yet very . . . present, painfully connected to what was happening, and in between contractions I just decided I should be able to inhabit that space myself, in a soothing way; a therapeutic way, I guess you could call it. Shouldn't the haven we give others be available for us too? Doesn't that seem right to you, Mama? Anyway, suddenly I was in a place I'd never known but wanted to come back to, and when I saw you now, I knew I had to bring you with me. I'm very glad you agreed to come." The two women had no suspicion that they were in some fashion exposed to the practiced ear of a man whose profession is to listen through a membrane to all the world's secrets.

"No one would ever think to look for us here."

"I suppose you're right, dear. But what if someone should need either of us? I don't feel right to be unavailable. We do have company, after all. I've always prided myself on being a perfect hostess."

"But Mother, we've only just arrived. Stay awhile. Besides, it's only fair I reciprocate," the bride said, after a brief pause. "My first journey in this world was through a room just like this, that you guided me through. Then somehow we grew estranged from one another."

"You make it all sound a bit tragic, Kathleen, when we've been having such a pleasant, such an interesting visit. I really don't know what you are referring to. And might I suggest you consider the word estrangement in relation to your own son and husband? But you always take offense when I try to remind you of your responsibilities, even though my only concern is your happiness."

"Oh yes, let's not get into it, Mother, I didn't mean anything by it. I love being here with you where it's so embracing, yet expansive too, as if it might extend beyond infinity."

"Such a lovely way of putting it; you are your mother's daughter, aren't you? And I will certainly come again, if I'm invited. If nothing else, it's educational. It shows me just how much we have in common."

It seemed their session had terminated but it was hard to assess, something of the sensation one has during an overseas phone conversation: its disorienting static and delays in transmission of sound.

"Is this the exit, honey?"

"You go first, Mama."

Mrs. Callahan's next words were clearly articulated; no longer did they sound submerged, murky, as I watched the mesmerizing reemergence of the two women. The bride seemed to turn inside out; I have no other words, as inadequate, as pedestrian as these are; I was reminded of the way certain of nature's creatures shed their skins. The bride was again lying in the bed; indeed she had never stood during the entire expedition, and her mother was back at her side, seated, now dabbing inside the bodice of the bride's dressing gown with a linen cloth.

"My breasts feel so swollen." The daughter's plaintive voice addressed her mother.

"Of course they do; they *are* swollen," the latter replied as she continued to execute the dainty motion with the cloth, the inadequacy of which brought to mind the image of the Dutch boy's finger in the dike.

"It's a pity you destroyed that breast pump, dear; rather reckless of you."

"It was in a moment of passion."

"Ah, yes. Where did you say David went? Not to mention my grandchild."

"To investigate something, I think. I'm not really sure. Things are a bit strained between us, actually."

"No doubt. Well, if we don't do something soon I'm afraid you're going to burst, and we can't have that. There is mess enough around here as it is. I suppose that midwife gave you some lactating stimulant. I've never heard of milk coming in quite this early in such . . . volume. I'm going to have to take matters into my own . . ." She hesitated, looking uncharacteristically tentative, for clearly she lacked a destination or function for the parts of herself to which her ellipsis metaphorically alluded. As her voice trailed off, I saw Mrs. Callahan gently, furtively affix her mouth to her daughter's breast, to relieve it of the nourishment meant for another which burdened it so. The bride winced. "Could you try to be gentler, Mother?" she asked. "They're a bit tender, since this is the first time."

The bride's mother obligingly removed her lips from the darkened protuberance no longer veiled by white fabric. She awaited permission as an accompanist awaits the signal from another instrumentalist to initiate music, so as to create, all the more precisely, unity of sound and feeling.

And when that signal came, and she lowered again her head to grasp with her lips what hands would not be useful for, a stream of pale white squirted out, startling us all. I nearly toppled over but repositioned to correct myself, careful to utter no sound. The bride's mother also made adjustments; she appeared to take a deep breath and then, after one unsuccessful attempt, arrested the stream. With enviable dexterity, she reached, while thus occupied, toward the couple's dressing table to retrieve a crystal bowl, into which she released, in an astoundingly refined fashion, the translucent whitish liquid from her mouth, the latter which she dabbed with the same linen cloth. Ignoring the unimpeded flow, she breathed again, and said, "I only wish I had two mouths." Valiantly she resumed her relief measures, acquiring an almost graceful regimen of intake and release, growing, it seemed to me, increasingly acclimated, mother and daughter both, approaching a state of trance-like serenity.

Now I am an efficient man, as I have said, and it troubled me to think of the ignored twin of the bride's mammae, engorged as it was, unattended. Mrs. Callahan, pragmatic woman that she was, had obviously elected not to attempt a system of alternation, fearing the rhythmic complications of leaking and squirting. It had never occurred to me, until that moment, that a baby might nurse from both a mother's breasts, in careful sequencing. Already today I had learned a great deal, primarily with the aid of sight, the sense that is not usually my instructor. But having thus benefited from observation, was it not my duty, now, to intervene? So often we men of cloth are accused of being "out of touch" with the pragmatic needs of our parishioners, particularly alienated from the needs of women, and inhabiting a comfortably ethereal realm. I looked into my heart and knew I had to overcome my resistance; sometimes matters far less grand than exorcising demons were well worthy of a priest. Such contact, though it be ostensibly at odds with propriety, and with my own inclinations, would be the gift that I could offer. The analogy of artificial respiration seemed fitting: this sort of detachment, yet commitment and intensity.

I crept into the room, literally, for I would need to remain on my knees—I am well practiced—for this novel process. Neither stirred and I made only the softest sounds.

"I am here." I whispered it so softly that it might have been an angel's voice, or strand of dream. And the bride's gasp was likewise a subterranean response to dreamt image or sensation, when I took into my mouth the darkened mounded center of the aureole, controlling my distress to find it already wet, leaking in fact, all the while that Mrs. Callahan attended its twin. The breast itself was hard, like a boulder, but with a quality of translucence, blue veins protruding through the flesh. I had the unique opportunity to use as visual instruction the template across from me, and let this be my focus, rather than the disconcerting image immediately before me. I was prepared now for the energy with which its contents would gush forth. I moved my lips, and not my teeth, in time with Mrs. Callahan's, and found, by some small miracle, a rhythm that seemed appropriate to Kathleen's needs. Inadvertently I glanced at the crystal bowl to see that within the clearer fluid, resembling white watercolor paint, some globules of fat had collected. I managed to check, at first, an impulse to gag, but after this sight, the taste—for I could not approximate Mrs. Callahan's demure dexterity in spitting out every drop of the substance to make room for more—of the cloyingly sweet liquid overwhelmed me. Already, it took all my concentration to be one with it. But certainly my training should have equipped me with the discipline required to transcend my squeamishness, to put mind and spirit over matter, in order to overcome the body's limitations.

And so I did, offering a silent prayer of thanks. And just as when one engages in physical exercise, and after passing a certain threshold of pain, gains momentum and achieves sustained transcendence, I too felt altogether delivered from my limitations. Such a strange suspension this state was, to be intensely present yet entranced: unique in my adventures as a servant. I felt no impatience whatsoever, only a curiosity as to how long a milk-filled mother's breast required to empty its contents. My only reference was a single farming experience one summer as a boy, tentatively touching a cow's udder—the farmhand laughing, "That won't get you anywhere, little feller, ya gotta use some muscle," as she squeezed my arm to add emphasis before demonstrating the far more vigorous maneuvers required to make the milk squirt into the silver pail. She might, I supposed, be proud of me now—though the bishop would demand an explanation.

Most unfortunately, the indigestion—which was engendered when I indulged in gluttony over Mrs. Callahan's repast, followed by hearing the bride's reproach, and finally by coming to the aid of a woman—who happened to be the same as she who had reproached me—in distress—now welled up in my gut anew, and I was ashamed of my weakness. Mortal that I was, I would have to admit my subservience to the body. Such a vast intake of milk for an unaccustomed adult system was bound to result in some degree of gastric distress. I thought it best to absent myself before either woman "awakened," for certainly my becoming ill would be no contribution to the situation. My gift would be left unsigned, as it were, and how happy this made me, for this is the joy of my vocation: to help without ostentation, to offer subtle assistance without expectation of boast or virtue. We must give freely even when—especially when—the gift entails sacrifice; even when we would wish nothing so much as to have the cup pass from our lips.

It seemed in many ways the opportune time to go. I am a man of God and I had done what I could for the family. There were other families: a vast world in need of instruction, and I myself with so much to learn. In some other sense, however, I had just arrived; for my observance of these women, and the unique form of my participation in physiological processes that had remained for the greater part of my life abstract, had been instructive in a way I could not define or assimilate. Feeling thus overwhelmed made me want to flee, and yet I was to an equal degree entranced. Perhaps if I rested here with them, as quiet as I had been all this time, I could become for them a part of their landscape, a part of their life. I had the sense that they had been changed by their visit with each other, as most certainly had I by my covert interaction.

Here the undertaker had no place, it seemed. And my own truths seemed disturbingly incomplete. What could I learn from this? How could I apply these lessons? In so many senses, failure felt the order of the day.

Why, then, could I not pull myself from the room, from the sight of the two women, one of with whom I had had particular and unprecedented carnal interaction, for which I had no reference and lacked all vocabulary. I wished her to regain normal consciousness; felt, in fact, that I kept vigil to it—and yet it was this very transformed appearance that mesmerized me—for I am a man of ritual, am I not, performing every day again and again an invisible transformation of the ordinary into the extraordinary: bread into body, bread into body, but that body seen only in mind. Was my nausea and near-vertigo perhaps my own body's excuse to remain?—weakness a catalyst for instruction: address your ignorance, servant, in order to better be that which you were meant? Humble yourself before the creatures made of Adam's rib, made of man, but who themselves make men?

I myself had seen the process; participated, in some sense, in its perpetuation—though all my efforts likely misinterpreted as thwarting. From sacred texts, from prayer, and from my superiors, had come my instruction in the past, but where was I now led? As they reclined, I too would recline, but apart from the bed, here in the corner, where I would witness, but not disturb; reflect upon the role I had played in their sustained interaction. Instinctively I took out my pen: "My children, ladies and gentlemen, good people"—I put a line through each in turn—"brothers and sisters in Christ"—all addresses seemed prosaic, formulaic—"I would ask that you reflect today on something rather esoteric, something challenging and perhaps initially off-putting. Christian responsibilities are far more complex than they first appear, than we might have learned through the catechism lessons of our youth. Consider me, if you would, a kind of . . . midwife, who mediates collectively your birth in Christ, your baptism into new life. You must remind yourselves, should you ever feel mistrustful toward me, that my sole purpose on this earth is to assist you, as your servant."

No sooner had I penned the words than I began to feel some mitigation of the turbulence within my bowels. Realizing that these were indeed the means through which I could calm myself and my digestion, I proceeded with the outline for my homily.

THE LIFE AND WORK OF ALPHONSE KAUDERS

ALEKSANDAR HEMON

Alphonse Kauders is the creator of *The Forestry Bibliography, 1900–1948*, published by the Engineers and Technicians Association, in Zagreb, 1949. This is a special bibliography related to forestry. The material is classified into seventy-three groups and encompasses 8,800 articles and theses. Bibliographical units are not numbered. The creator of *The Forestry Bibliography* was the first to catalog the entire forest matter in a single piece of work. The work has been viewed as influential.

Alphonse Kauders had a dog by the name of Rex, whose whelp, in the course of time, he gave to Josip B. Tito.

Alphonse Kauders had a mysterious prostate illness and, in the course of time, he said: "Strange are the ways of urine."

Alphonse Kauders said to Rosa Luxemburg: "Let me penetrate a little bit, just a bit, I'll be careful."

*   *   *

Alphonse Kauders said: "And what if I am still here."

Alphonse Kauders was the only son of his father, a teacher. He was locked up in a lunatic asylum, having attempted to molest seven seven-year-old girls at the same time. Father, a teacher.

Alphonse Kauders said to Dr. Joseph Goebbels: "Writing is a useless endeavor. It is as though we sign every molecule of gas, say, of air, which—as we all know—cannot be seen. Yet, signed gas, or air, is easier to inhale."

Dr. Joseph Goebbels said: "Well, listen, that differs from a gas to a gas."

Alphonse Kauders was the owner of the revolver used to assassinate King Alexander.

One of Alphonse Kauders's seven wives had a tumor as big as a three-year-old child.

Alphonse Kauders said: "People are so ugly that they should be liberated from the obligation to have photos in their identity cards. Or, at least, in their Party cards."

Alphonse Kauders desired, passionately, to create a bibliography of pornographic literature. He held in his head 3,700 pornographic books. Plus magazines.

Richard Sorge, talking about the winds of Alphonse Kauders, said: "They sounded like sobs, sheer heartrending sorrow, which, resembling waves, emerged from the depths of one's soul, and, then, broke down, someplace high, high above."

Alphonse Kauders, in the course of time, had to crawl on all fours for seven days, for his penis had been stung by seventy-seven bees.

*   *   *

Alphonse Kauders owned complete lists of highly promiscuous women in Moscow, Berlin, Marseilles, Belgrade, and Munich.

Alphonse Kauders was a Virgin in his horoscope. And in his horoscope only.

Alphonse Kauders never, never wore or carried a watch.

There are records suggesting that the five-year-old Alphonse Kauders amazed his mother by making "systematic order" in the house pantry.

Alphonse Kauders said to Adolf Hitler, in Munich, as they were guzzling down their seventh mug of beer: "God, mine is always hard when it is needed. And it is always needed."

Alphonse Kauders:
a) hated forests
b) loved to watch fires
These proclivities were happily united in his notorious obsession with forest fires, which he would watch, with great pleasure, whenever he had a chance.

Josip B. Tito, talking about the winds of Alphonse Kauders, said: "They sounded like all the sirens of Moscow on May 1, the International Labor Day."

Alphonse Kauders impregnated Eva Braun, and she, in the course of time, delivered a child. But after Adolf Hitler began establishing new order and discipline and seducing Eva Braun, she, intoxicated by the Führer's virility, sent the child to a concentration camp, forcing herself to believe it was only for the summer.

*   *   *

Alphonse Kauders hated horses. Oh, how Alphonse Kauders hated horses.

Alphonse Kauders, in the course of time, truly believed that man created himself in the process of history.

Alphonse Kauders stood behind Gavrilo Princip, whispering—as urine was streaming down Gavrilo's thigh, as Gavrilo's sweating hand, holding a weighty revolver, was trembling in his pocket—Alphonse Kauders whispered: "Shoot, brother, what kind of a Serb are you?"

Alphonse Kauders described his relationship with Rex: "We, living in fear, hate each other."

There are records that Alphonse Kauders spent some years in a juvenile delinquents' home, having set seven forest fires in a single week.

Alphonse Kauders said: "I hate people, almost as much as horses, because there are always too many of them around, and because they kill bees, and because they fart and stink, and because they always come up with something, and it is the worst when they come up with irksome revolutions."

Alphonse Kauders wrote to Richard Sorge: "I cannot speak. Things around me do not speak. Still, dead, like rocks in a stream, they do not move, they have no meaning, they are just barely present. I stare at them, I beg them to tell me something, anything, to make me name them. I beg them to exist—they only buzz in the darkness, like a radio without a program, like an empty city, they want to say nothing. Nothing. I cannot stand the pressure of silence, even sounds are motionless. I cannot speak, words mean nothing to me. At times, my Rex knows more than I do. Much more. God bless him, he is silent."

Alphonse Kauders knew by heart the first fifty pages of the Berlin phone book.

Alphonse Kauders was the first to tell Joseph V. Stalin: "No!" Stalin asked him: "Do you have a watch, Comrade Kauders?" and Alphonse Kauders said: "No!"

Alphonse Kauders, in the course of time, told the following: "In our party, there are two main factions: the Maniacs and the Killers. The Maniacs are losing their minds, the Killers are killing. Naturally, in neither of these two factions are there any women. Women are gathered in the faction called the Women. Chiefly, they serve as an excuse for bloody fights between the Maniacs and the Killers. The Maniacs are the better soccer team, but the Killers can do wonders with knives, like nobody else in this modern world of ours."

Alphonse Kauders had gonorrhea seven times and syphilis only once.

Alphonse Kauders does not exist in the *Encyclopedia of the USSR.* Then again, he does not exist in the *Encyclopedia of Yugoslavia.*

Alphonse Kauders said: "I am myself, everything else is stories."

Dr. Joseph Goebbels, talking about the winds of Alphonse Kauders, said: "They were akin to the wail of an everlastingly solitary siren, sorrow in the purest of forms."

*   *   *

One of the seven wives of Alphonse Kauders had a short leg.
Then again, the other leg was long. The arms were, more or less,
of the same length.

In the Archives of the USSR, there is a manuscript which is
believed to have originated from Alphonse Kauders:
"1) shoot under the tongue (?);
  2) symbolism (?); death on the ground (?); in the forest
     (??); by an anthill (?); by a beehive;
  3) take only one bullet;
  4) the sentence: I shall be reborn if this bullet fails,
     and I hope it won't;
  5) lie down, so all the blood flows into the head;
  6) burn all manuscripts => possibility of someone
     thinking they were worth something;
  7) invent some love (?);
  8) the sentence: I blame nobody, especially not Her (?);
  9) tidy up the room;
 10) write to Stalin: Koba, why did you need my death?
 11) take a bottle of water with me;
 12) avoid talking until the certain date."

One of Alphonse Kauders's seven best men was Richard Sorge.

Alphonse Kauders regularly subscribed to all the pornographic magazines of Europe.

Alphonse Kauders removed his own appendix in Siberia, and
he probably would have died, had he not been transferred to the
camp hospital at the very last moment. And that was only because
he had informed on a bandit in the bed next to his for secretly
praying at night.

Alphonse Kauders said to Eva Braun: "Money isn't everything. There is some gold too."

*   *   *

Alphonse Kauders was a fanatic beekeeper. In the course of his life, he led fierce and merciless battles against parasitic lice that ruthlessly exploit bees, and are known as "varoa."

Alphonse Kauders said: "The most beautiful fire (not being a forest one) I have ever seen, was when the Reichstag was ablaze."

The very idea of creating Alphonse Kauders occurred for the first time to his (future) mother. She said to the (future) father of Alphonse Kauders: "Let's make passionate love and create Alphonse Kauders."

Father said: "All right. But let's watch some, you know, pictures."

Alphonse Kauders was a member of seven libraries, of seven apicultural societies, of seven communist parties, and of a national-socialist one.

Alphonse Kauders told the following: "In elementary school, I attracted attention by stuffing my fist into my mouth. Girls from other classes would rush in droves to see me stuff my fist into my mouth. My father, a teacher, glowed with a bliss, seeing all those girls swarming around me. Once, a girl that I wished to make love to approached me. And I was so excited that I tried to shove both of my fists into my mouth. I sacrificed my two front teeth for my passion. Ever since I have been noticed for my insanity. This strange event probably determined the course of my life. Ever since I haven't talked."

On one copy of *The Forestry Bibliography, 1900–1948,* kept in Zagreb, there is the following handwritten remark: "Since the day I was born, I have been waiting for the Judgment Day. And the

Judgment Day is never coming. And, as I live, it is becoming all too clear to me. I was born after the Judgment Day."

Alphonse Kauders told the following: "When Rex and I had a fight, and that happened almost every day, he would stray and would be gone for days. And he would tell me nothing. Except once. He said: 'The stray-dog shelter is full of spies.'"

On the eve of World War II, in Berlin, Alphonse Kauders said to Ivo Andric: "A firm system still exists only in the minds of madmen. In other people's minds, there's nothing but chaos, as well as around them. Perhaps art is one of the last pockets of resistance to chaos. And then again, maybe it isn't. Who the hell cares?"

On the eve of World War I, Alphonse Kauders said to Archduke Franz Ferdinand's pregnant wife: "Let me penetrate a little bit, just a little, I'll be careful."

On one of Alphonse Kauder's seven tombs, it is written: "I have vanished and I have appeared. Now, I am here. I shall disappear and I shall return. And then, again, I shall be here. Everything is so simple. All one needs is courage."

Alphonse Kauders wrote to one of his seven wives letters "full of filthy details and sick pornographic fantasies." Stalin forbade such letters to be sent by Soviet mail, because "among those who open and read letters there are many tame, timid family people." So then Alphonse Kauders sent his letters through reliable couriers.

Alphonse Kauders said: "I—I am not a human being. I—I am Alphonse Kauders."

Alphonse Kauders said to Richard Sorge: "I doubt there exists an emptiness greater than that of empty streets. Therefore, it is better to have some tanks or bodies on the streets, if nothing else is possible. Because Anything is better than Nothing."

Alphonse Kauders, in the course of time, put a revolver on Gavrilo Princip's temple, for he had burned a bee with his cigarette.

Alphonse Kauders, in the course of time, said to Stalin: "Koba, if you shoot Bukharin ever again, we shall have an argument." And Bukharin was shot only once.

Alphonse Kauders said to Eva Braun—in bed, after seven mutual, consecutive orgasms, four of which had gone into the annals—Alphonse Kauders said to Eva Braun: "One should find a way of forbidding people to talk, especially to talk to each other. People should be forbidden to wear watches. Anything should be done with people."

It is widely believed that the little-known pornographic work *Seven Sweet Little Girls,* signed by pseudonym, was written by Alphonse Kauders.

Alphonse Kauders told, in the course of time, about the first days of the Revolution: "We killed all mad horses. We set empty houses on fire. We saw soldiers weeping. Crowds gushed out of prisons. Everybody was scared. And we had nothing but a bad feeling."

Albeit Alphonse Kauders hated folk from the depths of his soul, almost as much as he hated horses (Good God, how Alphonse Kauders hated horses!), he was the creator of a folk proverb: "Never a bee from a mare."

Joseph V. Stalin, talking about the winds of Alphonse Kauders, said: "Many a time, in the course of our Central Committee sessions, Comrade Kauders would, well, cut a wind, and a few moments later, all comrades would be helplessly crying. Including myself, as well."

Alphonse Kauders owned the revolver used to murder Lola, a twelve-year-old prostitute from Marseilles.

Ivo Andric, talking about Alphonse Kauders, said: "His insides were removed by a secret operation. All that remained was a sheath of skin, within which he safely dreamt of a bibliography of pornographic literature."

Alphonse Kauders spent the night between April 5 and April 6, 1941, on the slopes of Avala, waiting to see Belgrade in flames.

Alphonse Kauders killed his dog Rex with gas after Rex had tried to slaughter him in his sleep because Alphonse Kauders had set mousetraps all over their place to take revenge on Rex for having pissed on his new, pristine uniform.

Alphonse Kauders, in the course of time, was engaged in painting. The only painting that has been preserved, oil on canvas, is called *The Class Roots of Tattooing* and is kept in the National Museum in Helsinki.

Alphonse Kauders said to Josip B. Tito: "A few days, or years, hell, ago, I noticed that a tree under the window in one of my seven rooms had grown some ten goddamn meters. There aren't many people who notice trees growing at all. And those who do are likely to be lumberjacks."

Gavrilo Princip, talking about the winds of Alphonse Kauders, said: "They sounded like this: Pffffffuuummmmiiuujmmsghhhss."

*   *   *

Alphonse Kauders had two legal sons and two legal daughters. The rest were illegal. One son was shot as a war criminal in Madona, Lithuania; the other was a distinguished member of the Australian national cricket team. One daughter was an interpreter at the Yalta conference; the other discovered, in the Amazon rain forests, a hitherto unknown species of an insect resembling the bee, labeled eventually Virgo Kauders.

Alphonse Kauders said: "Literature has nothing human in itself. Nor in myself."

Alphonse Kauders never finished work on the bibliography of pornographic literature.

NOTES

J. B. Tito was the Yugoslav communist leader for thirty-five long years. My childhood was saturated with histories of his just enterprises. My favorite one has always been the one in which he, at the age of twelve, found a whole, cooked pig's head in the house pantry, hoarded for Christmas, and, without telling his brothers and sisters, gorged himself with it on his own—an ominous act for a future communist head of state. He was sick for days afterward (fat overdose), and was additionally punished by being banned from the Christmas dinner. Later on, he lost interest in Christmas, but never lost passion for pigs and heads.

Rosa Luxemburg was a German communist who attempted, with Karl Liebknecht, a socialist revolution in Germany after the end of World War I, and then withered with it. Rosa Luxemburg was a terribly nice name for a revolutionary.

King Alexander was a Yugoslav king and was assassinated in Marseilles, in 1934, by a Macedonian nationalist, with a generous support of Croatian fascists. Rickety propaganda machinery of the first Yugoslavia sermonized that his last words were: "Take care of my Yugoslavia." The likely truth, however, was that he gobbled and bolted his own blood, while a sweaty French secret policeman was protecting, with his own body, Alexander's ex-body, corpse-to-be. I always thought that the fact that an Alexander was assassinated by a Macedonian was as close as you can get to a nice touch in a farce.

Richard Sorge was a Soviet spy in Tokyo, undercover as a journalist, eventually becoming a press attaché in the German embassy. He informed Stalin that Hitler was going to attack the Motherland, but Stalin trusted Hitler and disregarded the information. The first time I read about Sorge I was ten and, not even having reached the end of the book, decided to become a spy. At the age of sixteen, I wrote a poem about Sorge entitled "The Loneliest Man in the World." The first verse: "Tokyo is breathing and I am not."

Gavrilo Princip was the young Serb who assassinated the Austrian Archduke Franz Ferdinand Habsburg and Sophia, his pregnant wife, thus effectively commencing World War I. He was eighteen at the time (I think) and had the first scrub over his thin lip and dark ripples around his eyes. He was incarcerated for life, which lasted only a few more years, and died of tuberculosis, blessed by repeated beatings, in an obscure imperial prison. In Sarajevo, by the Latin Bridge, at the corner from which he sent those historical bullets into the fetus's brain, his footprints were immortalized in concrete (left foot W–E, right foot SE–NW). When I was a little boy, I imagined him waiting for the Archduke's coach, waiting to change the course of history, stuck up to his ankles in wet concrete. When I was sixteen, my feet fit perfectly into his feet's tombs.

The Encyclopedia of the USSR is a book whose different editions are innumerable and often obscure. Historical characters (like Stalin's Secret Police chiefs) would be praised in one edition and then would be vanished in another. There are countries whose precious minerals (with annual production in parentheses) would be minutely listed by the encyclopedia's sanguine world map, and in another edition they would be swallowed by an ocean, much like Atlantis, without the bubble-burps ever reaching the surface of the map world. This great book teaches us how the verisimilitude of fiction is achieved by the exactness of the detail.

The Encyclopedia of Yugoslavia, on the other hand, was never even close to being entirely published, because of so many conflicting histories involved, so there really isn't any encyclopedic Yugoslavia, which by a snide turn of history, couldn't matter less, since Yugoslavia is not much of a country anymore.

Nikolai Bukharin, dubbed by Lenin "the darling of the Party," was a member of the Politburo and probably the main Soviet ideologue (save the great Stalin) in the thirties, for which he was rewarded with an accusation of spying, simultaneously, for the United States, Great Britain, France, and Germany. No one was surprised, but everyone was terrified when he was sentenced to death, for that was the beginning of one of Stalin's greatest purges. From his death cell, he sent a letter to Stalin, beginning with the words: "Koba, why did you need my death?", which Stalin is believed to have kept in his desk drawer for a long time. Bukharin voluntarily cooperated with his inquisitors and refused to be used as the martyr of Stalin's tyranny. If he is in a Dantesque inferno, he'll eternally bang his porcine head against the walls of hell's pantry.

Ivo Andric, a Bosnian, was the only Yugoslav author who has ever been awarded the Nobel Prize. In 1941, he worked in the Yugoslav embassy in Berlin, and helped organize trysts of cringing Yugoslav politicians with Hitler. He was a gentleman and wrote novels about the ways people are entangled with history. At the acceptance ceremony, he talked about the importance of bridges. In his youth, he was involved in organizing the Archduke's assassination.

On April 6, 1941, at dawn, Belgrade was relentlessly bombed by the Luftwaffe. That was the beginning of the German attack on the Kingdom of Yugoslavia, which lasted for eleven more hapless days.

Avala is a breast-like mountain near Belgrade, with the tomb-tumor for the Unknown Serbian Soldier, built after World War I.

The Yalta Conference brought together Churchill, Roosevelt, and Stalin. The end of the war was in sight and they appeared to be the victors ("I'd like some Germany").

When I was thirteen, I saw a photo of those three great men in Yalta, sitting in three wicker chairs, against the background of standing people whose names were as insignificant as their deeds. The three heads of the free world had something like a dim grin on their round faces, as though they had done a good, hard work ("Have some Germany"). When I was thirteen, I thought that the picture was taken right after their lunch, because—as my father claimed—right after lunch is the best time, for people are "full and happy." I thought that behind their dim grins they were trying to get out last bits of food from between their teeth. They gaze at me, full of borscht, sweet Crimean wine, and plans for the world. Within a few moments Churchill will be asleep, and I'll be old, lacking significance, but not memories.

Now keep reading the book.

THE PAPERHANGER

WILLIAM GAY

The vanishing of the doctor's wife's child in broad daylight was an event so cataclysmic that it forever divided time into the then and the now, the before and the after. In later years, fortified with a pitcher of silica-dry vodka martinis, she had cause to replay the events preceding the disappearance. They were tawdry and banal but in retrospect freighted with menace, a foreshadowing of what was to come, like a footman or a fool preceding a king into a room.

She had been quarreling with the paperhanger. Her four-year-old daughter, Zeineb, was standing directly behind the paper-hanger where he knelt smoothing air bubbles out with a wide plastic trowel. Zeineb had her fingers in the paperhanger's hair. The paperhanger's hair was shoulder length and the color of flax and the child was delighted with it. The paperhanger was accustomed to her doing this and he did not even turn around. He just went on with his work. His arms were smooth and brown and corded with muscle and in the light that fell upon the paper-hanger through stained-glass panels the doctor's wife could see that they were lightly downed with fine golden hair. She studied these arms bemusedly while she formulated her thoughts.

You tell me so much a roll, she said. The doctor's wife was from Pakistan and her speech was still heavily accented. I do not know single-bolt rolls and double-bolt rolls. You tell me double-bolt price but you are installing single-bolt rolls. My friend has told me. It is cost me perhaps twice as much.

The paperhanger, still on his knees, turned. He smiled up at her. He had pale blue eyes. I did tell you so much a roll, he said. You bought the rolls.

The child, not yet vanished, was watching the paperhanger's eyes. She was a scaled-down clone of the mother, the mother viewed through the wrong end of a telescope, and the paperhanger suspected that as she grew neither her features nor her expression would alter, she would just grow larger, like something being aired up with a hand pump.

And you are leave lumps, the doctor's wife said, gesturing at the wall.

I do not leave lumps, the paperhanger said. You've seen my work before. These are not lumps. The paper is wet. The paste is wet. Everything will shrink down and flatten out. He smiled again. He had clean even teeth. And besides, he said, I gave you my special cockteaser rate. I don't know what you're complaining about.

Her mouth worked convulsively. She looked for a moment as if he'd slapped her. When words did come they came in a fine spray of spit. You are trash, she said. You are scum.

Hands on knees, he was pushing erect, the girl's dark fingers trailing out of his hair. Don't call me trash, he said, as if it were perfectly all right to call him scum, but he was already talking to her back. She had whirled on her heels and went twisting her hips through an arched doorway into the cathedraled living room. The paperhanger looked down at the child. Her face glowed with a strange constrained glee, as if she and the paperhanger shared some secret the rest of the world hadn't caught on to yet.

In the living room the builder was supervising the installation of a chandelier that depended from the vaulted ceiling by a long golden chain. The builder was a short bearded man dancing about, showing her the features of the chandelier, smiling obsequiously. She gave him a flat angry look. She waved a dismissive hand toward the ceiling. Whatever, she said.

She went out the front door onto the porch and down a makeshift walkway of two-by-tens into the front yard where her car was parked. The car was a silver-gray Mercedes her husband had given her for their anniversary. When she cranked the engine its idle was scarcely perceptible.

She powered down the window. Zeineb, she called. Across the razed earth of the unlandscaped yard a man in a grease-stained T-shirt was booming down the chains securing a backhoe to a lowboy hooked to a gravel truck. The sun was low in the west and bloodred behind this tableau and man and tractor looked flat and dimensionless as something decorative stamped from tin. She blew the horn. The man turned, raised an arm as if she'd signaled him.

Zeineb, she called again.

She got out of the car and started impatiently up the walkway. Behind her the gravel truck started, and truck and backhoe pulled out of the drive and down toward the road.

The paperhanger was stowing away his T square and trowels in his wooden toolbox. Where is Zeineb? the doctor's wife asked. She followed you out, the paperhanger told her. He glanced about, as if the girl might be hiding somewhere. There was nowhere to hide.

Where is my child? she asked the builder. The electrician climbed down from the ladder. The paperhanger came out of the bathroom with his tools. The builder was looking all around. His elfin features were touched with chagrin, as if this missing child were just something else he was going to be held accountable for.

Likely she's hiding in a closet, the paperhanger said. Playing a trick on you.

Zeineb does not play tricks, the doctor's wife said. Her eyes kept darting about the huge room, the shadows that lurked in corners. There was already an undercurrent of panic in her voice and all her poise and self-confidence seemed to have vanished with the child.

The paperhanger set down his toolbox and went through the house, opening and closing doors. It was a huge house and there were a lot of closets. There was no child in any of them.

The electrician was searching upstairs. The builder had gone through the French doors that opened onto the unfinished veranda and was peering into the backyard. The backyard was a maze of convoluted ditch excavated for the septic-tank field line and beyond that there was just woods. She's playing in that ditch, the builder said, going down the flagstone steps.

She wasn't, though. She wasn't anywhere. They searched the house and grounds. They moved with jerky haste. They kept glancing toward the woods where the day was waning first. The builder kept shaking his head. She's got to be *somewhere*, he said.

Call someone, the doctor's wife said. Call the police.

It's a little early for the police, the builder said. She's got to be here.

You call them anyway. I have a phone in my car. I will call my husband.

While she called, the paperhanger and the electrician continued to search. They had looked everywhere and were forced to search places they'd already looked. If this ain't the goddamnedest thing I ever saw, the electrician said.

The doctor's wife got out of the Mercedes and slammed the door. Suddenly she stopped and clasped a hand to her forehead. She screamed. The man with the tractor, she cried. Somehow my child is gone with the tractor man.

Oh Jesus, the builder said. What have we got ourselves into here.

* * *

The high sheriff that year was a ruminative man named Bell-wether. He stood beside the county cruiser talking to the paper-hanger while deputies ranged the grounds. Other men were inside looking in places that had already been searched numberless times. Bellwether had been in the woods and he was picking cockleburs off his khakis and out of his socks. He was watching the woods, where dark was gathering and seeping across the field like a stain.

I've got to get men out here, Bellwether said. A lot of men and a lot of lights. We're going to have to search every inch of these woods.

You'll play hell doing it, the paperhanger said. These woods stretch all the way to Lawrence County. This is the edge of the Harrikin. Down in there's where all those old mines used to be. Allens Creek.

I don't give a shit if they stretch all the way to Fairbanks, Alaska, Bellwether said. They've got to be searched. It'll just take a lot of men.

The raw earth yard was full of cars. Dr. Jamahl had come in a sleek black Lexus. He berated his wife. Why weren't you watching her? he asked. Unlike his wife's, the doctor's speech was impeccable. She covered her face with her palms and wept. The doctor still wore his green surgeon's smock and it was flecked with bright dots of blood as a butcher's smock might be.

I need to feed a few cows, the paperhanger said. I'll feed my stock pretty quick and come back and help hunt.

You don't mind if I look in your truck, do you?

Do what?

I've got to cover my ass. If that little girl don't turn up damn quick this is going to be over my head. TBI, FBI, network news. I've got to eliminate everything.

Eliminate away, the paperhanger said.

The sheriff searched the floorboard of the paperhanger's

pickup truck. He shined his huge flashlight under the seat and felt behind it with his hands.

I had to look, he said apologetically.

Of course you did, the paperhanger said.

Full dark had fallen before he returned. He had fed his cattle and stowed away his tools and picked up a six-pack of San Miguel beer and he sat in the back of the pickup truck drinking it. The paperhanger had been in the Navy and stationed in the Philippines and San Miguel was the only beer he could drink. He had to go out of town to buy it, but he figured it was worth it. He liked the exotic labels, the dark bitter taste on the back of his tongue, the way the chilled bottles felt held against his forehead.

A motley crowd of curiosity seekers and searchers thronged the yard. There was a vaguely festive air. He watched all this with a dispassionate eye, as if he were charged with grading the participants, comparing this with other spectacles he'd seen. Coffee urns had been brought in and set up on tables, sandwiches prepared and handed out to the weary searchers. A crane had been hauled in and the septic tank reclaimed from the ground. It swayed from a taut cable while men with lights searched the impacted earth beneath it for a child, for the very trace of a child. Through the far dark woods lights crossed and recrossed, darted to and fro like fireflies. The doctor and the doctor's wife sat in folding camp chairs looking drained, stunned, waiting for their child to be delivered into their arms.

The doctor was a short portly man with a benevolent expression. He had a moon-shaped face, with light and dark areas of skin that looked swirled, as if the pigment coloring him had not been properly mixed. He had been educated at Princeton. When he had established his practice he had returned to Pakistan to find a wife befitting his station. The woman he had selected had been chosen on the basis of her beauty. In retrospect, perhaps more consideration should have been given to other qualities. She was still beautiful but he was thinking that certain faults might outweigh this. She seemed to have trouble keeping up with her children. She could lose a four-year-old child in a room no larger than six hundred square feet and she could not find it again.

The paperhanger drained his bottle and set it by his foot in the bed of the truck. He studied the doctor's wife's ravaged face through the deep blue light. The first time he had seen her she had hired him to paint a bedroom in the house they were living in while the doctor's mansion was being built. There was an arrogance about her that cried out to be taken down a notch or two. She flirted with him, backed away, flirted again. She would treat him as if he were a stain on the bathroom rug and then stand close by him while he worked until he was dizzy with the smell of her, with the heat that seemed to radiate off her body. She stood by him while he knelt painting baseboards and after an infinite moment leaned carefully the weight of a thigh against his shoulder. You'd better move it, he thought. She didn't. He laughed and turned his face into her groin. She gave a strangled cry and slapped him hard. The paintbrush flew away and speckled the dark rose walls with antique white. You filthy beast, she said. You are some kind of monster. She stormed out of the room and he could hear her slamming doors behind her.

Well, I was looking for a job when I found this one. He smiled philosophically to himself.

But he had not been fired. In fact now he had been hired again. Perhaps there was something here to ponder.

At midnight he gave up his vigil. Some souls more hardy than his kept up the watch. The earth here was worn smooth by the useless traffic of the searchers. Driving out, he met a line of pickup trucks with civil defense tags. Grim-faced men sat aligned in their beds. Some clutched rifles loosely by their barrels, as if they would lay to waste whatever monster, man or beast, would snatch up a child in its slaverous jaws and vanish, prey and predator, in the space between two heartbeats.

Even more dubious reminders of civilization as these fell away. He drove into the Harrikin, where he lived. A world so dark and forlorn light itself seemed at a premium. Whippoorwills swept red-eyed up from the roadside. Old abandoned foundries and furnaces rolled past, grim and dark as forsaken prisons. Down a ridge here was an abandoned graveyard, if you knew where to look. The paperhanger did. He had dug up a few of the graves, examined with curiosity what remained, buttons, belt buckles, a cameo brooch. The bones he laid out like a child with a Tinkertoy, arranging them the way they went in jury-rigged resurrection.

He braked hard on a curve, the truck slewing in the gravel. A bobcat had crossed the road, graceful as a wraith, fierce and lantern-eyed in the headlights, gone so swiftly it might have been a stage prop swung across the road on wires.

Bellwether and a deputy drove to the backhoe operator's house. He lived up a gravel road that wound through a great stand of cedars. He lived in a board-and-batten house with a tin roof rusted to a warm umber. They parked before it and got out, adjusting their gun belts.

Bellwether had a search warrant with the ink scarcely dry. The operator was outraged.

Look at it this way, Bellwether explained patiently. I've got to cover my ass. Everything has got to be considered. You know how kids are. Never thinking. What if she run under the wheels of your truck when you was backing out? What if quicklike you put the body in your truck to get rid of somewhere?

What if quicklike you get the hell off my property, the operator said.

Everything has to be considered, the sheriff said again. Nobody's accusing anybody of anything just yet.

The operator's wife stood glowering at them. To have something to do with his hands, the operator began to construct a cigarette. He had huge red hands thickly sown with brown freckles. They trembled. I ain't got a thing in this round world to hide, he said.

Bellwether and his men searched everywhere they could think of to look. Finally they stood uncertainly in the operator's yard, out of place in their neat khakis, their polished leather.

Now get the hell off my land, the operator said. If all you think of me is that I could run over a little kid and then throw it off in the bushes like a dead cat or something then I don't even want to see your goddamn face. I want you gone and I want you by God gone now.

Everything had to be considered, the sheriff said.

Then maybe you need to consider that paperhanger.

What about him?

That paperhanger is one sick puppy.

He was still there when I got there, the sheriff said. Three witnesses swore nobody ever left, not even for a minute, and one of them was the child's mother. I searched his truck myself.

Then he's a sick puppy with a damn good alibi, the operator said.

That was all. There was no ransom note, no child that turned up two counties over with amnesia. She was a page turned, a door closed, a lost ball in the high weeds. She was a child no larger than a doll, but the void she left behind her was unreckonable. Yet there was no end to it. No finality. There was no moment when someone could say, turning from a mounded grave, Well, this has been unbearable, but you've got to go on with your life. Life did not go on.

At the doctor's wife's insistence an intensive investigation was focused on the backhoe operator. Forensic experts from the FBI examined every millimeter of the gravel truck, paying special attention to its wheels. They were examined with every modern crime-fighting device the government possessed, and there was not a microscopic particle of tissue or blood, no telltale chip of fingernail, no hair ribbon.

Work ceased on the mansion. Some subcontractors were discharged outright, while others simply drifted away. There was no one to care if the work was done, no one to pay them. The half-finished veranda's raw wood grayed in the fall, then winter, rains. The ditches were left fallow and uncovered and half filled with water. Kudzu crept from the woods. The hollyhocks and oleanders the doctor's wife had planted grew entangled and rampant. The imported windows were stoned by double-dared boys who whirled and fled. Already this house where a child had vanished was acquiring an unhealthy, diseased reputation.

The doctor and his wife sat entombed in separate prisons replaying real and imagined grievances. The doctor felt that his wife's neglect had sent his child into the abstract. The doctor's wife drank vodka martinis and watched talk shows where passed an endless procession of vengeful people who had not had children vanish, and felt, perhaps rightly, that the fates had dealt her from the bottom of the deck, and she prayed with intensity for a miracle.

Then one day she was just gone. The Mercedes and part of her clothing and personal possessions were gone too. He idly wondered where she was, but did not search for her.

Sitting in his armchair cradling a great marmalade cat and a bottle of J&B and observing with bemused detachment the gradations of light at the window, the doctor remembered studying literature at Princeton. He had particular cause to reconsider the poetry of William Butler Yeats. For how surely things fell apart, how surely the center did not hold.

His practice fell into a ruin. His colleagues made sympathetic allowances for him at first, but there are limits to these things. He made erroneous diagnoses, prescribed the wrong medicines not once or twice but as a matter of course.

Just as there is a deepening progression to misfortune, so too there is a point beyond which things can only get worse. They did. A middle-aged woman he was operating on died.

He had made an incision to remove a ruptured appendix and the incised flesh was clamped aside while he made ready to slice it out. It was not there. He stared in drunken disbelief. He began to search under things, organs, intestines, a rising tide of blood. The appendix was not there. It had gone into the abstract, atrophied, been removed twenty-five years before, he had sliced through the selfsame scar. He was rummaging through her abdominal cavity like an irritated man fumbling through a drawer for a clean pair of socks, finally bellowing and wringing his hands in bloody vexation while nurses began to cry out, another surgeon was brought on the run as a closer, and he was carried from the operating room.

Came then days of sitting in the armchair while he was besieged by contingency lawyers, action news teams, a long line of process servers. There was nothing he could do. It was out of his hands and into the hands of the people who are paid to do these things. He sat cradling the bottle of J&B with the marmalade cat snuggled against his portly midriff. He would study the window, where the light drained away in a process he no longer had an understanding of, and sip the scotch and every now and then stroke the cat's head gently. The cat purred against his breast as reassuringly as the hum of an air conditioner.

He left in the middle of the night. He began to load his possessions into the Lexus. At first he chose items with a great degree of consideration. The first thing he loaded was a set of custom-made monogrammed golf clubs. Then his stereo receiver, Denon AC3, $1,750. A copy of *This Side of Paradise* autographed by Fitzgerald that he had bought as an investment. By the time the Lexus was half full he was just grabbing things at random and stuffing them into the backseat, a half-eaten pizza, half a case of cat food, a single brocade house shoe.

He drove west past the hospital, the country club, the city-limit sign. He was thinking no thoughts at all, and all the destination he had was the amount of highway the headlights showed him.

In the slow rains of late fall the doctor's wife returned to the unfinished mansion. She used to sit in a camp chair on the ruined veranda and drink chilled martinis she poured from the pitcher she carried in a foam ice chest. Dark fell early these November days. Rain crows husbanding some far cornfield called through the smoky autumn air. The sound was fiercely evocative, reminding her of something but she could not have said what.

She went into the room where she had lost the child. The light was failing. The high corners of the room were in deepening shadow but she could see the nests of dirt daubers clustered on the rich flocked wallpaper, a spider swing from a chandelier on a strand of spun glass. Some animal's dried blackened stool curled like a slug against the baseboards. The silence in the room was enormous.

One day she arrived and was surprised to find the paperhanger there. He was sitting on a yellow four-wheeler drinking a bottle of beer. He made to go when he saw her but she waved him back. Stay and talk with me, she said.

The paperhanger was much changed. His pale locks had been shorn away in a makeshift haircut as if scissored in the dark or by a blind barber and his cheeks were covered with a soft curly beard.

You have grown a beard.

Yes.

You are strange with it.

The paperhanger sipped from his San Miguel. He smiled. I was strange without it, he said. He arose from the four-wheeler and came over and sat on the flagstone steps. He stared across the mutilated yard toward the tree line. The yard was like a funhouse maze seen from above, its twistings and turnings bereft of mystery.

You are working somewhere now?

No. I don't take so many jobs anymore. There's only me, and I don't need much. What became of the doctor?

She shrugged. Many things have change, she said. He has gone. The banks have foreclose. What is that you ride?

An ATV. A four-wheeler.

It goes well in the woods?

It was made for that.

You could take me in the woods. How much would you charge me?

For what?

To go in the woods. You could drive me. I will pay you.

Why?

To search for my child's body.

I wouldn't charge anybody anything to search for a child's body, the paperhanger said. But she's not in these woods. Nothing could have stayed hidden, the way these woods were searched.

Sometimes I think she just kept walking. Perhaps just walking away from the men looking. Far into the woods.

Into the woods, the paperhanger thought. If she had just kept walking in a straight line with no time out for eating or sleeping, where would she be? Kentucky, Algiers, who knew.

I'll take you when the rains stop, he said. But we won't find a child.

The doctor's wife shook her head. It is a mystery, she said. She drank from her cocktail glass. Where could she have gone? How could she have gone?

There was a man named David Lang, the paperhanger said. Up in Gallatin, back in the late 1800s. He was crossing a barn lot in full view of his wife and two children and he just vanished. Went into thin air. There was a judge in a wagon turning into the yard and he saw it too. It was just like he took a step in this world and his foot came down in another one. He was never seen again.

She gave him a sad smile, bitter and one-cornered. You make fun with me.

No. It's true. I have it in a book. I'll show you.

I have a book with dragons, fairies. A book where Hobbits live in the middle earth. They are lies. I think most books are lies. Perhaps all books. I have prayed for a miracle but I am not worthy of one. I have prayed for her to come from the dead, then just to find her body. That would be a miracle to me. There are no miracles.

She rose unsteadily, swayed slightly, leaning to take up the cooler. The paperhanger watched her. I have to go now, she said. When the rains stop we will search.

Can you drive?

Of course I can drive. I have drive out here.

I mean are you capable of driving now. You seem a little drunk.

I drink to forget but it is not enough, she said. I can drive.

After a while he heard her leave in the Mercedes, the tires spinning in the gravel drive. He lit a cigarette. He sat smoking it, watching the rain string off the roof. He seemed to be waiting for something. Dusk was falling like a shroud, the world going dark and formless the way it had begun. He drank the last of the beer, sat holding the bottle, the foam bitter in the back of his mouth. A chill touched him. He felt something watching him. He turned. From the corner of the ruined veranda a child was watching him. He stood up. He heard the beer bottle break on the flagstones. The child went sprinting past the hollyhocks toward the brush at the edge of the yard, a tiny sepia child with an intent sloe-eyed face, real as she had ever been, translucent as winter light through dirty glass.

The doctor's wife's hands were laced loosely about his waist as they came down through a thin strand of sassafras, edging over the ridge where the ghost of a road was, a road more sensed than seen that faced into a half acre of tilting stones and fading granite tablets. Other graves marked only by their declivities in the earth, folk so far beyond the pale even the legibility of their identities had been leached away by the weathers.

Leaves drifted, huge poplar leaves veined with amber so golden they might have been coin of the realm for a finer world than this one. He cut the ignition of the four-wheeler and got off. Past the lowering trees the sky was a blue of an improbable intensity, a fierce cobalt blue shot through with dense golden light.

She slid off the rear and steadied herself a moment with a hand on his arm. Where are we? she asked. Why are we here?

The paperhanger had disengaged his arm and was strolling among the gravestones reading such inscriptions as were legible, as if he might find forebear or antecedent in this moldering earth. The doctor's wife was retrieving her martinis from the luggage carrier of the ATV. She stood looking about uncertainly. A graven angel with broken wings crouched on a truncated marble column like a gargoyle. Its stone eyes regarded her with a blind benignity. Some of these graves have been rob, she said.

You can't rob the dead, he said. They have nothing left to steal.

It is a sacrilege, she said. It is forbidden to disturb the dead. You have done this.

The paperhanger took a cigarette pack from his pocket and felt it, but it was empty, and he balled it up and threw it away. The line between grave robbing and archaeology has always looked a little blurry to me, he said. I was studying their culture, trying to get a fix on what their lives were like.

She was watching him with a kind of benumbed horror. Standing hip-slung and lost like a parody of her former self. Strange and anomalous in her fashionable but mismatched clothing, as if she'd put on the first garment that fell to hand. Someday, he thought, she might rise and wander out into the daylit world wearing nothing at all, the way she had come into it. With her diamond watch and the cocktail glass she carried like a used-up talisman.

You have broken the law, she told him.

I got a government grant, the paperhanger said contemptuously.

Why are we here? We are supposed to be searching for my child.

If you're looking for a body the first place to look is the grave-yard, he said. If you want a book don't you go to the library?

I am paying you, she said. You are in my employ. I do not want to be here. I want you to do as I say or carry me to my car if you will not.

Actually, the paperhanger said, I had a story to tell you. About my wife.

He paused, as if leaving a space for her comment, but when she made none he went on. I had a wife. My childhood sweetheart. She became a nurse, went to work in one of these drug rehab places. After she was there awhile she got a faraway look in her eyes. Look at me without seeing me. She got in tight with her supervisor. They started having meetings to go to. Conferences. Sometimes just the two of them would confer, generally in a motel. The night I watched them walk into the Holiday Inn in Franklin I decided to kill her. No impetuous spur-of-the-moment thing. I thought it all out and it would be the perfect crime.

The doctor's wife didn't say anything. She just watched him.

A grave is the best place to dispose of a body, the paperhanger said. The grave is its normal destination anyway. I could dig up a grave and then just keep on digging. Save everything carefully. Put my body there and fill in part of the earth, and then restore everything the way it was. The coffin, if any of it was left. The bones and such. A good settling rain and the fall leaves and you're home free. Now that's eternity for you.

Did you kill someone, she breathed. Her voice was barely audible.

Did I or did I not, he said. You decide. You have the powers of a god. You can make me a murderer or just a heartbroke guy whose wife quit him. What do you think? Anyway, I don't have a wife. I expect she just walked off into the abstract like that Lang guy I told you about.

I want to go, she said. I want to go where my car is.

He was sitting on a gravestone watching her out of his pale eyes. He might not have heard.

I will walk.

Just whatever suits you, the paperhanger said. Abruptly, he was standing in front of her. She had not seen him arise from the headstone or stride across the graves, but like a jerky splice in a film he was before her, a hand cupping each of her breasts, staring down into her face.

Under the merciless weight of the sun her face was stunned and vacuous. He studied it intently, missing no detail. Fine wrinkles crept from the corners of her eyes and mouth like hairline cracks in porcelain. Grime was impacted into her pores, in the crepe flesh of her throat. How surely everything had fallen from her: beauty, wealth, social position, arrogance. Humanity itself, for by now she seemed scarcely human, beleaguered so by the fates that she suffered his hands on her breasts as just one more cross to bear, one more indignity to endure.

How far you've come, the paperhanger said in wonder. I believe you're about down to my level now, don't you?

It does not matter, the doctor's wife said. There is no longer one thing that matters.

Slowly and with enormous lassitude her body slumped toward him, and in his exultance it seemed not a motion in itself but simply the completion of one begun long ago with the fateful weight of a thigh, a motion that began in one world and completed itself in another one.

From what seemed a great distance he watched her fall toward him like an angel descending, wings spread, from an infinite height, striking the earth gently, tilting, then righting itself.

*   *   *

The weight of moonlight tracking across the paperhanger's face awoke him from where he took his rest. Filigrees of light through the gauzy curtains swept across him in stately silence like the translucent ghosts of insects. He stirred, lay still then for a moment getting his bearings, a fix on where he was.

He was in his bed, lying on his back. He could see a huge orange moon poised beyond the bedroom window, ink-sketch tree branches that raked its face like claws. He could see his feet book-ending the San Miguel bottle that his hands clasped erect on his abdomen, the amber bottle hard-edged and defined against the pale window, dark atavistic monolith reared against a harvest moon.

He could smell her. A musk compounded of stale sweat and alcohol, the rank smell of her sex. Dissolution, ruin, loss. He turned to study her where she lay asleep, her open mouth a dark cavity in her face. She was naked, legs outflung, pale breasts pooled like cooling wax. She stirred restively, groaned in her sleep. He could hear the rasp of her breathing. Her breath was fetid on his face, corrupt, a graveyard smell. He watched her in disgust, in a dull self-loathing.

He drank from the bottle, lowered it. Sometimes, he told her sleeping face, you do things you can't undo. You break things you just can't fix. Before you mean to, before you know you've done it. And you were right, there are things only a miracle can set to rights.

He sat clasping the bottle. He touched his miscut hair, the soft down of his beard. He had forgotten what he looked like, he hadn't seen his reflection in a mirror for so long. Unbidden, Zeineb's face swam into his memory. He remembered the look on the child's face when the doctor's wife had spun on her heel: spite had crossed it like a flicker of heat lightning. She stuck her tongue out at him. His hand snaked out like a serpent and closed on her throat and snapped her neck before he could call it back, sloe eyes wild and wide, pink tongue caught between tiny seed-pearl teeth like a bitten-off rosebud. Her hair swung sidewise, her head lolled onto his clasped hand. The tray of the toolbox was out before he knew it, he was stuffing her into the toolbox like a rag doll. So small, so small, hardly there at all.

He arose. Silhouetted naked against the moon-drenched window, he drained the bottle. He looked about for a place to set it, leaned and wedged it between the heavy flesh of her upper thighs. He stood in silence, watching her. He seemed philosophical, possessed of some hard-won wisdom. The paperhanger knew so well that while few are deserving of a miracle, fewer still can make one come to pass.

He went out of the room. Doors opened, doors closed. Footsteps softly climbing a staircase, descending. She dreamed on. When he came back into the room he was cradling a plastic-wrapped bundle stiffly in his arms. He placed it gently beside the drunk woman. He folded the plastic sheeting back like a caul.

What had been a child. What the graveyard earth had spared the freezer had preserved. Ice crystals snared in the hair like windy snowflakes whirled there, in the lashes. A doll from a madhouse assembly line.

He took her arm, laid it across the child. She pulled away from the cold. He firmly brought the arm back, arranging them like mannequins, madonna and child. He studied this tableau, then went out of his house for the last time. The door closed gently behind him on its keeper spring.

The paperhanger left in the Mercedes, heading west into the open country, tracking into wide-open territories he could infect like a malignant spore. Without knowing it, he followed the selfsame route the doctor had taken some eight months earlier, and in a world of infinite possibilities where all journeys share a common end, perhaps they are together, taking the evening air on a ruined veranda among the hollyhocks and oleanders, the doctor sipping his scotch and the paperhanger his San Miguel, gentlemen of leisure discussing the vagaries of life and pondering deep into the night not just the possibility but the inevitability of miracles.

PEOPLE SHOULDN'T HAVE TO BE THE ONES TO TELL YOU

GARY LUTZ

He had a couple of grown daughters, disappointers, with regretted curiosities and the heavy venture of having once looked alive. One night it was only the older who came by. It was photos she brought: somebody she claimed was more recent. He started approvingly through the sequence. A man with capped-over hair and a face drowned out by sunlight was seen from unintimate range in decorated settings out-of-doors. The coat he wore was always a dark-blue thing of medium hang. But in one shot you could make out the ragged line of a zipper, and in another a column of buttons, and in still another the buttons were no longer the knobby kind but toggles, and in yet another they were not even buttons, just snaps. Sometimes the coat had grown a drawstring. The pockets varied by slant and flapwork. The man advanced through the stack again. His eye this time was caught in doubt by the collar. A contrastive leather in this shot, common corduroy in that one, undiversified cloth in a third. And he was expected to make believe they were all of the same man? He swallowed clumsily, jumbled through the photographs once more.

"But you'll still have time for your sister?" he said.

Her teeth were off-colored and fitted almost mosaicwise into the entire halted smile.

A few nights later, the younger. A night class was making her interview a relation for a memory from way back and then another from only last week. He was not the best person to be in recall, but he thought assistively of a late afternoon he had sat at a table outside a gymnasium and torn tickets off a wheel one at a time instead of in twos and threes for the couples and threesomes. He had watched them file arm in arm into the creped-up place with a revived, stupid sense of how things ought to be done. A banquet? A dance? He never stayed around for things.

He saw his words descend into the whirling ungaieties of her longhand.

"And one from just last week?"

Easier.

At the Laundromat, he had chosen the dryer with a spent fabric-softener sheet teased behind inside it. He brought the sheet home afterward to wonder whether it was more a mysticization of a tissue than a denigration of one. It was sparser in its weave yet harder to tear apart, ready in his hand when unthrobbing things of his life could stand to be swabbed clean.

(He watched his daughter wait a considerate, twinging minute before she set down the tumbler from which she had been sipping her faucet water.)

"Your sister's the one with the head for memory," he said. "You ever even once think to ask her?"

Most nights, the man's hair released its oils into the antimacassar at the back of his chair. The deepening oval of grease could one day be worth his daughters' touch.

He got the two of them fixed in his mind again.

The older went in for dolled-up solitude but was better at batting around the good in people. Her loves were always either six feet under or ten feet tall because of somebody else.

The younger was a rich inch more favored in height, but slower of statement. Men, women, were maybe not her type. But she was otherwise an infatuate of whatever you set before her— even the deep-nutted cledges of chocolate she picked apart for bits of skin.

They had tilted into each other early, then eased off, shied aside.

Then they were wifely toward him for a night, poising curtains at his streetward windows, hurrying the wrinkles out from his other good pants, running to the bathroom between turns at his dirt. The older holding the dustpan again, the younger the brush—a stooped, ruining twosome losing balance in his favor.

They were on the sofa afterward, each with a can of surging soda.

"Third wheel," he said, and went into his bedroom to sit. Were there only two ways to think? One was that the day did not come to you whole. It was whiffled. Things were blowing out of it already. Or else a day was actually two half-days, each half-day divided into dozenths, each dozenth corrugated plentifully into its minutes. There was time.

He sat, stumped.

When he looked in on them again, they had already started going by their middle names—hard-pressed, standpat single syllables. Barb and Dot.

The next couple of nights he kept late hours, pulling his ex-wife piecemeal out of some surviving unmindedness. The first night it was only the lay of her shoulders.

On the next: the girlhood browniness still upheld in her hair—a jewelried uprisal of it.

The souse of the cologne she had stuck by.

Budgets of color in her eyelids.

The night it was the downtrail of veins strung in her arms, he had had enough of her to reach at least futilely for the phone.

It was the younger's number he dialed.

It was a different, lower voice he brought the words up inside of. She had never been one to put the phone down on a pausing stranger.

"People shouldn't have to be the ones to tell you," he said.

One night, he went over their childhoods again. Had he done nearly enough?

Their mother had taught them that you can ask anybody anything, but it can't always be "Do I know you?"

That you had arms to bar yourself from people.

That you had to watch what you touched after you had already gone ahead and touched some other thing first.

That the most pestering thing on a man was the thing that kept playing tricks with how long it actually was.

For his part, he had got it across that a mirror could not be counted on to give its all. If they should ever need to know what they might look like, they were to keep their eyes off each other and come right to him. He would tell them what was there. In telling it, he put flight and force into the hair, nursed purpose into the lips, worked a birthmark into the shape of a slipper.

Each had a room to roam however she saw fit in either fickleness or frailty.

Rotten spots on the flesh of a banana were just "ingrown cinnamon."

The deep well of the vacuum cleaner accepted any runty jewelry they shed during naps.

The house met with cracks, lashings.

They walked themselves to his chair one day as separates, apprentices at the onrolling household loneliness. The older wanted to know whether it was more a help or a hindrance that things could not drop into your lap if you were sitting up straight to the table. The younger just wanted ways to stunt her growth that would not mean spending more money.

When they were older, and unreproduced, he figured they expected him to start taking after them at least a little. So he now and then let his eyes slave away at the backs of his fingers in the manner of the younger. He raised the older's keynote tone of gargly sorrow up as far into his voice as it deserved when it came time again to talk about his car, any occult change in how the thing took a curve.

Some nights he saw his ex-wife's face put to fuming good use on each of theirs. His failings? A waviness around all he felt bad about, a slovenry mid-mouth. Timid, uncivic behaviors that went uncomprehended. Before the layoffs, he'd been a subordinate with at least thorny standing among the otherwise harmable. He had left it to others to take everything the wrong way. (Tidy electrical fires, backups downstairs, wastepaper calculations off by one dim digit.)

From where they had him sitting, to see a thing through meant only to insist on the transparency within it, to regard it as done and gone.

But adultery? It was either the practice, the craft, of going about as an adult, or there had been just that once. Poles above the woman's toilet had shot all the way up to the ceiling, hoisting shelves of pebble-grained plastic. The arc of his piss was at least a suggestion of a path that thoughts could later take. He went back to the bed and found her sitting almost straight up in her sleep. Her leg was drawn forward: a trough had formed between the line of the shinbone and some flab gathered to the side. It needed something running waterily down its course. All he had left in him now was spittle.

At home afterward: unkindred totes and carryalls arranged in wait beside the door. He poked into the closest one to see whose clothing it might be. His fingers came up with the evenglow plush and opponency of something segregatedly hers. A robe, or something in the robe family.

One night he paid a visit to the building where the two of them lived on different floors. First the older: buttons the size of quarters sewn at chafing intervals into the back panels of what she showed him to as a seat. He had to sit much farther forward than ordinarily. He gave her money to take the younger one out for a restaurant supper. "How will I know what she likes?" she said. Then two flights up to the younger, but she was on the phone. A doorway chinning bar hangered with work smocks blocked him from the bedroom. The bathroom door was open. Passages of masking tape stuck to the plastic apparatus of her hygiene, but unlabeled, uncaptioned. Everything smacked of what was better kept to herself. When she got away from the phone, he gave her money to pick something nice out for her sister. "But what?" she said. "You've known her all your life," he said. "But other than that?" she said.

No sooner did he have the two of them turning up in each other's feelings again than his own days gave way underneath.

The library switched to the honor system. You had to sign the books out yourself and come down hard when you botched their return shelving. (He gawked mostly at histories, stout books full of people putting themselves out.) He recovered a gorge of hair from the bathroom drain and set it out on the soap dish to prosper or at least keep up. There were two telephone directories for the hallway table now—the official, phone-company one and the rival, heavier on front matter, bus schedules, seating charts. You had to know where to turn. He began breaking into a day from odd slants, dozing through the lower afternoon, then stepping out onto the platform of hours already packed beneath him. It should have put him on a higher footing. He started collecting sleeveless blouses—"shells" they were called. Was there anything less devouring that a woman could pull politely over herself? The arms swept through the holes and came right out again, unsquandered. He tucked the shells between the mattress pad and the mattress and barged above them in his sleep.

The younger showed up with an all-occasion assortment of greeting cards from the dollar store. She fanned them out on the floor so that only the greetings would show.

"Which ones can't I send?" she said.

"What aren't you to her?" he said.

"I'm not 'Across the Miles.'"

"Mail that when you're at the other end of town, running errands."

Then the movie house in his neighborhood reduced the ticket price to a dollar. It was a thrifty way to do himself out of a couple of hours. He followed the bad-mouthing on-screen or just sat politely until it was time to tip the rail of the side door.

He became a heavier dresser, a coverer.

The older called to say that while the younger was away, she had sneaked inside to screw new brass pulls into the drawer-fronts of her bureau.

"It'll all dawn on her," she said.

Before the week wore out, the two of them came by together one night, alike in the sherbety tint to their lips, the violescent quickening to the eyelids. Identical rawhide laces around their necks, an identical paraphernalium (something from a tooth?) suspended from each. Hair toiled up into practically a bale, with elastics.

High-rising shoes similar in squelch and hectic stringage. They were both full of unelevated understanding of something they had each noticed on TV—a substitution in the schedule. He had noticed it too. It hadn't improved him.

They were holding hands.

Each finger an independent tremble.

He had to tell them: "This is not a good time."

How much better to get the door shut against them now!

His nights were divided three ways. This was the hour for the return envelopes that came with the bills. The utilities no longer bothered printing the rubrics "NAME," "STREET," "CITY, STATE, ZIP" before the lines in the upper-left corner. The lines were yours to fill out as you wished.

Tonight: Electric.

_____

_____

_____

He wrote:

Who sees?

Who sees?

Who sees?

The night his car had to be dropped off for repairs, the older one offered to give him a ride home. He faced a windshield-wiper blade braced to its arm by garbage-bag ties. Come a certain age, she was saying, you start thinking differently of the people closest to hand. You dig up what you already know, but you turn it over more gently before bringing it all the way out. It might be no more than that she catches a cold at every change of the seasons. But why had it taken you this long to think the world of it?

He started listening to just the vowelly lining in what she said.

He skipped the casing consonants that made each word news.

It was carolly to him, a croon.

*   *   *

The daughters had wanted their ceremony held in the lunchroom where they worked. Other than him, it was only women who showed—a table's worth of overfragrant, older coworkers. The officiating one, the day supervisor, wanted to first run down her list of what she was in no position to do. It was a long, hounding list of the "including but not limited to" type. (This was not "espousage"; it was not "jointure"; it was "not in anywise matrimoniously unitudinal.") Then she turned to the daughters and read aloud from her folder to steepening effect that no matter where you might stand on whether things should come with time, it was only natural for you to want to close up whatever little space is left between you and whoever has been the most in your way or out of the question all this long while, and let a line finally be drawn right through the two of you on its quick-gone way to someplace else entirely. Nobody was twisting your arm for you to finish what you should have been screaming your lungs out for in public since practically day one.

The kiss was swift but depthening.

Then the reception. He was a marvel for once, waving himself loose from the greetings and salutes every time he realized anew that they were intended for the person beside him, or behind.

HISTORIES OF THE UNDEAD

KATE BRAVERMAN

When Erica took a leave of absence to complete her research she knew almost immediately that she would fail. She devised lists of people to telephone, penciled in a schedule of interviews and columns with questions. Her handwriting seemed small and bruised. She called no one.

She remembers now, in the long mornings when Flora and Bob are gone, that she always detested fragments. Or more accurately, the need to order them, to invent a spine, a progression, a curve that resolves.

She is, at her core, too nervous, restless, and cynical. There is something within her that can only say no. It's odd that she thought she had subdued this, found her own rain forest, slashed and burned it to the last acre of cold ash. She wonders if she should be grateful. Perhaps somewhere on a balcony, in a permanently ocher-tinted city she isn't certain of, there is more air for someone, a woman standing mute and confused in a scented dusk, a woman searching for something.

It was late morning. Day was elbowing clouds above glazed roofs of orange tiles, and she feels startled and amazed. Seen from the right angle, the city is a sequence of seashells, glistening abalone, their bellies an offering of mother-of-pearl. She became aware of the fact that she wasn't worried about abandoning her project or the implications this might have on her tenure profile. She had always sensed a rainy day coming. It would be an afternoon in winter when some massive typhoon would speak her name. There would be a new fluid language, a kind of cursive rendered in acid. Then it would invade her lungs, she would be singed, and it would be the time of the drowning.

It occurred to her that the suddenness with which her behavior altered had a predestined quality. It was as if she had been secretly engaged in a dress rehearsal for precisely this abandonment and divestiture all of her life. This knowledge entered her with a fierce urgency. It felt perpetual and alluring, like sin or revelation. It was inescapable. She recognized it as a kind of return. It had always been there. This was the cove where she was meant to anchor.

This must be what she was thinking about at traffic lights, why she didn't play her car radio and was never bored, why the static in the air seemed a kind of hieroglyphic she tried to decipher. This must be why she would walk out of theaters and not remember the title of the play, the setting, or even the genre. Had it been a musical, a love story, or a comedy? She would walk across a parking lot shaking her head.

Perhaps she had been tuned into another station entirely. There was something on the margin that attracted her, something in the extreme edge of the register where you couldn't be certain of dates or motives or outcome. She could never understand, really, why the motion picture was more interesting than sitting in the lobby with the carpet that looked like stained glass in reverse, deco blood petals, panels of crimson and lime that marked not translucency but rather the end of the line. Here couples glared at each other above the too-yellow popcorn and all things were random, vaguely metallic and swollen. She thought of hooks that were swallowed. And why was this less significant than the other images, the ones you sat in dark rooms for, sat as if a subliminal force were fattening you for a harvest or a kill.

Erica realized that time would pass and her grant would expire. The questions she had planned to examine seemed distant and trivial. She wondered if it were possible to be defined by refusal. Certainly the most brilliant of her subjects would listen to her questions, run a slow hand across a soft mouth, and remain silent. She was looking out the kitchen window when she realized this. There were five pigeons on a strip of grass, and the red bands around their necks were exactly the same shade of corrupted pink as the red *no stopping* lines painted on the curb in front of their house. Had she finally discovered something?

She began to sleep past eight o'clock. She could not drive her daughter to school. She was no longer reliable. Now she called a taxicab for her daughter the night before, gave Flora ten dollars, told her to wait outside, and to keep the change. She reminded Flora not to mention this to Bob. She squeezed Flora's shoulder with her fingers when she said this.

When Erica woke up late she made a second pot of coffee, put brandy in it, ate an extra piece of toast, layered it with jam. She turned on the stereo. The concept of rock and roll in the morning by sunlight was stunning.

Her husband came home for lunch. She hadn't expected him. She was looking out the kitchen window. There was a tarnish in the air, a sort of glaze.

Perhaps it was part of a complicated cleaning solution with invisible ammonia. It was designed to bring out the shine, but the sky was overcast.

"You seem troubled," Bob said. He put his briefcase on the table. Its proportion seemed monumental. "Is it the research?"

She shook her head, no. It was nearly noon. It was the hour the workingmen sat on lawns smoking cigarettes and eating lunches that looked too meager to sustain them. They leaned close to one another, planning burglaries and trading lies about women.

"You aren't yourself," Bob decided. He paused and studied her face. "I don't have to go to Seattle. Christ. I don't even have a paper to present."

Erica said, "Don't be silly. I'm perfectly fine."

Later, she stood in the backyard where the bushes were trimmed and resembled elongated skulls. She had forgotten he was going to a conference. Now that she knew he would be gone this night and the next, she wondered if his absence mattered. Was it fundamental, was it definitive, would there be change? She leaned against the side of the house. These were the stark fragments that bruised, made you fall, made you hoarse. It was best to create methods of walking with your eyes shut.

Bob noticed that she was different but his conclusion was wrong. He could observe but not interpret. She was merely in transition. She was returning to a version of a former self. And Erica wondered how she would devise a process of clarification, how she would problem-solve this small confusion of who she was.

Whenever she encountered enormities, Erica could only think of walking beside water, a bay or a rocky stretch of coast, or finding her daughter, holding Flora and breathing in the scent of her black hair, which was the spiced essence of night rivers. They were the only two manifestations in the landscape that were indisputable, like a certain sequence of spires, of bridges or plazas. This was how she could know where she was. Geography would form a rudimentary net, the first in a series of coordinates. Later she could build a landing strip.

Erica walks into the early afternoon, uncertain of where she is going. There is only a sense of fluid depth and the realization that she is again thinking about her sister Ellen. Her sister has two best friends and both of them are dying. These two other women, barely nodding acquaintances, have somehow achieved a massive presence in Erica's life. Often her sister will telephone with frantic updates on the brutal unravelings of the other women. It is curious how Lillian and Babette seem more vivid to Erica than her actual friends.

Erica is given the details of their deterioration and she absorbs these fragments without effort. They arrange themselves, as if she has an innate capacity for this ordering. She understands these proportions, their facets, how they must be viewed and composed. She envisions Babette, the French skier, frail now, ninety-three pounds. Babette, who never married or had children, who chose instead an intimacy with mountains, a life of suitcases and hotels facing ridges of white, is now confined to a wheelchair.

Erica has memorized the saga of Lillian, shunned by her oncologist, left without a referral for three months, and finally sent to an experimental chemotherapy program. The doctor tells her they expect the treatment to fail.

In the long mornings of waxy stray sunlight across the camellias, she finds herself waiting for Ellen to telephone, to recite the most recent conversations, to impart the medical data and the second and third opinions. How Lillian, only a year before the vice president of a stock brokerage, a woman with 275 employees, called in the predawn, terrified. They had removed the plug from her arm. They wanted her to get out of bed and into a wheelchair.

"They're dismissing me, and I'm too sick to go home," Lillian realized and wept. "I'm afraid. I keep drifting off."

"What did you do?" Erica asks. She can see part of the street from her living room window. The leaves on the orange trees look artificial, landscaped beyond recognition. They are not trees, but someone's concept of how trees should look.

"I tracked down the resident. He said Lillian could die any minute. She doesn't have a month left." Her sister sounds broken. "I told him Lillian lives alone. I said he couldn't send her home alone, not like this."

She imagines Lillian, whom she has only met twice and cannot clearly remember, as a tall woman with white hair and a straw hat with yellow silk flowers. Now this Lillian is shrunken, ordered into a wheelchair and pushed to the front of a building she cannot recognize. She has no hair, she is too weak to fasten her wig, it's become too complicated. A nurse who barely speaks English—is from the Philippines or Guatemala—deposits the wheelchair at the curb where a taxi attempts to take Lillian to an apartment she cannot provide adequate directions to.

After all, north or south of Wilshire are an immensity of possibility, everything writhes, stung by citrus and pastel, who could draw the line? Lillian knows there are indications. Poinsettias in a cluster might be December. There are lilies at Easter. That comes in April. Of course vegetation is a kind of compass that rises from the ground. There is always a chorus of pigments. This is why we believe in resurrection. And Lillian couldn't get out of a taxi, walk across a lobby, wait for an elevator, open the many locks of the heavy front door she had insisted on. And there's no food there, there hasn't been food in weeks. She just eats through a plug. She can't remember how to turn on appliances or who she gave her cat to.

Erica wonders if these are parables. Is this what happens to women who dare to live alone, even the good ones, like Lillian, a churchgoer who doesn't sin, ever? Her sister is adamant. Lillian is from the South for God's sake, she wears gloves and gives money to an organization to protect stray animals.

The air smells scrubbed, polished, and detoxed. It is a winter that has been taught a lesson. And Erica doesn't want Flora to be left like this, in some remote time, when she can't be there to protect her, to make sure about release forms, wheelchairs, plugs, the administration of morphine, a bed with a view of the tops of palms, the secret avenues in the air where they open their fans and do their ancient naked dance that has nothing to do with love.

Suddenly Erica remembers when she decided to murder her daughter. They were living in northern California. It was the winter it never stopped raining. It would be the coldest and wettest winter on record. She was going to graduate school and they didn't know anyone in the county. Erica was still smoking three packs of cigarettes a day. She had bronchitis again. It was her fourth bout of bronchitis that year and she refused to take a chest X-ray. The doctor in the student clinic said she was killing herself, pointed his long white arm at the door, placed her chart on the counter next to her purse, turned his back, walked away.

Erica was convinced she had lung cancer. She could sense the blue particles like a glacial stream, trickling and widening. The rain made them grow. They were sensitive to water. She could feel inside her veins to a fluid she imagined was the color of chilled larkspur. She was certain she wouldn't survive this California winter.

It was before she married Bob. She lay awake listening to the rain and considering her daughter Flora without her, a four-year-old orphan, a ward of the state. A child to be adopted by foster parents who would sexually abuse her, fail to provide piano lessons and poetry. A child to be raised in apartments where she was the entertainment for the brothers and uncles, and the television set was always on.

There was only one possible solution. She would take Flora into her bed, curve into her body, hold her beneath the quilt. They would both take sleeping pills and the winter would be over. But she didn't kill Flora that night, didn't kill herself, and now it is Los Angeles in early February.

Everything feels and tastes like spring. The afternoon dissolves into impressions, phantom images. We give them anchors, we give them language, she thinks. We practice acts of anthropomorphism, we wield the rules of grammar, but they are still creatures, pulsing.

She needs to see Flora. She is nine blocks from her school. It is afternoon and at 2:30 the fourth graders have gym on North Field.

Erica can sit behind a clump of oleander and watch her daughter play volleyball near the fence. The day has become simple, transparent. She can either walk along the ocean or watch Flora move through lacquered sunlight. These are the only two indisputable activities in this world.

She walks past an orange tree, then a tree with lemons that look distended, and one with tangerines that are a sharp red. They would sting the mouth. You could bite into them and burn or bleed. You could serve such fruit at weddings or wakes. Yesterday she watched Bob pack. He was going to a meeting in Washington. He said she seemed different. "I'm fine. I'm perfectly fine," she had replied.

She remembers saying this to her mother. She had employed exactly the same cadence, the precise rise and fall of her voice like a series of bells in a plaza passed by in a speeding night train. This is a lie she has long ago engraved within herself. This is the way she imagines grown-ups speak. And her mother said, "Don't make me laugh."

"I'm getting myself together," she had told her mother. It might have been at the end of graduate school, during her first divorce. It might have been the winter she almost murdered her daughter.

"It's going to take you a lifetime," her mother said. Her mother was drinking vodka. She surveyed her coolly, evaluated her like a suit she didn't consider worth buying. Then she smiled.

Of course, her mother and father are dead now. They are dead but not quite gone. There is an entire substratum of people like this, people she doesn't quite know and yet they somehow linger. There is the matter of her sister with the two best friends who are dying. There are her daughter's mystery friends that surface and are erased, names she has never heard before suddenly brandished as best friends.

"You know Alexa?" Flora begins. Erica says no. "Alexa, my best friend," Flora continues, highlighting each of her words, obviously annoyed.

This name is not familiar. She feels defensive and afraid. "I know Robin and Claudia," she reminds her daughter. "I know the twins. But not Alexa."

She is combing Flora's hair. It is night. She winds strands into tiny black braids. In the morning when the braids are undone, Flora will be adorned with vast complexities of curl. Now Flora looks like her head is a nest of snakes. We give birth to mythology over and over, Erica realizes, almost trembling with terror. We are the dried riverbeds where they hatch, where they drag their cold bodies across sand. It is from our bellies that they come.

"You're lying," Flora says. "All you do is talk on the phone. You don't even drive me to school anymore." Then she slams her bedroom door.

Now it is important that she find Flora and tell her she wasn't lying. There are protocols for the keeping of names. These syllables are sacred. When the winds have taken everything, even the buildings and the stones and the bark, these names will remain. These are the perpetually open graves. She is going to explain this to her daughter. She will defend herself against this suggestion of desecration.

Last night her sister called with more information about Babette. She can no longer sit. She has to sleep strapped to a board, upright, held by buckles. Her bones are turning to a kind of tin. Her sister cannot pronounce the name of the new disease. She can only say that Babette is rusting. She has nightmares filled with liquids, rain, waterfalls, a recurrent beach where she watches the approach of a tidal wave. Ellen has just visited her. She says Babette's skin smells like dust. She creaks when she breathes.

Erica knows both women were misdiagnosed, twice. Somewhere there are four mistakes and someone must be counting. Last night she asked her sister, "Do you ever talk to Lillian about death? About dying?" Erica was lying on her bed. She wanted to know. Bob had not yet gone to Seattle. Erica had shut her bedroom door.

Her sister thought for a moment. She said, "No."

"What do you talk about?" Erica asks.

"Ordinary things," her sister told her. "Who's playing good tennis. Who got a face-lift. Whose kid is in jail. The weather, the economy. You know."

Erica does know. When her father was dying, when he was decaying in front of them inches from their faces and almost in slow motion, it was the one thing no one ever spoke about. Father had the cancer stench. It was a kind of rancid yellow that made her think of tortured fruit and strange rotting cargoes abandoned at sea and something terrible done in rooms with unshaded lightbulbs, abortions, perhaps, or children being photographed naked. Her father's skin became translucent. He was a region of rivers. You could look inside and see his infinity of blue sins.

Erica wants to ask her sister if she remembers this but she doesn't. They never speak about their parents or the way they died or what their lives might have meant. Their parents simply disappeared, like a species that vanished overnight. It's as if they never were.

Erica realizes there is an entire ghost substratum inhabiting her. She's become aware of how much time she spends thinking about people she doesn't know and will never know, doesn't even want to meet once. Not just Lillian and Babette, these secondary tragedies she's internalized, not just Flora's profusion of suddenly found and lost best friends, but how she thinks about movie stars and European royalty and the state of their marriages.

She doesn't do this consciously, she would never permit herself to do this consciously. But when she takes her emotional pulse, when she looks directly inside, what she's been thinking about during a three-way traffic light, during a wait in a line at the bank, is Elizabeth Taylor and her new husband, the former carpenter and drug dealer. What do they do together? Do they attend AA meetings? Do they work the twelve-step recovery program? Do they promptly admit mistakes and answer crisis hotlines? She thinks they secretly drink and take drugs. Liz shows him what she has learned about pain pills and champagne. And he initiates her into the sordid avenues of hard-faceted white, the great internal winter, cocaine.

Now, during her leave of absence, when she can take her emotional pulse repeatedly with concentrated deliberation, she realizes she has been colonized by the insubstantial, something leaking, broken and generic, out of the self-destructing culture. It's a kind of collective virus.

She used to think about Virginia Woolf and Sylvia Plath. That was when she lived with painters, when she lived in lofts above Indian restaurants and afternoons smelled of curry and the sun set in a sequence of saffrons, when she thought the bungalows behind hedges of sunflowers along the Venice canals were holy and her parents were not yet dead.

She didn't try to imagine Sylvia Plath and her husband in bed. She didn't envision Virginia wrapped in the arms of a woman, rain falling, and what they might have done with their mouths. She visualized instead the kitchens where they brewed tea, the patterns of painted pink rosebuds on the cups, and the way the wind sounded as if it had just been eating ships. But the graphic couplings she now considers, the intricacies of bodies and proclivities, this she has saved for television stars.

It is 1:30 and she is four blocks from Flora's school. She can sense that Lillian is going into a coma. That's what Lillian was afraid of when she telephoned Ellen and wept, "Don't let them send me home. I feel like I'm drifting in and out."

Erica closes her eyes and there are acres of faces within her. She is even replete with the spouses of men she barely knows. How many afternoons had she imagined her lawyer's wife? She did this for months during her first divorce, staring at the photograph on his desk. A blond woman with ice skates balanced over her right shoulder. A woman wearing a green wool sweater and sunglasses.

She was often tempted to ask her name. She finally decided it was Ingrid or Justine. She was good with dogs and gardens, never got migraines, enjoyed baking.

It occurs to Erica that what she wants to research is not history as it actually is or was, but some more fragile peripheral version, in its own way filled with untamed ambiguity. It would be a history of the undead, the flickering partials and the almost.

In these regions of ambivalence are the men she almost married. Erica has reconstructed pieces of their lives, a conversation, a newspaper clipping, an accidental sighting, something overheard. She might have stayed with Derek in Maui. Or the photographer in Spain. There are the lingering pulsings of these multiple almost-hers, standing on balconies of apartments and villas, watering geraniums, wearing a white slip above cobblestone alleys, above a plaza or a bay.

Jason, telephoning her at the university two years ago. She was working late. He was drunk. "I'm drinking fifteen-year-old scotch and it's been fifteen years since I fucked you. Come over."

Erica looked out her office window, noted the low soiled mountains and considered it. It was August in Southern California and everything seemed burned, even at night. It was the time of the avenues of scorch and the unraveling of an indelible yellow.

She could reach into the substrata of the barely known, make a date, meet in a motel in Long Beach, maybe, or in the Valley, Van Nuys, perhaps. It would have to be an urban suburb where no landscape could intrude, where it wouldn't be about beaches and palm trees, but California as it really was, back roads the color of mustard, smelling of onions and vinegar below hills where nothing could grow. In a valley of brush and sage and sand they could know the real nature of their hearts. It wasn't the stuff of postcards. But they knew this already. That's why she hung up.

We carry the undead with us, she thinks. That's why it's so hard to walk, why her boots hurt and the sun sears. She still packs for Jason, still takes him to Hawaii and London with her. She stands at her closet, one closet or another, hearing him say, only red or black. You're a Toulouse-Lautrec whore. Anything else on your skin is an atrocity. And she finds herself repeatedly choosing these colors, in nightgowns and coats, tablecloths and socks.

Maybe she will tell her colleagues it is the history of the partial she wishes to explore, the terrain without specific intentions or borders. This is what she is thinking as she approaches Flora's school, as she sits on a lawn next to a rock with a bronze plaque nailed to it. "Dedicated to Maurice J. Finelander, 1918–1964." What did that forty-six-year-old man die from? Did he suffer, turn translucent, did he drift, could you look inside his chest and chart the avenues of his disgrace?

After she sees Flora, she will go home and wait for her sister to call. Afternoons are punctuated with desperate news about Lillian. Sometimes Erica telephones first. She has never called her sister so often, not even when their mother had a heart attack. They haven't spoken this often since they shared a room in the summer house.

"What's the latest with Lillian?" she will ask. Her eyes will be abnormally wide, she will take big breaths, as if there is some quality in the late afternoon wind that she requires.

Perhaps it has something to do with the enormous subterranean architecture she is discovering with its roots, shadows, and branching networks. This is beneath her feet all the time. This is what children sense under the bed. This is the secret structure of the world, and children feel this hidden spine. This is why they need stuffed pandas and teddy bears. This is why she has walked to the school to find her daughter, to tell Flora she would never lie about the names of the almost-known.

Suddenly, Erica recognizes a complexity that makes her decide to turn back. She wants to tell Flora that certain fragments seem like lies but they are not. It is simply the other world with its decaying possibilities casting luminous debris. It is not deliberate. There is no malice. But names get lost here. They are like seashells washed up on a wide night shore in a season of not enough moon. Inside each shell is a name, and the sea speaks it clearly, says Alexa, Flora, Lillian. But there are winds, the intrusion of partially forgotten winters that in memory are a stark and insinuating blue. And Erica realizes that she cannot tell this to Flora. This is a stretch of beach you must find for yourself and then only in a drowning season.

Erica walks home on a boulevard where the sidewalk is planted with rosebuds, bird-of-paradise, and iris, and she is thinking about events in the subterranean world. Here are the traffic accidents we almost had, but didn't.

Here are the planes we missed that might have carried bombs on them. Do the almosts form an architecture? Is that how you navigate in the cities of the undead?

Later that week, her sister calls, desperate. Lillian has run away. She's had a paranoid seizure, perhaps from the drugs, or maybe the cancer has metastasized into her brain. No one knows. She just took her raincoat and wallet and disappeared from the hospital. Her neighbor saw her get out of a cab. Lillian explained that she had come back for her cat.

"What should I do?" her sister Ellen asks.

She imagines her sister holding the phone, pacing, staring out the balcony. The wind has been blowing, a Santa Ana from the desert. Everything seems a form of fleshy yellow. It is a night of skin. Lamps are insignificant. The moon is so inordinately bright she thinks the savanna must have been like this, rocked by streaks of yellow with the intensity of seduction and prophecy.

"We'll drive the streets and find her," Erica decides. "I'll pick you up."

Flora has suddenly appeared. She is always barefoot, soundless. She simply materializes. She is holding her math book open at her hip. Flora could survive in the night, with her head of uncoiling snakes. She seems to be waiting for something. Erica knows what her daughter is doing. Flora is stalking.

Bob has returned from his conference in Seattle. He is staring at her, watching her assemble car keys, wallet, jacket, watch. He studies the objects she is sliding into her pockets as if he plans to collect evidence. He is standing in front of the living room door as if he intends to guard it.

Earlier, when she was cooking dinner, Bob asked if she had gone to the library. He had telephoned and she wasn't home. She examined the tip of the knife. Her husband didn't understand that she was never going back to the library. It didn't contain the artifacts she needed. Then he asked what she had done all day.

"I don't remember," she said. She was holding a knife. It felt hard in her hand. She put it down. She could feel the moon through the window. It occurred to her that there was no history, only the etiology of yellow.

Now Bob says, "Where are you going?"

There is always this moment, she realizes. The where and the why. The demand for coordinates and specifics, the number of acres, who saw the troops, which direction and how many. There is always this and the way sometimes you don't answer.

"It's Lillian," she says, walking quickly toward the door. He is heavier but he has trouble with his knees. She could outflank him if she had to. "She's roaming the streets. She's lost her mind."

Erica considers the invisible artifacts she has recently unearthed. She thinks about mapping the subterranean strata. What sort of tools would she need, what form of illumination?

"But you don't even know that woman," her husband says.

"I do know her," Erica replies. "I've never known anyone so well."

Flora is staring at her. They look into one another's eyes and Erica realizes communication is dimensional, like something knitted, a rope or a net. Then she is walking into the yellowed night where the wind sounds like a rushing river, there is a lashing of branches, and the leaves are clinging to stay on.

YOU DRIVE

C H R I S T I N E   S C H U T T

She brought him what she had promised, and they did it in his car, on the top floor of the car park, looking down onto the black flat roofs of buildings, and she said, or she thought she said, "I like your skin," when what she really liked was the color of her father's skin, the mottled white of his arms and the clay color at the roots of the hairs along his arms. Long hair along his arms it was, hair bleached from sun and water—sun off the lake, and all that time he spent in water, summer to summer abrading the wild dry hair on his head, turning the ends of his hair, which was also red, and deeply so, quite white. "You look healthy," she said to her father, and he did, in high color, but the skin on his face also seemed coarse to her— not boy's skin, her father's, not glossy, close-grained skin, but pitted and stubbled under all that color, rashed along his jaw and neck, her father's skin: rough. She touched him, and it was rough skin, his cheek. "Just testing," she said, and smiled at her father. "Shaving," she said. "I used to watch Mother's guys at it."

Her father said, "My youngest daughter still"; then he took hold of her hand and kissed it. He was quiet. Holding her hand against his leg and looking out at a roof where a fat woman waited for her dog, her father was quiet. "What a dirty place this is," he said. "That poor dog is ashamed of himself."

"Look at my hands," she said. "I have seen lots of things," she said, changing the sheets of incontinent patients on rounds made twice a night—all of them up, anyway, these old howlers, mean and balked and full of worry. The naked woman with her pocketbook is crying after baby while the farmer at the nurses' station slaps the counter for a drink. "Where the fuck," the farmer says over and over. "You should know this about me," she said to her father. "I can take care of myself."

"So tell me what you have seen," her father said, and she told him about her mother and the guy with the criminal haircut. "Can you imagine?" she asked her father. Imagine the two of them, inviting her in after, turning over the pillows and fanning at their chests by lifting up the sheet. And there was more, she said, a lot more, but it was her father's turn. "You promised," she said. "The wife."

"The wife," he said.

The wife has see-through skin and grainy eyelids bruised by nature. When she wakes, there is all this sand between her lashes. Daughters, too, there are—brown and knobby daughters, dozens of them, Scotch-taping bangs and walking through the house in their underwear.

She told her father a girl had kissed her once, and not a girl really, but a woman, a teacher, a small, dark, trembly woman who followed all the games at school, running herself breathless up and down the playing field.

"How did it feel," her father asked, "to kiss a woman?"

"I don't remember," she said. "The woman turned teacherly and took me by the shoulders."

*   *   *

"You are such a show-off," T said. "You are vain. You are braggy."

She told her father about these girls she knew who were in love with each other. They let her watch them kiss at the lake after swimming. Their kissing was not so dry or hard-seeming as the kissing she remembered with her teacher, and she spoke of the blond abundance of the girl-girl curled outside a high-cut suit; but there was so much smoke in the car by then, she did not know if she imagined the square and heavy ends of her father's fingers, or if she saw or had hold of his fingers, of the whorled dead-white ends of his fingers, tips weighted as surely as a line, deep fishing, plummet of fat in the black-green water—what was that thing he said he caught? Lifted out of the water and beating against her as it had, the fish curling and uncurling in the heat of her hand, did it have a name?

"Tell me about your boyfriends," her father said. Her father asked, "Who else besides the character who gets you this stuff?"

"Just the character," she said, and she called the character T because she didn't want to give him a name. A name could get them all in trouble. "T is just a hairless boy—doesn't need to shave," she said. Same age, but not her size. Smaller, prettier—T had a lean girl's face, sharp angles, good bones. The hammocked skin underneath his eyes fluttered when he kissed. "I look," she said.

Her father kissed her, his dry lips slack against her own and soft. Gentle enough, this time; she could have looked, but she was shy: ready to move in what ways he moved, toward her or away, a lot depending on the things she brought him. That is what she thought at least, that is what she told him, but her father said, "No, no, no."

Her father said, "My problem is, I'm tired."

Another boy, another car, she used to let him feel her up just so long as she could sleep. "The night shift," she said to her father, "is such a bitch. You're always tired. I can't talk," she said, and she kissed her father. She opened her mouth to him and worried her hand inside his coat and felt the warm damp of his shirt, the hard back and heat of her father. Here was no girl-boy, but heavy muscle and bone, soft, wide shoulders and something like breasts. She liked to push against and rub her face between her father's breasts. She rubbed her face in him: lemons and gin and earth and smoke. His springy hair was in her teeth, everywhere springy, and fragrant and wet and tasting of nails. Yes, the metals in my mouth, she said, are singing.

She told T she couldn't remember where she had parked her car.

That was why she was late, she told T. This was another time she couldn't remember. They had driven around and around, she and her father, looking for the street. "Honest," she said, but T didn't believe her, and he put his hand under her skirt to prove it.

T said, "You are so fucking easy to get at," which she supposed was true, the way she dressed, the way she Velcroed shut, ready to unravel at a tab for a boy—any boy, or that was what T said. "I can see through your dress," T said. "I know what you've been doing."

Under the watchful eye of a man whose name she did not remember, she took off her skinny bra. He only wanted to look, the man said, and touch her, just a little.

"You would like my mother," she said to the man. "You should see my mother."

"Should I be ashamed?" she asked her father. The lady and her dog were gone; only skin-colored fence acted guardrail on a road: no view.

"Of what?" he asked.

Third party to things, watching, scattering other women's charms like seed and clucking in a backward shuffle was how she saw herself, asking, "Do you like that woman? Did you see her breasts?"

Her father said, "I like your breasts."

* * *

Full snub-nosed breasts, nipples tightened to the size of quarters in the cold, she liked these breasts, too, and girls with boy chests and ribs showing through, which wasn't the way she was made, or maybe it was—she wasn't sure, even though she looked when she was being touched. She knew these feelings. The damp press and hurtful weight of a man's head against her collar—beard, no beard—she had known this.

"Everyone else," she told her father, "seems to have what I want."

Her father said, "My daughters are the same." Spoiled girls, they were using Daddy's credit cards to clean beneath their nails, asking, Can we? Why don't we? We should. Her father said, "I don't think of you that way," and he pressed the heel of his hand against her hip as he might to push away, to push off, hard body arched, moving stiffly in the cold waters just off the rocks.

The summer houses were shut up for the winter. November, midday, and the black lake level against the yellow shore. "We could go there," her father said, but they stayed put, in his car, and used the things she brought.

T said, "Even your mother wants it," and she was surprised.

T said, "Oh, come on, everything you fucking do on that night-shift fucking job is crooked."

"What do you do," she asked her father, "when you are not with me?"

He said, "You don't really want to know," and he drove her to an unfinished place and pointed. "I have something to do with that." She saw a building, girders, rags, nets, menacing vacancies. Her father pointed. "Nobody's home," he said, "but that's not my job." Rocking the car easy over the scrub-board road, raising dust, her father said, "We'll never get this thing finished."

Dust settling on the canvased shapes, Dumpsters and cinder block, the whole wild modern array of it—amazing.

"Amazing," she said to her father, looking out the window and back at him: the whiteness of his collar against the blaze of neck, the creases darkened, almost black. At his throat, he wore a tie knotted tight as a knuckle.

Maybe he draws the buildings; maybe he warehouses nails and joints, figure-eight pieces, metal supports. Who knows? The way her father palmed the wheel of his fat car, he might very well be a crook with a crook's car, much like an office, plush and neutral, her father's make, coppery glitter and paneling that might or might not be real wood. Black and gold buttons for everything; the music on the radio—never clearer. Only decide, decide, please. You pick, no you, was the way she was with her father, first word always *yes* to everything he asked about. Yes, I did. Yes, I will.

Yes when he surprised her, coming up almost to her house and pointing to a shut eye. "Do you believe my wife did this?" he asked, the good eye blinking and teary and strained. "Can you come out with me for just a while?" Yes.

Yes, Dad: The name warmed her every time she used it to his face, so that she rarely used this name—or any other to his face. Instead, she signaled him. She gave directions in the way she touched him, sometimes saying, "You" and "You" when she was tired and wanted to let him know she would, all he had to do was ask, but not tonight. Tonight she wasn't feeling well.

"But yes," she said to her father. She was always saying yes to her father, and only when she was away from him did she wonder, Does this make sense, my father? Driving all the way to her and home again and to her again in a night, driving to where she worked and waiting for her in the lot until the morning—did her father make sense?

"Twice in a night, it happened," she said to T. "I get confused."

She said, "But I like what I am doing. I wanted to be in something hard. I wanted to be up all night."

* * *

"You're so fucking out of it," T said, and all the other boys said, too. "How do you know one man from another?"

The heavy-lidded eyes, the brittle hair and color of her father: first off, these things, and his voice she knew. The juicy sweetness of his voice when her father was drinking, the way even the words came unbuttoned, the way he said her name, she could be done in by this much about him.

Also the money he gave her—and why not?—presents between the covers of oversized matches: *Don't strike* in gold from O'Something's bar.

"Are these from us?" she asked her father, holding up matches. "Have we been here?"

"You," she said, in the car again, free to speak and ready—even her earlobes oiled, every part of her clean and cleaned. She could get off looking at and petting the hair on her arms. "I don't understand," she said. "What are you doing with a wife who beats you?"

"Oh," her father said, and he was sad, or he was tired. Hard to give it up, the look out onto water, someplace to go. Neighbors far apart on either side—not seen until the winter, then sighted in the forked spaces: women standing at windows waiting to be seen. "But it is hard to see them," her father said. "The glare hurts my eyes, and the bog of common plants—the sappy heart-shaped greeny danglers—beads the windows. Nothing happens, besides," he said. "I don't know why the wife is jealous."

She said, "The light in rooms like that puts me to sleep. I know the daughters," she said. From schools and summers, she knew them, diving for soap chips in the boathouse, she and the daughters playing to know what it felt like. The winner held the soap between her legs the longest—oh, yes, she remembered everything about this game. The way it ticked inside of her. "I wanted to melt down soap," she said. "But all of us girls got to play," she said. "We all got to fold our hands over the burning part."

They switched places. Her father tipped the seat and shut his eyes. She said, "I'm my mother's daughter. I want more than others." The way it was for her to wake up in the morning: the reason you think you have been here is you have been here. "I don't want it the same," she said.

"Everyone I know is broke," she said. "The night shift doesn't pay much. My boyfriends never work."

"And your mother?" her father asked when she had already told her stories: grandfather and uncles making house calls on her mother and scolding the poor woman before they made it better, every day less charmed by her mother, opening their wallets, saying, "This has got to stop. There is only so much we can take."

"Do you remember at all? Do you remember her at all?" She said, "Nothing has changed."

Her father said, "I can't get excited when I think about your mother."

"I am shivering," she said, and he was, too. She could see the cold in his shoulders and in her arms resting on his shoulders; and both of them, she and her father, white, blue-white—November still—and the horizon cindered thin, burnt-out, quite black. She put her bare foot against the car-door window and said, "Look at my leg." No-color sky, battered grasses. After a while, she asked, "Is this doing anything for you?"

Her father smiled. He said, "I've had better," which made her laugh, his saying, when what did he know?

"Just ask me how many times," she said. "I couldn't tell you."

She said, "I'm always in love with someone."

*　　*　　*

Her father said he meant it, he was tired, and she put her hands on his face to feel the bristle grown in driving just to get away—a day, a night, another day, as he had said.

"We don't have to do anything," she said.

Her father asked her, "Do you think I look young, or do you think I look like some old guy who got his eyes done cheap?"

"Look at my feet," she said, parked near the boat launch to a lake they didn't know, iced over, gray-white, no clear shoreline. "Look at the footmarks I've left on the window."

"Such white feet," her father said, and he put his foot over hers.

"Have I told you this before?" she asked.

But T didn't answer, bapping pencils against her head and dancing to his made-up music.

Her father said, "Find some music."

"Not that," her father said. "And no to that, no, no"; then he forgot about the music or was indifferent to it; she could stop at anything she liked.

"But do you like it?" she asked her father.

"Do you like this dress?" she asked. "These shoes?"

Her father said, "It's hard for me to see. My eye still hurts." So she drove again, and she told her father what it was as they passed it, and in what connection to him were these women at the end of narrow drives in houses near the water. She spoke of aproned Annes and pretty Susies. "You knew them," she told her father.

Her father said, "Did I?"

Her father said, "I don't miss many people."

*   *   *

She said, "I don't understand how you can stay with a wife who beats you." There, running after her father down the hallway in his story, was a small woman with a small head and a racket in her hand. Why did he stay with this woman? she wanted to know, and he never answered her, or not that she remembered. What could he have answered, besides, married to a woman such as this: marigoldy hair and bright mouth. After all those daughters, the wife still blushed. Some sweet name it was, flicked loose from the roll, a Cathy, a Jane, ring guards clanking on her wedding finger.

She said, "You should live with me."

She said, "Maybe you don't want to know this, but it doesn't take much." She was talking numbers—two and three a week, once that many in a day. "And I'm not very big," she said. "A bigger woman could take more."

"Once, here at the park," she said, driving her father slowly through the main streets of the town, pointing out where she had been. Here, the last time, with some doper—boots and lots of hair—the two of them on the roof, overlooking the entire fucking wayward county. She said, "Oh, Dad, anyone with what we had could have seen everything, too." Mother and one of her guys in her Mustang or her Bronco—the woman turning in cars as fast as she did men—grandfather and the uncles honking close behind. Keep your wallet shut; sign nothing; say you don't speak the language. She said, "What do I care about those guys? They're not looking out for me."

"I know who lives there," she said, and she pointed to insinuating driveways, raked gravel, money. She told her father she was easily coaxed into cars, at times even asking for it, waiting in obvious places for something to happen, in bedrooms and bathrooms, at doorways with lots of traffic. She said, "I can be dumb sometimes. I don't always know what I am thinking."

Look at the shoes she wore and the dresses.

Mother's mother was still sewing flaps on the cups of the girl's brassieres, so she would look flat, more boy-girl than girl, as if that were going to change things, as if there weren't other ways to do it. "I know lots of ways," she said to her father. "Look," she said, and she lifted up her shirt. "Look at what the lawn did to my back."

She showed her father something else that she had brought, but he said, "No." Her father said, "I don't feel like it today."

T said, "The shit you deal wears off too fast."

"What do I care?" she said. "There are always men somewhere with money. I've got my grandfather, remember. I've got my uncles."

A friend of a friend had a place for them to go in a big-enough town where a lot went unnoticed, but her father said, "No. I don't feel like it today."

"No," her father said. "No, I have no place to keep it. Just let me kiss you," he said, which she did. Arms crossed and eyes shut tight in the cold of the car, she moved a little closer to him and waited for the blow.

WHEN MR. PIRZADA CAME TO DINE

JHUMPA LAHIRI

In the autumn of 1971 a man used to come to our house, bearing confections in his pocket and hopes of ascertaining the life or death of his family. His name was Mr. Pirzada, and he came from Dacca, now the capital of Bangladesh, but then a part of Pakistan. That year Pakistan was engaged in civil war. The eastern frontier, where Dacca was located, was fighting for autonomy from the ruling regime in the west. In March, Dacca had been invaded, torched, and shelled by the Pakistani army. Teachers were dragged onto streets and shot, women dragged into barracks and raped. By the end of the summer, three hundred thousand people were said to have died. In Dacca Mr. Pirzada had a three-story home, a lectureship in botany at the university, a wife of twenty years, and seven daughters between the ages of six and sixteen whose names all began with the letter *A*. "Their mother's idea," he explained one day, producing from his wallet a black-and-white picture of seven girls at a picnic, their braids tied with ribbons, sitting cross-legged in a row, eating chicken curry off of banana leaves. "How am I to distinguish? Ayesha, Amira, Amina, Aziza, you see the difficulty."

Each week Mr. Pirzada wrote letters to his wife, and sent comic books to each of his seven daughters, but the postal system, along with most everything else in Dacca, had collapsed, and he had not heard word of them in over six months. Mr. Pirzada, meanwhile, was in America for the year, for he had been awarded a grant from the government of Pakistan to study the foliage of New England. In spring and summer he had gathered data in Vermont and Maine, and in autumn he moved to a university north of Boston, where we lived, to write a short book about his discoveries. The grant was a great honor, but when converted into dollars it was not generous. As a result, Mr. Pirzada lived in a room in a graduate dormitory, and did not own a proper stove or a television set. And so he came to our house to eat dinner and watch the evening news.

At first I knew nothing of the reason for his visits. I was ten years old, and was not surprised that my parents, who were from India, and had a number of Indian acquaintances at the university, should ask Mr. Pirzada to share our meals. It was a small campus, with narrow brick walkways and white pillared buildings, located on the fringes of what seemed to be an even smaller town. The supermarket did not carry mustard oil, doctors did not make house calls, neighbors never dropped by without an invitation, and of these things, every so often, my parents complained. In search of compatriots, they used to trail their fingers, at the start of each new semester, through the columns of the university directory, circling surnames familiar to their part of the world. It was in this manner that they discovered Mr. Pirzada, and phoned him, and invited him to our home.

I have no memory of his first visit, or of his second or his third, but by the end of September I had grown so accustomed to Mr. Pirzada's presence in our living room that one evening, as I was dropping ice cubes into the water pitcher, I asked my mother to hand me a fourth glass from a cupboard still out of my reach. She was busy at the stove, presiding over a skillet of fried spinach with radishes, and could not hear me because of the drone of the exhaust fan and the fierce scrapes of her spatula. I turned to my father, who was leaning against the refrigerator, eating spiced cashews from a cupped fist.

"What is it, Lilia?"

"A glass for the Indian man."

"Mr. Pirzada won't be coming today. More importantly, Mr. Pirzada is no longer considered Indian," my father announced, brushing salt from the cashews out of his trim black beard. "Not since Partition. Our country was divided. 1947."

When I said I thought that was the date of India's independence from Britain, my father said, "That too. One moment we were free and then we were sliced up," he explained, drawing an X with his finger on the countertop, "like a pie. Hindus here, Muslims there. Dacca no longer belongs to us." He told me that during Partition Hindus and Muslims had set fire to each other's homes. For many, the idea of eating in the other's company was still unthinkable.

It made no sense to me. Mr. Pirzada and my parents spoke the same language, laughed at the same jokes, looked more or less the same. They ate pickled mangoes with their meals, ate rice every night for supper with their hands. Like my parents, Mr. Pirzada took off his shoes before entering a room, chewed fennel seeds after meals as a digestive, drank no alcohol, for dessert dipped austere biscuits into successive cups of tea. Nevertheless my father insisted that I understand the difference, and he led me to a map of the world taped to the wall over his desk. He seemed concerned that Mr. Pirzada might take offense if I accidentally referred to him as an Indian, though I could not really imagine Mr. Pirzada being offended by much of anything. "Mr. Pirzada is Bengali, but he is a Muslim," my father informed me. "Therefore he lives in East Pakistan, not India." His finger trailed across the Atlantic, through Europe, the Mediterranean, the Middle East, and finally to the sprawling orange diamond that my mother once told me resembled a woman wearing a sari with her left arm extended.

Various cities had been circled with lines drawn between them to indicate my parents' travels, and the place of their birth, Calcutta, was signified by a small silver star. I had been there only once and had no memory of the trip. "As you see, Lilia, it is a different country, a different color," my father said. Pakistan was yellow, not orange. I noticed that there were two distinct parts to it, one much larger than the other, separated by an expanse of Indian territory; it was as if California and Connecticut constituted a nation apart from the U.S.

My father rapped his knuckles on top of my head. "You are, of course, aware of the current situation? Aware of East Pakistan's fight for sovereignty?"

I nodded, unaware of the situation.

We returned to the kitchen, where my mother was draining a pot of boiled rice into a colander. My father opened up the can on the counter and eyed me sharply over the frames of his glasses as he ate some more cashews. "What exactly do they teach you at school? Do you study history? Geography?"

"Lilia has plenty to learn at school," my mother said. "We live here now, she was born here." She seemed genuinely proud of the fact, as if it were a reflection of my character. In her estimation, I knew, I was assured a safe life, an easy life, a fine education, every opportunity. I would never have to eat rationed food, or obey curfews, or watch riots from my rooftop, or hide neighbors in water tanks to prevent them from being shot, as she and my father had. "Imagine having to place her in a decent school. Imagine her having to read during power failures by the light of kerosene lamps. Imagine the pressures, the tutors, the constant exams." She ran a hand through her hair, bobbed to a suitable length for her part-time job as a bank teller. "How can you possibly expect her to know about Partition? Put those nuts away."

"But what does she learn about the world?" My father rattled the cashew can in his hand. "What is she learning?"

We learned American history, of course, and American geography. That year, and every year, it seemed, we began by studying the Revolutionary War. We were taken in school buses on field trips to visit Plymouth Rock, and to walk the Freedom Trail, and to climb to the top of the Bunker Hill Monument. We made dioramas out of colored construction paper depicting George Washington crossing the choppy waters of the Delaware River, and we made puppets of King George wearing white tights and a black bow in his hair. During tests we were given blank maps of the thirteen colonies, and asked to fill in names, dates, capitals. I could do it with my eyes closed.

The next evening Mr. Pirzada arrived, as usual, at six o'clock. Though they were no longer strangers, upon first greeting each other, he and my father maintained the habit of shaking hands.

"Come in, sir. Lilia, Mr. Pirzada's coat, please."

He stepped into the foyer, impeccably suited and scarved, with a silk tie knotted at his collar. Each evening he appeared in ensembles of plums, olives, and chocolate browns. He was a compact man, and though his feet were perpetually splayed, and his belly slightly wide, he nevertheless maintained an efficient posture, as if balancing in either hand two suitcases of equal weight. His ears were insulated by tufts of graying hair that seemed to block out the unpleasant traffic of life. He had thickly lashed eyes shaded with a trace of camphor, a generous mustache that turned up playfully at the ends, and a mole shaped like a flattened raisin in the very center of his left cheek. On his head he wore a black fez made from the wool of Persian lambs, secured by bobby pins, without which I was never to see him. Though my father always offered to fetch him in our car, Mr. Pirzada preferred to walk from his dormitory to our neighborhood, a distance of about twenty minutes on foot, studying trees and shrubs on his way, and when he entered our house his knuckles were pink with the effects of crisp autumn air.

"Another refugee, I am afraid, on Indian territory."

"They are estimating nine million at the last count," my father said.

Mr. Pirzada handed me his coat, for it was my job to hang it on the rack at the bottom of the stairs. It was made of finely checkered gray-and-blue wool, with a striped lining and horn buttons, and carried in its weave the faint smell of limes. There were no recognizable tags inside, only a hand-stitched label with the phrase "Z. Sayeed, Suitors" embroidered on it in cursive with glossy black thread. On certain days a birch or maple leaf was tucked into a pocket. He unlaced his shoes and lined them against the baseboard; a golden paste clung to the toes and heels, the result of walking through our damp, unraked lawn. Relieved of his trappings, he grazed my throat with his short, restless fingers, the way a person feels for solidity behind a wall before driving in a nail. Then he followed my father to the living room, where the television was tuned to the local news. As soon as they were seated my mother appeared from the kitchen with a plate of mincemeat kebabs with coriander chutney. Mr. Pirzada popped one into his mouth.

"One can only hope," he said, reaching for another, "that Dacca's refugees are as heartily fed. Which reminds me." He reached into his suit pocket and gave me a small plastic egg filled with cinnamon hearts. "For the lady of the house," he said with an almost imperceptible splay-footed bow.

"Really, Mr. Pirzada," my mother protested. "Night after night. You spoil her."

"I only spoil children who are incapable of spoiling."

It was an awkward moment for me, one which I awaited in part with dread, in part with delight. I was charmed by the presence of Mr. Pirzada's rotund elegance, and flattered by the faint theatricality of his attentions, yet unsettled by the superb ease of his gestures, which made me feel, for an instant, like a stranger in my own home. It had become our ritual, and for several weeks, before we grew more comfortable with one another, it was the only time he spoke to me directly. I had no response, offered no comment, betrayed no visible reaction to the steady stream of honey-filled lozenges, the raspberry truffles, the slender rolls of sour pastilles. I could not even thank him, for once, when I did, for an especially spectacular peppermint lollipop wrapped in a spray of purple cellophane, he had demanded, "What is this thank-you? The lady at the bank thanks me, the cashier at the shop thanks me, the librarian thanks me when I return an overdue book, the overseas operator thanks me as she tries to connect me to Dacca and fails. If I am buried in this country I will be thanked, no doubt, at my funeral."

It was inappropriate, in my opinion, to consume the candy Mr. Pirzada gave me in a casual manner. I coveted each evening's treasure as I would a jewel, or a coin from a buried kingdom, and I would place it in a small keepsake box made of carved sandalwood beside my bed, in which, long ago in India, my father's mother used to store the ground areca nuts she ate after her morning bath. It was my only memento of a grandmother I had never known, and until Mr. Pirzada came to our lives I could find nothing to put inside it. Every so often before brushing my teeth and laying out my clothes for school the next day, I opened the lid of the box and ate one of his treats.

That night, like every night, we did not eat at the dining table, because it did not provide an unobstructed view of the television set. Instead we huddled around the coffee table, without conversing, our plates perched on the edges of our knees. From the kitchen my mother brought forth the succession of dishes: lentils with fried onions, green beans with coconut, fish cooked with raisins in a yogurt sauce. I followed with the water glasses, and the plate of lemon wedges, and the chili peppers, purchased on monthly trips to Chinatown and stored by the pound in the freezer, which they liked to snap open and crush into their food.

Before eating Mr. Pirzada always did a curious thing. He took out a plain silver watch without a band, which he kept in his breast pocket, held it briefly to one of his tufted ears, and wound it with three swift flicks of his thumb and forefinger. Unlike the watch on his wrist, the pocket watch, he had explained to me, was set to the local time in Dacca, eleven hours ahead. For the duration of the meal the watch rested on his folded paper napkin on the coffee table. He never seemed to consult it.

Now that I had learned Mr. Pirzada was not an Indian, I began to study him with extra care, to try to figure out what made him different. I decided that the pocket watch was one of those things. When I saw it that night, as he wound it and arranged it on the coffee table, an uneasiness possessed me; life, I realized, was being lived in Dacca first. I imagined Mr. Pirzada's daughters rising from sleep, tying ribbons in their hair, anticipating breakfast, preparing for school. Our meals, our actions, were only a shadow of what had already happened there, a lagging ghost of where Mr. Pirzada really belonged.

At six thirty, which was when the national news began, my father raised the volume and adjusted the antennas. Usually I occupied myself with a book, but that night my father insisted that I pay attention. On the screen I saw tanks rolling through dusty streets, and fallen buildings, and forests of unfamiliar trees into which East Pakistani refugees had fled, seeking safety over the Indian border. I saw boats with fan-shaped sails floating on wide coffee-colored rivers, a barricaded university, newspaper offices burnt to the ground. I turned to look at Mr. Pirzada; the images flashed in miniature across his eyes. As he watched he had an immovable expression on his face, composed but alert, as if someone were giving him directions to an unknown destination.

During the commericals my mother went to the kitchen to get more rice, and my father and Mr. Pirzada deplored the policies of a general named Yahyah Khan. They discussed intrigues I did not know, a catastrophe I could not comprehend. "See, children your age, what they do to survive," my father said as he served me another piece of fish. But I could no longer eat. I could only steal glances at Mr. Pirzada, sitting beside me in his olive green jacket, calmly creating a well in his rice to make room for a second helping of lentils. He was not my notion of a man burdened by such grave concerns. I wondered if the reason he was always so smartly dressed was in preparation to endure with dignity whatever news assailed him, perhaps even to attend a funeral at a moment's notice. I wondered, too, what would happen if suddenly his seven daughters were to appear on television, smiling and waving and blowing kisses to Mr. Pirzada from a balcony. I imagined how relieved he would be. But this never happened.

That night when I placed the plastic egg filled with cinnamon hearts in the box beside my bed, I did not feel the ceremonious satisfaction I normally did. I tried not to think about Mr. Pirzada, in his lime-scented overcoat, connected to the unruly, sweltering world we had viewed a few hours ago in our bright, carpeted living room. And yet for several moments that was all I could think about. My stomach tightened as I worried whether his wife and seven daughters were now members of the drifting, clamoring crowd that had flashed at intervals on the screen. In an effort to banish the image I looked around my room, at the yellow canopied bed with matching flounced curtains, at framed class pictures mounted on white and violet papered walls, at the penciled inscriptions by the closet door where my father recorded my height on each of my birthdays. But the more I tried to distract myself, the more I began to convince myself that Mr. Pirzada's family was in all likelihood dead. Eventually I took a square of white chocolate out of the box, and unwrapped it, and then I did something I had never done before. I put the chocolate in my mouth, letting it soften until the last possible moment, and then as I chewed it slowly, I prayed that Mr. Pirzada's family was safe and sound. I had never prayed for anything before, had never been taught or told to, but I decided, given the circumstances, that it was something I should do. That night when I went to the bathroom I only pretended to brush my teeth, for I feared that I would somehow rinse the prayer out as well. I wet the brush and rearranged the tube of paste to prevent my parents from asking any questions, and fell asleep with sugar on my tongue.

No one at school talked about the war followed so faithfully in my living room. We continued to study the American Revolution, and learned about the injustices of taxation without representation, and memorized passages from the Declaration of Independence. During recess the boys would divide in two groups, chasing each other wildly around the swings and seesaws, Redcoats against the colonies. In the classroom our teacher, Mrs. Kenyon, pointed frequently to a map that emerged like a movie screen from the top of the chalkboard, charting the route of the *Mayflower,* or showing us the location of the Liberty Bell. Each week two members of the class gave a report on a particular aspect of the Revolution, and so one day I was sent to the school library with my friend Dora to learn about the surrender at Yorktown. Mrs. Kenyon handed us a slip of paper with the names of three books to look up in the card catalog. We found them right away, and sat down at a low round table to read and take notes. But I could not concentrate. I returned to the blond-wood shelves, to a section I had noticed labeled "Asia." I saw books about China, India, Indonesia, Korea. Eventually I found a book titled *Pakistan: A Land and Its People.* I sat on a footstool and opened the book. The laminated jacket crackled in my grip. I began turning the pages, filled with photos of rivers and rice fields and men in military uniforms. There was a chapter about Dacca, and I began to read about its rainfall, and its jute production. I was studying a population chart when Dora appeared in the aisle.

"What are you doing back here? Mrs. Kenyon's in the library. She came to check up on us."

I slammed the book shut, too loudly. Mrs. Kenyon emerged, the aroma of her perfume filling up the tiny aisle, and lifted the book by the tip of its spine as if it were a hair clinging to my sweater. She glanced at the cover, then at me.

"Is this book a part of your report, Lilia?"

"No, Mrs. Kenyon."

"Then I see no reason to consult it," she said, replacing it in the slim gap on the shelf. "Do you?"

As weeks passed it grew more and more rare to see any footage from Dacca on the news. The report came after the first set of commercials, sometimes the second. The press had been censored, removed, restricted, rerouted. Some days, many days, only a death toll was announced, prefaced by a reiteration of the general situation. More poets were executed, more villages set ablaze. In spite of it all, night after night, my parents and Mr. Pirzada enjoyed long, leisurely meals. After the television was shut off, and the dishes washed and dried, they joked, and told stories, and dipped biscuits in their tea. When they tired of discussing political matters they discussed, instead, the progress of Mr. Pirzada's book about the deciduous trees of New England, and my father's nomination for tenure, and the peculiar eating habits of my mother's American coworkers at the bank. Eventually I was sent upstairs to do my homework, but through the carpet I heard them as they drank more tea, and listened to cassettes of Kishore Kumar, and played Scrabble on the coffee table, laughing and arguing long into the night about the spellings of English words. I wanted to join them, wanted, above all, to console Mr. Pirzada somehow. But apart from eating a piece of candy for the sake of his family and praying for their safety, there was nothing I could do. They played Scrabble until the eleven o'clock news, and then, sometime around midnight, Mr. Pirzada walked back to his dormitory. For this reason I never saw him leave, but each night as I drifted off to sleep I would hear them, anticipating the birth of a nation on the other side of the world.

One day in October Mr. Pirzada asked upon arrival, "What are these large orange vegetables on people's doorsteps? A type of squash?"

"Pumpkins," my mother replied. "Lilia, remind me to pick one up at the supermarket."

"And the purpose? It indicates what?"

"You make a jack-o'-lantern," I said, grinning ferociously. "Like this. To scare people away."

"I see," Mr. Pirzada said, grinning back. "Very useful."

The next day my mother bought a ten-pound pumpkin, fat and round, and placed it on the dining table. Before supper, while my father and Mr. Pirzada were watching the local news, she told me to decorate it with markers, but I wanted to carve it properly like others I had noticed in the neighborhood.

"Yes, let's carve it," Mr. Pirzada agreed, and rose from the sofa. "Hang the news tonight." Asking no questions, he walked into the kitchen, opened a drawer, and returned, bearing a long serrated knife. He glanced at me for approval. "Shall I?"

I nodded. For the first time we all gathered around the dining table, my mother, my father, Mr. Pirzada, and I. While the television aired unattended we covered the tabletop with newspapers. Mr. Pirzada draped his jacket over the chair behind him, removed a pair of opal cuff links, and rolled up the starched sleeves of his shirt.

"First go around the top, like this," I instructed, demonstrating with my index finger.

He made an initial incision and drew the knife around. When he had come full circle he lifted the cap by the stem; it loosened effortlessly, and Mr. Pirzada leaned over the pumpkin for a moment to inspect and inhale its contents. My mother gave him a long metal spoon with which he gutted the interior until the last bits of string and seeds were gone. My father, meanwhile, separated the seeds from the pulp and set them out to dry on a cookie sheet, so that we could roast them later on. I drew two triangles against the ridged surface for the eyes, which Mr. Pirzada dutifully carved, and crescents for eyebrows, and another triangle for the nose. The mouth was all that remained, and the teeth posed a challenge. I hesitated.

"Smile or frown?" I asked.

"You choose," Mr. Pirzada said.

As a compromise I drew a kind of grimace, straight across, neither mournful nor friendly. Mr. Pirzada began carving, without the least bit of intimidation, as if he had been carving jack-o'-lanterns his whole life. He had nearly finished when the national news began. The reporter mentioned Dacca, and we all turned to listen: An Indian official announced that unless the world helped to relieve the burden of East Pakistani refugees, India would have to go to war against Pakistan. The reporter's face dripped with sweat as he relayed the information. He did not wear a tie or a jacket, dressed instead as if he himself were about to take part in the battle. He shielded his scorched face as he hollered things to the cameraman. The knife slipped from Mr. Pirzada's hand and made a gash dipping toward the base of the pumpkin.

"Please forgive me." He raised a hand to one side of his face, as if someone had slapped him there. "I am—it is terrible. I will buy another. We will try again."

"Not at all, not at all," my father said. He took the knife from Mr. Pirzada, and carved around the gash, evening it out, dispensing altogether with the teeth I had drawn. What resulted was a disproportionately large hole the size of a lemon, so that our jack-o'-lantern wore an expression of placid astonishment, the eyebrows no longer fierce, floating in frozen surprise above a vacant, geometric gaze.

For Halloween I was a witch. Dora, my trick-or-treating partner, was a witch too. We wore black capes fashioned from dyed pillowcases and conical hats with wide cardboard brims. We shaded our faces green with a broken eye shadow that belonged to Dora's mother, and my mother gave us two burlap sacks that had once contained basmati rice, for collecting candy. That year our parents decided that we were old enough to roam the neighborhood unattended. Our plan was to walk from my house to Dora's, from where I was to call to say I had arrived safely, and then Dora's mother would drive me home. My father equipped us with flashlights, and I had to wear my watch and synchronize it with his. We were to return no later than nine o'clock.

When Mr. Pirzada arrived that evening he presented me with a box of chocolate-covered mints.

"In here," I told him, and opened up the burlap sack. "Trick or treat!"

"I understand that you don't really need my contribution this evening," he said, depositing the box. He gazed at my green face, and the hat secured by a string under my chin. Gingerly he lifted the hem of the cape, under which I was wearing a sweater and a zipped fleece jacket. "Will you be warm enough?"

I nodded, causing the hat to tip to one side.

He set it right. "Perhaps it is best to stand still."

The bottom of our staircase was lined with baskets of miniature candy, and when Mr. Pirzada removed his shoes he did not place them there as he normally did, but inside the closet instead. He began to unbutton his coat, and I waited to take it from him, but Dora called me from the bathroom to say that she needed my help drawing a mole on her chin. When we were finally ready my mother took a picture of us in front of the fireplace, and then I opened the front door to leave. Mr. Pirzada and my father, who had not gone into the living room yet, hovered in the foyer. Outside it was already dark. The air smelled of wet leaves, and our carved jack-o'-lantern flickered impressively against the shrubbery by the door. In the distance came the sounds of scampering feet, and the howls of the older boys who wore no costume at all other than a rubber mask, and the rustling apparel of the youngest children, some so young that they were carried from door to door in the arms of their parents.

"Don't go into any of the houses you don't know," my father warned.

Mr. Pirzada knit his brows together. "Is there any danger?"

"No, no," my mother assured him. "All the children will be out. It's a tradition."

"Perhaps I should accompany them?" Mr. Pirzada suggested. He looked suddenly tired and small, standing there in his splayed, stockinged feet, and his eyes contained a panic I had never seen before. In spite of the cold I began to sweat inside my pillowcase.

"Really, Mr. Pirzada," my mother said, "Lilia will be perfectly safe with her friend."

"But if it rains? If they lose their way?"

"Don't worry," I said. It was the first time I had uttered those words to Mr. Pirzada, two simple words I had tried but failed to tell him for weeks, had said only in my prayers. It shamed me now that I had said them for my own sake.

He placed one of his stocky fingers on my cheek, then pressed it to the back of his own hand, leaving a faint green smear. "If the lady insists," he conceded, and offered a small bow.

We left, stumbling slightly in our black pointy thrift-store shoes, and when we turned at the end of the driveway to wave good-bye, Mr. Pirzada was standing in the frame of the doorway, a short figure between my parents, waving back.

"Why did that man want to come with us?" Dora asked.

"His daughters are missing." As soon as I said it, I wished I had not. I felt that my saying it made it true, that Mr. Pirzada's daughters really were missing, and that he would never see them again.

"You mean they were kidnapped?" Dora continued. "From a park or something?"

"I didn't mean they were missing. I meant, he misses them. They live in a different country, and he hasn't seen them in a while, that's all."

We went from house to house, walking along pathways and pressing doorbells. Some people had switched off all their lights for effect, or strung rubber bats in their windows. At the McIntyres' a coffin was placed in front of the door, and Mr. McIntyre rose from it in silence, his face covered with chalk, and deposited a fistful of candy corns into our sacks. Several people told me that they had never seen an Indian witch before. Others performed the transaction without comment. As we paved our way with the parallel beams of our flashlights we saw eggs cracked in the middle of the road, and cars covered with shaving cream, and toilet paper garlanding the branches of trees. By the time we reached Dora's house our hands were chapped from carrying our bulging burlap bags, and our feet were sore and swollen. Her mother gave us bandages for our blisters and served us warm cider and caramel popcorn. She reminded me to call my parents to tell them I had arrived safely, and when I did I could hear the television in the background. My mother did not seem particularly relieved to hear from me. When I replaced the phone on the receiver it occurred to me that the television wasn't on at Dora's house at all. Her father was lying on the couch, reading a magazine, with a glass of wine on the coffee table, and there was saxophone music playing on the stereo.

After Dora and I had sorted through our plunder, and counted and sampled and traded until we were satisfied, her mother drove me back to my house. I thanked her for the ride, and she waited in the driveway until I made it to the door. In the glare of her headlights I saw that our pumpkin had been shattered, its thick shell strewn in chunks across the grass. I felt the sting of tears in my eyes, and a sudden pain in my throat, as if it had been stuffed with the sharp tiny pebbles that crunched with each step under my aching feet. I opened the door, expecting the three of them to be standing in the foyer, waiting to receive me, and to grieve for our ruined pumpkin, but there was no one. In the living room Mr. Pirzada, my father, and mother were sitting side by side on the sofa. The television was turned off, and Mr. Pirzada had his head in his hands.

What they heard that evening, and for many evenings after that, was that India and Pakistan were drawing closer and closer to

war. Troops from both sides lined the border, and Dacca was insist-
ing on nothing short of independence. The war was to be waged
on East Pakistani soil. The United States was siding with West
Pakistan, the Soviet Union with India and what was soon to be
Bangladesh. War was declared officially on December 4, and
twelve days later, the Pakistani army, weakened by having to fight
three thousand miles from their source of supplies, surrendered in
Dacca. All of these facts I know only now, for they are available to
me in any history book, in any library. But then it remained, for
the most part, a remote mystery with haphazard clues. What I
remember during those twelve days of the war was that my father
no longer asked me to watch the news with them, and that Mr.
Pirzada stopped bringing me candy, and that my mother refused
to serve anything other than boiled eggs with rice for dinner. I
remember some nights helping my mother spread a sheet and
blankets on the couch so that Mr. Pirzada could sleep there, and
high-pitched voices hollering in the middle of the night when my
parents called our relatives in Calcutta to learn more details about
the situation. Most of all I remember the three of them operating
during that time as if they were a single person, sharing a single
meal, a single body, a single silence, and a single fear.

In January, Mr. Pirzada flew back to his three-story home in
Dacca, to discover what was left of it. We did not see much of him
in those final weeks of the year; he was busy finishing his manuscript, and we went to Philadelphia to spend Christmas with
friends of my parents. Just as I have no memory of his first visit, I
have no memory of his last. My father drove him to the airport one
afternoon while I was at school. For a long time we did not hear
from him. Our evenings went on as usual, with dinners in front of
the news. The only difference was that Mr. Pirzada and his extra
watch were not there to accompany us. According to reports Dacca
was repairing itself slowly, with a newly formed parliamentary government. The new leader, Sheikh Mujib Rahman, recently re-

leased from prison, asked countries for building materials to replace more than one million houses that had been destroyed in the war. Countless refugees returned from India, greeted, we learned, by unemployment and the threat of famine. Every now and then I studied the map above my father's desk and pictured Mr. Pirzada on that small patch of yellow, perspiring heavily, I imagined, in one of his suits, searching for his family. Of course, the map was outdated by then.

Finally, several months later, we received a card from Mr. Pirzada commemorating the Muslim New Year, along with a short letter. He was reunited, he wrote, with his wife and children. All were well, having survived the events of the past year at an estate belonging to his wife's grandparents in the mountains of Shillong. His seven daughters were a bit taller, he wrote, but otherwise they were the same, and he still could not keep their names in order. At the end of the letter he thanked us for our hospitality, adding that although he now understood the meaning of the words "thank you" they still were not adequate to express his gratitude. To celebrate the good news my mother prepared a special dinner that evening, and when we sat down to eat at the coffee table we toasted our water glasses, but I did not feel like celebrating. Though I had not seen him for months, it was only then that I felt Mr. Pirzada's absence. It was only then, raising my water glass in his name, that I knew what it meant to miss someone who was so many miles and hours away, just as he had missed his wife and daughters for so many months. He had no reason to return to us, and my parents predicted, correctly, that we would never see him again. Since January, each night before bed, I had continued to eat, for the sake of Mr. Pirzada's family, a piece of candy I had saved from Halloween. That night there was no need to. Eventually, I threw them away.

DOWN THE ROAD

STEPHEN DIXON

Just as it's starting to get dark, the stick falls out of her hand, and she drops. "I told you to be more careful," I say. "There are stones all over the road, cracks every third step. You all right?" She doesn't answer. I shake her, try to wake her. She seems dead. I put my head close to her nose, hand on her wrist and then her temple. I hold my breath while I press my ear to her lips, put a finger in my ear and the other ear to her chest, but I still can't hear her breathe or hear or feel any pulse or heartbeat.

"Then I guess I'll have to try to make it alone," I say. Louder: "Alone. I'm going. Leah, I said I'm going, I have to, I can't carry you and try to make it also. You're too heavy. Not 'too heavy,' meaning overweight. Just that I've been weakened by this trip too and can barely make it on my own. We've both been weakened. We've had little food these last few days, not much to drink. Both of us have walked three times the amount someone our age and particularly in our physical condition would normally be able to walk in the last three days. Monday . . . Thursday. Four days. This is our fourth day on the road. We're weak in just about every way, that's all. You can't carry me, and I can't carry you. I might be able to help you up, but that's about all I can do for you. All right, I'll not only help you up but help you walk as long as I'm able to. But I can't carry you, remember that. I just can't."

She's on her back. I lift her up so she's in a sitting position and keep her up. Her eyes are closed. She still doesn't seem to be breathing. "Leah, you alive or not? Because we can't stay here. Night's just fallen. It's what I'd call semidark. It's dusk, that's the word, but a dark dusk, almost completely dark so almost not dusk. It's already about five degrees colder than it was a half hour ago. We have to find shelter in the next hour, or we'll freeze to death. We certainly won't last the night. Or if we do, we'll be so weak by morning that neither of us will be able to walk a single step or at least go very far, even on our knees. So try to stand up. All right, I'll help you all the way up and help you walk, if that's what you think it'll take to get you to walk, but also because I said I would. But I won't carry you—we agreed on that."

I pull her up by her wrists. I say, "Walk. Walk with me. Or first try to walk on your own. Let's just see if you can." I let her go. She starts to fall. I catch her and hold her up. I put my arm around her waist, hold one of her hands, and start to walk. I have to drag her along, but we are now walking. Or moving. Slowly. Moving step by step, but my steps. Five steps already, six. It's dark. Few stars out. I don't know where there'll be shelter ahead. There wasn't any shelter the last mile or two. I don't know this area. I might have been over it years ago in a car, but I forget. "There seem to be fewer and fewer trees," I say to her, "and more and more rocks. But no tree or rock with any shelter underneath and no rock with a space for even one of us to crawl into. What do you make of it? Well, it's the only way we could come. They say we couldn't go the other way—or rather shouldn't. That the other way would even be worse for us. 'Worse' meaning less chance to get food, fewer places to rest and find shelter for the night or from the rain.

That it'd be colder, rainier, snowier. How it could be rainier than it's been or snowier or colder, I don't know. Of course I know. It's not raining or snowing now, though the ground's so soaked we could never be able to rest on it for the next couple of days or so or rest without getting wet and sick or just wet, and it could always be colder. If it's thirty degrees now, it could be twenty degrees in an hour and ten degrees and then zero degrees later on and so forth. I'm saying it could always get colder. Maybe fifty degrees below, sixty, seventy degrees below is the limit, or has been the limit as far as I know, but only for the coldest regions on earth, which this area isn't one. And snowier. It could snow for days. Could have snowed a couple of inches an hour for days. It didn't. It just snowed, a moderate snow. Five inches one day, six? Rained a lot, though. I'd say two or three inches a day for the last three days. That's a lot of rain. Maybe a record of rain in that time period for this area. How did we stand it? We just said, 'It isn't raining.' Or 'The rain can't hurt us—our skins are unalterably waterproof.' Or 'You say that's rain? That's not rain. Those are sun rays coming down on us that only look like rain. So it's sunny, and we should get out of the sun, or we'll get a bad burn.' Foolish, right, but it worked, didn't it? And now the rain's stopped. But it is getting colder. So we should do the same thing with the cold that we did with the rain. Call the cold 'warmth.' Say, 'My, but it's getting warm. Very comfortable. What a welcome change.' Then when it gets much colder, say, 'It's getting too warm. I'd call it hot. We should get out of the heat. It's beginning to stifle us. It's at least stifled me. We should remove some of our clothes, in fact.' Without doing it, of course. In other words, work the reverse. That's a good self-preserving philosophy for now. Or self-surviving, self-sustaining, but you know what I mean. How you doing, by the way?"

I've been dragging her along for the last fifty feet. Her eyes have stayed shut. "Just sleep, Leah. Continue to sleep. It's all right. You're just sleepwalking. Sleepwalking is as good as regular awake-walking as long as you're going at the same pace with the person you're walking with and using most to all your own energy, as you would when you walk while you're awake. In ways it might be better than awake-walking, since you're also probably getting some rest. And you need the rest. I do too, but one of us has to stay awake. For suppose we strayed off the road while both of us were sleepwalking and, instead of going in the right direction, we went back where we came from? Who wants that? I don't. I'm sure you don't. So sleep. You're lucky. But when you wake up, mind if I fall asleep and sleepwalk with you but with you awake and leading the way? Because I can certainly use the sleep. I'm very tired, sleepy, and weak."

We walk another thirty or so feet. It starts to rain. I set her down on the soaked ground right off the road. I sit beside her, cover her with my body. I lie on top of her. I say, "Let's just go to sleep. I know it's not that late, but there's something about country air that makes me sleepier much earlier than I get in the city. Is it the same way with you? And it's a nice house. Good thing we found shelter in time. I don't much like the furniture—the style, I mean, for the furniture itself seems comfortable enough and clean. And the room's warm, no leaks in the roof where we'd have to run around looking for pots and pans, and enough food here to keep us for a week. Also, the bed's soft, sheets seem fresh and no more than a few days old, covers seem to be filled with real down. Let's even try having that baby we said we'd try to have if things got better for us, and then we'll go to sleep for the night. The weather outlook is very good. Clearing tonight, sunny and warm tomorrow, and the extended forecast calls for continued fair skies and low humidity through the weekend. We can even plant some flowers outside tomorrow and maybe occupy this house free for the next year. I doubt the owners or renters or whoever they are will come back for it that soon. And it's a decent area, neighborhood seems pleasant and safe, neighbors seem like hardworking honest people, and I hear the shopping's good, and a car's been left outside with a tankful of gas in it and the keys on top of the dashboard. And lots of other things we've been dreaming of having the last few days. And here they all are, suddenly available to us. Good thing I brought along our credit cards, or rather, that you reminded me to bring them along. So, like to start now? Having a baby I mean. No matter how tired and sleepy I said I was, I always have energy for that. There, what heaven. The good things in life are free. Want to wash up now? You'd rather just go to sleep? Fine with me. I love cuddling up in bed with you. You're so soft, you smell so nice, I love you more than I've loved any one thing. Any one person I mean. Oh, maybe as much as I loved my parents when I was a boy. Whatever, I love you more than I've loved any one person since I was a teen. So good night, all right? One last kiss? Now have sweet dreams."

I get up, walk another hundred feet in the direction we were going, look back, see her lying by the road, run back, lie beside her, put my arms around her, say, "Dearest, you don't know how good it is to be back. Been away I can't say how long, but that's the last time I'll ever do that. I've seen lots of things, met lots of people, but found I can't live without you, can't leave without you, can't live or leave or even love without you, or at least for very long, no matter how many interesting places I go to and people I meet. And since you don't want to leave here, nothing I can do but stay here with you and call this home. It's not a bad place, as I said. Better than most places, in fact, when you consider all it offers in just natural surroundings and comforts and that by my staying here the kids will have both parents to dote on them till they're grown-up. So I'm staying unless you say it's a better idea that I leave. You don't want to answer that right now—that's certainly your right. You want to hold off your decision about my decision to stay here, do so for as long as you like. But believe me, staying here with you and our kids in this home is really the only thing I want to do. Okay, no more yap. Just give me a little hug, because I need one." And I squeeze her into me, press my cheek to hers, put the side of my lips on the side of hers, and shut my eyes. "Sleep. Boy, do I need to, too. But I said enough already for one night. Sleep tight."

ALL AMERICAN

DIANE WILLIAMS

The woman, who is me—why pretend otherwise?—wants to love a man she cannot have. She thinks that is what she should do. She should love a man like that. He is inappropriate for some reason. He is married.

When she thinks of the man, she thinks *force,* and then whoever has the man already is her enemy—which is the man's wife.

The woman makes sure the man falls in love with her. She has fatal charm. She can force herself to have it. Then she tells the man she cannot love him in return. She says, "You are in the camp with the enemy."

Of course, the woman knew the man was sleeping with the enemy before she ever tried to love him, and the word *enemy* gives joy—the same as I get when the wrong kind of person calls me *darling,* as when my brother says, "Okay," to me, "good-bye, darling," before he hangs up the phone, after we have just made some kind of pact, which is what we should do, because I have to force myself to love the ones I am supposed to love, and then I have to force myself on the ones I am not supposed to love.

I got my first real glimpse of this kind of thing when I was still a girl trying to force myself on my sister. I didn't know what I was doing until it was obvious. We were in the backseat of the family car. The car had just been pulled into the garage. The others got out, but we didn't. I thought I was not done with something. Something was not undone yet—something like that—and I was trying to kiss my sister, and I was trying to hug my sister, and she must have thought it was inappropriate, like what did I think I was a man and she was a woman?

I must have been getting rough, because she was getting hysterical. I remember I was surprised. I remember knowing then that I was applying force and was getting away with it.

X NUMBER OF POSSIBILITIES

JOANNA SCOTT

Theodore von Grift lives a counterfeit life neither out of habit nor choice but out of self-defense. His tastes have been carefully acquired. Soft-boiled eggs, steak tartare, the fragrance of peonies, lawn tennis: the list has nothing genuine about it, since appreciation for Theodore von Grift is only an act. He abandoned his authentic self so long ago that he wouldn't recognize him if they met on a street in downtown Baltimore. That he lives at number fifty-five Penrose Street in Baltimore, Maryland, is as unnatural as any other aspect of his life. His position as a bank officer, his wife and two children, his four-bedroom house—all contribute to the elaborate composition. He is not who he is and doesn't try to resolve the paradox. Instead, he fills in the role he originated, each day adds new details, and by 1927 has grown so intricate, so complex, that the many people who early on recognized his personality as a mask have dwindled to one.

Theodore is being revealed, investigated, stripped, and examined by a mere child. He doesn't even know the boy's name, nor have they ever spoken. But every morning the boy is sitting on the porch steps of number sixty-three when Theodore walks by on his way to the trolley stop on Fulton Avenue. Sixty-three is the most dilapidated house on the block, the shingles sloughing, the shutters hanging crookedly, and ordinarily Theodore would have ignored these neighbors. But there is something about the way the boy looks up from the scab on his knee and stares: a wise, unnerving stare, as though he can see beneath Theodore's clothes. Theodore has spent half his lifetime protecting himself from observation, has perfected impenetrability and is to acquaintances and family what lead is to the X-ray. And now, in his forty-ninth year, he has met his match in an unkempt little boy.

He could easily take a roundabout route and avoid the child. But the challenge is too compelling: he walks by number sixty-three in order to test himself, and though he continues to fail the test, he has not given in to discouragement. If one sheet of lead doesn't shield him from those prying eyes, he will try two; if two don't suffice, he will try platinum. Eventually he will be to the child what he is to everyone else—only surface—and the boy will forget what he has seen. Young children have short, selective memories. There will be enough distractions in his life, and Theodore von Grift will fade with most of the boy's past, just as he has faded from himself.

"I should remember," Wilhelm Conrad Röntgen, inventor of the X-ray, once wrote to a friend, "where there is much light there is also much shadow." Theodore's adult life remains clear in his memory, but the years of his childhood are hidden in shadow. It is not *as if* he died on or around his eighteenth birthday. The figurative expression is nearly literal in his case, a case notable enough to be written up in *Scientific American,* earning him invitations to lecture at two German universities. But because the fame of the case was inspired by the new Röntgen rays rather than by his remarkable recovery, and, more important, because he had to reconstruct his personality from scratch, he had declined the invitations, booked a passage to the United States, and under a pseudonym (now his permanent name, thirty-one years later) began life over again.

He remembers the first days of adulthood only through a few stark impressions: the face of an old woman, her crooked teeth which looked as soft as hot tallow. A man, presumably his doctor, breathing stale tobacco as he peered into his ear. And nuns, dozens of nuns bustling about the room—like gray rats, Theodore had thought as he sleepily watched them from his bed.

He had been living in Munich; where he'd come from he didn't know. The doctor could tell him only this: that he'd been found lying in a park, his hair matted with blood, his fingers still tangled around the trigger of a pistol. No identification was found. He'd been transported to a nearby hospital. A surgeon neatly sutured the wound after deciding that the bullet was too deeply embedded to be removed, and Theodore remained an invalid at the hospital for five months.

The hospital nuns called him Anton because he often murmured the name in his sleep. They grew fond of him, intrigued, perhaps, by his amnesia, and when he was strong enough to leave, they gave him a wallet full of money to maintain him until he could find work. They offered to love him like a son if he couldn't locate his own parents, told him to consider the hospital his permanent home. But life on the busy city streets absorbed him as soon as he walked out into daylight, and he left the hospital behind forever.

While he had been convalescing, the police had made inquiries and advertised in newspapers for any information concerning the young man known as Anton, age approximately eighteen. But no one had come forward. He must have been a stranger in Munich, without friends or relatives in the city. And Theodore, then Anton, found himself increasingly grateful for the mystery of his past. Whatever he'd been in his previous life, he'd been driven to suicide. So it was best to forget that life, along with the nuns, the hospital, the bullet in his head. The German language and an impressive mathematical ability were the only souvenirs from his youth. At the age of eighteen (approximately), he had thirty crowns to his name, whatever name he chose. Even as he'd boarded a train for Hamburg the day he was released from the hospital, he gave himself a new name, Hermann, as though this were enough to dismiss the former self entirely, the self hidden just beyond the boundary of his awareness.

Can the child sitting on the steps of number sixty-three Penrose Street in Baltimore see what Theodore can't see? The secrets of his past, which are to Theodore no more than countless possibilities? He is like a pocket watch and the boy does what most children will do if given the chance. He smashes the watch so he can investigate its parts. Smashes Theodore every time he walks by. Twirls his dirty little forefinger in his cowlick and stares at Theodore with smug innocence, which makes the man, by contrast, guilty.

What have I done? Theodore has been wondering since the boy first stationed himself on the steps last August. His first memory is of the old woman's teeth. Before that, his recollections are all speculative. He imagines himself sprawled on the ground, spread-eagle, blood crusted on his brow. Is this what the little boy sees? Or worse? And what came before? What crime did Theodore commit that drove him to the crime of suicide?

Try this, he tells himself repeatedly. *Make your mind blank. White.* Beyond the oranges and reds of Baltimore row houses he sees white walls, four windowless walls as white as paper. Anton, Hermann, Theodore. Anton's eyes were covered with white bandages. Hermann was surrounded by whitewashed walls. Theodore's mind is nearly blank, dominated by these memories of blankness, and what he wants is identical to what he wanted: to escape. His was a wild animal's rage. As Hermann he had leaped at a man, gripped his throat, throttled him, all the while blinded by the intensity of white. *This is what I will do to you, boy,* Theodore von Grift thinks, flexing his fingers as he walks on. *Don't touch me. They called me mad once. Come too close and you won't live to tell what happened.*

It is the same sequence every morning, and by the time Theodore has reached State Street, his face shines with perspiration, his chest heaves, the design of his life has begun to unravel.

In truth, he was never mad, or at least no more mad than a man strung on the rack. He had a bullet in his head, and Theodore—rather, Hermann—believed that if the bullet were removed he would regain control over himself. But he was living in Hamburg by then, and he couldn't recall the name of the hospital where he'd been treated. He could only point to the side of his head and insist repeatedly, "Here, I shot myself here." The Hamburg doctors, seeing no sign of a scar, labeled him insane.

The fault was his. Without references or personal history— before he'd invented a story for himself—he'd been unable to find a job, so in the beginning he'd done nothing but wander the streets, spending his money on coffee, bread, and rent. Soon the headaches began, and after three months, when the pain grew too intense to bear, he'd gone to a doctor and asked him to remove the bullet. The doctor asked for a detailed account, so Theodore explained how at the age of eighteen he had tried to kill himself.

It was in the doctor's office where Theodore first lost control. In the middle of his visit, without provocation, he suddenly seized the doctor by his neck, nearly strangling him to death. He attacked the policemen who came to carry him off to jail. He fought with the attendants transporting him to the asylum. He even sprang at a nurse, a young woman who, with astonishing strength, subdued him with a punch that split his lower lip. Not until the director informed him that he'd been committed to the Hamburg asylum did he realize what he'd done.

I have a bullet embedded in my head. I am not mad; the bullet makes me crazy, blinds me, all I can see is the white light of my pain. I want to stop the pain, nothing else. Don't blame me—blame the bullet in my head. You think these are a lunatic's ravings. Cut me open, see for yourself. I don't remember who I was, how I survived. I know I shot myself. I can't explain why there is no scar. The nuns, ask the nuns. I don't remember where they were, but they must be somewhere still. Let me out and I'll find them. They'll assure you that I'm speaking the truth. My name is Hermann Glasser. I give you my permission to operate. I implore you. Go ahead—for curiosity's sake, then, if for no other reason. I want to live a normal life, work hard all week and on Sundays shoot woodcocks from the window of a little bird-branch hut. But I cannot acquire a hunting license as long as I am legally insane. Help me.

For ten years he had raged, begged, wept, but the doctors remained unmoved. In their informed opinion everything he said was governed by the skewed logic of his main delusion: the patient named Hermann believed he had a bullet in his head. After extensive examination the doctors proclaimed him incurable, and he became just another inmate of the asylum, another child-man to hide from his easily disgusted fellow Germans.

Against all odds he had survived, emerged from the asylum at the age of twenty-nine—approximately—not only sane but famous enough to share a page in *Scientific American* with an English swallow. The swallow's feat was to fly from London to its nest on a Shropshire farm at a speed of two miles per minute. Theodore's feat was to be among the first to demonstrate the usefulness of the recently discovered X-ray.

"A Hamburg young man has just had his sanity proved by the Röntgen rays. He declared ten years ago that he had a bullet in his head which he had fired into it in trying to commit suicide. He complained of pain, and as he attacked his keepers and the doctors could find no trace of the wound, was locked up as a dangerous lunatic. The Röntgen rays have now shown the exact place of the bullet." *Scientific American,* November 7, 1896.

This is the only true story of his life. Thirty-one years later Theodore von Grift, the former phenomenon, is an average man weighing 140 pounds and composed of enough water to fill a ten-gallon barrel, enough fat for seven cakes of soap, enough carbon for nine thousand lead pencils, enough phosphorus to make twenty-two hundred match heads, sufficient magnesium for one dose of salts, enough iron to make one medium-sized nail, sufficient lime to whitewash a chicken coop, and enough sulfur to rid one dog of fleas. An average man who is an average combination of nutrients and poisons. What more is there to know?

Ask the boy.

But Theodore has seen into his own head; he doesn't want to see any more. The bullet was removed over three decades ago, and the only pain he felt for years, before the boy at number sixty-three began to haunt him, was the occasional late-afternoon stab of hunger. Typical pain. Eight hours a day he has devoted himself to balancing the debit and credit columns. He eats lunch at Estes Grill with three or four colleagues, always ordering the same chowder and the same beer. He leaves work at six, buys the evening paper, and walks to the trolley station alone.

The porch steps of number sixty-three are empty in the evening, the house as unconcerned as a drunk sleeping on the street. His own home, number fifty-five, is always tidy on the outside and bustling inside, his ten-year-old son flying paper airplanes in the living room, his eight-year-old daughter screaming at her mother because she doesn't like onions, her mother knows she doesn't like onions yet still she puts chopped onions in the meat loaf.

You shouldn't speak to your mother that way.

Always the same routine, which is just how Theodore von Grift wants it, with occasional delicacies to relieve the tedium and distinguish him from the lower classes. Soft-boiled eggs, steak tartare . . . He is a naturalized American now. His wife knows the few facts of her husband's life and is content with the mystery of his youth, perhaps even intrigued by it, like the nuns had been.

Easily satisfied, she fills her days with household chores and as a hobby raises African violets. Nothing makes her prouder than a blue ribbon in the annual garden competition. His son wants to be a fighter pilot; his daughter wants to grow her hair to her ankles.

What more is there to know? Or tell? Theodore's story begins and ends in a single paragraph in the November 7, 1896, issue of *Scientific American.* He has served his purpose and wants to be left alone. And whatever happens, whatever other injuries he sustains, he will never submit to an X-ray again. He hadn't anticipated the consequences or even understood at the time what an X-ray meant. X stood for unknown character. Because of the X-ray— he'd had thirty-two X-rays taken before the doctors had finished with him—the bullet had been located and removed, and he no longer explodes in violent rages. But in recent months, ever since the impertinent boy assumed his place on the front steps of sixty-three Penrose, Theodore has rarely enjoyed a full night's rest. In the early-morning hours he is awakened by the same panic that he feels when he walks past the boy.

The dream recurs, with minor variations: he is herded with a group of people, about two dozen in all, into a large examination room. A doctor directs the group to chairs arranged opposite the long, tubular lens of an X-ray machine. The doctor turns the machine on, aims the lens, and after a few seconds—just long enough for him to reach the exit—hot light washes over the rows of patients.

What unnerves Theodore in the dream is the doctor's hasty retreat. Why must he leave the room when he turns on the machine? Theodore will puzzle over this, his confusion will escalate under the heat of the X-ray, and he will have to grip the seat of his chair in order to keep himself steady. Panic wakes him and keeps him awake for an hour or more, and the light that fills his mind during this time is not the familiar light of pain but of unspeakable fear.

In 1927, Theodore's forty-ninth year, most scientists believe that light is only beneficial: light cures rickets in young children, protects against scurvy, regulates the absorption and metabolism of calcium, prevents pellagra in man and black tongue in animals. Light is necessary to life, and the X-ray, thirty-two years after its discovery, is essential to medical diagnosis. Decades will pass before opinions change and the dangers of light, even life-sustaining sunlight, are identified. So why does Theodore feel that he has been poisoned? Theodore has thirty-two X-rays inside his head. All it takes is a single able interpreter to see what the light exposes: the first eighteen years of his life, eighteen years of secrets.

It is the middle of December, ten days before Christmas, when Theodore finally decides to confront the boy at number sixty-three. He passes a restless night; awakened at 3:00 A.M. by his dream, he lies awake until dawn imagining various retaliations against the boy. His visions disgust and delight him. Since the bullet had been removed, he has steadily gained self-control and rarely even engages in an argument. He knows he could never harm an innocent child. But it is this very innocence that gives the boy his power, Theodore believes. The child sees what the light exposes. Theodore must be reasonable; instead of confronting the boy he will befriend him. He will convince the boy that he, Theodore von Grift, is hiding nothing. Children are gullible. In the name of self-defense Theodore will take advantage of the boy's trusting nature.

After a breakfast of toast—the crust slightly burnt, just the way he likes it—rich black coffee, and a soft-boiled egg in a silver-plated eggcup, he props his hat at a thirty-degree tilt from left to right, winds his pocket watch, and sets off: a thoroughly average man on an average day. His breath frosts in the winter air. He feels both uneasy and capable—his enemy is only a child, after all. But wouldn't it be easier if the child were an adult, Theodore's equal? He's not sure how he will open the conversation, decides too late that he should have brought some candy to use as bait.

The boy is there, sitting on the second step of number sixty-three, pulling at a loose thread hanging from the cuff of his plaid jacket. He turns up his face at the tap of Theodore's footsteps on the sidewalk, and his eyes settle into that offensive stare.

Hello there, Theodore intends to begin. But the conversation needs direction. *Hello there, young man, fine day today.* No, this won't do at all—it is too stiff, too mature. *And how are you this morning?* Too intimate for a child. *Hello there. Tell me, shouldn't someone be looking after you?* Too accusatory. Try this: *Hello there, early riser.*

"Hello there, early riser."

"Hello."

Just then Theodore sees a woman cross behind the front window, and he hurries on, all too aware of the hint of impropriety in his address to the boy. There is more than neighborly cheer in his intentions. But what, exactly, does he intend? He still isn't certain, though he imagines that the boy's mother would not approve. As he rounds the corner, he grinds his fist into his open hand, furious at his stupidity. The child is not alone in the world—he'd forgotten this. If he's going to make a companion of the boy he'll have to contend with the mother. Or befriend the mother first. Now here's an idea: seduce the mother, and the boy will follow. Theodore has no interest in other women, though. His wife fits perfectly into his life, and he knows better than to take a risk that might lead to ruin. All he really needs to do is to convince the mother that he wants to help.

Help me.

To help himself—like a glutton at the dinner table, pleasure-seeker that he is, or so she might conclude and warn her boy away from him. That won't do. It's best to avoid the mother and go straight to the child. He shouldn't have hurried away so quickly this morning. The mother probably hadn't even noticed him.

By the time he arrives at his office building, he has decided to be honest with the boy, the most difficult approach, since his honesty is rooted in an intricate deception. He is not who he is. If the boy sees this, then surely he will see Theodore's true motives.

Stop looking at me. This is what he wants to tell the boy. But how to work his way toward the command? It is a difficult task, far more difficult than subtracting expenditures from income, so Theodore can fulfill his duties at the office even while his mind wanders and he contemplates various approaches to the dangerous little gorgon at number sixty-three.

By this point in the year Sacco and Vanzetti are dead, Trotsky has been expelled from the Communist party, the German economic system has collapsed, and Lindbergh has landed the *Spirit of St. Louis* in Paris. These are the subjects of lunchtime conversation, but today Theodore skips lunch, for he wants to be alone. He walks with shoulders hunched along Patapsco Street wishing he were entirely invisible. Because of the X-rays inside him his bones show through his transparent skin. No one notices except the boy. Theodore feels him watching from every downtown window.

He pauses in front of a toy shop, locks himself in place, and faces the display as though it were the child. *We'll see who falters first.* He is looking at a Christmas scene: wooden elves at work, Santa bulging like a ripe red bud from a chimney, reindeer on the roof, cotton snow on the ground, a wooden locomotive stalled on wooden tracks, its tiny conductor standing inside, gazing at the world. Christmas in Toyland, and Theodore's thoughts grind to a halt, as though he himself has changed from flesh to wood, transformed into a toy himself. He has been struck by an idea, a masterful idea, and he feels safer than he's felt in years. He sees his answer here in the conductor's eyes, painted beads no bigger than pinheads. How long has it been since he understood an image so completely, in its full meaning and potential?

He leaves work half an hour early that evening. Wouldn't it be wonderful if the streets were covered with cotton snow and reindeer were pulling the jalopies? There is no snow in Baltimore. Still, that doesn't mean a man can't celebrate tradition. In front of number sixty-three Theodore tucks the package inside his coat and clumps loudly up the warped porch steps. The woman has opened the door before he's had a chance to knock. Theodore is not afraid. He removes his hat and asks to see her little boy. He notices that she looks too elderly to be the mother of such a young child. Perhaps she is his grandmother. With gray hair in a bun pulled so tight that it seems to stretch the wrinkles of her forehead into broad dents, she squints at Theodore, arms folded, and clears her throat as if to speak. Then she changes her mind and disappears, leaving the door open. Theodore steps into the front hallway. The house is rank with the smells of cooking fat, kerosene, stale wine. In a moment the woman returns, pushing the boy ahead of her. Perhaps she thinks that Theodore is a benefactor; she wouldn't be far from the truth.

Now Theodore may study the boy up close. The child has a plump, round face that looks so young Theodore is almost surprised to see teeth when the boy smiles. He must be five years old, at least, but there is something oddly infantile about him, and with his aged guardian behind, the pair seems laughably anachronistic. She stands with her arms folded, waiting.

"Hello there, early riser."

Theodore and the boy grin at each other like distrustful competitors. For the first time Theodore can meet the assault with impervious good humor. It is time to make his offering. He removes the package from inside his coat and hands it to the boy, who gingerly peels off the wrapping, not taking his eyes from Theodore until he has dropped the paper to the floor.

At first Theodore imagines that it is himself being unwrapped, the boy peeling away the lies of his life with cruel, deliberate slowness. But it turns out just as he had hoped: the boy's attention shifts completely, he forgets about Theodore, forgets all that he knows about the man and gives himself over to childish delight. Already he is rolling the locomotive across the chipped ceramic tiles of the floor, bringing the wooden train to life with his voice: "Chuchu, chug-chug." He's a child again, thoroughly a child, with all his interest devoted to a toy.

In returning the boy to his childhood, Theodore has freed himself. The mother needs an explanation, and then Theodore will dance up the street and enjoy his easily won freedom.

"I wanted . . ." Unexpectedly, he falters. But the woman nods, still unsmiling yet with a reassuring expression. She may not understand the reason for the gift, but she doesn't object.

Before he turns to leave Theodore squats, rests his elbows on his knees, and asks the boy his name. The child is too absorbed in play to notice, so Theodore asks again.

"The man wants to know your name." The woman blocks the train with her foot, and the boy stops just long enough to reply. "Tim," he snaps impatiently. Chuchu. Chug-chug.

Tim. It's a fine name, pristine and to the point. Tim. Theodore looks admiringly at the child bending over his new toy. The straw-haired boy called Tim. Theodore almost wishes the child belonged to him. His hand hovers an inch above the boy's head, palm open. Then he remembers where he is. He hastily bids good-bye with a slight nod, positions his hat, and leaves.

He descends the steps two at a time and hurries along the sidewalk with such high-stepping vigor that he looks like he might break into a skip. By the time he has reached number fifty-five, his pleasure has turned to glee. He's solved his problem, safely enclosed himself. Patting his coat collar to straighten it, he unlatches the picket gate and marches up the walk, thinking of young Tim, savoring the image of the boy bent over his wooden train. What is more satisfying than the sight of a delighted child? Theodore's only regret is that his own emotions are not equally instinctive, that he's had to forsake childish spontaneity along with his past. But he reminds himself that he's forty-nine years old, a fair representative of a type of man, precise, dependable, with distinguished tastes. He's completely filled himself in, and now, with the last threat averted, his mind is at ease. He has never felt more confident.

TWO BROTHERS

BRIAN EVENSON

I. DADDY NORTON

Daddy Norton had fallen and broken his leg. He lay on the floor of the entry hall, the rug bunched under his back, a crubbed jab of bone tearing his trousers at the knee.

"I have seen all in vision," he said, grunting against the pain. "God has foreseen how we must proceed."

He forbad Aurel and Theron to depart the house, for God had called them to witness and testify the miracles He would render in that place. Mama he forbad to summon an ambulance on threat of everlasting fire, for his life was God's affair alone.

He remained untouched on the floor into the evening and well through the night, allowing Mama near dawn to touch his face with a damp cloth and to slit back his trouser leg with a butcher knife. Aurel and Theron slept fitfully, leaning against the front door, touching shoulders. The leg swelled and grew thick with what to Aurel appeared flies but which were, before Daddy Norton's pure spiritual eye, celestial messengers cleansing the wound with God's holy love. Dawn broke and the sun reared suddenly up the side of the house to flood the marbled glass at the peak of the door, creeping across the floor until it struck the broken leg. Daddy Norton beheld unfurled in the light the face of God, and spoke with God of his plight, and felt himself assured.

When the light fell beyond the leg and Daddy Norton lay silent and panting, Theron called for his breakfast. Mama had stood to go after it when Daddy Norton raised his hand and denied him, for *He that trusteth in the Lord is nourished by his word alone.*

"Bring us rather the Holy Word, Mama," Daddy Norton said. "Bring us the true book of God's aweful comfort. We shall feast therein."

Theron declared loudly that he loved God's Holy Word as good as any of God's anointed, but that he wanted some breakfast. Daddy Norton feigned not to hear, neglecting Theron until Mama returned armed with the Holy Word. She spread it before him, beside his face, tilting the book so her husband could read from it prone.

Daddy Norton tightened his eyes.

"Jesus have mercy," he said. "I can't find the pages."

Mama brought the book closer, kept bringing it closer until the pages were pressed against Daddy Norton's face. "Closer!" he called, "Closer!", until his head rolled to one side and he stopped altogether.

"Make me some breakfast, Mama," said Theron.

"You heard what Daddy Norton said," said Mama.

"I'm starved, Mama," said Theron.

She took up the Holy Word and began to read, though without the lilt and fall of voice which Daddy Norton had learned to afflict on the words. Aurel did not feel the nourishment in Mama's voice, sounding as it did as mere words rattling forth without the spirit squiring them. He made to listen but after a few words paid heed only to Daddy Norton's leg. He crawled closer to the leg and looked at it, watching God's holy love seethe.

"Goddamn if I don't make my own breakfast," Theron said, standing.

"Theron," said Mama. "Be Mama's good boy and sit."

Theron ventured a step. Mama heaved her bulk up and stood filling the hallway, the Holy Word raised over her head.

"Damned if I won't brain you," she said.

"Now, Mama," said Theron. "It's your Theron you're talking to. You don't want to hurt your sweet child."

In his dreams Daddy Norton gave utterance to some language devoid of distinction, spilling out a continual and incomprehensible word. He lifted his head, his eyes furzing about the sockets, his tongue thrust hard between his teeth. He tried to pull himself up, the bone thrusting up through the flesh and blood welling forth anew.

"Listen to what he's saying, Theron," said Mama. "It is for you."

Theron looked at Daddy Norton, carefully sat down.

Daddy Norton continued to speak liquids, his mouth flecked with blood. Aurel and Theron stayed against the outer door, silent, watching the light slide across the floor and vanish up over the house. Aurel's mouth was dry enough he couldn't swallow. He kept clearing his throat and trying to swallow for hours, until the sun streamed in the window at the other end of the hall and began its descent.

"Tell Daddy to ask God when lunch is served, Mama," said Theron.

Mama glared at him. She opened the *Holy Word of God as revealed to Daddy Norton, Beloved* and read aloud from the revelations of the suffering of the wicked. As she read, Daddy Norton's voice grew softer, then seemed to stop altogether, though the lips never stopped moving. The light made its way toward them until they could see, through the glass at the end of the hall, the sun flatten onto the sill and collapse.

Mama clutched the Holy Word to her chest and rocked back and forth, her eyes shut. Theron nudged Aurel, then arose and edged past Daddy Norton. He skirted Mama, his boots creaking, without her eyes opening. He strode down the hall and into the kitchen, the door banging shut behind him.

Mama started, opening her eyes.

"Where's Theron?" she asked.

Aurel shook his head.

"That boy is godless," she said. "And you, Aurel, hardly better. A pair of sorry sinners, the goddamn both of you."

She closed her eyes and rocked. In the dim, Aurel examined Daddy Norton. The man's face had gone pale and floated in the coming darkness like a buoy.

Theron returned, carrying half a loaf of bread and a bell jar of whiskey. He edged past Mama and straddle-stepped over Daddy Norton, sitting down against the door.

He ripped the loaf apart, gave a morsel to Aurel. Aurel took it, tore off a mouthful. Mama watched them dully. They did not stop chewing. She closed her eyes, clung tighter to the Holy Word.

"Holy Word won't save you now, Mama," said Theron. "You need bread."

"Shut up," said Aurel. "Leave her alone."

"Won't save Daddy either," said Theron. "Nor angels neither."

"Shut up!" shouted Aurel, hiding his ears in his hands.

Theron unscrewed the lid of the whiskey, took a swallow.

"Drink, Mama?" he asked, holding the jar out.

She would not so much as look at him. He offered the jar to Aurel, who removed his hands from his ears long enough to take it and drink.

"Aurel knows, Mama," said Theron. "He don't like it, but he knows."

Turning away from them, she lay down on the floor. Aurel swallowed his bread and lay down as well. Theron swallowed the last of the whiskey. He leaned back against the door, whispering softly to himself, and watched the others sleep.

* * *

Aurel awoke in the early light. Daddy Norton, he saw, had risen to standing and was leaning against the wall on one leg. He held a butcher knife awkwardly, trying to hack off the other leg just above the joint, crying out with each blow.

He stopped to regard Aurel with burning, red-rimmed eyes, the knife poised, his gaze drifting slowly upward. He shook his head, continued to gash the leg, the dull knife making poor progress, at last turning skew against the bone and clattering from his fingers.

Bending his good leg, he tried to take the blood-smeared knife off the floor. He could not reach it. He cast his gaze about until it stuck on Aurel.

"Aurel," he said, his voice greding high. "Be a good boy and hand Daddy the knife."

Aurel did not move. They looked at one another, Aurel unable to break Daddy Norton's gaze. He began to move slowly across the floor, pulling himself backward until he struck against the door.

"Aurel," Daddy Norton said. "God wants you to pick up the knife."

Aurel swallowed, stayed pressed to the door.

"Shall I damn you, Aurel?" said Daddy Norton.

Daddy Norton extended an arm, pointing a finger at Aurel, his other hand raised open-palmed to support the heavens. He stepped onto the injured leg, listing toward the boy, and fell. His leg folded, turning under him so that he looked like he was attempting to couple with it. He lay on the floor slick-faced with sweat, his eyes misfocused.

"Give me the knife, Aurel," he said.

He began to pull himself around by his fingers, turning his body around until it became wedged between the hall walls. Grunting, he rolled over, twisting the broken leg, and fainted.

Aurel shook Theron. Theron blinked his eyes and mumbled, his voice still thick with liquor. Aurel motioned to Daddy Norton, who came conscious again and stared them through with God's awful hate.

"Stop staring at me," said Theron.

Daddy Norton neither stopped nor moved. There was a smell coming up from him, from his leg too. Theron stood, plugging his nose, and stepped over him, taking up the knife, Daddy Norton's eyes following him almost in reflex. "Stop staring," Theron said again, and pushed the knife in.

Aurel closed his eyes and turned his face to the door. He could hear a dozen times the damp sound of Theron pushing the knife in and pulling it out, then the noise of it stopped.

He opened his eyes to see Theron leaning over Daddy Norton, holding what remained of the eyelids fixed with his fingertips, though when he released them the eyelids crept up to reveal the emptied sockets. Theron twisted the man's neck and rolled the head, directing the face toward the floor. He wiped the knife on Daddy Norton's shirt. Putting the knife into the man's hand, he stood back. The fingers straightened and the knife slipped out. He folded the fingers around the haft, watched them straighten again.

"Theron?" said Aurel.

"Not now, Aurel," said Theron.

"What about Mama?" asked Aurel.

Theron seemed to consider it, then stood and took the knife in his own hands and approached Mama.

"Don't kill her, Theron," said Aurel. "Not Mama."

"Be quiet about it," said Theron. He prodded her head with his boot. "Wake up, Mama," he said.

She did not move. Theron pushed her head again.

"Daddy needs you, Mama," he said.

"I can't bear to have you do it," said Aurel.

"You don't know at all what you can bear," said Theron.

He knelt down beside her. He took the Holy Word out of her hands and dropped it aside. He placed the knife into her hand, carefully, so as not to awaken her. The knife fit, held.

"You can have only one of us, Aurel," said Theron. "Me or Mama?"

"Mama," said Aurel.

"It's me you want," said Theron. "You aren't thinking straight. Let me think for you."

He picked up Mama under the shoulders and dragged her closer to Daddy Norton. He took her wrists and pushed her hands into Daddy Norton's body until they came away stained, the knife gory too.

"Besides," said Theron. "You don't have a choice. Mama gone and died while we were jawing. You got only me."

II. THE FUNERAL

For the funeral, Preacher Thrane collected from his congregation enough for a shirt and a pair of presentable trousers for each boy—though, he said, they would have to secure collar and cravat of their own initiative, did they care for them. This he suggested they find the means to do by taking up the cup and pleading door for door to members of Daddy Norton's former congregation.

"But," said Thrane, "I want you to give by any plans you have of being after the manner of Daddy Norton. You aren't Daddy Nortons. You come worship with me from now on."

"We should carry on Daddy Norton's work," said Aurel.

"Don't listen to Aurel," said Theron. "We've had enough Daddy to last a lifetime."

Thrane patted them both on the shoulders, passed to Theron a brown paper package wrapped in twine.

"There are good hidden boys in you somewhere," Thrane said, touching their hair. "All you got to do is let them out."

They took a tin cup from beneath the sink and left it before the house beneath a hand-lettered placard reading "Comfort for the Bereav'd" with a crude arrow pointing down. They wore their new clothes to loosen them a little before the funeral. They wore the clothes in the hall, sitting on the floor, admiring what they could see. Each time the clock chimed they stood on their toes and looked out the panes along the top of the door, but never saw that anyone approached the cup to give into it.

"Thrane should damn well have the decency to buy us some collars and cravats too," said Theron. "I have a mind not to attend their funeral at all."

Aurel said nothing to this. Theron strode up and down the entry hall. He snatched his hat and coat from their pegs and went out.

Aurel stood tiptoed at the door and watched his brother take up the tin cup, stare into it, set it back down. Theron put the hat on, then the coat, then stood on the porch looking out into the fields. He stood like that for a long while, then came back inside.

"Hell if I'll beg," said Theron. "You?"

"I don't want to go to any funeral," said Aurel.

"What?" asked Theron.

"I don't want to go," Aurel said.

Theron stripped off his hat, his coat, hanging them from their pegs. He sat down on the floor, began to work off his boots.

"I am not going," said Aurel. "Theron, you heard me?"

"I heard you, Aurel," said Theron.

"We could stay here," said Aurel. "Nobody would know the difference."

"Preacher Thrane would," said his brother.

"What do we care about Preacher Thrane?" asked Aurel.

"He gave us these clothes, didn't he?"

"He only wants us coming to his church," said Aurel. "He wants us to be his boys."

"We aren't nobody's boys," said Theron.

"We are Daddy Norton's boys," said Aurel.

"No," said Theron. "Don't say that, Aurel."

He looked briefly into his boots, then set them to one side. He slid back and leaned against the door.

"I am not going," said Aurel, "I mean it."

"Nobody said you were," said Theron. "We'll stay," he said. He stretched his hands toward his brother. "Come sit with me," he said.

Aurel looked at him as if pained, but came and sat down next to him.

Theron made a point of looking up and down his brother's body.

"Fine clothing," said Theron. "But if we aren't going to the funeral, take them off. They reek of Thrane's God."

Aurel began to unbutton the shirt, stopped.

"You aren't taking yours off," he said.

"All in time, brother," said Theron. "You first."

Aurel stood and turned into the corner. He unbuttoned the shirt, stripped it off his shoulders, let it fall. He unbuttoned the trousers and stepped out of them.

"Briefs, too," said Theron.

"The briefs are mine," said Aurel. "No preacher gave them to me."

"You got them from Daddy Norton, didn't you?" said Theron. "You better do all I say."

"I don't want it," said Aurel.

"Doesn't matter," said Theron. He stood and shook loose his own belt. "This is my church now. I take what I want."

They sat against the door, touching each other, staring down the hall. Preacher Thrane came and pounded on the door and cursed them, but they did not open for him, and once they dropped the clothes he had given them out the window he took his leave. Others came by, and knocked, and called out, but the two brothers remained silent and holding each other and did not respond.

Near evening someone knocked, and, when they did not answer, tried to turn the knob, then began to throw a shoulder against the door, weakly.

Theron stood and looked out to see a woman there, rubbing her shoulder. She stood rubbing it for some time then turned the other shoulder to the door and started again.

"By God," whispered Theron, crouching. "She thinks she can break down the door."

"Can she?" said Aurel.

Theron snorted. "Not her," he said.

"I heard that!" the woman yelled from the outside. "Open the door!"

"She knows we're here," whispered Aurel.

"Let's see her do anything about it," Theron said.

"You got to let her in," said Aurel.

"Let her in?" said Theron. "And then what are we to do with her?"

Aurel looked. Theron, he saw, was bare of body, his sides scarred where Daddy Norton had beat the devil out of him to make way for the penetration of God. He looked down at himself, saw his red hands fidget and swim on his pale thighs, his belly slack, the dull tip of his sex prodding the floorboards between his legs.

"I am naked," said Aurel.

"I want to know what you think you are going to do to her after we let her in."

"Don't let her in," pleaded Aurel, covering his crotch with his hands.

Theron stood and turned to the door. "Just a minute," called Theron. "A moment please."

"No," said Aurel. "Please, Theron."

"Who do you love, Aurel?"

"What?" said Aurel.

"Do you love her?"

"I don't love her," said Aurel.

"Nobody said you did, Aurel," said Theron. "But who?"

Aurel brought his head down against his knees, tipped over onto his side. "Don't ask me that, Theron," he said.

"Think about it," said Theron. "Think it through."

The thumping at the door resumed.

"Who do you love? Who is all you have in this world, Aurel?" asked Theron. "With Mama and Daddy Norton dead and gone?"

"God?" said Aurel.

"In *this* world," said Theron, kicking Aurel in the face. "God isn't in this world. Think, goddamn it."

Aurel remained silent a long time, his face darkening where Theron had kicked him. He kept touching his cheek and pulling his fingers away and staring at them. Theron took his hands, held them away from his face, stilled them.

"You?" asked Aurel. "Is it you?"

Theron let go of the hands, cupped his own hands around Aurel's face. He drew the face forward, kissed it on the mouth.

"Yes," said Theron. "Me."

He let Aurel's head go and watched Aurel collapse, his eyes rolling back into his head. He went and unlocked the door. He opened it.

"God almighty," said the woman outside.

Aurel came conscious and tried to crawl out of line of the woman's voice, but Theron kept opening the door wider until the door was pressed against the wall and there was nowhere left to crawl. Aurel got up and stumbled down to the far end of the hall, covering his sex, then came stumbling back, moaning.

"Won't you please come in?" asked Theron.

The woman seemed to be trying to keep her eyes on his face. "Will you put on some clothing?" she asked.

"No," he said. "I will not."

"We are clothed in God's spirit," said Aurel.

"Shut up, Aurel," said Theron. He rendered his best smile. "What can we do for you?" he asked the woman.

She looked at Aurel, then back to Theron, then at Aurel again, her eyes drawing down. "I am here about the property," she said.

"Won't you come in?" Theron said.

He stretched his hand toward her, his palm opening and closing. Aurel came up behind Theron and hid behind his body, his sex beginning to exsert itself more severely. He peered over Theron's shoulder at her. He tried to push the door shut, but Theron kept it blocked open with his foot.

"No," she said, stepping backward, "I don't think I can."

"What's thinking got to do with it?" asked Theron.

She took a few more steps backward until she stepped off the edge of the porch and fell hard.

"The property," said Theron. "We'll pay you whatever you want. We have it inside."

"We don't have any money, Theron," said Aurel.

"Shut up, Aurel," said Theron. "Soon," he said to the woman. "We'll pay you soon. Is it money you want?"

She sat in the weeds holding her ankle, rocking back and forth, her face grimaced.

"I think she likes you, Aurel," said Theron.

Aurel just watched until Theron nudged him. "What's her name?" Aurel said.

"What's your name?" Theron asked the woman.

She had taken the shoe off and was rotating the foot manually and with care, wincing. She did not choose to answer.

"My name is Theron," said Theron. "This is my brother Aurel. Our daddy and mama are dead."

"Pleased to meet you," Aurel said, trying to shut the door.

"Maybe you have a name too?" said Theron. He stared at her, watched her stand and put her weight tenuously on the foot. "Looks like she's hurt, Aurel," he said. "She won't get far."

"I bet her name is Arabella," said Aurel. "That's a pretty name."

"Is that your name?" asked Theron.

She looked at them. Slowly, as if to avoid startling them, she began to limp away, flimmering her hands for balance.

"Go fetch her, Aurel," said Theron. "Bring her back here."

Aurel did not move.

"I mean it, Aurel," said Theron.

Aurel went back into the house. He went to the far end of the hall and crouched there, shaking, and hugged himself around the knees. Theron watched the woman stumble away for a while and then came back into the hall, closing and locking the door.

He came down the hall toward his brother.

"You'll have to do," said Theron.

He sat on the floor beside him, leaning in, putting his hand inside his brother's thigh. He kissed Aurel on the shoulder, the cheek, the neck.

"See now," he said throatily, "we only got each other. Nobody in the world but you and me."

III. THE DOG

Aurel would hardly leave the hall, at most taking two steps out onto the front porch or going through the extreme door into the bathroom. He would not enter the kitchen. Theron had to bring food out to him, though he swore each time that he would not bring it the next.

Theron left him to rummage through the rest of the rooms—except for Daddy Norton's private room, the door to that room being locked and he (though he dared not admit so before Aurel) not having quite the nerve to kick it down. Had it been open, he told himself, he would have entered. But he could not bring himself to break in.

The sprawling house was even larger than he had imagined, running into a half-dozen levels and half-levels, and strung into labyrinths of makeshift rooms, especially on the upper floors, that could not be made sense of or later recovered. He at first made some effort to remain on the two lower floors, as he had done when

Daddy Norton was alive, but as the days passed he went farther up. To make sense of the upper levels, he tried to trace his way in and then out of a floor along the same path, but this proved impossible. Often he found himself in trying to leave passing through chambers that seemed not to have existed before.

He searched through the rooms and found clothing which seemed to belong neither to him nor his brother, nor Mama, nor Daddy Norton. He could not make sense of it nor piece it together in complete outfits, for no matter how many times he coupled articles of clothing, they seemed mismatched in color, style, size. He abandoned clothing and took to gathering objects that interested him, carrying them with him for fear that he would never find them again. He gathered them and then, when sufficiently burdened, tried to find his way back, in the process discovering more than he could ever hope to carry. He heaped what he could in the kitchen and hall, dividing them into piles according to an interior logic he could not fathom but felt compelled to obey.

Aurel sat almost entirely still, and seemed hardly to breathe. He could still arise to walk up and down the hall when he chose, though he moved now with an excess of precision, as if even his most subtle motions were the result of a tremendous and impeccable focusing of the will. He spoke in a similar way, his voice measured and taut, his inflection oddly spaced but so well controlled as to impact much harder upon the words.

"You have begun to talk like Daddy Norton," said Theron. "Are you thinking of reopening the ministry?"

"No," said Aurel. "Daddy Norton has begun to talk like me."

Since Theron could not puzzle through what Aurel meant, he began to watch him more closely. He noticed that when his brother moved it was as if he were hardly resident within his own body, or was resident only in a strictly mechanic sense. When Aurel was motionless, he did not seem present at all.

He took to nudging Aurel when he came into the hall, prodding him gently until the eyes focused in. He kept this up for a few days, until Aurel learned to ignore it.

In one of the upper rooms, Theron found an air rifle and a box of hard plastic pellets. He pumped the gun and shot off into a rat-eaten mattress, raising puffs of dust. Taking the rifle downstairs, he showed it to Aurel.

"Where was it?" said Aurel.

"Upstairs," said Theron. "One of the rooms."

"Daddy Norton's room?" said Aurel.

"No."

"What is in Daddy Norton's room?" asked Aurel.

Theron claimed that he had entered the room but could not remember precisely what was there. Nothing much, he told Aurel. The next time, he thought, I will go in.

The next time, he did not go in. He stood for some time beside the door and even tried to twist the knob again, but it did not turn. He bent down and applied his eye to the keyhole, but found the aperture blocked. He shot the doorknob with the air rifle, listening to the pellets ping off and roll about the floor.

He began, to please Aurel, to imagine Daddy Norton's room, to flesh it forth out of nothing in his head and then regurgitate it. It was, he claimed, a simple room, spare in decor, austere, little substance to it, a few books, a few ordinary objects. When he described Daddy Norton's room, Aurel seemed almost attentive and even asked a few questions. It became so that Theron had to keep a series of notes in the kitchen and review them frequently, for Aurel noticed any inconsistency. He seemed to remember every detail, even to the point of requesting certain items from the room itself, asking for the private trinity of holy books that Theron claimed Daddy Norton had written: *Unaccustomed Sinners, Fathers of Light, Body of Lies.*

"I won't bring his rubbish to you," said Theron. "Get it yourself."

Aurel came to his feet, his knees crackling, and swayed down the hall. Before he got to the door, he slowed, sat deliberately down.

"What's the matter?" asked Theron.

"I am not ready," said Aurel. "Not yet."

At times Theron left the hall not to wander the upper rooms, but to remain behind one of the five doors leading off the main hall, his ear pressed to the door or the door cracked open slightly and he peering through, observing Aurel. Aurel did not appear to notice him, nor in fact to notice anything. Each time Theron returned to the hall and shook him conscious, Aurel would say, "You've been to Daddy Norton's room?" and, when Theron shook his head, "I'll have to go myself."

"Why don't you go?" Theron asked.

"I am going," said Aurel. "Here I go," he said, but did not rise.

The pantry was nearly empty. Creditors and bastards of the slickest varieties took to coming to the door and posting notices. The brothers did not answer. A wet-haired man in a tennis shirt tried to break the door open with a crowbar until Theron opened it and threatened him with the air rifle.

"You are naked," said the man. "You can't shoot me."

Theron shot the man point-blank in the belly, the pellet burying itself shallowly in the fat. Pressing his hands to his belly, the man backed away.

The food in the kitchen ran out. Theron searched the upper rooms for food, found nothing. He returned to the entrance hall.

He grabbed the air rifle, pulling Aurel to his feet and toward the front door. Aurel leaned against him, moving languidly, as if drugged. He allowed himself to be propelled through the door, onto the porch, and then began weakly to resist.

"Where are we going?" he managed.

"To kill something," said Theron.

"We need clothes," Aurel said.

Theron leaned his brother over the porch rail, went back into the house. Kicking through the piles in the hall and kitchen, he uncovered a pair of bathing trunks and a pair of briefs. He slipped into the bathing trunks, carried the briefs outside.

Aurel had fallen off the porch, was lying curled up and hardly moving in the dirt.

"What's wrong with you, brother?" said Theron.

"What do you mean?" said Aurel.

Theron stepped off the porch and slipped the briefs over Aurel's feet, working them up to rim about the knees. He lifted his brother off the ground, pulled the briefs up until they caught on his sex, then lifted the elastic out and over.

"I have to go back inside," said Aurel.

"We need something to eat," said Theron.

Supporting Aurel, he dragged him forward until Aurel began to move his legs of his own accord. He slowly slacked his support until Aurel tottered forward on his own.

"I want to go home," said Aurel.

They traveled alongside the town road for a time then cut away into the fields. They waded through a vacant plot, the ground dawked and uneven. Theron stuffed Aurel through a barbed-wire fence, holding the wires apart, then crawled through himself. Passing through wheat fields, they fell onto a dirt track and were led to a house. They went around to the back.

In the shade of one of the trees was a dog on a chain. He got to his feet when he saw them, stretched. Theron started pumping the air rifle. The dog came forward, wagging its tail, the chain paying out.

Theron steadied Aurel against the side of the house and leveled the air rifle at the dog's head. The dog sniffed at the muzzle, licked the tip of it, tried to pass under it. Theron pushed the barrel flush against the dog's forehead. Closing his eyes, he shot.

Opening them, he found the dog's eye burst and bubbling,

the dog staggering and beginning to turn a circle, its paws tangling in the chain. He pumped the rifle. The dog moaned, started wavering its way back toward the tree.

He followed it, pumping the rifle. He put barrel's end between the shoulder blades. As the dog turned to snap at it, he jerked the trigger.

The dog stumbled to its belly and lay spread a moment, then got back up. Theron could see a small burr of blood rising where the pellet had gone in, the pale lump of it resting just under the skin.

"This dog doesn't want to die," Theron called.

"Leave it alone," said Aurel.

Theron pumped the rifle and got around by the dog where it was sitting under the tree and on its side, palsied. He reached his bare foot out and put it against the dog's jaw, pushing the head down, exposing the throat.

"I want to go home," said Aurel.

Theron pointed the gun and fired, shooting the dog through the throat, the pellet lodging somewhere within the breathpipe. The dog whimpered, the fur of its throat darkening slowly with blood. Theron pushed his foot down and lined up the gun again, pumping. Wriggling beneath him, the dog shook its jaw free and bit him.

He cried out and began to jab at its nose with the barrel, the dog chacking its jaws tighter. He reversed the rifle to bring the gunstock down hard across the dog's skull. The dog shuddered, let go.

Theron limped back a little distance and dropped to examine the wound, blood pushing up in the teethmarks and running streaks down the side of the foot. The dog tried to get to its feet but could not and just stayed pawing the ground in front of it until it could not do that either, and curled its legs underneath and died.

He looked up for Aurel and found Aurel gone. He left the dog and the gun beside it and hobbled around to the front of the house. Aurel he found on the porch clawing at a window.

"What is it?" said Theron.

"I need air," said Aurel. "Let me out."

"Come off of there," said Theron, taking him by the hair and dragging him down. "This is not even our house."

Limping, he pulled Aurel back to the dog and let go. He unchained the dog and took it by the hind legs and began to drag it away.

"Come on, Aurel," said Theron. "Time to go home."

Aurel stayed put, watching him. "I don't want to go," he said.

"Jesus F. Christ," said Theron. "First you don't want to leave, then you don't want to go back. What's the matter with you?"

"The middle name isn't F.," said Aurel.

"The Jesus I'm talking about is," said Theron.

"Stop it, Theron," said Aurel. "You want to go to hell?"

"Are you walking or do I have to drag you?" asked Theron.

Aurel remained a moment standing and then sat down. Theron let go of the dog's legs and came over to hit Aurel in the face until he was lying down. He picked his brother up under the arms and found him light and cold to the touch. When Theron lifted and carried him, Aurel did not seem to notice, but lay in his arms without regard for anything.

Theron stumbled past the dead dog and a few meters later set Aurel down on the ground. He went down stiffly. He went back for the dog, dragged it alongside his brother. He crouched down and stared at first one then the other.

"Can you walk?" he asked Aurel.

"I won't," said Aurel.

He alternated between lugging Aurel and the dog's carcass until he reached the main road, and then gave it up to carry the one while dragging the other. He tried to drag the dog and carry

Aurel, but kept dropping his brother. He found it easier to drag Aurel by the feet, Aurel's head jouncing across the asphalt, while he slung the dog over his shoulders.

He could hardly walk for the pain in his foot. People slowed as they passed in cars, at times even pointing, shouting. He cursed them thoroughly and kept on.

The dog grew heavy around his neck, his chest and shoulders spattering with blood and foam. Behind, Aurel seemed to have fallen asleep, though his eyes were still open. Theron kept turning around and asking, *Hey, you dead? Hey, you dead? Hey, you dead?* After a while, Theron stopped asking.

IV. THE HOLY WORD

The foot festered, and soon he could not walk on it. He left the carcass in the hall, slitting the skin and fur off it with an old kitchen knife and eating raw hunks until it was too hard to pick out the maggots. He pulled himself back a few yards, watching the flesh vanish and the bones push through, the structure collapsing into a mere arthritic pile, flies turning circles on the walls. Maggots struck blindly across the floor out from the carcass and Theron was hungry enough to drag himself to them.

Soon both dog and maggots seemed gone, though Theron discovered no inclination to leave the hall. Aurel, on the contrary, seemed to have regained his strength. He had risen suddenly to his feet, and was now rarely found in the hall. He had acquired color in his cheeks, and his eyes seemed less inclined to delirium. He roamed the upper levels of the house, though unlike Theron he never returned with anything. He would vanish for days, and then Theron would awaken to find him crouched and peering over him. Then Aurel would vanish again.

The maggots returned, this time pushing their way out of Theron's injured foot. He scraped them from the wound and swallowed them, but they originated deeper within the foot than he dared scrape, and kept returning. The smaller, individual wounds became a single wound, the wound growing purple and deep, the flesh sloughing away almost painlessly at a touch.

He faded in and out of consciousness, Aurel seeming to grow immense. He could hear his brother's feet creak through the ceiling above, the structure of the house swaying beneath his weight.

He took to not seeing things, then to not hearing them. He kept his eyes closed and pulled himself to a corner and leaned into it, and soon thereafter his nerves dried out and his skin ceased to feel. His thoughts ran on for a while in all directions and then seemed to establish an equilibrium of sorts, and then fell silent.

He felt himself shaken. After some time, he brought himself to open his eyes. He looked up to see Aurel.

He tried to turn his head. He swallowed, coughed forth a web of phlegm, spread it onto the wall.

"What did you do with Daddy Norton's eyes?" asked Aurel.

"His eyes?"

"You removed them," said Aurel. "Where are they?"

Theron fumbled his hand into the corner behind him and seemed to fall asleep. Aurel nudged him and he brought his hand forth and opened his palm out, an irregular mass within.

Aurel took the eye from Theron's hand and examined it, the surface withered and collapsed, the lens sunken in and grown opaque.

"Where's the other one?" he said.

"This is the one that has been watching me," said Theron. "I think it is his. It might be the dog's."

Aurel sniffed it. He lifted it, held it against first one of his eyes then the other, then stretched it toward Theron. Theron let it come close, then closed his eyes.

"Look," said Aurel. "Please look."

He brought the eye toward Theron slowly and Theron let him do it. He brought the eye up near to Theron's living eye.

"What do you see?" he said.

"Nothing," said Theron. "Not a goddamn thing."

Upstairs, Aurel broke down Daddy Norton's door by simply leaning into it, the cheap hinges shearing away. The room inside was dark and damp, reeking of Daddy Norton's pomade. He left the door open and felt around beside the door for a light mechanism, but did not find one. He took a few steps in and stood there, waiting for the dark to acquire depth and texture. He took a few more steps, then a few more. He stood still until he began to see.

One side of the room was lined with religious tokens of all sects and creeds, strung along the wall. There were, as well, holy books, many of them still in wrapping and apparently never opened, scattered over the floor.

The other side of the room was nearly empty—a stiff austere bed, a low basin, a lectern which supported Daddy Norton's Holy Word.

He went to the Holy Word and opened it up. He began to read.

Those who strike against God's True and Everlasting Covenant as revealed by Him to Daddy Norton shall be numbered among the damned and cast into the outer dark.

Those who have known God's Own Truth, as revealed to Daddy Norton and written by his hand, guided by God's hand, in this holy book, and who turn against it, shall be numbered most visibly among the damned and cast into the outer dark.

To afflict Daddy Norton is to afflict God himself. Those who, knowingly or unknowingly, in faith or outside of it, challenge Daddy Norton on his sacred path toward Truth, will be damned with the damnation that sticks and cast well beyond the outer dark.

He took the book downstairs and shook Theron alive and read the verses to him.

"It's a good thing the bastard's dead," said Theron.

"Be quiet," said Aurel. "Do you want to be cast into the outer dark?"

"As long as Daddy Norton isn't there waiting for me."

Aurel shook his head. In closing the book, his eye passed across a line, and he opened the book again and began to read the verse in its full body.

He who converses with my enemies, though he claim loyalty to me and every whit of doctrine, is my enemy, for the law must be fulfilled. Brother shall turn against brother for my sake, and father against child.

He studied the verse out and pondered it in his mind and wondered upon its application until the hall had fallen dark.

"Theron," he said. "Let me read this to you."

Theron did not answer yea or nay. Aurel read the passage slowly, haltingly, in his own voice, then looked up to see what his brother would say. Theron didn't say anything, just stayed pressed up into the corner, silent.

"I'm sorry, brother," said Aurel. "I must leave."

He closed the book. He stood and looked down at Theron. He prodded the festered leg with his own foot, his toes sinking into the flesh. He stood and left the hall.

He traveled through the upper rooms, the air hardly breathable, at one time stumbling into an attic filled with dead swallows, their heads screwed off and heaped in a corner. He lived for some time on the armload of swallows he carried out, stripping them free of their larger feathers and choking them down whole as he wandered on.

He could feel the house creak and sway beneath him, the wood groaning as if the rooms were never meant to be walked in. Many of the rooms were dark, and he found in these his eyes could not gather sufficient light to glean wisdom from the Holy Word, so he began to avoid them. Others rippled with heat, and these he came to avoid as well. He kept instead to the narrow and rickety rooms nearest the top, chinks in their walls and ceilings, their floors as well, which howled with wind and in which he had to hold the pages of the Holy Word pressed flat so they could not go adrift.

He read the book from cover to cover, reading a little in each room, and quickly came to believe in the divinity of the book and in the divine election of Daddy Norton, and in his own divine election as Daddy Norton's disciple, called of God in this, God's only true church. And then he read the book a second time and found himself no longer certain. It did not seem to him the same book the second time, for it began to reveal to him faces that he had not wanted to perceive before. He saw that his faith would fall in jeopardy were he to continue to read, and so, to preserve his faith, he abandoned the book in one of the upper rooms and never saw it again.

He lived on what scraps he could find, when these were gone peeling off the wallpaper and eating the paste underneath. He began to find other books in the rooms. These at first he left where they were, passing along the walls of the room and into other rooms beyond. But when he began to find them more often, he took to picking them up and hiding them beneath beds and tables, so as not to have to see them again. Still, the books appeared everywhere, in each new room he entered as well as in rooms he thought he had entered before, as if someone were moving them.

He stopped trying to hide the books and left them where they were. He tried to find his way downstairs but had no inkling of the way. He came into a room with a split-board floor where he thought the stairs should be. Light shone up hard through the floorcracks, the walls musted and blotched with mold. Kicking a hole through a wall, he crawled out into a narrow room, a globed glass fixture hanging from the ceiling and aglow. Lying on the floor, he watched the light and listened to fleas ping inside the globe, and fell asleep.

He awoke to find fleas strung up and down his veins and grown fat upon him. He began to crush them with stiff thumbs, leaving smears of blood. Getting to his feet he saw a book on a table, and this he took up and opened and read from silently without avail or feeling though like every other book it was most likely some god or other's sacred word. He read on blankly for many pages, until was given to him:

He that loveth his brother abideth in light, and there is none occasion of stumbling in him.

He put the book down as if struck and then as quickly scooped it up again. He took Daddy Norton's dessicated eye out of his underwear and held it toward the words, then put the eye away. Putting the book under his arm, he went out of the room through a door and from there through chambers with irregular floors and from there fell down a ramshackle staircase face-first. He found himself in a room that seemed familiar to him, though he could place nothing about it. He made his way out through a door broken from its hinges and through a hall and down a staircase missing its treads. He entered what seemed at one time to have been a kitchen but which now seemed a repository for refuse of all kinds.

Wading across the room, he opened a door and came out into a long hall, a door at one end of it, a window at the other. In the corner, beneath the window, was a figure, vaguely human. The smell of it was hard to breathe at first, and then became sweet and made his head dance with light.

He could feel God watching. He approached the figure and sat beside it, pulling it over to lean against him. What he touched was soggy in his hands, as if impregnated with water, and it left portions of itself adhered to the wall even as it came away.

He read the verse aloud, but his brother did not respond. He pulled him closer and felt him come apart in his hands.

He gathered what he could and pushed it back into the corner. He took off the briefs he wore, Daddy Norton's eye falling out and dropping away. He beat the pile in the corner like a pillow and lay his head onto it.

"Brothers always," he said. And closed his eyes.

TINY, SMILING DADDY

MARY GAITSKILL

He lay in his reclining chair, barely awake enough to feel the dream moving just under his thoughts. It felt like one of those pure, beautiful dreams in which he was young again, and filled with the realization that the friends who had died, or gone away, or decided that they didn't like him anymore, had really been there all along, loving him. A piece of the dream flickered, and he made out the lips and cheekbones of a tender woman, smiling as she leaned toward him. The phone rang, and the sound rippled through his pliant wakefulness, into the pending dream. But his wife had turned the answering machine up too loud again, and it attacked him with a garbled, furred roar that turned into the voice of his friend Norm.

Resentful at being waked and grateful that for once somebody had called him, he got up to answer. He picked up the phone, and the answering machine screeched at him through the receiver. He cursed as he fooled with it, hating his stiff fingers. Irritably, he exchanged greetings with his friend, and then Norm, his voice oddly weighted, said, "I saw the issue of *Self* with Kitty in it."

He waited for an explanation. None came, so he said, "What? Issue of *Self*? What's *Self*?"

"Good grief, Stew, I thought for sure you'd of seen it. Now I feel funny."

The dream pulsed forward and receded again. "Funny about what?"

"My daughter's got a subscription to this magazine, *Self*. And they printed an article that Kitty wrote about fathers and daughters talking to each other, and she, well, she wrote about you. Laurel showed it to me."

"My God."

"It's ridiculous that I'm the one to tell you. I just thought—"

"It was bad?"

"No, she didn't say anything bad. I just didn't understand the whole idea of it. And I wondered what you thought."

He got off the phone and walked back into the living room, now fully awake. His daughter, Kitty, was living in South Carolina, working in a used-record store and making animal statuettes, which she sold on commission. She had never written anything that he knew of, yet she'd apparently published an article in a national magazine about him. He lifted his arms and put them on the windowsill; the air from the open window cooled his underarms. Outside, the Starlings' tiny dog marched officiously up and down the pavement, looking for someone to bark at. Maybe she had written an article about how wonderful he was, and she was too shy to show him right away. This was doubtful. Kitty was quiet, but she wasn't shy. She was untactful and she could be aggressive. Uncertainty only made her doubly aggressive.

He turned the edge of one nostril over with his thumb and nervously stroked his nose hairs with one finger. He knew it was a nasty habit, but it soothed him. When Kitty was a little girl he would do it to make her laugh. "Well," he'd say, "do you think it's time we played with the hairs in our nose?" And she would giggle, holding her hands against her face, eyes sparkling over her knuckles.

Then she was fourteen, and as scornful and rejecting as any girl he had ever thrown a spitball at when he was that age. They didn't get along so well anymore. Once, they were sitting in the rec room watching TV, he on the couch, she on the footstool. There was a Charlie Chan movie on, but he was mostly watching her back and her long, thick brown hair, which she had just washed and was brushing. She dropped her head forward from the neck to let the hair fall between her spread legs and began slowly stroking it with a pink nylon brush.

"Say, don't you think it's time we played with the hairs in our nose?"

No reaction from bent back and hair.

"Who wants to play with the hairs in their nose?"

Nothing.

"Hairs in the nose, hairs in the nose," he sang.

She bolted violently up from the stool. "You are so gross you disgust me!" She stormed from the room, shoulders in a tailored jacket of indignation.

Sometimes he said it just to see her exasperation, to feel the adorable, futile outrage of her violated girl delicacy.

He wished that his wife would come home with the car, so that he could drive to the store and buy a copy of *Self*. His car was being repaired, and he could not walk to the little cluster of stores and parking lots that constituted "town" in this heat. It would take a good twenty minutes, and he would be completely worn out when he got there. He would find the magazine and stand there in the drugstore and read it, and if it was something bad, he might not have the strength to walk back.

He went into the kitchen, opened a beer, and brought it into the living room. His wife had been gone for over an hour, and God knew how much longer she would be. She could spend literally all day driving around the county, doing nothing but buying a jar of honey or a bag of apples. Of course, he could call Kitty, but he'd probably just get her answering machine, and besides, he didn't want to talk to her before he understood the situation. He felt helplessness move through his body the way a swimmer feels a large sea creature pass beneath him. How could she have done this to him? She knew how he dreaded exposure of any kind, she knew the way he guarded himself against strangers, the way he carefully drew all the curtains when twilight approached so that no one could see them walking through the house. She knew how ashamed he had been when, at sixteen, she announced that she was lesbian.

The Starling dog was now across the street, yapping at the heels of a bowlegged old lady in a blue dress who was trying to walk down the sidewalk. "Dammit," he said. He left the window and got the afternoon opera station on the radio. They were in the final act of *La Bohème.*

He did not remember precisely when it had happened, but Kitty, his beautiful, happy little girl, turned into a glum, weird teenager that other kids picked on. She got skinny and ugly. Her blue eyes, which had been so sensitive and bright, turned filmy, as if the real Kitty had retreated so far from the surface that her eyes existed to shield rather than reflect her. It was as if she deliberately held her beauty away from them, only showing glimpses of it during unavoidable lapses, like the time she sat before the TV, daydreaming and lazily brushing her hair. At moments like this, her dormant charm broke his heart. It also annoyed him. What did she have to retreat from? They had both loved her. When she was little and she couldn't sleep at night, Marsha would sit with her in bed for hours. She praised her stories and her drawings as if she were a genius. When Kitty was seven, she and her mother had special times, during which they went off together and talked about whatever Kitty wanted to talk about.

He tried to compare the sullen, morbid Kitty of sixteen with the slender, self-possessed twenty-eight-year-old lesbian who wrote articles for *Self*. He pictured himself in court, waving a copy of *Self* before a shocked jury. The case would be taken up by the press. He saw the headlines: Dad Sues Mag—Dyke Daughter Reveals . . . reveals what? What had Kitty found to say about him that was of interest to the entire country, that she didn't want him to know about?

Anger overrode his helplessness. Kitty could be vicious. He hadn't seen her vicious side in years, but he knew it was there. He remembered the time he'd stood behind the half-open front door when fifteen-year-old Kitty sat hunched on the front steps with one of her few friends, a homely blond who wore white lipstick and a white leather jacket. He had come to the door to view the weather and say something to the girls, but they were muttering so intently that curiosity got the better of him, and he hung back a moment to listen. "Well, at least your mom's smart," said Kitty. "My mom's not only a bitch, she's stupid."

This after the lullabies and special times! It wasn't just an isolated incident, either; every time he'd come home from work, his wife had something bad to say about Kitty. She hadn't set the table until she had been asked four times. She'd gone to Lois's house instead of coming straight home like she'd been told to do. She'd worn a dress to school that was short enough to show the tops of her panty hose.

By the time Kitty came to dinner, looking as if she'd been doing slave labor all day, he would be mad at her. He couldn't help it. Here was his wife doing her damnedest to raise a family and cook dinner, and here was this awful kid looking ugly, acting mean, and not setting the table. It seemed unreasonable that she should turn out so badly after taking up so much of their time. Her afflicted expression made him angry too. What had anybody ever done to her?

*   *   *

He sat forward and gently gnawed the insides of his mouth as he listened to the dying girl in *La Bohème.* He saw his wife's car pull into the driveway. He walked to the back door, almost wringing his hands, and waited for her to come through the door. When she did, he snatched the grocery bag from her arms and said, "Give me the keys." She stood openmouthed in the stairwell, looking at him with idiotic consternation. "Give me the keys!"

"What is it, Stew? What's happened?"

"I'll tell you when I get back."

He got in the car and became part of it, this panting mobile case propelling him through the incredibly complex and fast-moving world of other people, their houses, their children, their dogs, their lives. He wasn't usually so aware of this unpleasant sense of disconnection between him and everyone else, but he had the feeling that it had been there all along, underneath what he thought about most of the time. It was ironic that it should rear up so visibly at a time when there was in fact a mundane yet invasive and horribly real connection between him and everyone else in Wayne County: the hundreds of copies of *Self* magazine sitting in countless drugstores, bookstores, groceries, and libraries. It was as if there were a tentacle plugged into the side of the car, linking him with the random humans who picked up the magazine, possibly his very neighbors. He stopped at a crowded intersection, feeling like an ant in an enemy swarm.

Kitty had projected herself out of the house and into this swarm very early, ostensibly because life with him and Marsha had been so awful. Well, it had been awful, but because of Kitty, not them. As if it weren't enough to be sullen and dull, she turned into a lesbian. Kids followed her down the street, jeering at her. Somebody dropped her books in a toilet. She got into a fistfight. Their neighbors gave them looks. This reaction seemed only to steel Kitty's grip on her new identity; it made her romanticize herself, like the kid she was. She wrote poems about heroic women warriors, she brought home strange books and magazines, which, among other things, seemed to glorify prostitutes. Marsha looked for them and threw them away. Kitty screamed at her, the tendons leaping out on her slender neck. He punched Kitty and knocked her down. Marsha tried to stop him, and he yelled at her. Kitty jumped up and leapt between them, as if to defend her mother. He grabbed her and shook her, but he could not shake the conviction off her face.

Most of the time, though, they continued as always, eating dinner together, watching TV, making jokes. That was the worst thing; he would look at Kitty and see his daughter, now familiar in her withdrawn sullenness, and feel comfort and affection. Then he would remember that she was a lesbian, and a morass of complication and wrongness would come down between them, making it impossible for him to see her. Then she would just be Kitty again. He hated it.

She ran away at sixteen, and the police found her in the apartment of an eighteen-year-old bodybuilder named Dolores, who had a naked woman tattooed on her sinister bicep. Marsha made them put her in a mental hospital so psychiatrists could observe her, but he hated the psychiatrists—mean, supercilious sons of bitches who delighted in the trick question—so he took her out. She finished school, and they told her if she wanted to leave it was all right with them. She didn't waste any time getting out of the house.

She moved into an apartment near Detroit with a girl named George and took a job at a home for retarded kids. She would appear for visits with a huge bag of laundry every few weeks. She was thin and neurotically muscular, her body having the look of a fighting dog on a leash. She cut her hair like a boy's and wore black sunglasses, black leather half-gloves, and leather belts. The only remnant of her beauty was her erect, martial carriage and her efficient movements; she walked through a room like the commander of a guerrilla force. She would sit at the dining-room table with Marsha, drinking tea and having a laconic verbal conversation, her body speaking its precise martial language while the washing machine droned from the utility room, and he wandered in and out, trying to make sense of what she said. Sometimes she would stay into the evening, to eat dinner and watch *All in the Family.* Then Marsha would send her home with a jar of home-made tapioca pudding or a bag of apples and oranges.

One day, instead of a visit they got a letter postmarked San Francisco. She had left George, she said. She listed strange details about her current environment and was vague about how she was supporting herself. He had nightmares about Kitty, with her brave, proudly muscular little body, lost among big fleshy women who danced naked in go-go bars and took drugs with needles, terrible women whom his confused, romantic daughter invested with oppressed heroism and intensely female glamour. He got up at night and stumbled into the bathroom for stomach medicine, the familiar darkness of the house heavy with menacing images that pressed about him, images he saw reflected in his own expression when he turned on the bathroom light over the mirror.

Then one year she came home for Christmas. She came into the house with her luggage and a shopping bag of gifts for them, and he saw that she was beautiful again. It was a beauty that both offended and titillated his senses. Her short, spiky hair was streaked with purple, her dainty mouth was lipsticked, her nose and ears were pierced with amethyst and dangling silver. Her face had opened in thousands of petals. Her eyes shone with quick perception as she put down her bag, and he knew that she had seen him see her beauty. She moved toward him with fluid hips; she embraced him for the first time in years. He felt her live, lithe body against his, and his heart pulsed a message of blood and love. "Merry Christmas, Daddy," she said.

Her voice was husky and coarse; it reeked of knowledge and

confidence. Her T-shirt said "Chicks with Balls." She was twenty-two years old.

She stayed for a week, discharging her strange jangling beauty into the house and changing the molecules of its air. She talked about the girls she shared an apartment with, her job at a coffee shop, how Californians were different from Michiganders. She talked about her friends: Lorraine, who was so pretty men fell off their bicycles as they twisted their bodies for a better look at her; Judy, a martial-arts expert; and Meredith, who was raising a child with her husband, Angela. She talked of poetry readings, ceramics classes, workshops on piercing.

He realized, as he watched her, that she was now doing things that were as bad as or worse than the things that had made him angry at her five years before, yet they didn't quarrel. It seemed that a large white space existed between him and her, and that it was impossible to enter this space or to argue across it. Besides, she might never come back if he yelled at her.

Instead, he watched her, puzzling at the metamorphosis she had undergone. First she had been a beautiful, happy child turned homely, snotty, miserable adolescent. From there she had become a martinet girl with the eyes of a stifled pervert. Now she was a vibrant imp, living, it seemed, in a world constructed of topsy-turvy junk pasted with rhinestones. Where had these three different people come from? Not even Marsha, who had spent so much time with her as a child, could trace the genesis of the new Kitty from the old one. Sometimes he bitterly reflected that he and Marsha weren't even real parents anymore but bereft old people rattling around in a house, connected not to a real child who was going to college, or who at least had some kind of understandable life, but to a changeling who was the product of only their most obscure quirks, a being who came from recesses that neither of them suspected they'd had.

*   *   *

There were only a few cars in the parking lot. He wheeled through it with pointless deliberation before parking near the drugstore. He spent irritating seconds searching for *Self,* until he realized that its airbrushed cover girl was grinning right at him. He stormed the table of contents, then headed for the back of the magazine. "Speak Easy" was written sideways across the top of the page in round turquoise letters. At the bottom was his daughter's name in a little box. "Kitty Thorne is a ceramic artist living in South Carolina." His hands were trembling.

It was hard for him to rationally ingest the beginning paragraphs, which seemed, incredibly, to be about a phone conversation they'd had some time ago about the emptiness and selfishness of people who have sex but don't get married and have children. A few phrases stood out clearly: ". . . my father may love me but he doesn't love the way I live." ". . . even more complicated because I'm gay." ". . . because it still hurts me."

For reasons he didn't understand, he felt a nervous smile tremble under his skin. He suppressed it.

"This hurt has its roots deep in our relationship, starting, I think, when I was a teenager."

He was horribly aware of being in public, so he paid for the thing and took it out to the car. He drove slowly to another spot in the lot, as far away from the drugstore as possible, picked up the magazine, and began again. She described the "terrible difficulties" between him and her. She recounted, briefly and with hieroglyphic politeness, the fighting, the running away, the return, the tacit reconciliation.

"There is an emotional distance that we have both accepted and chosen to work around, hoping the occasional contact—love, anger, something—will get through."

He put the magazine down and looked out the window. It was near dusk; most of the stores in the little mall were closed. There were only two other cars in the parking lot, and a big, slow, frown-

ing woman with two grocery bags was getting ready to drive one
away. He was parked before a weedy piece of land at the edge of
the lot. In it were rough, picky weeds spread out like big green
tarantulas, young yellow dandelions, frail old dandelions, and
bunches of tough blue chickweed. Even in his distress he vaguely
appreciated the beauty of the blue weeds against the cool white-
and-gray sky. For a moment the sound of insects comforted him.
Images of Kitty passed through his memory with terrible speed:
her nine-year-old forehead bent over her dish of ice cream, her tiny
nightgowned form ran up the stairs, her ringed hand brushed her
face, the keys on her belt jiggled as she walked her slow blue-
jeaned walk away from the house. Gone, all gone.

The article went on to describe how Kitty hung up the phone
feeling frustrated and then listed all the things she could've said to
him to let him know how hurt she was, paving the way for "real
communication"; it was all in ghastly talk-show language. He was
unable to put these words together with the Kitty he had last seen
lounging around the house. She was twenty-eight now, and she no
longer dyed her hair or wore jewels in her nose. Her demeanor was
serious, bookish, almost old-maidish. Once, he'd overheard her
saying to Marsha, "So then this Italian girl gives me the once-over
and says to Joanne, 'You 'ang around with too many Wasp.' And I
said, 'I'm not a Wasp, I'm white trash.'"

"Speak for yourself," he'd said.

"If the worst occurred and my father was unable to respond to
me in kind, I still would have done a good thing. I would have
acknowledged my own needs and created the possibility to connect with what therapists call 'the good parent' in myself."

Well, if that was the kind of thing she was going to say to
him, he was relieved she hadn't said it. But if she hadn't said it to
him, why was she saying it to the rest of the country?

He turned on the radio. It sang: "Try to remember, and if you
remember, then follow, follow." He turned it off. The interrupted

dream echoed faintly. He closed his eyes. When he was nine or ten, an uncle of his had told him, "Everybody makes his own world. You see what you want to see and hear what you want to hear. You can do it right now. If you blink ten times and then close your eyes real tight, you can see anything you want to see in front of you." He'd tried it, rather halfheartedly, and hadn't seen anything but the vague suggestion of a yellowish-white ball moving creepily through the dark. At the time, he'd thought it was perhaps because he hadn't tried hard enough.

He had told Kitty to do the same thing, or something like it, when she was eight or nine. They were sitting on the back porch in striped lawn chairs, holding hands and watching the fireflies turn on and off.

She closed her eyes for a long time. Then very seriously, she said, "I see big balls of color, like shaggy flowers. They're pink and red and turquoise. I see an island with palm trees and pink rocks. There's dolphins and mermaids swimming in the water around it." He'd been almost awed by her belief in this impossible vision. Then he was sad, because she would never see what she wanted to see. Then he thought she was sort of stupid, even for a kid.

His memory flashed back to his boyhood. He was walking down the middle of the street at dusk, sweating lightly after a basketball game. There were crickets and the muted barks of dogs and the low, affirming mumble of people on their front porches. Securely held by the warm night and its sounds, he felt an exquisite blend of happiness and sorrow that life could contain this perfect moment, and a sadness that he would soon arrive home, walk into bright light, and be on his way into the next day, with its loud noise and alarming possibility. He resolved to hold this evening walk in his mind forever, to imprint in a permanent place all the sensations that occurred to him as he walked by the Oatlanders' house, so that he could always take them out and look at them. He dimly recalled feeling that if he could successfully do that, he could stop time and hold it.

*   *   *

He knew he had to go home soon. He didn't want to talk about the article with Marsha, but the idea of sitting in the house with her and not talking about it was hard to bear. He imagined the conversation grinding into being, a future conversation with Kitty gestating within it. The conversation was a vast, complex machine like those that occasionally appeared in his dreams; if he could only pull the switch, everything would be all right, but he felt too stupefied by the weight and complexity of the thing to do so. Besides, in this case, everything might not be all right. He put the magazine under his seat and started the car.

Marsha was in her armchair, reading. She looked up, and the expression on her face seemed like the result of internal conflict as complicated and strong as his own, but cross-pulled in different directions, uncomprehending of him and what he knew. In his mind, he withdrew from her so quickly that for a moment the familiar room was fraught with the inexplicable horror of a banal nightmare. Then the ordinariness of the scene threw the extraordinary event of the day into relief, and he felt so angry and bewildered he could've howled.

"Everything all right, Stew?" asked Marsha.

"No, nothing is all right. I'm a tired old man in a shitty world I don't want to be in. I go out there, it's like walking on knives. Everything is an attack—the ugliness, the cheapness, the rudeness, everything." He sensed her withdrawing from him into her own world of disgruntlement, her lips drawn together in that look of exasperated perseverance she'd gotten from her mother. Like Kitty, like everyone else, she was leaving him. "I don't have a real daughter, and I don't have a real wife who's here with me, because she's too busy running around on some—"

"We've been through this before. We agreed I could—"

"That was different! That was when we had two cars!" His voice tore through his throat in a jagged whiplash and came out a cracked half scream. "I don't have a car, remember? That means

I'm stranded, all alone for hours, and Norm Pisarro can call me up and casually tell me that my lesbian daughter has just betrayed me in a national magazine and what do I think about that?" He wanted to punch the wall until his hand was bloody. He wanted Kitty to see the blood. Marsha's expression broke into soft, open-mouthed consternation. The helplessness of it made his anger seem huge and terrible, then impotent and helpless itself. He sat down on the couch and, instead of anger, felt pain.

"What did Kitty do? What happened? What does Norm have—"

"She wrote an article in *Self* magazine about being a lesbian and her problems and something to do with me. I don't know; I could barely read the crap."

Marsha looked down at her nails.

He looked at her and saw the aged beauty of her ivory skin, sagging under the weight of her years and her cockeyed bifocals, the emotional receptivity of her face, the dark down on her upper lip, the childish pearl buttons of her sweater, only the top button done.

"I'm surprised at Norm, that he would call you like that."

"Oh, who the hell knows what he thought." His heart was soothed and slowed by her words, even if they didn't address its real unhappiness.

"Here," she said. "Let me rub your shoulders."

He allowed her to approach him, and they sat sideways on the couch, his weight balanced on the edge by his awkwardly planted legs, she sitting primly on one hip with her legs tightly crossed. The discomfort of the position negated the practical value of the massage, but he welcomed her touch. Marsha had strong, intelligent hands that spoke to his muscles of deep safety and love and the delight of physical life. In her effort, she leaned close, and her sweatered breast touched him, releasing his tension almost against his will. Through half-closed eyes he observed her sneakers on the floor—he could not quite get over this phenomenon of adult women wearing what had been boys' shoes—in the dim light, one toe atop the other as though cuddling, their laces in pretty disorganization.

Poor Kitty. It hadn't really been so bad that she hadn't set the table on time. He couldn't remember why he and Marsha had been so angry over the table. Unless it was Kitty's coldness, her always turning away, her sarcastic voice. But she was a teenager, and that's what teenagers did. Well, it was too bad, but it couldn't be helped now.

He thought of his father. That was too bad too, and nobody was writing articles about that. There had been a distance between them, so great and so absolute that the word "distance" seemed inadequate to describe it. But that was probably because he had known his father only when he was a very young child; if his father had lived longer, perhaps they would've become closer. He could recall his father's face clearly only at the breakfast table, where it appeared silent and still except for lip and jaw motions, comforting in its constancy. His father ate his oatmeal with one hand working the spoon, one elbow on the table, eyes down, sometimes his other hand holding a cold rag to his head, which always hurt with what seemed to be a noble pain, willingly taken on with his duties as a husband and father. He had loved to stare at the big face with its deep lines and long earlobes, its thin lips and loose, loopily chewing jaws. Its almost godlike stillness and expressionlessness filled him with admiration and reassurance, until one day his father slowly looked up from his cereal, met his eyes, and said, "Stop staring at me, you little shit."

In the other memories, his father was a large, heavy body with a vague oblong face. He saw him sleeping in the armchair in the living room, his large, hairy-knuckled hands grazing the floor. He saw him walking up the front walk with the quick, clipped steps that he always used coming home from work, the straight-backed choppy gait that gave the big body an awesome mechanicalness. His shirt was wet under the arms, his head was down, the eyes were abstracted but alert, as though keeping careful watch on the outside world in case something nasty came at him while he attended to the more important business inside.

"The good parent in yourself."

What did the well-meaning idiots who thought of these phrases mean by them? When a father dies, he is gone; there is no tiny, smiling daddy who appears, waving happily, in a secret pocket in your chest. Some kinds of loss are absolute. And no amount of self-realization or self-expression will change that.

As if she had heard him, Marsha urgently pressed her weight into her hands and applied all her strength to relaxing his muscles. Her sweat and scented deodorant filtered through her sweater, which added its muted wooliness to her smell. "All righty!" She rubbed his shoulders and briskly patted him. He reached back and touched her hand in thanks.

Across from where they sat had once been a red chair, and in it had once sat Kitty, looking away from him, her fist hiding her face.

"You're a lesbian? Fine," he said. "You mean nothing to me. You walk out that door, it doesn't matter. And if you come back in, I'm going to spit in your face. I don't care if I'm on my deathbed, I'll still have the energy to spit in your face."

She did not move when he said that. Tears ran over her fist and down her arm, but she didn't look at him.

Marsha's hands lingered on him for a moment. Then she moved and sat away from him on the couch.

SOMEONE TO TALK TO

DEBORAH EISENBERG

"Are you going to be all right, Aaron?" Caroline said.

Shapiro saw himself, as if in a dream, standing on a dark shore. "Yes," he heard himself say.

"Are you sure?" Caroline said.

Lady Chatterley leaned herself thuggishly against Shapiro's shin and began to purr. "Hello, there," he said. He reached down and patted her gingerly.

Caroline hesitated at the door, then took a few steps back toward Shapiro, and her delicious, clean fragrance spilled over him. "Your big concert's in less than a month now . . ." She tilted her head and managed a little smile.

Was she going to touch him? Shapiro went rigid with alarm, but she just looked vaguely around the room. "You know, it's supposed to be a beautiful country . . ." She scooped up Lady Chatterley and nuzzled the orange fur. "Chat. Dear little Chat. Are you going to take care of Aaron?" She took a paw in her hand. "Are you?"

Lady Chatterley wrenched herself free and bounded back to the floor. Caroline's eyes—like Lady Chatterley's—were large and light and spoked with black. Her small face was pale, always, as though with shock.

"Shall I help you with your things?" Shapiro said.

There was really only one suitcase, a good one—leather, old, genteel—which had probably accompanied Caroline to college; the rest had gone on before. "No need," she said. Tears wavered momentarily in her eyes. "Jim's picking me up."

The suitcase appeared to be heavy. Shapiro watched Caroline's thin legs as she struggled slightly with it. At the door she turned back. "Aaron?" she said.

He waited to hear himself answer, but this time no words came.

"Aaron, I know this is probably not what you want to hear right now, but I think it's important for me to say it—I'll always care about you, you know. I hope you know that."

Shapiro awoke suddenly and unpleasantly, as though a crateful of fruits had been emptied out on him. There was an unfamiliar wall next to him, and the window was all wrong. He heard footsteps, a snicker. A hotel room wobbled into place around him—yes, Richard Penwad would be coming to pick him up, and Caroline wasn't even in this country.

The night had been crowded with Caroline and endless versions of her departure—dreamed, reversed in dreams, modified, amended, transfigured, made tender and transcendently beautiful as though it had been an act of sacral purification. For a week or so he had been free of her, or at least anesthetized. But this morning he was battered by her absence; in this distant place his body and mind didn't know how to protect themselves.

As soon as she'd left that day, he'd closed his eyes. An afterimage of the door glowed. When he'd opened his eyes again, the room seemed strange in an undetectable way, as though he were seeing it after a hiatus of years. Hesitantly, he brushed cat fur from the armchair and sat down.

Six years. Six years of life that belonged to them both, out the door in the form of Caroline's fragile person. If only there'd been less . . . tension about money. Caroline, from many generations of a background she referred to as "comfortable," was deeply sympathetic with, and at the same time deeply insensitive to, the distress of others. "Why not, Aaron?" she would say. "Why don't I just take care of the rent from now on?" Or, when she felt like going to some morbidly expensive restaurant, "I could treat. Wouldn't it be fun, for a change? Of course"—she would gaze at him with concern—"if you're not going to enjoy it . . ." Sometimes, when she noticed him grimly going through the mail or eyeing the telephone, she would say gently, "Something will turn up."

Though not quite a prodigy, Shapiro had been received with great enthusiasm at the youthful start of his career. He'd been shy and luminously pale, with dark curls and almost freakish technical abilities that delighted audiences. But the qualities he greatly admired and envied in other pianists—varieties of a profound musicianship which focused the attention on the ear, hearing, rather than on the hand, executing—were ones he lacked. He practiced, he struggled, he cultivated patience, and he was rewarded—minimally. By just the faintest flicker of heat in his crystalline touch.

His curls, pallor, and technique lost some of their brilliance; his audience was distracted by newcomers and dispersed, and a sudden increase in the velocity of the earth's spin dumped Shapiro into his thirty-eighth year. *Aaron Shapiro*. Caroline had been starry-eyed when they'd met, although by that time he'd already moved out to the margin of the city and was beginning to take on private students, startlingly untalented children who at best thought of the piano as a defective substitute for something electronic. Gradually he ceased to be the sort of pianist who might expect to make recordings, give important concerts, be interviewed, hold posts at conservatories. His name, once received like a slab of precious metal, was now received like a slip of blank paper.

"Things will work out," Caroline said, although "things," in Shapiro's estimation, were deteriorating. She touched him less often. Her smiles became increasingly lambent and forbearing. Sometimes she called in the afternoon to say she'd be held up at work. Her voice would be hesitant, apprehensive; her words floated in the air like dying petals while he listened, reluctant to hang up but unable to think of anything to say.

Recently, he'd been silent for whole evenings, reading, or simply sitting. Rent, plus utilities, plus insurance, minus lessons, plus food—columns of figures went marching through his head, knocking everything else out of it. Once, after he'd had a day of particularly demoralizing students, Caroline perched on the arm of his chair. "Things will work out," she said, and touched his cheek.

She might just as well have socked him. "Things will work out?" he said. He was ready to weep with desire that this be true, yet it was manifestly not. "You mean—Ah. Perhaps what you mean is that things will work out for some other species. Or on some other planet. In which case, Caroline, you and I are in complete accord. After all, life moves on."

She was staring at him, her hand drawn back as though she'd inadvertently touched a hot stove. Was that his voice? Were those his words? He could hardly believe it himself. Those stiff words, like stiff little soldiers, stiff with shame at the atrocities they were committing.

"Life moves on," he continued, ruthless and miserable, "but not necessarily to the benefit of the individual, does it? Yes, things will work out eventually, I suppose. But do you think they'll work out for the guy who sleeps in front of our building? Do you think—" The danger and excitement of probing his terror narrowed his vision into a throbbing circle, from which Caroline, imprisoned, stared back. "Do you think they'll work out for me?"

She'd retreated to the other room, and he sat with his head in his hands. Evidently, Caroline herself did not understand or accept

the very thing she had just forced him to understand and accept—
that he, like most humans, was an experiment that had never been
expected to succeed, a little padding around some evolutionary
thrust, a scattershot nubbin of DNA. It was a matter of huge biological importance, for some reason, that he be desperate to meet
the demands of his life, but it was a matter of no biological importance whatever that he be *able* to meet them.

. But that week—that very week—an airmail letter arrived
from a Richard Penwad inviting Shapiro to play Umberto García-
Gutiérrez's Second Piano Concerto at a Pan-American music
festival.

An amazing occurrence. Though one that, having occurred,
was—like every other occurrence—plausible. The terrible feeling
hanging over the apartment began to evaporate. Shapiro was embarrassed by his recent behavior and feelings, which now seemed
absurdly theatrical, absurdly childish. Of course things would work
out. Why wouldn't things work out? Why shouldn't he and Caroline go to whatever restaurant she pleased? And enjoy it. Order some
decent wine, attend concerts, travel . . . Check in hand, he would
lead Caroline into the bower of celebrity and international convivi-
ality from which he'd been exiled. However gradually, in due course
things would work out.

In the days that followed, Shapiro felt by turns precariously
elated and violently dejected, as though he were emerging from
the chaos of an accident that had left him impaired in as yet un-
disclosed ways. He would catch Caroline gazing at him soberly
with her great, light-filled eyes. She mentioned the invitation
frequently. "Isn't it terrific?" she said. "Aaron. How terrific." Her
voice was tender and lingering—remote, the voice in which, when
they'd first met, she'd recounted to Shapiro tales of her idyllic
childhood. Then, one evening, when he came home with a guide-
book, she said, "Listen, Aaron." And her voice had been especially
gentle. "We have to talk."

*   .   *   *

Shapiro checked the clock by his uncomfortable bed; it would be a relief to go downstairs and meet Penwad. His brain felt unbalanced by Caroline's precipitous entrances and exits; anything to block them. He shut the door of his dark, cramped room behind him, and descended to the restaurant; yes, unbalanced! The corridors themselves seemed to buckle underfoot.

The festival would have been an attractive proposition even at the best of times. Shapiro had played once before in Latin America—a concert in Mexico City many years earlier. The air in the hall had been velvety with receptivity, the audience ideal, and although his piece had been first on the program, they had demanded an encore from him right then and there.

The García-Gutiérrez concerto had furnished other happy occasions in his career. He'd performed its United States premiere some seventeen years earlier. The piano part was splashy and difficult, perhaps not terribly substantial, but an excellent vehicle for Shapiro; it glittered in his hands. García-Gutiérrez had been there to congratulate him with a quiet intensity. What would he look like now, Shapiro wondered. At that time he'd been handsome—silvery hair, tall, hooded eyes. How young Shapiro must have seemed, with his abashed, eager gratitude!

Penwad was already downstairs at the restaurant drinking a coffee. He extended, with official enthusiasm, a carefully manicured but stubby hand, and grimaced as Shapiro shook it. "We're pleased we could get you down," he said, and glanced at his palm. "This is our first go at the festival, I think I must have written you, but we're hoping to bring people such as yourself annually, from all over the Americas—especially the States. We're starting out with García-Gutiérrez as our star attraction, you see, because he's a local boy."

On the walls were posters of palm-fringed lakes, frosted volcanoes, and Indians smiling regal, slightly haughty smiles. Interspersed with the posters were magnificent examples of Indian textiles.

"Charming, isn't it?" Penwad said. "Not a—an *ostentatious* place, but we felt you'd find it charming."

Charming, Shapiro thought. Well, probably the other hotels were even worse. He glanced at the walls again. Charming! It was well known, what was happening in this country to the descendants of its earliest inhabitants—massacres, internment, debt slavery, torture—and, *naturally,* the waiters who scurried around beneath the smiling posters, looking raddled and grief-stricken, were Indians, ceremonial costumes draping their skinny bodies.

"People don't tend to be aware how vigorous our sponsorship of the arts is," Penwad was saying. "We're hoping the festival will help to . . . rectify the, ah, perception that we're identified with the military here."

Shapiro's attention was wrenched from the waiters. "The perception that . . ."

"Rectify that perception," Penwad said.

Fee, Shapiro reminded himself. Fee plus lessons, minus rent, minus utilities . . . Well, and besides, there would be the credit. In a program note, even the most dubious event acquired grandeur. And why not? Concerts and exhibitions from the beginning of time had been funded by villains in search of endorsement, apologists, a place in history, or simple self-esteem. "Incidentally," Shapiro said, "who is 'we'?"

Penwad raised his eyebrows. "Who is we?" he said.

"That is, when you say 'we'—"

"Ah," Penwad said. "Well, I'm not including myself, actually. I'm just a liaison, really, between the Embassy and various local committees and groups concerned with the arts."

"I see," Shapiro said, with no attempt at tact.

"So," Penwad said. "We'll get you a bit of breakfast, then go on over to the Arts Center, take a little look around— Rehearsal all day, rather strenuous, I'm afraid. After that we've fixed up a little interview for you—I trust that's all right—around dinnertime.

Friday's free until the concert. Joan and I will pick you up first thing in the morning to show you around." He smiled. "Joan has her own ideas, but you must say what interests *you*. Then, after the concert, there's to be a party, a reception for you, essentially, at the home of some friends of ours, very fine people here. Then plane, yes? Very next morning." He already, Shapiro noticed, looked relieved. "Quite a whirlwind."

"Wonderful," Shapiro said. "But no need, you know, to take me over to the . . . Arts Center. Why don't I just grab a taxi?"

Penwad waved his hand. "I'm afraid the Center is difficult to find. Most of the drivers are unfamiliar with it. Besides," he added, "enjoy your company." He narrowed his eyes at his coffee cup, and raised it to his mouth.

There was something anatomical about the Center's great concrete sweeps and protuberances. Like all Arts Centers and Performing Arts Complexes and National Centers for the Performing Arts, though futuristic in design, it had a look of ancient decay, being left over from a period when leisure time and economic abundance were considered an imminent menace. How quaint a notion that now seemed! Shapiro almost laughed to think there had been a period, the period in which he'd grown up, no less, when it had been feared that wealth would soon cause humanity to devolve into a grunting mass sprawled in front of blood-drenched TV screens. But, no—*Art* (whatever that was), encouraged to flourish in its Centers, would prevent people from becoming intractable, illiterate, fat! And all the while poverty was accomplishing the devolution by itself.

"I see you're enjoying the, ah, prospect," Penwad said.

Shapiro became aware that he was staring down over toothy crenellations into a city cleaved by deep ravines and encircled by mountains.

"Those tall buildings are the downtown area, of course," Penwad said. "And to the right and left, obviously, are residential sectors. Our place is over there—that's pretty much where the whole English-speaking community has . . . put down its little roots. And up there on the slopes is what we call the Gold Zone."

Shapiro, shading his eyes, noticed that the ravines below were encrusted with fuming slums. "My God," he said.

"Incredible, isn't it," Penwad said, "what an earthquake can do? You can really see the damage from up here. You probably noticed the floor of your hotel. The Center survived intact, though. We're very proud of the Center. The architect was truly successful, we feel, the way he . . . Yes, actually. You might be interested. A fellow named Santiago Méndez. He's done most of the better hotels in town, and our museum. There was a lecture last year. One of our events. It was explained. The way Méndez— Well, this was some time ago, of course—Joan would be better able to . . . But . . . the . . . combined influences." He gestured toward several concrete mounds. "The modernistic, the indigenous . . . well, *motifs.* A cross-fertilization, as Joan says."

Shapiro hesitated. A bunting-like stupefaction had enveloped him. "Of . . . what?" he asked.

"Of . . . ? What of what?" Penwad asked.

"Of . . ." Shapiro had lost the thread of his own question. "Of what . . . does *Joan* . . . say 'cross-fertilization'?"

"Joan *says* it . . ." Penwad glared at him. "She says it of . . . mo*tifs.*"

The orchestra was from a small, nearby dictatorship, and the musicians had a startled appearance, as though a huge claw had snatched them from their beds and plonked them into their chairs. The conductor, a delicate and intelligent-looking man, welcomed Shapiro with reassuring collegiality, but when he brought down his baton Shapiro almost cried out; the sound was so peculiar that he feared he was suffering from some neurological damage.

How had the conductor come to find himself in his profession, Shapiro wondered. The man's waving arms seemed to be signaling for help rather than leading an orchestra. The poor musicians clutched their instruments, staring wildly at their sheet music as they played. But then it was Shapiro's entrance; notes began to leap froggily from his own fingers, and he understood: clearly the hall was demonic.

How to outwit these acoustics? As if this concerto were not difficult enough under the best of circumstances, with all its flash and bombast! But, of course, there was always something. Even in the loftiest, the most competently administered concerts, catastrophes invented themselves from the far reaches of possibility. The piano bench would fall into splinters at seven forty-five, or the other musicians turned out to have a new version of the score, three measures shorter than one's own, or there was a bank holiday and it was impossible to retrieve one's tuxedo from the cleaner's—catastrophes far beneath the considerations of music, and yet!

How synthetic the concerto sounded in this inhospitable hall! Shapiro was surprised to find himself disliking it so. He had never tremendously admired it, exactly, but he'd always enjoyed playing it: he'd enjoyed the athletic challenge of its surface complexities; he'd enjoyed the response of the audience. It was *affirming,* people said upon hearing it, and their faces had the shining, decisive expressions of people who feel their worth to be recognized. *Affirming,* Shapiro thought, as sound sloshed and bulged, gummed up in clumps, liquefied, as though the air were full of whirling blades.

The interview that had been arranged for Shapiro was with an English journalist named Beale. An interview: implied interest on the part of someone. There would be clippings, at least, and, perhaps, therefore some shadowy retention of his name in the minds of those people—"we"—who put these festivals together.

Shapiro located Beale in a restaurant of the hotel, much larger than his own, where they'd been scheduled to meet. "Are you tired of it?" Beale inquired anxiously. "I was hoping not. In my opinion it's the best food in town, and the station will reimburse if it's an interview."

Beale's head was an interesting spaceship shape. Colorless and sensitive-looking filaments sprouted from it, and his ears looked like receiving devices. Sensors, transmitters, Shapiro thought, noting Beale's other large, responsive-looking features and his nervous, hesitant fingers. Beale's suit was faintly mottled by traces of stains; his shirt, from the evidence of his wrists, was short-sleeved, and he wore, incredibly, a tie that appeared to be made of rope.

"I'm not tired of it yet," Shapiro said. "I've never been here."

Beale squinted distrustfully at Shapiro. "They didn't put you here? They put a lot of guests here . . ."

Shapiro glanced around. So this was where they'd put an *important* musician. It was ugly and grandiose, with slippery-looking walls—the very air seemed soaked with a venal, melting luxe. "Santiago Méndez?" he said.

"Oh, you're good," Beale said with delight. "Seriously. If they bring you down again, insist. Nice, isn't it? They all speak English, and the furniture doesn't just"—he lunged toward Shapiro in illustration—"loom up at you. Now, will you drink something?"

Shapiro saw that two glasses already sat in front of Beale, one emptied and the other containing hardly more than a gold film. "Just water, thanks," Shapiro said.

"Oh, you can, here," Beale said. "Rest assured. Ice and all. I, on the other hand," he informed a waiter, "will have a whiskey, why not."

"And perhaps we could order," Shapiro added. Well, at least someone had seen fit to arrange a party for him.

Beale studied the menu worriedly, running his finger along the print. He had quantities of advice for Shapiro about it but seemed unable to make up his own mind. "A nice chop, perhaps," Beale said. "You know, this is the one place where it's perfectly safe to eat pork. That is, if you—" His eyes blinked and reset themselves furiously, like lights on an overtaxed instrument panel.

While Beale entrusted his order to the waiter, Shapiro's attention wandered to posters on the wall. Plenty of charm here, too: more lakes, more volcanoes, more smiling Indians . . . Beale dove abruptly beneath the table, resurfacing with a tape recorder as primitive-looking as a trilobite. "I hope you don't mind if I . . . There are several publications that are reasonably, well . . . friendly to me, but mostly I do radio."

"Radio," Shapiro agreed politely. "And this would be for . . . the English-speaking community, I presume."

Beale looked at him blankly. "Not really. There are telephones for that sort of thing. Oh! No." His voice became gluey with attempted modesty. "No, this is a show back home in England, you see. They often ask me for a little story."

England. So, this was a bit more promising. "A show . . . about the arts," Shapiro suggested.

"The arts?" Beale said. "Well, there's not really too much scope for that sort of thing here. This country isn't just churning out the artists, you know. Not a very . . . well, 'favorable climate' I suppose is the expression. Actually, it's a show about just whatever happens to come up. I was glad when your Embassy called and put me on to this one, because there's not really a fantastic amount. You can file only just so often about dead students before people get sick of it. Still, don't think I'm complaining—I'm lucky to be here at all. When I was young, I was simply frantic to get to this part of the world. Astonishing place. Have you had much chance to get around? See the sights, meet the people?"

"I got in last night," Shapiro said.

"Ah," Beale said. "Oh, yes. Well, it is truly staggering. Very beautiful, as I'm sure you know. And the highlands—when I first came it was like the dawn of the earth up there, really. Oh, if I could only . . ." He sighed. "You know, the Indians here had simply everything at one time. A calendar. A written language—centuries, centuries, *centuries* before the Spanish came. And all sorts of

other magnificent, um—appurtenances. While *we* were still running around in—" He cast a veiled glance at Shapiro. "Yes. Well,
and the Spanish actually destroyed it all. But you know that.
Burned their books, herded them into villages with Spanish over-
seers. Isn't it amazing? The written language was actually de*stroyed,*
do you see. The calendar, the architecture, the books . . . And so, I
mean, we're slaughtering these people and so forth, but we don't
really know anything about them. And if they know anything
about themselves they're not letting on. Who *are* they? That is,
who are *we*? I mean, *they're* here, *we're* here . . . It's just terribly
strange." He smiled a misty, wondering smile, then frowned. "Oh
dear. *Any*how, I tried and tried to get people to send me here. They
said, 'But *why*? Where *is* it? Nothing *happens* there.' Then, fortunately, there were all these insurrections and repressions and what-
not, and that created demand, and so now I've been here over
fifteen years!"

Shapiro opened his mouth; a blob of sound came out.

"I tried to reach García-Gutiérrez yesterday," Beale said. "But
I gathered he hadn't arrived yet. He lives in Europe a lot of the
time now, you know. They told me he'd be in today, but I thought
I'd talk to you instead. I'm sure he's a wonderful composer. They
say he is. But, to tell you the truth, the man gives me the shivers.
I've seen him around, at parties here, and I just don't like his sort.
You know what I mean—well-fed, a bit of a dandy. *Suave.* Eye
always on the main chance. A big smile for every colonel. Ladies
all love him. Government always showing him off like a big,
stuffed . . ." Beale brooded at his drink, then waved over a new
one. "Anyhow," he said unhappily, "I've got you."

Shapiro took a sip of water. He would have liked a drink, too,
but alcohol affected him unpredictably. Even Beale's alcohol
seemed to be making Shapiro mentally peculiar. "Let me ask you,"
he said. "It isn't actually dangerous here, I suppose."

"Dangerous?" Beale said. "Why? What do you mean? Not for

you, it isn't. You know"—he sat back and looked at Shapiro with drunken coldness—"I find it *most* comical. How Americans come down here, and they talk about danger. And they talk about *this,* and they talk about *that.* Well, I don't endorse slavery and torture myself, but who are you, may I ask, to talk? Dare I mention who kicked off all this ha-ha 'counterinsurgency' business here in the first place? Dare I mention whose country it was that killed *all* their Indians?"

"Now, look—" Shapiro began.

"A thousand apologies," Beale said. "How true. You're no more responsible for your country than I am for mine. But all this simply jerks my chain, I'm afraid. It simply does. And I mean *dangerous!* I mean this place is hardly in the league of—I mean, one's forever reading, isn't one? How some poor tourist? Who's saved his pennies for years and years and years. Who then *goes* to New York, to see a show on your great Broad*way,* and virtually the instant he arrives gets stabbed in the . . ." He took a violent gulp of his drink. "The—"

"Liver," Shapiro said.

"*Sub*way," Beale said. "Yes." He beamed at Shapiro in surprise. "I don't know why that's so difficult to . . . Oh, look," he exclaimed, as the waiter set down their plates. "Oh, my darling! That *is* nice." He extracted a pair of glasses from his pocket, put them on to peer at his plate, then removed them to clean them on his ropy tie.

Shapiro took a bite of his meal, but Beale's grubbiness had damaged his appetite.

"Of course the highlands are another story," Beale said. "The highlands, the whole countryside, really—still sheer carnage. But here in the city it's just sporadic violence. Of a whatsit sort. Really, about the worst that can happen to you here is Protestants. Random. Of a random sort."

"Protestants?" Shapiro said.

"Evangelicals," Beale said. "So bloody noisy. Haranguing in the streets, massive convocations every which place, speaking in tongues—YAGABAGABAGAGABAGAGA." He sighed. "Now, don't think I'm prejudiced, please. I'm Protestant myself. But that's the point, isn't it? That one can slag off one's own group, though one would never— That is, I, for instance, would never, oh, say, call . . . a Jew, for example, a '*kike*'—that's *your* prerogative. But all that shouting is simply not the point of speech. I mean, the point of speech is— Well, that is just very simply not the point. And it can be terribly, just terribly annoying when you're trying to conduct an interview or what have you, as you and I are here today."

"Perhaps . . ." Shapiro began with difficulty. "That is, perhaps, speaking of the interview, perhaps there's something you'd like to ask me."

"Ah," Beale said. "Right you are." He smiled, then frowned. "But the thing is, old man—I'm afraid I'm not all that familiar with . . . If you could help me out a bit. That is, perhaps we'd best stick to rather general concepts."

Shapiro nodded. "If you wish. What . . . for example, were you thinking we might—"

"Yes," Beale said. "Hmm. Well, I suppose we might talk about your . . . oh, impressions, for example, of the country . . ."

Shapiro looked at him. "I only arrived last—"

"Last night," Beale said impatiently. He drummed his fingers on the tape recorder. "Well, but just generally, you know. Just something . . . spontaneous."

Shapiro pressed his fingers to the corners of his eyes.

"Not acceptable. I see, not acceptable," Beale said, bitterly. "Well, in that case . . . we could talk, for example, about what it feels like to come down here as an American."

"As an American?" Shapiro said. "I'm not *down* here as an American. I'm not down here *as* anything. I'm down here as a *pianist*."

"Yes," Beale said. "Quite."

Heat began to creep over Shapiro's skin as Beale stared at him.

"You know," Beale said, "I've always wondered. And this is something that I think would be very interesting to the radio audience. How do instrumentalists feel about their relationship—that is, via music, of course—to the composer?"

"What are you—" Shapiro began.

"Well, the very *word*—" Beale said. "That is, the word *literally*, well, it literally *means*—well, instru*men*talist. I mean, you're a—"

"Excuse me," Shapiro said. "I've got to . . . get to a phone."

Shapiro fled into a system of corridors and polyp-like lobbies or reception rooms. Oh, to be alone! The men's room? Maybe not. Well, actually, there was a phone booth. Shapiro sat down inside it, shutting himself into an oceanic silence. Beyond the glass wall people floated by—huge, serene, assured, like exhibits. Shapiro leaned against the wall. He rested his hand on the phone as though it were the hand of an old lover. Absently, he stroked the receiver, then lifted it, releasing a loud electronic jeer—the sound, as silence is not, of emptiness. He would tell Beale that he was unwell, that he had to go rest.

Shapiro paused at the entrance to the restaurant. Beale was sitting at the table alone, his narrow shoulders hunched and his spaceship head bent over the tape recorder as he spoke into it. There was urgency in Beale's posture, and his face was anguished. What could he be saying? Shapiro took a step closer.

"Ah!" Beale said, clicking off the machine with a bright smile, as though he'd been apprehended in some mild debauchery. "Get through?"

"Excuse me?" Shapiro said.

"Get your call through?"

"Oh," Shapiro said. He sat down and passed his hands across his face. "No."

"No," Beale agreed with unfocused sympathy. "Oh, it's all so difficult. *So* difficult. Now—" He smiled sentimentally. Amazingly, he appeared to have completely forgotten he'd been in the process of attacking Shapiro. "Not to worry—we're going to get a very nice little segment about you. In fact"—he twinkled slyly— "I've already done something by way of an intro. Your name and so on, you're down here for the festival, you'll be playing the García-Gutiérrez . . . Hmm." He removed his glasses to study a crumpled piece of paper. "And, let's see." He turned on the machine and spoke into it again. "You've played the piece before with great success . . . Mr. Shapiro, I understand." He nodded encouragingly and indicated the machine.

Shapiro looked at it. "Yes," he said, wearily.

Beale gave him a wounded glance. "In fact, you premiered the piece in the U.S., I believe."

Shapiro closed his eyes.

"Yes," Beale said. He took a deep breath through his nose. "Well, *any*how, that was back in, let's see . . . nineteen . . . goodness me! You must be very fond of it."

"Well," Shapiro said, "I mean, it *is* in my repertory . . ."

Beale emitted a giggle, or hiccup. "I have a set of little spoons," he said. "Tiny little silver things. For olives or something of the sort, that someone gave a great-aunt of mine as a wedding present. And somehow *I've* ended up with them."

Shapiro opened his eyes and looked at Beale.

"Well, I don't throw them out, I mean, do I?" Beale said. "I say." He frowned. "Are you not going to . . . ?" He waved at Shapiro's plate.

"No, no," Shapiro said. "Go ahead. Please."

"Thank you." Beale switched off the tape recorder and placed Shapiro's full plate on top of his own empty one. "We'll go on in a minute. And I think we'll get something nice, don't you? Most people like doing radio. It's a lovely medium, lovely. Do you know what I especially like about it?" He interrupted himself to eat, then continued. "One meets people. Oh, I know one does in any profession—it can hardly be avoided. But I mean one *gets out* to meet people, on an equal basis. The voice—it's freeing, wouldn't you agree? Yet intimate. There one is, a great glob of . . . oh . . . pork pie!" His eyes gleamed briefly with lust. "But I mean all one's qualities and circumstances just . . . globbed together, if you see what I mean. The good, the bad, the . . . pointless . . ." He paused again, and rapidly forked food into his mouth. "But with radio, you see, there's a way to separate out the real bit. And all the rest of it—I mean one's body, one's face, one's age . . . even, even"—he glanced around as though bewildered—"even the place where one is sitting! Well, one is free of it, isn't one? One sees how free one really is.

"Great *leaps.* Teleportation. The world is so . . . *roomy.* So full of oddments. But there's that now-you-see-it, now-you-don't quality about life that makes one so very nervous. Danger, as you pointed out just now, yourself. Danger simply everywhere. Everything destroyed, lost, forgotten . . . Well, that's what they want, you know, most of them. *'There's nothing about it in the reports,'* they'll tell you. They'll say it straight to your face. Of course there are ghosts, people say. I suppose that's some help. But a ghost is simply not terribly . . . *communicative.* They haunt, they grieve, that sort of thing. But it's all rather general, you see. Because they don't much really talk.

"Oh, didn't you just love it when you were a boy? It's raining outside, your mum's still working in the shop, you haven't a friend in the world, then you turn on the radio, and someone's talking— to *you.* Oh, my darling! Someone is talking to you, and you don't know, before you turn that radio on, who will be there, or what thing they've found to tell you on that very day, at that very moment. Maybe someone will talk to you about cookery. Maybe someone will talk to you about a Cabinet minister. And then that particular thing is *yours,* do you see what I mean? Who *knows* whether it's something worth hearing? Who *knows* whether there's someone out there to hear it! It's a leap of faith, do you see? That both parties are making. Really the most enormous leap of faith."

He paused to devour the food remaining on Shapiro's plate, and then looked helplessly into Shapiro's eyes. "I mean, I find that all enormously, just enormously . . ." He shook his head and turned away.

Shapiro set his alarm for 6:00 a.m., and slipped out of the hotel before Penwad could come for him, consequences be damned. *Haha*—the day was his! Screechy traffic flew cheerfully through the streets, and toxins gave the air a silvery, fishlike flicker as the sun bobbed aloft on waves of industrial waste.

Shapiro walked and walked. He passed through grand neighborhoods, where armed guards lounged in front of high, white walls. And he passed through poor neighborhoods, where children, bloated with hunger, played in the gutters, their eyes dreamy and wild with drugs. Beyond the surrounding slopes lay the countryside—the gorgeous, blood-drenched countryside.

In some parts of the city Indians congregated on the sidewalk. Some sold chewing gum or trinkets on the corners, some seemed to be living the busy and inscrutable life of the homeless. Their clothing was filthy and tattered, but glorious nonetheless, Shapiro thought, glorious, noble, celebratory—like the banners of an army in rout.

Shapiro considered them with terror. The destitute. People who were almost invisible, almost inaudible. People to whom almost anything could be done: *other* people. At home, in the last five or ten years they had encamped in Shapiro's neighborhood. At first he thought of them as a small and temporary phenomenon. But now they were everywhere—sleeping in parks or on the pavement, ranging through the city night and day, hungry and diseased, in ragged suits and dresses acquired in some other life.

Everyone had become used to them; no one remembered how shocking it had been only a few years earlier to see someone curled up in a doorway, barefoot in freezing temperatures. Most of the time they were just a group at the periphery of Shapiro's vision. But when a student failed to show up for a lesson, or no concert work materialized, or the price of the newspaper went up, or some unexpected expense arose, Shapiro's precious hands would tingle. Injury? Arthritis? Even as it was, daily life was beginning to eat away at Shapiro's small savings. And at such times Shapiro would see those *other* people with an individualized and frigid clarity, would search their faces for proof that each was in some reliable way different from him, as though he were a dying man approaching the gauzy crowds waiting for judgment.

And they—what were they seeing? Perhaps he and his kind seemed a ghostly population to *them*—distant, fading . . . Perhaps at some terrible border you'd simply leave behind everything that you now considered life, forget about once precious concerns, as though they were worn-out shirts or last year's calendar or old lists of things that long ago it had seemed important to accomplish.

Oh, it was probably true, as Caroline had sometimes said, that his fears were irrational. That he'd always find some way to manage. But when the door closed behind her that day he ought to have understood—yes, he thought, that was the moment he ought to have understood—that success, the sort of success Penwad's letter seemed to promise for him again, was something he could just, finally, forget about.

But he had understood nothing; he'd simply sat there numb—for hours—until Lady Chatterley threw herself forward in a frenzy of carpet shredding. "Stop that," he'd said. "Stop, O.K., please?" He'd flicked a finger at her rear, and she'd leapt, snarling. The truth was he had always been a little afraid of the cat. She was Caroline's, but Jim, evidently, was allergic.

Shapiro supposed that, to whatever extent Caroline was thinking about *him,* she would be imagining him in debonair company here, taking part in animated and witty conversations of a sort no living person had ever experienced. Shapiro felt short of breath, as though Caroline were suffocating him with a pillow. "This is a wonderful opportunity for Aaron," she could be assuring Jim at this very instant. "Really it is." Oh, yes. *He,* Shapiro, must be happy so she could be.

An Indian child playing nearby in the street skinned a knee and howled for his mother. Shapiro felt an almost uncontainable sorrow, as though he were just about to cry himself. But to cry it's necessary to imagine the comforter.

Caroline had never cared what things were really like. He'd once overheard her saying thank you to a recorded message. Everything was nice, pleasant, good. If he spoke truthfully to her, she couldn't hear him. She despised no one. Those who were not nice, pleasant, happy simply ceased to exist.

Shapiro was ravenous. He entered an inviting little restaurant. Inside, it was very dark, but low-hanging, green-shaded lamps made a pool of light over each table.

The waiter spoke no English, but was agreeable when Shapiro pointed at a nearby diner's plate of soup. But there had been a time—truly there had—when Caroline actually loved him, had been fascinated by him, not just by his reputation. For a moment he saw her distinctly. She stood holding Lady Chatterley, gazing into space with a baffled sorrow. "Caroline—" he said.

Had he spoken aloud? Three men at a neighboring table were staring at him with a volatile blend of loathing and amusement. All three were mammoth. One appeared to be a North American; he and one of the others wore pistols, visible even in the restaurant's pleasant gloom, beneath their shirttails.

The waiter, bearing soup, interposed himself; Shapiro gestured fervent thanks. He took a spoonful of the soup. It was clear, and delicious. *Food,* he thought.

Plus rent. Plus utilities . . . Yes, tonight the stage of a concert hall, a tuxedo. A party, champagne, adulation. But tomorrow it was back to cat fur.

The waiter arrived with a second plate for him, huge and unexpected. A pretty selection of things that seemed to have been cooked in the broth. Mmm. Shapiro leaned into the light of his hanging lamp to poke around at it—carrots, onions, white beans, cabbage, celery, a small . . . haunch, something that looked . . . like . . . a snout . . .

One of the men at the next table chuckled softly. Shapiro glanced at them involuntarily again, and they stared back, their faces framing the teardrop of light from their hanging lamp. Then one of them, still staring, reached up and unscrewed the bulb.

The enfeebled musicians threw themselves on García-Gutiérrez's last, idiotic, triumphal chord. What had happened? Shapiro felt as though he'd awakened to find himself squatting naked in a glade, blinking up at a chortling TV crew that had just filmed him gnawing a huge bone. Had he played well or badly? He hardly knew. He'd played in a frenzy—the banal sonorities, the trivial purposes, the trashy approximations of treasures forged in the inferno of other composers' souls. Lacerating ribbons of notes streamed from his hands as he tried to flog something out of the piece, but it had simply sat there over them all—a great, indestructible, affirming block of suet.

The sparse audience stopped fanning themselves with their programs and made some little applause. Seething with confusion and misery, Shapiro stood to take his bow, and caught a glimpse of a man who could only be García-Gutiérrez, opaque and dignified in the face of tribute. At the sight, Shapiro reexperienced the frictional response of his skin, seventeen years earlier, to the man's blandishments, like an acquiescence to unwelcome sensual pleasure.

Outside, Penwad resumed his post at Shapiro's elbow. "We'll just stick around here for a few minutes," he said nervously, "then round everyone up and get going to the reception. Oh. I don't believe you've met. Joan."

"That was lovely," Joan said. "Just lovely. You know, we looked for you at your hotel today. We felt sure you'd want to see our Institute of Indigenous Textiles."

"Oh, Lord—" Shapiro floundered. "Yes! No, absolutely. I—"

"We left messages at the desk," Penwad said.

"Well," Joan said. "Those *people* at the desk . . ."

Night had ennobled the Center. Musicians and members of the audience milled about in the uncertain radiance of stars and klieg lights. A slow, continuous combustion of garbage sent up bulletins of ruin from the hut-blistered gorges, which were quickly snuffed out by the fragrance drifting down from the garlanded slopes of the Gold Zone.

Penwad pointed out various luminaries. There was a Cultural Attaché, a Something Attaché, several Somethings from the Department of Something—it was all a matter for experts.

"And do you see the lady over there?" Joan said, nodding discreetly in the direction of a stunning woman with arched eyebrows and a bloodred mouth. She was bending toward a boy who appeared to be about fifteen. "Our hostess. The reception for you is at her house. And her son. Well, as you see. They're identical. You'll enjoy talking to him. Perfect English—he's going to boarding school up in the States, and he just loves it. He loves to meet our visitors. The father's cattle, you know. Special, special people. Josefina's a marvel. You're not going to believe the house. She's a real force behind culture here. And, you can imagine, *some* of these wives . . ."

"Wonderful people," Penwad said. "And of course *you* two know each other from way back."

García-Gutiérrez had joined them, murmuring thanks to Shapiro. He was as handsome as before, though he'd be over sixty—a great tree of a man, at which age was hacking away fruitlessly. His loaflike body was still powerful; his long arms and legs, the musculature so emphatic one felt aware of its operations beneath the very correct clothing, the straining neck and jaws, the hooded eyes. "I feel that you brought something new to my music tonight," he was saying. "Something of a darkness, perhaps." In the man's lingering examination Shapiro felt the blind focusing, adversarial and comprehending, the arousal of the hunter. "Very interesting . . ."

Oh, that night seventeen years earlier! When it was reasonable for Shapiro to assume that he himself was going to be one of the favored. That he, too, would be respected, dignified, happy . . . The audience that night! How gratifying Shapiro had found their ardor then, how loathsome now, in memory. How thrilled they had been, seeing their own bright reflection in all the weightless glitter.

"We'll talk more, you and I, at the reception," García-Gutiérrez whispered, and glided off with Penwad and Joan to a huddle of musicians, who watched their approach with alarm.

Shapiro's heart jumped and blazed. People were beginning to float toward the parking lot. He played *better* now than he had then, but it made no difference—*no difference at all*. And those nights at the stage door; the faces, golden in the light, diamond earrings winking in the gold light . . . All the beautiful women. Gone now. No matter. What was it they'd adored? Those ardent glances, warm in the glow of his fame, the first shock, at the stage door, of Caroline's great, light eyes. A*ffirm*ing, a*ffirm*ing—oh, what was he to *do*? They couldn't even put him in the decent hotel! Caroline was walking down the street. She wore a dainty little dress. The sun was on her hair, but black shadows swung overhead, and battling armies clanged behind her in the dust. Men and women lay on the sidewalk, their torn clothing exposing sticky lesions. One of them shifted painfully and held out a disintegrating paper cup. Caroline paused, opened her purse, and took out a quarter.

"Are you all right?" someone asked. Shapiro blinked, and saw the boy, the son of the woman who was having the reception. "You must be famished." He regarded Shapiro with the merry, complicitous look of a young person who anticipates approval. "What a workout for you, I think, that piece of G.-G.'s. But we'll have plenty of food back at home—the cooks have been racing around all day. Oh! Well, look at this. *He's* smart. He brought his own." The boy directed an amused glance toward Beale, who was ambling toward them, disemboweling an orange.

"Hello," Shapiro said. The boy's tone—despicable. He hoped Beale hadn't caught it.

"Would you care for any?" Beale said. "I'm afraid it's somewhat . . ." He nodded to the boy, who nodded distantly back. "You know," he said to Shapiro, "I'm sorry if I lost my bottle a bit last night. I tend to go on, from time to time, about one thing and another. Hope I said nothing to offend."

"Not at all," Shapiro said. *It made no difference at all.*

"Good good." A pink and rumpled smile wandered across Beale's face. "Goody goody."

Beale was making a complete mess of his orange. A small piece of peel had lodged in his webby tie. The boy was looking at it. "Oh," Beale said, glancing up. "Sorry. Difficult to handle. You know, it's strange about oranges, isn't it? They're so alluring. Irresistible, really. I mean, that color, for example—*orange.* And the *glossiness.* And that delicious smell they have. But it's all very strange. I mean, what good does it do them? They can't enjoy it. At least, so one supposes. All their deliciousness, do they get any fun out of it? No. It only gets them eaten. Isn't that strange? I mean, what is it for, from their point of view? I suppose you might ask the same of a flower. Flowers have sort of got it all, don't they. Looks, scent . . . But they have absolutely no way to appreciate that!" He giggled. "For all we know, they think of themselves as grotesque."

The boy was considering Beale with a dreamy, meditative look. His stare idled among the stains on Beale's suit. "Excuse me," he said. He smiled briefly at Shapiro. "I should go find some of our"—he glanced at Beale—"guests."

Beale gasped. "Did you hear that?" he said. "Little swine. Vicious little prick. As if I were going to crash the party! As if anyone *could* crash their fucking miserable party—they'll have half the fucking *army* at the gate."

"Mr. Shapiro, Mr. Shapiro," someone was calling.

"It's Joan," Shapiro said, hesitating. He heard his name again. "Just a moment!" he called out. "Just a moment," he said to Beale. "I've got to—"

"Little putrid viper," Beale was saying, as Shapiro hurried off.

"We're ready to leave now," Joan said cheerily as Shapiro approached. "Everyone's gone down to the parking lot."

"Just a moment," he said. "I'll be right—"

"Don't be long," she sang with warning gaiety, and tweaked the lapel of his tuxedo.

"I'll be right—" he said. A tuxedo! He might just as well be wearing grease-stained overalls with his name embroidered on the pocket. "One more minute." He hurried back to find Beale, but Beale had disappeared.

"Hello?" Shapiro said. "Hello? I just wanted to—" But where could Beale have gone to? How arrogant that young boy was! How— Well, and the fact was, Shapiro thought, a man in livery could hardly afford to turn up his nose at a sloppy suit. "Hello?" he said again.

For a moment there was just a gentle surf of night noises, but then Shapiro made out Beale's voice, faint, very faint. Following the sound, he saw Beale, a dark shape, crouched in the corner of a concrete trough that must have been intended as some sort of reflecting pool.

Beale was speaking into his tape recorder. His voice had a stealthy, incantatory tone. "And now . . ." But the little noises of the night were washing away his words. ". . . take you to the party I promised you. It's . . . prominent family here."

There was an oily stain, or fissure, Shapiro saw, at the bottom of the trough. "And any important artist from . . . And what a beautiful . . . high, white . . . and tasteful objets d'art. But tonight . . . to take you out into the . . ."

Shapiro stood as still as he could and strained to hear.

"How lovely it . . ." Beale crooned into the machine. "Fountains, flowers . . . And . . . of chirpings! Croakings! Can you hear, my darling?"

Beale held the tape recorder up in the lifeless trough. Shapiro shuddered—a slight chill was coming down from the mountains.

"And those other sounds—do you hear?" Beale said. His voice was growing louder or Shapiro's ears were adjusting, seeking out the words. "The little plashings?" Beale said. "The fountain, yes, but what else? Not Spanish. But a language, yes! Just so. A language that's much, much older.

"Yes, because we're right across from the servants' quarters. And right there, on the servants' portico, the children are playing. The Indian children. Their mothers are all inside, serving little goodies to the guests. Can you hear the chatter behind us, of the guests?" Shapiro closed his eyes. Yes, he could hear it, the chatter, the pointless chatter. And smell the orange-scented garden. Yes—and he could see the children, just beyond the fountain, with their black, black hair, and shrewd, ravishing little faces.

"Good," Beale said. "Yes. And one of the children has a piece of stone or crockery. The others whisper together. They're joining hands—they seem to be inventing a game, don't they? Or reinventing. Some sort of game. Maybe they remember . . ."

Shapiro's name floated up from the parking lot. They were beginning to shout for him. *Yes, yes,* he thought fiercely, and held up a hand as though both to forestall and to shush them. *In a moment . . .* He sat down, as quietly as he could manage, on the cool concrete. Another moment and he'd go.

"When I first came to this country," Beale was telling the tape recorder, "the sky was a blue dome over the highlands. People had more food then, and weren't so afraid. When you went hiking through the villages, suddenly there would be a waterfall, and fifty, a hundred, two hundred women, swaying along the mountain, coming to do their washing."

Ah! Along the mountain, coming closer. Their faces were in shadow still, and indistinct. But any minute, any minute now . . .

"I wanted to speak to them," Beale said. "But how could I? I was only an apparition! But—are you listening, my darling? I know they're still there—they'll always be there, beyond the curtain of blood." Beale stretched himself out in the trough, tucking the tape recorder under his head like a pillow, and a delicious sensation of rest poured into Shapiro's body. "I'm tired now." Beale patted the tape recorder. "I think I'll sleep. But it's going to be all right. Because the first thing. In the morning. When the sun is up again and shining? I'll start back off to them. And finally we'll speak. Please be there with me. They'll be so happy. I know they will. Because everyone has something, some little thing, my darling, they've been waiting so long to tell you . . ."

BRIEF INTERVIEWS WITH HIDEOUS MEN

DAVID FOSTER WALLACE

B.I. #59 04-98
Harold R. and Phyllis N. Engman Institute
for Continuing Care
Eastchester NY

'As a child, I watched a great deal of American television. No matter of where my father was being posted, it seemed always that American television was available, with its glorious and powerful women performers. Perhaps this was one more advantage of the importance of my father's work to the defenses of the state, for we had privileges and lived comfortably. The television program I most preferred then was to watch *Bewitched,* featuring the American performer Elizabeth Montgomery. It was as a child, while watching this television program, that I experienced my first erotic sensations. It was not for several years, until late in my adolescence, that I was able, however, to trace my sensations and fantasies backward to these episodes of *Bewitched* and my experiences as the viewer when the protagonist, Elizabeth Montgomery, would perform a circular motion with her hand, accompanied by the sound of a zither or harp, and produce a supernatural effect in which all motion ceased and all the television program's other characters suddenly were frozen in mid-gesture and were oblivious and rigid, lacking all animation. In these instances time itself appeared to cease, leaving Elizabeth Montgomery free alone to maneuver at her will. Elizabeth Montgomery employed this circular gesture within the program only as a desperate resort to help save her industrialist husband, Darion, from the political disasters which would come if she were exposed as a sorcerer, a frequent threat in the episodes. The program of *Bewitched* was poorly dubbed, and many details of the narratives I, at my age, did not understand. Yet my fascinations were attached to this great power to freeze the time of the program in its tracks, and to render all the other witnesses frozen and oblivious while she went about her rescue tactics among living statues whom she could again reanimate with the circular gesture when the circumstances called for this. Years later, I began, like many adolescent boys, to masturbate, creating erotic fantasies of my own construction in my imagination as I did so. I was a weak, unathletic, and somewhat sickly adolescent, a scholarly and dreamy youth more like my father, of nervous constitution and little confidence or social outgoingness in those years. It is little wonder that I sought compensation for these weaknesses in erotic fantasies in which I possessed supernatural powers over the women of my choosing in these fantasies. Linked heavily to this childhood program of *Bewitched,* these masturbation fantasies' connection to this television program were unknown to me. I had forgotten this. Yet, I learned too well the insupportable responsibilities which come along with power, responsibilities whose awesomeness I have since learned to decline in my adult life since arriving here, which is a story for another time. These masturbation fantasies took their setting from the settings of our actual existences during these times, which were located at the many different military posts to which my father, a great mathe-

matician, brought us, his family, along. My brother and I, separated in age by less than one year, were nevertheless dissimilar in
most things. Often, my masturbation fantasies took their settings
from the State Exercise Facilities which my mother, a former competitive athlete in youth, religiously attended, exercising enthusi-
astically each afternoon no matter of where my father's duties
brought us to live for that time. Willingly accompanying her to
these facilities on most afternoons of our lives was my brother, an
athletic and vigorous person, and often myself as well, at first with
reluctance and direct force, and then, as my erotic reveries set
there evolved and became more complex and powerful, with a
willingness born of reasons of my own. By custom, I was permitted to bring my science books, and sat reading quietly upon a
padded bench in a corner of the State Exercise Facility while my
brother and mother performed their exercises. For purposes of
envisioning, you may imagine these State Exercise Facilities as
your nation's health spa of today, although the equipment used
there was less varied and maintained, and an air of heightened
security and seriousness was due to the military posts to which the
facilities were attached for the uses of personnel. And the athletic
clothing of women at the State Exercise Facilities was very different from today, constituting full suits of canvas with belts and
straps of leather not unlike this, which was far less revealing than
today's exercise clothing and leaving more to the mind's eye. Now
I will describe the fantasy which evolved at these facilities as a
youth and became my masturbation fantasy of those years. You are
not offended by this word, masturbate?'

Q.

'And this is an adequate pronunciation of it?'

Q.

'In the fantasy which I am describing, I would envision myself
on such an afternoon at the State Exercise Facilities, and, as I mas-
turbated, I envision myself gazing out across the floor of vigorous

exercises to let my gaze fall upon an attractive, sensual, but vigorous and athletic and so highly concentrated on her exercises as to appear unfriendly woman, often resembling many of the attractive, vigorous, humorless young women of the military or civilian atomic engineering services who possessed access to these facilities and exercised with the same forbidding seriousness and intensity as my mother and my brother, who spent long periods of their time often hurling a heavy leather medicine ball between them with extreme force. But in my masturbation fantasy, the supernatural power of my gaze would rattle the chosen woman's attention, and she would look up from her piece of exercise equipment, gazing around the facility for the source of the irresistible erotic power which had penetrated her consciousness, finally her gaze locating me in my corner across the activity-filled room, such that the object of my gaze and I locked both eyes in a gaze of strong erotic attraction to which the remainder of the vigorously exercising personnel in the room were oblivious. For you see, in the masturbation fantasy I possess a supernatural power, a power of the mind, of which the origin and mechanics are never elaborated, remaining mysterious even to I who possess this secret power and can employ it at my will, a power through which a certain expressive, highly concentrated gaze on my part, directed at the woman who was the object of it, renders her irresistibly attracted toward me. The sexual component of the fantasy, as I masturbate, proceeds to depict this chosen woman and myself copulating in variations of sexual frenzy upon an exercise mat in the room's center. There is little more to these components of this fantasy, which are sexual and adolescent and, in retrospect, somewhat average, I now realize. I have not yet explained the origins of the American program of *Bewitched* of my early youth for these fantasies of seduction. Nor of the great secondary power which I also possess in the masturbation fantasy, the supernatural power to halt time and magically to freeze all other of the room's exercisers in their tracks with a covert circular motion of my hand, to cause all motion and activity in the State Exercise Facility to cease. You must envision these: heavily muscled missile officers held motionless beneath the barbell of a lift, wrestling navigators frozen complexly together, computer technicians' whirling jump ropes frozen into parabolas of all angle, and the medicine ball hanging frozen between the outstretched arms of my brother and my mother. They and all other witnesses in the exercise room are rendered with but one gesture of my will petrified and insensate, such that the attractive, bewitched, overpowered woman of my choice and myself only remain animated and aware in this dim wooden room with its odors of liniment and unwashed sweating in which now all time has ceased—the seduction occurs outside of the time and movement of the most very basic physics—and as I beckon her to me with a powerful gaze and perhaps as well a slight circular motion of just one finger, and she, overpowered with erotic attraction, comes toward me, I also in turn arise from my bench in the corner and come also toward her as well, until, as in a formal minuet, the woman of the fantasy and I both meet together upon the exercise mat at the room's exact center, she removing the straps of her heavy clothing with a frenzy of sexual mania while my schoolboy's uniform is removed with a more controlled and amused deliberation, forcing her to wait in an agony of erotic need. To compress the matters, then there is copulation in varied indistinct positions and ways among the many other petrified, unseeing figures for whom I have stopped time with my hand's great power. Of course, it is here you may observe this linkage with the program of *Bewitched* of my childhood sensations. For this additional power, within the fantasy, to freeze living bodies and halt time in the State Exercise Facility, which began merely as a logistical contrivance, became swiftly I think the primary fuel source of the entire masturbation fantasy, a masturbation fantasy which was, as any onlooker can easily be able to tell, a fantasy much more of power than merely of copulation. By this I am saying that envisioning my own great powers—over citizens' wills and motion, over the flowing of time, the frozen obliviousness of witnesses, over whether my brother and my mother even may move the robust bodies of which they were so justly proud and vain—soon these formed the true nucleus of the fantasy's power, and it was, unknown to me, to fantasies of this power that I was more truly masturbating. I understand this now. In my youth I did not. I knew, as an adolescent, only that the sustaining of this fantasy of overpowering seduction and copulation required some strict logical plausibility. I am saying in order to masturbate successfully, the scene required a rational logic by which copulation with this exercising woman is plausible in the public of the State Exercise Facility. I was responsible to this logic.'

Q.

'This may appear so outlandish, of course, from the perspective of how little logic is in envisioning a sickly youth causing sexual desire with only a hand's motion. I have really no answer for this. The hand's supernatural power was perhaps the fantasy's First Premise or *aksioma,* itself unquestioned, from which all else then must rationally derive and cohere. Here, you must say I think *First Premise.* And all must cohere from this, for I was the son of a great figure of state science, thus if once a logical inconsistency in the fantasy's setting occurred to me, it demanded a resolution consistent with the enframing logic of the hand's powers, and I was responsible for this. If not, I found myself distracted by nagging thoughts of the inconsistency, and was unable to masturbate. This is following for you? By this I am saying, what began only as a childish fantasy of unlimited power became a series of problems, complications, inconsistencies, and the responsibilities to erect working, internally consistent solutions to these. It was these responsibilities which swiftly expanded to become too insupportable even within fantasy to permit me ever to exercise again true power of any type, hence placing me in the circumstances which you see all too plainly here.'

Q.

'The true problem begins for me in soon recognizing that the State Exercise Facility is in truth public, open to all those of the post's personnel with proper documentation desiring to exercise; therefore, some person at any time could with ease stride into the facility in the midst of the hand's seduction, witnessing this copulation amidst a surreal scene of frozen, insensate athletics. To me this was not acceptable.'

Q.

'Not because of so much anxiety at being caught or exposed, which had been the concerns of Elizabeth Montgomery in the program, but for myself more because this represented a loose thread in the tapestry of power which the masturbation fantasy, of course, represented. It seemed ridiculous that I, whose circular hand's gesture's power over the facility's physics and sexuality was so total, should suffer interruption at the hands of any random military person who wanders in from outside wishing to perform calisthenics. This was the first-stage indication that the metaphysical powers of my hand were, though supernatural, nevertheless too limited. A yet more serious inconsistency occurred to me soon in the fantasy, as well. For the immobile, oblivious personnel of the exercise room—when the woman of my choice under my power and myself had now satiated one another, and dressed, and returned to our two positions across the wide facility from one another, with she, her, recalling now of the interval now only a vague but powerful erotic attraction toward the pale boy reading across the room, which would permit the sexual relation to occur again at whatever future time I would choose, and I then performed the reversed second hand gesture which permitted time and conscious motion in the facility to again begin—the now-resumed personnel in the midst of their exercises would, I realized, merely by glancing at their wristwatches, then they would be made aware that an inexplicable amount of time had passed. They would, therefore, be, in truth, not truly oblivious that something unusual had occurred. For instance, both my brother and our mother wore Pobyeda wristwatches. All witnesses were not truly *oblivious*. This inconsistency was unacceptable in the fantasy's logic of total power, and soon made successful masturbation to envisioning it impossible. Here you must say *distraction*. But it was more, yes?'

Q.

'Expanding the hand's imagined powers to stop all clocks, timepieces, and wristwatches in this room was the initial solution, until the nagging realization occurred that, just at the moment the room's personnel, afterward, left the State Exercise Facility and reentered the external flow of the military post outside, any first glance at some other clock—or, for example, the remonstrance of an appointment with a superior for which they were too late—this nevertheless would once again bring them to realize that *something* strange and inexplicable had taken place, which once again compromised the premise that all are *oblivious*. This, I naggingly concluded, was the fantasy's more serious inconsistency. Despite my circular gesture and the brief harp which accompanied its power, I had not, as I had naively at the outset believed, caused time's flow to cease and taken myself and the bewitched, athletic women out of time's physics. Trying to masturbate, I was agitated that my fantasy's power had in reality succeeded only in halting the superficial *appearance* of time, and then only within the limited arena of the fantasy's State Exercise Facility. It was at this time that the imaginative labor of this fantasy of power became exponentially more difficult. For, within the enframing logic of the fantasy's power, I now required this circular hand's gesture to halt all time and freeze all personnel upon the entire military post of which the exercise facility was a part. The logic of this need was clear. But also it was incomplete.'

Q.

'Excellent, yes. You see where this is now heading for, this logical problem whose circumference will continue expanding as each solution discloses further inconsistencies and further needs for the exercise of my fantasy's powers. For, yes, because the posts to which my father's duties to the computers brought us along were in strategic communications with the entire defense apparatus of the state, thus I soon was required to fantasize that only my one single hand's gesture—taking place in only one bleak Siberian defense outpost, and for the sake of entrancing the will of merely one female programmer or clerical aide—nevertheless now must accomplish the instantaneous freezing of the entire state, to suspend in time and consciousness almost two hundred million citizens in the midst of whatever of their actions might happen to intrude upon my imaginations, actions as diverse as peeling an apple, traversing an intersection, mending a boot, interring a child's casket, plotting a trajectory, copulating, removing new-milled steel from an industrial forge, and so forth, unending and numberless sep—'

Q.

'Yes yes and because the state itself existed in close ideological and defensive alliance with many neighboring satellite states, and, of course, also was in communication and trade with countless other of the world's nations, I all too quickly as an adolescent, trying merely to masturbate in private, found out that my single fantasy of unknown seduction outside time required that the very world's entire population itself must be frozen by the single hand's gesture, all of the entire world's timepieces and activities, from the activities of yam farming in Nigeria to those of affluent Westerners purchasing blue jeans and Rock and Roll, on, on . . . and you see of course yes not merely all human motion and time-measurings but of course the very movements of the earth's clouds, oceans, and prevailing winds, for it is hardly consistent to reanimate the earth's population to awareness at a resumed time of two o'clock with the tides and weathers, whose cycles have been scientifically cataloged to an exacting specificity, now in conditions corresponding to three o'clock or four. This is what I was meaning in referring to the *responsibilities* which come with such powers, responsibilities which the American program of *Bewitched* had wholly suppressed and neglected during my childish viewing. For this labor of freezing and holding suspended of each element of the natural world of earth which intruded to occur to me as I only am attempting to envision the attractive, athletic, uncontrollable cries of passion beneath me on the worn mat—these labors of imagination were exhausting to me. Episodes of masturbation fantasy which used to take up only fifteen brief minutes were now requiring many hours and enormous mental labors. My health, never good, declined in a dramatic fashion in this period, so much so that I was often bedridden and absent from my schools and from the State Exercise Facilities which my brother attended with my mother after school period. Also, my brother began at this time to become a competitive power weight lifter in the light divisions of his age and weight, competitions of lifting which our mother often attended, traveling along with him, while my father remained on duty with the targeting programs and I in bed in our empty quarters alone for whole days in a row. Most of my times alone in the bed in our room in their absence were increasingly devoted, not to masturbating, but in the labor of imagination of constructing a sufficiently motionless and atemporal planet earth to allow my fantasy merely to take place at all. I do not, in fact, remember now whether the American program's implicit doctrine required the circular hand motion of Elizabeth Montgomery to deanimate the whole of humanity and the natural world outside the suburban home she shared with Darion. But I vividly do remember that a new, different television performer assumed the role of Darion late in my childhood, near the end of the American program's avail-

ability from transmitters in the Aleutian, and my discomfiture,
even as a child, at the inconsistency that Elizabeth Montgomery
would fail to recognize that her industrialist mate and sexual partner was now altogether a different man. He did not look similar at
all and she remained oblivious! This had caused me some great
distress. Of course, also there was the sun.'

Q.

'Our sun up above, overhead, whose seeming movement
across the southern horizon was, of course, time's first measure
among man. This too must be suspended in its apparent movement, as well, by the logic of the fantasy, which, in reality, this
entailed halting the very earth's own spin. Very well I recall the
moment this further inconsistency occurred to me, in the bed, and
the labors and responsibility it implied within the fantasy. Well,
too, do I remember this envy I felt of my brutish, unimaginative
brother, upon whom the excellent scientific instruction of so many
of the posts' schools was sheerly wasted, and he would not be in
the least overwhelmed by the consequences of realizing this further: that the earth's rotation was but one part of its temporal
movements, and that in order not to betray the fantasy's First
Premise through causing incongruities in the scientifically cataloged measurements of the Solar Day and the Synodic Period, the
earth's elliptical orbit around the sun must itself be halted by my
supernatural hand's gesture, an orbit whose plane, I had to my
misfortune learned in childhood, included a 23.53-degrees angle
to the axis of the earth's own spin, having as well variant equiva-
lents in the measurement of the Synodic Period and Sidereal
Period, which required then the rotational and orbital stopping of
all other planets and their satellite bodies in the Solar System, each
of which forced me to interrupt the masturbation fantasy to perform research and calculations based upon the varying planets' different spins and angles with respect to the planes of their own
orbits around the sun. This was laborious in that era of only very

simple handheld calculators . . . and beyond, for you see where this nightmare is heading for, since, yes, the sun itself is in many complex orbits relative to such nearby stars as Sirius and Arcturus, stars which must now be brought under the hegemony of the hand's circular gesture's power, as did the Milky Way Galaxy, upon whose edge the neighboring cluster of stars which includes our own sun both complexly spins and orbits the many other such clusters . . . and onward and onward, an ever-expanding nightmare of responsibilities and labor, because yes the Milky Way Galaxy of itself also orbits the Local Group of galaxies in counterpoint to the Andromeda Galaxy more than some two hundred million light-years distant, an orbit whose halting entails also a halt in the Red Shift and thus the proven and measured flight of the now-known galaxies from one another in an expanding bloom of expansion of the Known Universe, with innumerable complications and factors to include in the nightly calculations which kept me from the sleep my exhaustion cried increasingly out for, such as, for example, the fact that such distant galaxies as 3C295 receded at rapid rates exceeding one-third the speed of light while far closer-in galaxies, including the troublesome NGC253 Galaxy at merely thirteen million light-years, appeared mathematically to actually be *approaching* our Milky Way Galaxy through its own momentums more rapidly than the larger expansions of the Red Shift could impel it to recede from us, so that now the bed is so awash with the piles of science volumes and journals and sheafs of my calculations that there would be no space for me to masturbate even if I had been able to do so. And it was when it then dawned upon me, amidst an agitated half-sleep in the littered bed, that all these many months' datas and calculations had, so stupidly, been based upon published astronomic observations from an earth whose spin, orbits, and sidereal positions were in the naturally unfrozen, ever-changing mode of reality, and that all of it therefore must be recalculated from my fantasy's gesture's theoretical haltings of the earth and neighboring satellites if the seduction and copulation amidst the timeless obliviousness of all citizens were to avoid hopeless inconsistency—it was then I broke down from it. The fantasy's single gesture of one adolescent hand had proven to entail an infinitely complex responsibility more befitting of a God than a mere boy. These broke me. It was at this moment I renounced, resigned, became again merely a sickly and unconfident youth. I abdicated at seventeen years and four months and 8.40344 days, reaching up high with now both of my hands to make the reversing gesture of linked circles which set all of it free once again in a bloom of renunciation that commenced at our bed and opened swiftly out to include all known bodies in motion. I think you have no idea what this cost for me. Delirium, confinement, my father's disappointments—but these were as nothing compared to the price and rewards of what I underwent in this time. This American program of *Bewitched* was merely the spark behind this infinite explosion and contraction of creative energy. Deluded, broken or not broken—but how many other men have felt the power to become a God, then renounced it all? This is the theme of my power you say you wished to hear of: *renunciation.* How many know the true meaning of it? None of these persons here, I can assure you. Going through their oblivious motions outside of here, crossing streets and peeling apples and copulating thoughtlessly with women they believe they love. What do they know of love? I, who am by my choosing a celibate of all eternity, have alone seen love in all its horror and unbounded power. I alone have any rights to speak of it. All the rest is merely noise, radiations of a background which is even now retreating always further. It cannot be stopped.'

B.I. #72 08-98
North Miami Beach FL

'I love women. I really do. I love them. Everything about them. I can't even describe it. Short ones, tall ones, fat ones, thin. From drop-dead to plain. To me, hey: all women are beautiful.

Can't get enough of them. Some of my best friends are women. I love to watch them move. I love how different they all are. I love how you can never understand them. I love love love them. I love to hear them giggle, the different little sounds. The way you just can't keep them from shopping no matter what you do. I love it when they bat their eyes or pout or give you that little look. The way they look in heels. Their voice, their smell. Those teeny red bumps from shaving their legs. Their little dainty unmentionables and special little womanly products at the store. Everything about them drives me wild. When it comes to women I'm helpless. All they have to do is come into a room and I'm a goner. What would the world be without women? It'd—oh no not again behind you *look out!*'

B.I. #28 02-97
Ypsilanti MI [Simultaneous]

K——: 'What does today's woman want. That's the big one.'

E——: 'I agree. It's the big one all right. It's the what-do-you-call . . .'

K——: 'Or put another way, what do today's women *think* they want versus what do they really deep down *want.*'

E——: 'Or what do they think they're *supposed* to want.'

Q.

K——: 'From a male.'

E——: 'From a guy.'

K——: 'Sexually.'

E——: 'In terms of the old mating dance.'

K——: 'Whether it sounds Neanderthal or not, I'm still going to argue it's the big one. Because the whole question's become such a mess.'

E——: 'You can say that again.'

K——: 'Because now the modern woman has an unprecedented amount of contradictory stuff laid on her about what it is she's supposed to want and how she's expected to conduct herself sexually.'

E———: 'The modern woman's a mess of contradictions that they lay on themselves that drives them nuts.'

K———: 'It's what makes it so difficult to know what they want. Difficult but not impossible.'

E———: 'Like take your classic Madonna-versus-whore contradiction. Good girl versus slut. The girl you respect and take home to meet Mom versus the girl you just fuck.'

K———: 'Yet let's not forget that overlaid atop this is the new feminist-slash-postfeminist expectation that women are sexual agents, too, just as men are. That it's OK to be sexual, that it's OK to whistle at a man's ass and be aggressive and go after what you want. That it's OK to fuck around. That for today's woman it's almost *mandatory* to fuck around.'

E———: 'With still, underneath, the old respectable-girl-versus-slut thing. It's OK to fuck around if you're a feminist but it's also not OK to fuck around because most guys aren't feminists and won't respect you and won't call you again if you fuck around.'

K———: 'Do but don't. A double bind.'

E———: 'A paradox. Damned either way. The media perpetuates it.'

K———: 'You can imagine the load of internal stress all this dumps on their psyches.'

E———: 'Come a long way baby my ass.'

K———: 'That's why so many of them are nuts.'

E———: 'Out of their minds with internal stress.'

K———: 'It's not even really their fault.'

E———: 'Who wouldn't be nuts with that kind of mess of contradictions laid on them all the time in today's media culture?'

K———: 'The point being that this is what makes it so difficult, when for example you're sexually interested in one, to figure out what she really wants from a male.'

E———: 'It's a total mess. You can go nuts trying to figure

out what tack to take. She might go for it, she might not. Today's woman's a total crapshoot. It's like trying to figure out a Zen koan. Where what they want's concerned, you pretty much have to just shut your eyes and leap.'

K——: 'I disagree.'

E——: 'I meant metaphorically.'

K——: 'I disagree that it's impossible to determine what it is they really want.'

E——: 'I don't think I said *impossible.*'

K——: 'Though I do agree that in today's postfeminist era it's unprecedentedly difficult and takes some serious deductive firepower and imagination.'

E——: 'I mean if it were really literally *impossible* then where would we be as a species?'

K——: 'And I do agree that you can't necessarily go just by what they *say* they want.'

E——: 'Because are they only saying it because they think they're supposed to?'

K——: 'My position is that actually most of the time you *can* figure out what they want, I mean almost logically deduce it, if you're willing to make the effort to understand them and to understand the impossible situation they're in.'

E——: 'But you can't just go by what they say, is the big thing.'

K——: 'There I'd have to agree. What modern feminists-slash-postfeminists will *say* they want is mutuality and respect of their individual autonomy. If sex is going to happen, they'll say, it has to be by mutual consensus and desire between two autonomous equals who are each equally responsible for their own sexuality and its expression.'

E——: 'That's almost word for word what I've heard them say.'

K——: 'And it's total horseshit.'

E——: 'They all sure have the empowerment-lingo down pat, that's for sure.'

K——: 'You can easily see what horseshit it is as long as you remember to start by recognizing the impossible double bind we already discussed.'

E——: 'It's not all that hard to see.'

Q.

K——: 'That she's expected to be both sexually liberated and autonomous and assertive, and yet at the same time she's still conscious of the old respectable-girl-versus-slut dichotomy, and knows that some girls still let themselves be used sexually out of a basic lack of self-respect, and she still recoils at the idea of ever being seen as this kind of pathetic roundheel sort of woman.'

E——: 'Plus remember the postfeminist girl now knows that the male sexual paradigm and the female's are fundamentally different—'

K——: *'Mars and Venus.'*

E——: 'Right, exactly, and she knows that as a woman she's naturally programmed to be more high-minded and long-term about sex and to be thinking more in relationship terms than just fucking terms, so if she just immediately breaks down and fucks you she's on some level still getting taken advantage of, she thinks.'

K——: 'This, of course, is because today's postfeminist era is also today's postmodern era, in which supposedly everybody now knows everything about what's really going on underneath all the semiotic codes and cultural conventions, and everybody supposedly knows what paradigms everybody is operating out of, and so we're all as individuals held to be far more responsible for our sexuality, since everything we do is now unprecedentedly conscious and informed.'

E——: 'While at the same time she's still under this incredible sheer biological pressure to find a mate and settle down and nest and breed, for instance go read this thing *The Rules* and try to explain its popularity any other way.'

K——: 'The point being that women today are now expected to be responsible both to modernity and to history.'

E——: 'Not to mention sheer biology.'

K——: 'Biology's already included in the range of what I mean by *history*.'

E——: 'So you're using *history* more in a Foucaultvian sense.'

K——: 'I'm talking about history being a set of conscious intentional human responses to a whole range of forces of which biology and evolution are a part.'

E——: 'The point is it's an intolerable burden on women.'

K——: 'The real point is that in fact they're just logically incompatible, these two responsibilities.'

E——: 'Even if modernity *itself* is a historical phenomenon, Foucault would say.'

K——: 'I'm just pointing out that nobody can honor two logically incompatible sets of perceived responsibilities. This has nothing to do with history, this is pure logic.'

E——: 'Personally, I blame the media.'

K——: 'So what's the solution.'

E——: 'Schizophrenic media discourse exemplified by like for example *Cosmo*—on one hand be liberated, on the other make sure you get a husband.'

K——: 'The solution is to realize that today's women are in an impossible situation in terms of what their perceived sexual responsibilities are.'

E——: 'I can bring home the bacon mm *mm* mm *mm* fry it up in a pan mm *mm* mm *mm*.'

K——: 'And that, as such, they're naturally going to want what any human being faced with two irresolvably conflicting sets of responsibilities is going to want. Meaning that what they're really going to want is some way *out* of these responsibilities.'

E——: 'An escape hatch.'

K——:   'Psychologically speaking.'

E——:   'A back door.'

K——:   'Hence the timeless importance of *passion*.'

E——:   'They want to be both responsible and passionate.'

K——:   'No, what they want is to experience a passion so huge, overwhelming, powerful, and irresistible that it obliterates any guilt or tension or culpability they might feel about betraying their perceived responsibilities.'

E——:   'In other words what they want from a guy is *passion*.'

K——:   'They want to be swept off their feet. Blown away. Carried off on the wings of. The logical conflict between their responsibilities can't be resolved, but their postmodern *awareness* of this conflict can be.'

E——:   'Escaped. Denied.'

K——:   'Meaning that, deep down, they want a man who's going to be so overwhelmingly passionate and powerful that they'll feel they have no choice, that this thing is bigger than both of them, that they can forget there's even such a *thing* as postfeminist responsibilities.'

E——:   'Deep down, they want to be irresponsible.'

K——:   'I suppose in a way I agree, though I don't think they can really be faulted for it, because I don't think it's conscious.'

E——:   'It dwells as a Lacanian cry in the infantile unconscious, the lingo would say.'

K——:   'I mean it's understandable, isn't it? The more these logically incompatible responsibilities are forced on today's females, the stronger their unconscious desire for an overwhelmingly powerful, passionate male who can render the whole double bind irrelevant by so totally overwhelming them with passion that they can allow themselves to believe they couldn't help it, that the sex wasn't a matter of conscious choice that they can be held responsible for, that ultimately if *anyone* was responsible it was the *male*.'

E——:   'Which explains why the bigger the so-called feminist, the more she'll hang on you and follow you around after you sleep with her.'

K——: 'I'm not sure I'd go along with that.'

E——: 'But it follows that the bigger the feminist, the more grateful and dependent she's going to be after you've ridden in on your white charger and relieved her of responsibility.'

K——: 'What I disagree with is the *so-called.* I don't believe that today's feminists are being consciously insincere in all their talk about autonomy. Just as I don't believe they're strictly to blame for the terrible bind they've found themselves in. Though deep down I suppose I do have to agree that women are historically ill-equipped for taking genuine responsibility for themselves.'

Q.

E——: 'I don't suppose either of you saw where the Little Wranglers' room was in this place.'

K——: 'I don't mean that in any kind of just-another-Neanderthal-male-grad-student-putting-down-women-because-he's-too-insecure-to-countenance-their-sexual-subjectivity way. And I'd go to the wall to defend them against scorn or culpability for a situation that is clearly not their fault.'

E——: 'Because it's getting to be time to answer nature's page if you know what I mean.'

K——: 'I mean, even simply looking at the evolutionary aspect, you have to agree that a certain lack of autonomy-slash-responsibility was an obvious genetic advantage as far as primitive human females went, since a weak sense of autonomy would drive a primitive female toward a primitive male to provide food and protection.'

E——: 'While your more autonomous, butch-type female would be out hunting on her own, actually competing with the males for food.'

K——: 'But the point is that it was the less self-sufficient, less autonomous females who found mates and bred.'

E——: 'And raised offspring.'

K——: 'And thus perpetuated the species.'

E——: 'Natural selection favored the ones who found mates instead of going out hunting. I mean, how many cave-paintings of *female* hunters do you ever see?'

K——: 'Historically, we should probably note that once the quote-unquote *weak* female has mated and bred, she shows an often spectacular sense of responsibility where her offspring are concerned. It's not that females have no capacity for responsibility. That's not what I'm talking about.'

E——: 'They do make great moms.'

K——: 'What we're talking about here is single adult pre-primipara females, their genetic-slash-historical capacity for autonomy, for as it were *self*-responsibility, in their dealings with males.'

E——: 'Evolution has bred it out of them. Look at the magazines. Look at romance novels.'

K——: 'What today's woman wants, in short, is a male with both the passionate sensitivity and the deductive firepower to discern that all her pronouncements about autonomy are actually desperate cries in the wilderness of the double bind.'

E——: 'They all want it. They just can't *say* it.'

K——: 'Putting you, today's interested male, in the paradoxical role of almost their therapist or priest.'

E——: 'They want absolution.'

K——: 'When they say *"I am my own person," "I do not need a man," "I am responsible for my own sexuality,"* they are actually telling you just what they want you to make them forget.'

E——: 'They want to be rescued.'

K——: 'They want you on one level to wholeheartedly agree and respect what they're saying and on another, deeper level to recognize that it's total horseshit and to gallop in on your white charger and overwhelm them with passion, just as males have been doing since time immemorial.'

E——: 'That's why you can't take what they say at face value or it'll drive you nuts.'

K——: 'Basically it's all still an elaborate semiotic code, with the new postmodern semions of autonomy and responsibility replacing the old premodern semions of chivalry and courtship.'

E——: 'I really do have to see a man about a prancing pony.'

K——: 'The only way not to get lost in the code is to approach the whole issue logically. What is she really saying?'

E——: '*No* doesn't mean yes, but it doesn't mean no, either.'

K——: 'I mean, the capacity for logic is what distinguished us from animals to begin with.'

E——: 'Which, no offense, but logic's not exactly a woman's strong suit.'

K——: 'Although if the whole sexual *situation* is illogical, it hardly makes sense to blame today's woman for being weak on logic or for giving off a constant barrage of paradoxical signals.'

E——: 'In other words, they're not responsible for not being responsible, K——'s saying.'

K——: 'I'm saying it's tricky and difficult but that if you use your head it's not impossible.'

E——: 'Because think about it: if it was really *impossible* where would the whole species be?'

K——: 'Life always finds a way.'

WHERE I WORK

ANN CUMMINS

It's piecework that brings in the money. You get four bucks an hour or ten cents a pocket. The old-timers can sew two pockets a minute and make eighteen an hour. They're a whiz. Most get between ten and fifteen. Me, I get four, today maybe five. This is my third day. You don't worry if you're no good at first. You catch on. You're guaranteed the four bucks no matter if you can't get one pocket on in an hour.

Sam Hunt with the measuring tape comes to my machine and measures the straightness of my stitching. He wears the tan vest, tan creased pants, brown polished shoes, white shirt. He has a perfectly formed nose, neither upturning nor downturning, and when he stands in front of my machine, I can smell a mysterious cologne coming from him. When he comes this close, I can see that the white shirt does not stick to any part of his skin because he does not sweat.

But the fat sisters from Galveston sweat like pigs. Turn up the air-conditioning! they'll yell. Today at lunch, I sat with the fatties from Galveston, Texas. You can hear them all over the lunchroom, talking about our Oregon summers, complaining about the heat and rain. They say, My bones never ached like this in Texas, and they wish they could move back there. In Galveston, the fat sisters plopped their rumps on the beach and watched the hurricanes come in. I have never seen a hurricane. When I sit with the Texans they tell me all about it.

And they say, How's your love life, darling? These women mull things over.

It is my duty to make them laugh. This is a social skill my brother, Michael, taught me. Make them laugh, he said, and you won't get fired.

Make them laugh or compliment them. Don't tell lies. Don't say things like, "I'd like to tear her little twat out"; if you have to say something like this, say it approximately, not exactly, or you'll scare people. He told me I scare people, and that's one reason why I can't hold a job—and because I tell lies. If you have to tell lies, tell little ones, he says. Try not to talk out loud when you're not talking to anybody.

At lunch yesterday, when they asked me about my lover, I said, He has a waterbed on his roof.

A waterbed on his roof? they said. In this rain?

Some laughed, some didn't. It's difficult to say what will make the women around here laugh.

But I admire their industry. They hardly make mistakes. Sam Hunt docks you a pocket for every mistake, and these add up.

Sam Hunt drives a scooter to work, a very little one. I have seen him from the bus window. He drives on the edge of the road, on the white line, and the Sandy Street bus could squash him like a penny. Then who would see to the time cards? It takes a certain kind of man. Serious. Not a drinker, I'd say. Nice-fitting suit, gleaming face.

My brother says my face is better than what you usually see. I would marry my brother in an instant, though he's sinister and disrespectful.

Michael drives a taxi and knows the timing of the traffic lights by heart. He drives two-fingered, with his foot both on and off the gas pedal, never speeding up, never slowing down, through the city neighborhoods. Some nights I sit on the passenger's side and the customers sit in the back. My brother's taxi smells like fire. Cinder and ash. In the ashtrays, fat men have stuffed cigars.

I wouldn't mind a fat man. A fat man would be somebody you could wrap yourself around and never meet yourself coming or going. If I married a fat man, I'd draw stars on his back every night. I'd say, How many points does this star have? Now pay attention, termite, I'd say. How many points does this star have?

In his taxi, my brother totes around the downtown whores. Some have the names of the months, June, July, and August. Ask them how much they make a night. Depends on how fast your brother drives, they say. Hurry up, baby, time's money, they like to say. And they spend it in Riverside Park, just junkies in Riverside Park.

It smells like garbage under the bridges in Riverside Park, and those houses over there? In the housing projects, don't go up to a black woman's door. They don't want you. Don't go up to the men on the steps. Keep your hands at your sides. Walk fast or run. Don't look in the windows of a car slowing down. Walk slow if there're dogs or they'll chase you. Keep your hand on your purse. If somebody approaches you, if he gets within ten feet, say, I am fully proficient in the use of semiautomatic weapons. My brother bought me a gun when I moved out on my own, because a woman living alone in this city should be able to defend herself. You go for the knees. We put cardboard circles on a fence post in the country. I can hit them a majority of the time. If you go for the heart or head and murder a person, you could be held liable by the dead man's family, even if he broke into your apartment. This is the justice system in our country, my brother says, and he's right. The justice system in this country treats us like a bunch of stinking fish.

There. A perfect pocket. This is a keeper, so that's one. These are my practice days. They give you a couple of practice days to start out, and after the third day or so you begin to develop a system. Like, one thing is not to stop when you're coming to a corner—not to slow down or speed up and keep your hands going with your foot on the pedal, and just turn the corner without thinking. If you ruin one, put it in your purse—if it's really bad.

Next week we're moving to a new line. Sam Hunt said when he orientated me that we're moving out of the blue and into the white. We'll have enough blue by the end of the week. How's your eyes? he says. The white stitches on the white material can blind you, so remember to blink often.

There's something wrong with my eyes. I can't cry. I'm just a happy idiot, my brother says, but I say there's something wrong with my eyes. They are deteriorating in my head. I have that condition—you read about it, where the eyes dry out unnaturally. I don't cry.

All of the women at this table wear glasses. And smoke. The lunchroom's like a chimney. And they say, How's your love life, darling?

The reason I'm not married yet is because I haven't found the right man. I don't know who he is, but I'll know him when I see him, and he'll look like something, and he won't whore around. Which, I'd shoot him, any man who whored around on me. Like that man in the laundry room. He was married because I saw the ring. And he says, How thin are your wrists? Look at how thin your wrists are. See, he says, I can put my fingers around you and not touch any part. A married man said this.

A lot of the good ones are married. He had green eyes and a friendly manner, and he asked me which was my apartment. He lives right above me—him and his wife. Says, Come up and watch TV sometime. I may just do that. I would like to see their home and their furnishings.

I will ask him to help me move furniture in. When I get my first check I'm going to buy a lamp, a nice brass one, and when I save enough I'm going to buy a brass bed, too, and one of those checkerboard coffee tables, the kind with different colors of wood in squares, and some rugs, throw rugs, and ask them to dinner, the man and his wife, which, you could never ask anybody to dinner at Michael's house because nobody ever does the dishes, and there's nothing in that house but Bob Marley posters and dirt and screaming fits.

My brother has paid my rent for the last time. If he's got to have such a screaming fit about it.

Outside the window in my new apartment on the east side is a mystery tree. We don't know what it is. I've asked around but nobody knows. On a muggy night if you don't turn the light on, you can see animals in the tree. Opossum. Eight, nine, ten of them, gliding along the mystery tree and the tree's branches all in a panic. Black like tar, the branches gleam in the moonlight, all the little opossum claws scratching where you can't see or hear. Shall I open the window? my brother said when he came over. Want some pets? Hold on to your hair. They could get into your hair. He says they're rats, but I have seen them up close. On this, he's wrong. He says this because he's jealous.

Who pays your rent? he says. He says, Who the fuck pays your rent?

My brother has paid my rent for the last time if it's such a big deal.

"My brother had a fire in his taxi."

"What?"

"My brother drives a taxi and somebody started a fire in the backseat."

"Ain't that something." She's the nice one. She says, Sit with us, honey, and tells me about the Texas hurricanes. She's someone you can talk to. "Did he have insurance?"

"What's the difference between a tornado and a hurricane?" The woman has bitten her fingernails to the quick. You can see it from here.

"A tornado? You know, I never considered it. Hey, Lynn. What's the difference between a hurricane and a tornado?"

"One's by sea, one's by land."

"One thing I do know. They can both come up on you in a minute."

"Same with a fire. My brother had a fire in his taxi."

"Ain't that something."

"Somebody left a cigar or cigarette burning in the back. It went, just like that."

"Anybody hurt?"

"They're made of straw. That's why the seats can go just like that."

Then you're walking.

So let him walk. See how that feels.

In the projects a man came up to me. He said, Woman? Woman? He said, Where can I find a pepper grinder? He said for fish, that he was cooking fish and he wanted some fresh ground pepper, and then started laughing and laughed his fool head off.

In the projects, you can get shot and nobody's going to look for you. In the projects, someone has busted out every streetlight, and there's glass in the street, and children playing in it. In the projects, you can walk down one street, up another, a street without lights so you don't see the dirty yellow walls all alike, street after street, with dogs that'll chase you and black women who don't want you, and it smells like garbage in the projects. Those people are filthy.

I don't care if it is cheaper there. He says, You don't have to worry. I'm not going to let anything happen to you. Don't make me cry, Michael. Joyce, I'm not going to let anything happen to you, he says. I told him I'd cry, but there's something wrong with my eyes.

*   *   *

Damn! Now that thread's broken. Where's Sam Hunt? Where's that weasel? Run the flag. Got a problem, he says. Pull this little string. I'll see your flag and respond. They can't be having girls run up and down the aisles looking for the weasel. That way if anything's missing or disturbed anyplace in the vicinity, we'll blame it on Betsy Ross's ghost, he says to me. He has equipped every sewing machine in the place with a little flag. If you have to go to the bathroom, raise the flag, take your purse, don't put it on the floor in the stall because the weasel is not responsible for stolen or lost property.

Somebody should burn that man up.

There are instances where fires occur by spontaneous combustion, and instances where water will not put a fire out. There are oil slicks on the ocean. In dreams, too—there are people burning on the ocean or in impossible places, instances where burning oil floats on water and your clothes are on fire, and your hair is on fire, and in the water the fire goes inward. If it's dirty with oil and muck. Sometimes there's no way to put the fire out.

In such a dream, go into a well. Make it from rocks. The bottom of the well is very smooth, and the rocks are cool. Close your eyes. Put your cheek against a rock. If you're dizzy, reach your arm out. Touch the other side. Twirl in a circle. Put yourself in a blue well, and keep your eyes closed. Turn around and around until the fire stops.

"Joyce? What is it?"

"My thread broke."

"Your thread broke? Do you remember how I showed you to reload your thread? Did you try that? Here. Show me. Remember? Here, now, you hook it around this wire first. Remember. Okay, good. That's right. Yes. Down the pole, into the needle. You pull that back or it's going to knot when you begin to sew. Good. Very good. See? That wasn't so hard. Was it?

"How you doing? You getting along okay? You getting to know people?"

"Yes."

"Let's see what you've done today. No, now you're holding your material too tightly. That's what'll give you the tangled stitches. Remember how I told you to roll it under the foot—just like it's a rolling pin and you're making pie crusts. Remember? You bake, Joyce? Just roll it under the foot with a nice, steady movement."

"Yes, I bake."

"No, now this one's not going to work. See, you've got the X in the corner. You can't overshoot the pattern or you'll have a little X. See? And here's another one.

"Joyce, where are the rest of them? I counted sixty pockets out for you this morning. Now I count—let's see . . . Where're the rest of them?"

"That's all you gave me."

"No. This morning I counted out sixty, and now there are . . . They can't just disappear. Let's see. Forty-eight—

"This is your third day? You're not picking this up, are you? Maybe we should transfer you to pant legs. There aren't as many angles. Come and talk to me when your shift's over."

"I can't. I'll miss my bus."

"Catch the next bus. Come and talk to me. We'll take a look at your file. See what we can do."

I can do this.

This is a cinch. Go forward and backwards to lock in the stitch. Be careful not to overshoot the pattern—be careful not to overshoot the pattern because that's when the X occurs. You can't rip it out because the buying customer will see where the ripping occurred. Now that's ruined. Put it in your purse.

Here's the rest of them. These are ruined. I forgot about these in my purse.

Forgetting is not lying. I'll say, I didn't lie. I forgot, and that's the truth.

What's she smiling at? What's so funny about that pocket? That's a hilarious pocket. These women will laugh behind your back. They listen in on every conversation and then they laugh behind your back. Well, fuck them.

I can do this. So, let them laugh. You go forward and backwards. Every system has its routine. In a house when you live alone, you check the rock by the front door when you come home to see if it's been moved in your absence. If it's been moved, someone has gone in your house. This is just real funny. I'd like to squash her pea-brain. Now that's ruined.

Check the rock and you check for broken windows before you unlock the door, and you keep your gun in the drawer by your bed. I'm going to tell him to give me another chance. This wasn't so good today, but tomorrow's a different story. My brain's ruined for this day. That's a sad thing how a woman will just laugh in your face like that. They think they're so hot.

You keep your gun in the drawer by your bed. If, at three in the morning some person breaks in your house, you take the phone off the hook, dial 0. You don't have time to dial 911. You've got your gun and you're kneeling in bed or on the floor, and you say, I'm fully proficient in the use of semiautomatic weapons. I live at one-one-three-four East Holly. You're saying this to the operator who will call the cops.

Say, "I am fully proficient in the use of semiautomatic weapons—"

"What?"

"What are you looking at?"

"What did you say?"

"I didn't say anything."

"Yes, you did."

"What are you looking at?"

"Hey, don't worry about it. Don't sweat it. Sam's okay. Gets a bee in his lugudimous maximus every now and again, but he's okay."

"They're going to fire me from this job."

"Nah, they ain't going to fire you."

"He's going to look at my file."

"Listen—"

"They look at your file, and then they look at you."

"You've got to—"

"Don't look at me."

"Now, honey—"

"Don't look at me! Don't look in my face."

Don't look anywhere.

They open your file and then they fire you. Everything is ruined now. So who cares.

These are ruined. I've ruined these. Meaning to or not doesn't count. Did you or didn't you? Did you or didn't you? he'll say. He'll call me on the phone. Did you or did you not? Michael will say. I'll say—

When Michael calls—

I'll say, I didn't get to these yet. These were misplaced. I'll say. I'll say, I forgot about these in my purse.

This place is filthy. Somebody ought to clean this place up.

You just do your work. You just pay attention.

I'll leave my coat in the locker. I'll sneak out the back way, and I'll leave my coat in the locker.

I'll say, These are my practice days, Mr. Hunt. I can do this.

I'll sneak out the back way.

I'll catch the Sandy Street bus. If I miss the Sandy Street, I'll catch the Burnside. I won't look at the bums sleeping there. When I walk across the bridge, across the Burnside Bridge—if they ask me for money, I'll look straight ahead.

When Michael calls to ask me how it went—if my brother calls—

I'll say, Not too bad. That's what I'll say.

He'll say, Way to go, Joyce. That's money in the bank.

For dinner, I'll make mashed potatoes or I'll make rice. I'll sit at the table by the kitchen window. I'll watch the sun go down.

I will set my alarm for six so I can catch the Sandy Street bus at seven because the Burnside bus will get me here too late. Sam Hunt sees to the time cards. Don't be late or you're docked pockets, and these add up.

I will set the alarm for six and I'll go to bed at ten. If I wake up in the night—if a dream or nightmare wakes me . . . I must not wake up in the night. A working girl needs her sleep.

THE SOUND GUN

MATTHEW DERBY

We are dragging it by hand now. The engine gave out days ago in a ravine two kilometers south of the parallel. We managed to haul the weapon out of the deep, fecal muck with two stolen mules, which were of no use to us once we ran out of the dried ice cream, the only thing that would get them moving. We killed the mules and ate them, and now we are dragging the Sound Gun by hand, using the last of the rope and medical gauze. No one is happy about this, not even Shaving Gel, whom we call Shaving Gel because he always smells like shaving gel, although we should call him Bulk or Keg or Mountain because he is big. I speculated that he, out of any of them, would champion the cause, shouldering the weapon from behind, barking fiercely at the enlisted men. Instead, he just looked at me evenly from the other side of the campfire, chewing deliberately at his mule as I debriefed the group.

Nobody knows what we are doing here. We are not entirely sure that the war is still happening. Since the mules ate the communications array we have had only the color of the sky to guide us. Evenings, it will burst suddenly into a thin purple halo of dense mist. These rings, we believe, must be the fragrant shards of battles occurring elsewhere in secret. So we continue to plow through the jungle, convinced that, any day now, a dark, backlit man in a business suit will descend from the sky in a clear pod and usher us home.

It was fun to drive around in the Sound Gun until it stopped working. Now the people who are fighting us, and who we are pretty sure are still the enemy, are much more dangerous and harder to kill. They come rushing up at us in the night, tossing sticks and VCRs.

My men go on about the size of the Sound Gun. Everything else is smaller now than in previous wars, but the Sound Gun is unimaginably bigger. "Bigger than what?" I ask Danson in a fit, having overheard this complaint for the last time.

"It's just bigger than it should be, sir," says Danson, a slight, walleyed Presbyterian who carries his recently deceased mother's dialysis machine with him at all times in a bowling ball bag, just in case or as a memento—no one knows for sure. "It should be, like, calculator-size. The size of a handheld—help me someone— think of something handheld . . ."

"A gun," says Memorex.

"Yes, exactly. All we ask is that the Sound Gun be the actual size of a gun? Instead of, like, a whole building?"

"Write it down in your Wish Journal, Private," I tell him. Everyone has a Wish Journal. When we're sad or upset or feeling violent we write in the Wish Journal. "I wish I could wrap my feelings in burlap and throw them into the ocean," we might write, or "I wish the act of sleep actually came with a blanket" or "I wish just one of my fellow soldiers was even remotely as attractive as the ones in the advertisements on the cloud screens, the ones climbing wooden structures with their shirts off or getting pummeled with a long, padded brick."

*   *   *

The Sound Gun has four settings. The first one is Make Scared. Make Scared makes a big loud noise that makes people scared. It is louder and scarier than the noise a bomb makes as it explodes, because the people we're fighting have not been scared by that sound for three wars. The sound that Make Scared makes is like a herd of elk tumbling into a cauldron of hot, resonant dung or, at night, the frail puff of air conjured up by a dying child. Make Scared worked for a while, but then the enemy started putting soaked wheat pods in their ears, so we had to move on to Hurt.

Hurt feels like getting hit hard by a rubber blanket. Not that I'd know—this is what the instructions tell us: *"Stay out of the path of the Sound Gun when using Hurt mode; otherwise, you may be struck by the slug with the force of a large rubber blanket."* Hurt worked for a longer time than Make Scared, because nobody liked having these rubber blankets constantly hurled at her. But the enemy developed a flared aluminum instrument, worn on the hips, that sprayed a hard yellow foam so that they could build tall, ad hoc baffles while advancing on us. We were left with no alternative: we had to switch to Very Hurt.

All the officers have been given a captured enemy soldier as a pet. I'm sickened by this practice, but own one myself and have to admit I have grown considerably dependent on the little man. In an attempt to distance myself from some of the more undesirable aspects of the relationship, I've named him Constantine. It's a dignified name, I think—much more dignified than Bastard Face, Shovel, or Milk of Magnesia, names that have been bestowed upon others in our midst. He has not, as of yet, become comfortable with it. Otherwise, he plays the role of slave with outrageous conviction, leaning into his servitude with an enthusiasm that mars my ability to sympathize with his plight. I want him to be belligerent or distant—anything but eager. Each morning by the time I wake up he's already gone off looking for kindling or is turning the spit on which a tube of meat product sizzles over a roaring fire. It is the worst, most diabolical revenge, and he knows it.

Very Hurt mode kept the enemy at bay for a good while. During that time, though, we heard from headquarters less and less. We started getting stark, austere communiqués like "Swell forest," "Stab the fabric cone," and "Fork"—dense, barely pronounceable phrases, indicating a new plateau of military strategy no one in our ranks could unpack. Our objective here, once clear and urgent, had faded into obscurity. The mission had become so secret that it had disappeared altogether. This made us angry, and tired. No one wanted to deal with all of the Very Hurt soldiers lying around, as they had to be dragged out of the path of the Sound Gun before we could move it. With no one to instruct us otherwise, we cranked up the gun from Very Hurt to Make Dead. Make Dead ruptures the enemy's bowels as the blast hurls them twenty feet or more into the air. In Make Dead mode the frequency is so low that you can no longer hear the gun as it fires—only the sound the enemy soldiers make as they sail through the air, limbs flapping like damp cloth.

I do not miss home, but not for the usual reasons. I like home, generally, but I do not like home the way that I left it—with a large wild bobcat living there. I came home one night and found Gruver on all fours, peering under the couch, where the bobcat was hiding. As the bobcat was a very large animal, this was not the best place to hide. The couch was balanced on its back, seesawing back and forth while Gruver offered up warm, encouraging aphorisms.

"I do not want to hear it," he said when I asked what was under the couch. I did not then know that what was under the couch was, in actuality, a bobcat. A bobcat, at that time, was one of the very last things I was thinking of.

"I found this beautiful animal in the garbage can, and it is now mine," Gruver called out from the floor.

"Clearly," I said.

"I will not hear any arguments against my case."

I saw that Gruver's left arm was bandaged with a shredded, bloodied T-shirt. "It's nothing," he said preemptively, cupping the wounded elbow with his free hand.

I went upstairs and ate a Starburst on the bed.

"Why don't you come down here," Gruver shouted from the bottom of the stairs. "Why don't you come down and put your hand on this animal's flanks? Feel the strength just lying there, dormant."

"It's sulking," I called out. "It is bringing down the whole house with that attitude."

"He's been abandoned. I believe that this animal has got a definite right to sulk?"

I had been with Gruver for seven years. Suddenly, it did not seem like such a good idea.

"Constantine," I call out from my tent. He sits cross-legged by the fire, facing away from me, worrying the coals with a slender branch. His shadow flickers wildly on the green nylon wall of the tent, the shape of his body crassly drawing attention to itself, showboating there behind him on the makeshift scrim, taunting me with the suggestion that, given half the chance, it might swallow me whole, enveloping the tent itself, the camp, everything we have brought along. "Constantine, bring me my flask." He does not move. He wants me to call him by his given name, which is Idrissa. He sits and waits.

On my way to the latrine I see Memorex sitting on a felled tree, writing in his Wish Journal.

"Well, hard at work, I see," I say, trying to amount to something in his mind.

"I'm just writing," he says.

I kneel at his side, laying a hand on his thigh, giving it a brief, reassuring squeeze. It is not an advance; I'd rather dip my face into a bucket of glass shards than sidle up to Memorex's whitened, porous midriff, but it's taken as such, and I get a frightened grimace.

I pull my hand away. "Sometimes the hurt goes away when we talk, too."

Memorex rests his pen in the spine. "I wish we weren't killing people."

The phrase "killing people" jars me—in my mind it isn't so much killing people that we are engaged in as pushing them out of the way, except that they stay there, wherever they topple, forever. "Well, Memorex, you know that's not a Wish Journal wish. That's not a feeling. You can't, you know, put that anywhere."

"I feel something about it, though. To see all those people go flying up in the air, all, like, ruptured? I feel something when that happens. It's, like, really a feeling, like getting hit in the face with a basketball again and again—"

"Like the time at base camp—"

"Yes. Just like. What is that feeling?"

"I don't know, Memorex. But it doesn't sound like the kind of feeling that winners feel. Is it? Is that the way you think people who win feel? Do you think that General Custer, as he stood atop the mound of enemy corpses, felt the way that you're feeling?"

He rubs the side of his face where scabs from a constellation of wicked-huge spider bites pill and drift. "No, that's definitely not what winners feel."

"Well, you've answered your own question there, Memorex, haven't you?"

"Yeah?"

"Yes. The answer is, don't feel feelings that aren't winning feelings. Make sense?"

Memorex nods and continues his journal entry. I run to the latrine, buckling, suddenly, with waste. I fill to the brim nearly five mason jars.

*   *   *

The enemy is getting smarter. They start digging big holes, which they cover up with leafy tree branches. They dig the holes so well and disguise them so carefully that, eventually, we fall into one. I hit the ground shoulder first, half of me sucked instantly into a pool of mud. Conservarte falls on top of me, his left knee coming down directly on my solar plexus. "Sorry, sir," he whispers, splashing frantically in the thick puddle. I grip his upper arm to shush him, pointing up toward the mouth of the giant hole. Everything goes dark and quiet as the Sound Gun teeters at the edge. Danson and his slave, who are tethered to the machine with the medical gauze, dangle about four meters from the ground, flailing their limbs erratically. Slowly, with groaning indecision, the Sound Gun begins to tip forward, and then, with unimaginable speed, casting out a heavy sheet of debris, it falls, landing on top of the both of them.

When the cloud dissipates, all we can see of them are their legs, sticking out from the treads like beefy shards of driftwood. Constantine rushes over to help Danson's slave, who used to be his wife, but the upper half of her has been completely squashed. He pulls on one of the legs for a while, whimpering, desperately imploring us to join in. We all look down or away, or up at the mouth of the hole, anything to avoid his plaintive stare.

If dragging the Sound Gun out of the ravine with four sturdy, if belligerent, mules was difficult, dragging it out of a surprisingly deep, narrow hole with no mules is all but impossible, but in the afternoon Memorex gets the idea that we could blast a path out of the ground. We have never tried shooting at the ground before, but given what usually happens when we shoot the Sound Gun, what with the leveling of trees and barricades, the hoisting aloft of enemy soldiers, the hurling of bodies, high and far, and so forth, moving earth seems eminently feasible. We all grab our percussion suits and take off into the brush while Conservarte warms up the generator.

"Okay," he calls out when everyone is far enough away. "Christ if I'm not going to do this." He grunts for a while, fiercely turning switches.

We pull the rip cords on the inflatable suits, biting down on the hard plastic mouthpieces. Air rushes into the stiff fabric, puffing us up like ripe berries. There is a moment of absolute silence, and then a faint crackling sound before a fierce shock wave knocks us back on our asses. Snakes and other creatures start falling out of the trees. One falls on my face and I jump up, flailing wildly. We are safe because we are in the percussion suits. But still.

Momentarily, the earth settles. The creatures of the forest, those that survived, have been shocked into silence. By the tree line an enormous brown creature lies on its side, twitching. We deflate our suits and make our way back to the hole. Conservarte is peering out over the wide, dual barrel of the Sound Gun. The hole is measurably bigger. We walk its perimeter to make sure.

"Did you put it up all the way?" I ask, but, since I forgot to remove my mouthpiece, what it sounds like is "Duh duh duh duh duh duh duh duh?"

"She's cranked, sir."

"Let's give it another shot."

It is dark out. The hole is bigger, I tell them. Look. They only look down into their plates of gruel, willing it into anything but the gray assemblage steaming away before them. We can hear the enemy cackling in the distance. I climb into the cockpit and fire off a round into the trees, snapping the trunks in half. The cackling stops.

After dinner, gathered as we are around a pathetic campfire made from Danson's boots, Memorex carefully draws a small photograph from his breast pocket, cupping it gently in his palm. Shaving Gel and Orange Face sheepishly follow suit. It is against the rules for the men to carry photographs, but who am I to enforce rules? After ordering Conservarte to crank the settings of the Sound Gun from Very Hurt to Make Dead, a configuration that hadn't ever really been tested, let alone approved? After taking the men deeper and deeper into the unmapped wilderness, following a set of military objectives I'd constructed by vague speculation? Who am I to snatch the photographs the men have carried around with them at great risk, images of their dumb, savage loved ones, and toss them into the dwindling campfire?

I snatch the photographs the men have carried around with them at great risk and toss them into the dwindling campfire.

Gruver whispered something from across the room. It was my last night in New Jersey, one that I had willfully hacked away at on the Boardwalk, stuffing myself with sticky buns while standing in line for brightly lit amusement rides that, if successful, would bring the heavy pastry back up. I shouted and growled at anyone who dared occupy the vacant passenger seat of my bumper car—I arched my back like a banshee, if that is indeed what banshees do, and hissed at them, spraying their faces with murky brown mist. I wanted to ward off all human contact, to create the narrowest possible aperture in the world through which to jettison myself.

Things had not been going so well between the bobcat and me, so for the past week or so I'd been sleeping in the closet, curled up like a fetal chick in the corner. The two of them slept in the big yellow bed, the cat's disturbing, furry head nestled in the crook of Gruver's arm. Every night I watched them through the crack in the closet door until I fell unconscious, lulled to sleep by the animal's heavy breathing. On the last night, though, I left the closet door open. Should the cat climb onto my back and bounce repeatedly, as if I were an unsteady outcropping of rock, then so be it. There were more undignified ways to go out than to be crushed by a wild animal.

The cat, though, did not climb onto my back. Instead, I woke in a dyspeptic haze to Gruver's thick, malleable face staring at me from across the room, suspended, it seemed, from the doorframe. He whispered something, this head floating at the entrance to what had been our room. I could not hear him, though: what came out of his mouth sounded like "gretl balls."

"Come again?" I said, shooting up from the tangled sheets piled up on the closet floor, but it sounded more like a plea than a question, and before I had fully understood what was happening he was gone—the soft head withdrawn into the hallway and out the door.

The Sound Gun was made so that we could fight friendlier wars. The Wish Journals are so that we can fight with clean consciences. The no-pictures rule is so that we forget what we're missing. The slaves we made up. Also the deaths. And our reason for being here. That part was made up when the mules ate part of the communications array.

Eating the mules, we made up.

We have started digging a path with shovels fashioned from hollowed-out tree trunks. At the rate we're currently proceeding, we'll be finished by Saturday. The Sound Gun may not be working, though. It's settled into the hole at an angle, engine and auxiliary generators submerged in a clammy pool of mud. Whenever we turn the key it only shudders briefly, offering up a thin plume of green smoke, and then dies, leaving a deafening silence in its wake. Conservarte is inside the cockpit, working with an oversize wrench in an attempt to breathe some life into the machine.

"God, I'm starting to think of my house," Memorex blurts out suddenly, collapsing to his knees. "I'm thinking of my house with everything inside of it. I'm thinking of a piece of floor inside my house that has junk all over it and if someone cleans up the junk without me there I won't ever be able to find it again and put it together because it's not really junk it's my diabetes kit—"

"Hey, hey," I call over to him, "no need to panic, there. Let's all take out our Wish Journals, men, and start writing away Memorex's bad feelings. Get out your Wish Journals—"

"No," says Memorex, "no, I *want* to feel this way. I want to. Don't anybody put my feelings in a canvas bag." The rest of the men look up from their freshly opened journals, pens carefully poised over the ruled sheets. Memorex slides down the mud ramp on his knees, coming to rest underneath one of the enormous armored treads of the Sound Gun, where he slumps like an old, head-beaten pillow.

"Memorex," I say, crawling backward down the steep trail that he has just plowed with his body. "What's this bit of silliness? Come now, your house is not important anymore. Your car, your tile sample collection, your whole life just pales in comparison to what you're doing here. We're fighting a war here, Memorex."

"War? This is a war?"

"Yes, Memorex, of course."

"What is the war about?" he asks from under the tread. All we can see are his legs. Constantine turns away. "I can't remember what the war is about, so maybe you can just, like, tell me?"

"Memorex. It's not really our place to ask, is it? I mean, you wanted to disappear, correct? You wanted never to have happened, am I right? That is the reason you and the rest of us are here, correct? We are men in retreat, all of us. We are hiding from the rest of our lives. The terms have always been fairly well defined. Otherwise, they never would have signed you up. Now come on, Memorex, let's crawl our way out of the mud, shall we?"

The legs don't move. "I'm going to lie here until I get crushed."

Constantine turns back toward Memorex's legs, bending at the waist in prayer.

"What's that he's saying?" I ask Shaving Gel, who points the translation gun at Constantine's head.

"Says he's not leaving, either. He wants to die, too, so that he can be with his wife."

Memorex starts chanting along phonetically with Constantine. Constantine crawls in next to Memorex, so all that we can see are their legs, four sets now, poking out from underneath the tread.

We are there for a long time, watching the two of them shudder and yelp like Pentecostals under the Sound Gun. It is not clear what we should do at this point.

"Sir?" Shaving Gel asks, saluting halfheartedly as he approaches.

"Yes, Shaving Gel."

"With all due permission, sir, can we break from this, like, vigil-type thing?"

"Absolutely not."

"Sir, how come?"

"Because these two are being ridiculous, and we must show them that we, too, can be ridiculous. We must suffocate them with our will."

"Oh," Shaving Gel says, looking down at his feet. "Can I at least have a sandwich?"

I imagine the look I give Shaving Gel to be wild with disbelief. "Where did you get a sandwich from?"

"Well, sir, it's a dirt sandwich."

"A dirt sandwich."

"Yes, sir."

I take a survey of the other men. They are all watching, shovels pitched defiantly into the mud. Their eyes are black and distant, the opposite of stars. "Shaving Gel," I say, grasping his shoulder paternally, "by all means, go have yourself a dirt sandwich." He lopes off happily into the brush, disappearing behind a spray of wiry vines. The rest of the men do not move.

In the morning I am the only one left. Shaving Gel has not returned. I can see by the muddy prints left on the crispy shale that the Numismatist has scaled the high cliff wall to the east sometime during the night, last of the mule meat and ice tubes strapped to his back. Orange Face has left a small shrine fashioned from twigs and diaphanous gauze, the significance of which is not entirely lost on me. Half Brick and his two slaves are simply gone without a trace—they have even taken the body floss and the elimination hood.

Actually, I should not say that I am the only one left. Memorex and Constantine remain under the Sound Gun, keening like abandoned kittens. As far as anyone that matters is concerned, however, I am the only one left, where "anyone that matters" equals the part of me that does not go off like the others, abandoning the Sound Gun and the mission. Missions are important, I tell myself. They are important, and they are to be carried out. Every bit as important as a person.

I am resting on the gnarled trunk of a felled tree, and it has just occurred to me how comfortable an object it is, how well it accepts my intrusive ass, utterly without condescension, without the attendant grief brought on by contemporary furniture. How quiet a thing the world is without all these crude, puffy bodies flailing away at it. I long for a cigarette, and for the first time since I have been here, I long, also, for Gruver, towering over me, shaking me from my sleep for an early walk. I long for his fierce, stubbled head; his long, recriminatory stares; and the way that he would grasp my jaw when we coupled, his filthy fingers in my mouth, clamping my tongue flat, as though he could, by holding down my face, perform a hostile takeover of the burdensome life I'd absently flung at him, neutralizing, at last, the dull tyranny of language.

Let them pray, is what I am thinking here at the bottom of the enemy hole. Let them pray for atonement, and may the purest heart rise up, out of this flat land and back to the first place that seemed a good idea to stay away from.

SHORT TALKS

ANNE CARSON

Introduction

Early one morning words were missing. Before that, words were not. Facts were, faces were. In a good story, Aristotle tells us, everything that happens is pushed by something else. Three old women were bending in the fields. What use is it to question us? they said. Well it shortly became clear that they knew everything there is to know about the snowy fields and the blue-green shoots and the plant called "audacity," which poets mistake for violets. I began to copy out everything that was said. The marks construct an instant of nature gradually, without the boredom of a story. I emphasize this. I will do anything to avoid boredom. It is the task of a lifetime. You can never know enough, never work enough, never use the infinitives and participles oddly enough, never impede the movement harshly enough, never leave the mind quickly enough.

On *Homo Sapiens*

With small cuts Cro-Magnon man recorded the moon's phases on the handles of his tools, thinking about her as he worked. Animals. Horizon. Face in a pan of water. In every story I tell comes a point where I can see no further. I hate that point. It is why they call storytellers blind—a taunt.

On Chromoluminism

Sunlight slows down Europeans. Look at all those spellbound people in Seurat. Look at monsieur, sitting deeply. Where does a European go when he is "lost in thought"? Seurat—the old dazzler—has painted that place. It lies on the other side of attention, a long lazy boat ride from here. It is a Sunday rather than a Saturday afternoon there. Seurat has made this clear by a special method. *Ma méthode,* he called it, rather testily, when we asked him. He caught us hurrying through the chill green shadows like adulterers. The river was opening and closing its stone lips. The river was pressing Seurat to its lips.

On Gertrude Stein About 9:30

How curious. I had no idea! Today has ended.

On Disappointments in Music

Prokofiev was ill and could not attend the performance of his First Piano Sonata played by somebody else. He listened to it on the telephone.

On Trout

In haiku there are various sorts of expressions about trout—
"autumn trout" and "descending trout" and "rusty trout" are some
I have heard. Descending trout and rusty trout are trout that have
laid their eggs. Worn out, completely exhausted, they are going
down to the sea. Of course there were occasionally trout that spent
the winter in deep pools. These were called "remaining trout."

On Ovid

I see him there on a night like this but cool, the moon blowing
through black streets. He sups and walks back to his room. The
radio is on the floor. Its luminous green dial blares softly. He sits
down at the table; people in exile write so many letters. Now Ovid
is weeping. Each night about this time he puts on sadness like a
garment and goes on writing. In his spare time he is teaching himself the local language (Getic) in order to compose in it an epic
poem no one will ever read.

On Parmenides

We pride ourselves on being civilized people. Yet what if the names
for things were utterly different? Italy, for example. I have a friend
named Andreas, an Italian. He has lived in Argentina as well as in
England, and also Costa Rica for some time. Everywhere he lives,
he invites people over for supper. It is a lot of work. Artichoke
pasta. Peaches. His deep smile never fades. What if the proper
name for Italy turns out to be Brzoy—will Andreas continue to
travel the world like the wandering moon with her borrowed light?
I fear we failed to understand what he was saying or his reasons.
What if every time he said *cities,* he meant *delusion,* for example?

On Defloration

The actions of life are not so many. To go in, to go, to go in secret, to cross the Bridge of Sighs. And when you dishonored me, I saw that dishonor is an action. It happened in Venice; it causes the vocal cords to swell. I went booming through Venice, under and over the bridges, but you were gone. Later that day I telephoned your brother. What's wrong with your voice? he said.

On Major and Minor

Major things are wind, evil, a good fighting horse, prepositions, inexhaustible love, the way people choose their king. Minor things include dirt, the names of schools of philosophy, mood and not having a mood, the correct time. There are more major things than minor things overall, yet there are more minor things than I have written here, but it is disheartening to list them. When I think of you reading this, I do not want you to be taken captive, separated by a wire mesh lined with glass from your life itself, like some Elektra.

On the Rules of Perspective

A bad trick. Mistake. Dishonesty. These are the views of Braque. Why? Braque rejected perspective. Why? Someone who spends his life drawing profiles will end up believing that man has one eye, Braque felt. Braque wanted to take full possession of objects. He said as much in published interviews. Watching the small shiny planes of the landscape recede out of his grasp filled Braque with loss so he smashed them. *Nature morte,* said Braque.

On *Le Bonheur d'Etre Bien Aimée*

Day after day I think of you as soon as I wake up. Someone has put cries of birds on the air like jewels.

On Rectification

Kafka liked to have his watch an hour and a half fast. Felice kept setting it right. Nonetheless for five years they almost married. He made a list of arguments for and against marriage, including inability to bear the assault of his own life (for) and the sight of the nightshirts laid out on his parents' beds at 10:30 (against). Hemorrhage saved him. When advised not to speak by doctors in the sanatorium, he left glass sentences all over the floor. Felice, says one of them, had too much nakedness left in her.

On Sleep Stones

Camille Claudel lived the last thirty years of her life in an asylum, wondering why, writing letters to her brother the poet, who had signed the papers. Come visit me, she says. Remember, I am living here with madwomen; days are long. She did not smoke or stroll. She refused to sculpt. Although they gave her sleep stones— marble and granite and porphyry—she broke them, then collected the pieces and buried these outside the walls at night. Night was when her hands grew, huger and huger until in the photograph they are like two parts of someone else loaded onto her knees.

On Walking Backwards

My mother forbad us to walk backwards. That is how the dead walk, she would say. Where did she get this idea? Perhaps from a bad translation. The dead, after all, do not walk backwards but they do walk behind us. They have no lungs and cannot call out but would love for us to turn around. They are victims of love, many of them.

On the Mona Lisa

Every day he poured his question into her, as you pour water from one vessel into another, and it poured back. Don't tell me he was painting his mother, lust, et cetera. There is a moment when the water is not in one vessel nor in the other—what a thirst it was, and he supposed that when the canvas became completely empty he would stop. But women are strong. She knew vessels, she knew water, she knew mortal thirst.

On Waterproofing

Franz Kafka was Jewish. He had a sister, Ottla, Jewish. Ottla married a jurist, Josef David, not Jewish. When the Nuremberg Laws were introduced to Bohemia-Moravia in 1942, quiet Ottla suggested to Josef David that they divorce. He at first refused. She spoke about sleep shapes and property and their two daughters and a rational approach. She did not mention, because she did not yet know the word, Auschwitz, where she would die in October 1943. After putting the apartment in order she packed a rucksack and was given a good shoeshine by Josef David. He applied a coat of grease. Now they are waterproof, he said.

On the End

What is the difference between light and lighting? There is an etching called *The Three Crosses* by Rembrandt. It is a picture of the earth and the sky and Calvary. A moment rains down on them; the plate grows darker. Darker. Rembrandt wakens you just in time to see matter stumble out of its forms.

On Sylvia Plath

Did you see her mother on television? She said plain, burned things. She said I thought it an excellent poem but it hurt me. She did not say jungle fear. She did not say jungle hatred wild jungle weeping chop it back chop it. She said self-government she said end of the road. She did not say humming in the middle of the air what you came for chop.

On Reading

Some fathers hate to read but love to take the family on trips. Some children hate trips but love to read. Funny how often these find themselves passengers in the same automobile. I glimpsed the stupendous clear-cut shoulders of the Rockies from between paragraphs of *Madame Bovary.* Cloud shadows roved languidly across her huge rock throat, traced her fir flanks. Since those days, I do not look at hair on female flesh without thinking, Deciduous?

On Rain

It was blacker than olives the night I left. As I ran past the palaces, oddly joyful, it began to rain. What a notion it is, after all—these small shapes! I would get lost counting them. Who first thought of it? How did he describe it to the others? Out on the sea it is raining too. It beats on no one.

On the Total Collection

From childhood he dreamed of being able to keep with him all the objects in the world lined up on his shelves and bookcases. He denied lack, oblivion or even the likelihood of a missing piece. Order streamed from Noah in blue triangles and as the pure fury of his classifications rose around him, engulfing his life, they came to be called waves by others, who drowned, a world of them.

On Charlotte

Miss Brontë & Miss Emily & Miss Anne used to put away their sewing after prayers and walk all three, one after the other, around the table in the parlor till nearly eleven o'clock. Miss Emily walked as long as she could, and when she died, Miss Anne & Miss Brontë took it up—and now my heart aches to hear Miss Brontë walking, walking on alone.

On Sunday Dinner with Father

Are you going to put that chair back where it belongs or just leave it there looking like a uterus? (Our balcony is a breezy June balcony.) Are you going to let your face distorted by warring desires pour down on us all through the meal or tidy yourself so we can at least enjoy our dessert? (We weight down the corners of everything on the table with little solid-silver laws.) Are you going to nick your throat open on those woodpecker scalps as you do every Sunday night or just sit quietly while Laetitia plays her clarinet for us? (My father, who smokes a brand of cigar called Dimanche Eternal, uses them as ashtrays.)

On the Youth at Night

The youth at night would have himself driven around the scream. It lay in the middle of the city gazing back at him with its heat and rose-pools of flesh. Terrific lava shone on his soul. He would ride and stare.

On *The Anatomy Lesson of Dr. Deyman*

A winter so cold that, walking on the Breestraat and you passed from sun to shadow, you could feel the difference run down your skull like water. It was the hunger winter of 1656 when Black Jan took up with a whore named Elsje Ottje and for a time they prospered. But one icy January day Black Jan was observed robbing a cloth merchant's house. He ran, fell, knifed a man and was hanged on the twenty-seventh of January. How he fared then is no doubt known to you: the cold weather permitted Dr. Deyman to turn the true eye of medicine on Black Jan for three days. One wonders if Elsje ever saw Rembrandt's painting, which shows her love thief in violent frontal foreshortening, so that his pure soles seem almost to touch the chopped-open cerebrum. Cut and cut deep to find the source of the problem, Dr. Deyman is saying as he parts the brain to either side like hair. Sadness comes groping out of it.

On Orchids

We live by tunneling for we are people buried alive. To me, the tunnels you make will seem strangely aimless, uprooted orchids. But the fragrance is undying. A Little Boy has run away from Amherst a few Days ago, writes Emily Dickinson in a letter of 1883, and when asked where he was going, he replied, Vermont or Asia.

On Penal Servitude

Je haïs ces brigands! said an aristocrat named M-ski one day in Omsk as he strode past Dostoevski with flashing eyes. Dostoevski went in and lay down, hands behind his head.

On Hölderlin's World Night Wound

King Oedipus may have had an eye too many, said Hölderlin and kept climbing. Above the tree line is as blank as the inside of a wrist. Rock stays. Names stay. Names fell on him, hissing.

On Hedonism

Beauty makes me hopeless. I don't care why anymore I just want to get away. When I look at the city of Paris I long to wrap my legs around it. When I watch you dancing there is a heartless immensity like a sailor in a dead-calm sea. Desires as round as peaches bloom in me all night, I no longer gather what falls.

On the King and His Courage

He arose laden with doubt as to how he should begin. He looked back at the bed where the grindstone lay. He looked out at the world, the most famous experimental prison of its time. Beyond the torture stakes he could see, nothing. Yet he could see.

On Shelter

You can write on a wall with a fish heart, it's because of the phosphorus. They eat it. There are shacks like that down along the river. I am writing this to be as wrong as possible to you. Replace the door when you leave, it says. Now you tell me how wrong that is, how long it glows. Tell me.

UP THE OLD GOAT ROAD

DAWN RAFFEL

We are here on the peninsula, where pie is made from scratch and the goats are getting fatter on a nearby roof. It is an upwind roof. This is industry, my father says. Company, my sister says. This is not the dells. All the supper clubs are shut or tight. The falls are somewhere else we have not been. Overhead is where it's lusher, fresh—green above this hard-luck thumb. But the goats, my sister says, look overwarm. The water is our neighbor, and what washes up is sorry or worse.

There is the smell of the quick.

My mother is cooking in the kitchen again, and I do not know what. Something is chopping. Something is chirping. Something is black in a tree, and blue. A piano must be playing at a distance, someone four and twenty singing, someone whistling for dinner, someone cutting a rug, someone sweeping, and rinsing every dish in the sink. The kettle is on. The timer is off. Efficiency, my mother says, is why she keeps the pans, the pots, the spatulas and spoons, the metal platter for the fish, the cream clotting in the bottle, the needlepoint sampler, tongs, tins, mitts, and all the spices of our life on a hook.

We children are not children. We are sister and sister, face front and center, buttoned mother-of-pearl. Mother's oven is Dutch. The rattle of the boil is a sound we sisters prefer to ignore. We are waiting on the weather, my sister says. We are waiting for a fit like a fine kid glove. We are waiting for a higher tide to roll in.

It is a hook my mother says she nailed herself.

An unrelated rumor has been hanging in the air.

My mother keeps a basket by the door with nothing in it. It is there for the season, my mother says. She says, Go and fetch your father. He is salting the beach.

A job is a job. This could not be simpler.

But my sister and I are slow and slowest. We are in the wrong year. Our father is never in the place we expect. Father sickness-and-health, he is chewing the breeze. He is checking what is greener on the other side. He is butter through our fingers. Gone.

The rumor is bearing on the burial mounds. It is the clatter of change. There is talk of heads of arrows switching hands up the Old Goat Road. Somebody is selling precious pennies, it is said, and crooked corn. Somebody is selling beads of sweat, a little Pepsi in a cup. Somebody is marking down the souvenir bones of Paul Bunyan and his blue ox, Babe.

We do not investigate ourselves.

The stitching in the kitchen says nothing, is only p's and q's, is out-of-date.

It is winter already and the ice is full of fish, my mother says. We have the recipes engraved on a laminated log. We have lanyards and all-purpose holiday plums. We have edible leaves. We have drawstring hoods. This is smart, my mother says. But we are winded and it smells like snow.

All the stiffs are frozen stiff, my sister says. She is waiting on tables that are empty. She is waiting on a headdress, a puff-puff, a tepee for two. My mother's hair has turned to silver and we are scraping by.

I am making a crust. I am fluting the edge.

My father is sighted up the hill and in the road and on the lake. But it is never him. The party line is busy. There's a message in a bottle. A ship is on a shore.

My sister has begun to misremember. In the interest of time, my sister says, she has started seeing double. She is slugging the port. She is carrying a tune south across the border.

My mother has a suitor with a range.

There is a legend on the map.

There is something boiling over.

There has been a drowning.

We have prints. We have a photo of the Mona Lisa on a ring for keys. This is not Chicago. We have cherries by the peck.

There are stars for lying under.

There are stones.

My sister is impossible to call. We have gone too far. We are no longer listed. They have changed the exchange. The poor old goat, my mother says, is gouty, and spent.

But we are somewhere else. We are always somewhere else. We are in this plangent earth. We are going up the road. We are standing on the roof of the world, facing off.

SCARLIOTTI AND THE SINKHOLE

PADGETT POWELL

In the Pic N' Save Green Room, grits were free. Scarliotti, as he liked to call himself, though his real name was Rod, Scarliotti ate free grits in the Green Room. To Rod, grits were virtually sacramental; to Scarliotti they were a joke, and if he could not eat them for free in a crummy joint so down in the world it had to use free grits as a promotional gimmick, he wouldn't eat them. Scarliotti had learned that when he was Rod, treating grits as good food, *he* had been a joke, so he became Scarliotti. He wanted his other new name, his new given name, to come from the province of martial arts. Numchuks Scarliotti was strong but a little obvious. He was looking for something more refined, a name that would not start a fight but would prevent one from starting. He also thought a name from the emergency room might do: Triage Scarliotti, maybe. But he had to be careful there. Not many people knew what terms in the emergency room meant. Suture Scarliotti, maybe. Edema Scarliotti. Lavage Scarliotti. No, he liked the martial-arts idea better. With his new name he would be a new man, one who would never eat grits with a straight face again.

There were many things he never intended to do with a straight face again. One of them was ride Tomos, a Yugoslavian moped that would go about twenty miles per hour flat out, and get clipped in the head by a mirror on a truck pulling a horse trailer and wake up with a head wound with horseshit in it in the hospital. Another was to be grateful that at least Tomos had not been hurt. Now, his collection of a quarter million dollars in damages imminent, he didn't give a shit about a motorized bicycle. He wasn't riding that and he wasn't seriously eating grits anymore. He was going to take a cab the rest of his life and eat grits only if they were free. He would never again be on the side of the road and never pay for grits, and it might just be *Mister* Scarliotti. Deal with that.

The horse Yankees who clipped him were in a world of hurt and he wanted them to be. They were the kind of yahoos who leave Ohio and find a tract of land that was orange groves until 1985 and now is plowed out and called a horse farm and buy it and fence it and call themselves horse breeders. And somehow they breed Arabian horses, and somehow it is Arabs behind it all. Somehow Minute Maid, which is really Coca-Cola, leaves, and Kuwait and Ohio are here. And the Yankees are joking and laughing about grits at first, and then they wise up and try to fit in and start eating them every morning after learning how to cook them, which it takes them about a year to do it. And driving all over the state in diesel doolies with mirrors coming off them about as long as airplane wings, and knocking *people who live here* in the ditch.

Scarliotti is in his motorized bed in his trailer in Hague, Florida. It is only ten o'clock but the trailer is already ticking in the heat. Scarliotti swears it—the trailer—moves, kind of bends, on its own, when he is lying still in the bed, and not even moving the bed, which has an up for your head and an up for your feet and both together kind of make a sandwich out of you; hard to see the TV that way, which is on an arm just like at the hospital and controlled by a remote just like at the hospital, a remote on a thick white cord, which he doesn't understand why it isn't like a remote everybody else has at their house. When the trailer moves, Scarliotti thinks that a sinkhole might be opening up. Before his accident that would have been fine. But not now. Two hundred and fifty thousand dollars would be left topside if he went down a sinkhole today, and even if he *lived* down there, which he thought was possible, he knew he couldn't spend *that* kind of money down there. He thought about maybe asking Higgins, whom he worked for before the accident, if they could put outriggers or something on the trailer to keep it from going down. They could cable it to the big oak, but the big oak might go itself. He didn't know. He didn't know if outriggers would work or not. A trailer wasn't a canoe, and the dirt was not water.

There were about a hundred pills on a tray next to him he was supposed to take but he hadn't been, and now they were piled up and he had started throwing them out the back window and he hoped they didn't *grow* or something and give him away. You could get busted for anything these days. It was not like the old days.

Tomos was beside the trailer, and Scarliotti had asked his daddy to get it running, and if his daddy had, he could get to the Lil' Champ for some beer before the nurse came by. The bandages and the bald side of his head scared the clerk at the Lil' Champ, and once she undercharged him, she was so scared. He let that go, but he didn't like having done it because he liked her and she'd have to pay for it. But right now he couldn't afford to correct an error in his favor. Any day now, he'd be able to afford to correct all the errors in his favor in the world. He was going to walk in the Lil' Champ and buy the entire glass beer cooler, so he might as well buy the whole store and the girl with it. See how scared she got then.

He accidentally hit both buttons on the bed thing and squeezed himself into a sandwich and it made him pee in his pants before he could get it down, but he did not care. It didn't matter now if you peed in your pants in your bed. It did not matter now.

He tried to start Tomos by push-starting it, and by the time he gave up he was several hundred yards from the trailer. It was too far to walk it back and he couldn't leave it where it was so he pushed Tomos with him to the Lil' Champ. He had done this before. The girl watched him push the dead moped up and lean it against the front of the store near the paper racks and the doors so he could keep a eye on it.

Scarliotti did not greet her but veered to the cooler and got a twelve-pack of Old Mil and presented it at the counter and began digging for his money. It had gotten in his left pocket again, which was a bitch because he had to get it out with his right hand because his left couldn't since the accident. Crossing his body this way and prorating his arm to dig into his pocket threw him into a bent slumped contortion.

The girl chewed the gum fast to keep from laughing at Scarliotti. She couldn't help it. Then she got a repulsive idea, but she was bored so she went ahead with it.

"Can I help you?" she asked.

Scarliotti continued to wrestle with himself, looking like a horror-movie hunchback to her. His contorting put the wounded part of his head just above the countertop between them. It was all dirty hair and scar and Formica and his grunting. She came from behind the counter and put one hand on Scarliotti's little back and pulled his twisted hand out of his pocket and slipped hers in. Scarliotti froze. She held her breath and looked at his poor forlorn moped leaning against the brick outside and hoped she could get the money without touching anything else.

Scarliotti braced his two arms on the counter and held still and then suddenly stuck his butt out into her and made a noise and she felt, as she hoped she wouldn't, a hardening the size of one of those small purple bananas they don't sell in the store but are very good, Mexicans and people eat them. She jerked her hand out with a ten-dollar bill in it.

Scarliotti put his head down on the counter and began taking deep breaths.

"Do you want to go on a date?" he asked her, his head still down as if he were weeping.

"No." She rang up the beer.

"Any day now I will be pert a millionaire."

"Good."

"Good? *Good? Shit.* A *mil*lionaire."

She started chewing rapidly again. "Go ahead and be one," she said.

"You don't believe me?"

"You going be Arnold Schwarzenegger, too?"

This stopped Scarliotti. It was a direction he didn't understand. He made a guess. "*What?* You don't think I'm strong?" Before the girl could answer, he ran over to the copy machine and picked up a corner of it and would have turned it over but it started to roll and got away and hit the magazine rack. Suddenly, inexplicably, he was sad. He did not do sad. Sad was bullshit.

"Don't think I came," he said to the girl.

"What?"

"I didn't *come*. That's *pee!*" He left the store with dignity and pushed Tomos with the beer strapped to the little luggage rack over the rear wheel to the trailer and did not look back at approaching traffic. Hit him *again*, for all he cared.

In the trailer there wasn't shit on the TV, people in costumes he couldn't tell what they were, screaming, Come on down! or something. He put the beer in the freezer. He sat against the refrigerator feeling the trailer tick and bend. Shit like that wouldn't happen if his daddy would fix damn Tomos. His daddy was letting him down. He was—he had an idea something like he was letting himself down. This was preposterous. How did one do, or not do, that? Do you extend outriggers from yourself? Can a canoe in high water just grow its own outriggers? No, it can't.

A canoe in high water takes it or goes down. End of chapter. He drank a beer and popped a handful of the pills for the nurse and knew that things were not going to change. This was it. It was foolish to believe in anything but a steady continuation of things exactly as they are at this moment. This moment was it. This was it. Shut the fuck *up*.

He was dizzy. The trailer ticked in the sun and he felt it bending and he felt himself also ticking in some kind of heat and bending. He was dizzy, agreeably. It did not feel bad. The sinkhole that he envisioned was agreeable, too. He hoped that when the trailer went down it went smoothly, twisting, scraping. The sinkhole was the kind of thing he realized that other people had when they had Jesus. He didn't need Jesus. He had a *hole,* and it was a purer thing than a *man*.

He was imagining life in the hole—how cool? how dark? how wet? Bats or blind catfish? The most positive speculation he could come up with was it was going to save on air-conditioning, then maybe on clothes. Maybe you could walk around naked, and what about all the things that had gone down sinkholes over the years, *houses* and shit, at your disposal maybe—he heard a noise and thought it was the nurse and jumped in bed and tried to look asleep, but when the door opened and someone came in he knew it wasn't the nurse and opened his eyes. It was his father.

"Daddy," he said.

"Son."

"You came for Tomos?"

"I'mone Tomos your butt."

"What for?" Rather than have to hear the answer, which was predictable even though he couldn't guess what it would be, Scarliotti wished he had some of those sharp star things you throw in martial arts to pin his daddy to the trailer wall and get things even before this started happening. His father was looking in the refrigerator and slammed it. He had not found the beer. If you didn't drink beer you were too stupid to know where people who do drink it keep it after a thirty-minute walk in Florida in July. Scarliotti marveled at this simple luck of his.

He looked up and saw his daddy standing too close to him, still looking for something.

"The doctor tells me you ain't following directions."

"What directions?"

"*All* directions."

Scarliotti wasn't following any directions but didn't know how anybody knew.

"You got to be *hungry* to eat as many pills as they give me."

"You got to be *sober* to eat them pills, son."

"That, too."

The headboard above Scarliotti's head rang with a loudness that made Scarliotti jerk and made his head hurt, and he thought he might have peed some more. His father had backhanded the headboard.

"If we'd ever get the money," Scarliotti said, "but that lawyer you picked I don't think knows shit—"

"He knows plenty of shit. It ain't his fault."

"It ain't my fault."

"No, not beyond getting hit by a truck."

"Oh. That's *my* fault."

"About."

Scarliotti turned on the TV and saw Adam yelling something at Dixie. Maybe it was Adam's crazy brother. This was the best way to get his father to leave. "Shhh," he said. "This is my show." Dixie had a strange accent. "Don't fix it, then."

"Fix what?" his father said.

"Tomos."

"Forget that damned thing."

"I can't," Scarliotti said to his father, looking straight at him. "I love her."

His father stood there a minute and then left. Scarliotti peeked through the curtains and saw that he was again not taking the bike to get it fixed for him.

He got a beer and put the others in the refrigerator just in time. He wanted sometimes to have a beer joint and *really* sell the coldest beer in town, not just say it. He heard another noise outside and jumped back in bed with his beer. Someone knocked on the door. That wouldn't be his father. He put the beer under the covers.

"Come in."

It was the nurse.

"Come in, *Ma*ma," Scarliotti said when he saw her.

"Afternoon, Rod."

He winced but let it go. They thought in the medical profession you had mental problems if you changed your name. They didn't know shit about mental problems, but it was no use fighting them so he let them call him Rod.

The nurse was standing beside the bed looking at the pill tray, going "Tch, tch, tch."

"I took a bunch of 'em," Scarliotti said.

The nurse was squinching her nose as if she smelled something.

"I know you want to get well, Rod," she said.

"I am well," he said.

"Not by a long shot," she said.

"I ain't going *to the moon,*" he said.

The nurse looked curiously at him. "No," she said, "you're not."

Scarliotti thought he had put her in her place. He liked her but didn't like her preaching crap at him. He was well enough to spend the $250,000, and that was as well as he needed to be. It was the Yankee Arab horse breeders were sick, not well enough to pay their debts when they go running over people because they're retired and don't have shit else to do. The nurse was putting the arm pump-up thing on his arm. She had slid some of the pills around with her weird little pill knife that looked like a sandwich spreader or something. He wanted to show her his Buck knife, but would reveal the beer and the pee if he got it out of his pocket.

"It's high, again. If you have another fit, you're back in the hospital."

"I'm not having no nother fit."

Scarliotti looked at her chest. The uniform was white and ribbed, and made a starchy little tissuey noise when she moved, and excited him. He looked closely at the ribs in the material when she got near him.

"Them lines on your shirt look like, crab lungs," he said.

"What?"

"I don't know, like crab lungs. You know what I mean?"

"No, Rod, I don't." She rolled her eyes and he saw her. She shouldn't do that. That was what he meant when he said, and he was right, that the medical profession did not know shit about mental problems.

The nurse went over everything again, two this four that umpteen times ninety-eleven a day, which meant you'd be up at two and three and five in the morning taking pills if you bought the program, and left. He watched Barney Fife get his bullet taken back by Andy. He wanted to see Barney *keep* his bullet. Barney should be able to keep that bullet. But if Barney shot at his own foot like that, he could see it. Barney was a dumb fuck. Barney looked like he'd stayed up all night taking pills. There was another noise outside. Scarliotti had had it with people fucking with him. He listened. There was a timid knock at the door. He just lay there. Let them break in, he thought. Then, head wound or not, he would kill them.

The door opened and someone called Hello. Then: "Anyone home?"

Scarliotti waited and was not going to say anything and go ahead and lure them in and kill them, but it was a girl's voice and familiar somehow, but not the nurse, so he said, "If you can call it that."

The girl from the Lil' Champ stepped in.

"I'm down here."

She looked down the hall and saw him and came down it with a package.

"You paid for a case," she said.

"I could use a case," Scarliotti said.

"Pshew," the girl said. Even so, she was, it seemed, being mighty friendly.

"Well, let's have us one," Scarliotti said.

The girl got two beers out of the package.

"You like Andy Griffin?" he said.

"*Fith.* He's okay. Barney's funny. Floyd is creepy."

"Floyd?"

"Barber? In the chair?"

"Oh." Scarliotti had no idea what she was talking about. Goober and Gomer, he knew. The show was over anyway. He turned the set off, holding up the white remote rig to show the girl.

"They let you off to deliver that beer?"

"I'm off."

"Oh."

"On my way."

"Oh."

Scarliotti decided to go for it. "I would dog to dog you." He blushed, so he looked directly at her to cover for it, with his eyes widened.

"That's about the nastiest idea I ever heard," the girl said.

"My daddy come by here a while ago, took a *swang* at me," Scarliotti said. "Then the nurse come by and give me a raft of shit. I nearly froze the beer. Been a rough day."

"You would like to make love to me. Is that what you're saying?" Since she had touched him in the store and he had said what he said, the girl had undergone a radical change of heart about Scarliotti's repulsiveness. She did not understand it, exactly.

Scarliotti had never in his life heard anyone say, "You would like to make love to me," nor had he said it to anyone, and did not think he could, even if it meant losing a piece of ass. He stuck by his guns.

"I would dog to dog you."

"Okay."

The girl stood up and took her clothes off. Compared to magazines she was too white and puffy, but she was a girl and she was already getting in the bed. For a minute Scarliotti thought they were fighting and then it was all warm and solid and they weren't. He said "Goddamn" several times. "God*damn.*" He looked at the headboard and saw what looked like a dent where his father had backhanded it and was wondering if he was wearing a ring done that or just hit it that fucking hard with his hand when the girl bit his neck. "Ow!" he said. "*Goddamn.*"

"You fucker," the girl said.

"Okay," Scarliotti said, trying to be agreeable.

"*Good,*" she said.

Then it was over and she no longer looked too white and soft. She was sweaty and red. Some of Scarliotti's hair had fallen out on her from the good side of his head and he hoped nothing had fallen out of the bad side. The trailer had stopped moving from their exertions. There were ten beers sweating onto a hundred pills beside the bed. The nurse and his father would not be back before the trailer could start ticking in the heat and bending on its own, unless they bent it again themselves with exertions in the bed, but all in all Scarliotti thought it would be a good enough time to have some fun without being bothered by anyone before the trailer found its way down the hole.

*   *   *

Scarliotti woke up and took the sweating beers in his arms and put them in the refrigerator and came back with two cold ones. "They *look* like a commercial sitting there but they don't *taste* like a commercial," he said, waking and mystifying the girl. "Women," he said, feeling suddenly very good about things, "know what they want and how to get it. Men are big fucking babies."

"How do you come to know all that?" the girl asked.

"I know."

"How many women you had?"

"Counting you?"

"Yeah."

"Three."

"That explains how you know so much."

Scarliotti started laughing. "Heh, heh, heh . . . *heah, heahh, heahhh*—" and did not stop until he was coughing and slumped against the wall opposite the bed.

"Quailhead," he said.

"What?"

"Nothing."

"You call me quailhead?"

"No. You want to go down to the Green Room and eat free grits?"

"Eat free grits," she said flatly, with a note of suspicion.

"Yeah."

"I thought you were going to be a millionaire."

"I am. Pert near. That's why I don't pay for grits."

"Well, I still pay for grits. I ain't eating no free grits."

"See? Heh, heh . . . it proves what I said. Women know what they want."

"And men are babies."

Scarliotti started the laugh again and crawled into bed with the girl.

"Be still. Shhh!"

"What?" the girl asked.

"Listen to the trailer."

"I don't hear anything—"

"Listen! Hear that?"

"No."

"It's ticking. It's moving. You ever thought of living in a sink-hole?"

"No."

"You want to go down into a sinkhole with me?"

"No."

"You want to go to the Hank show?"

"Okay."

"I mean, us all, whole thing going. Trailer and all."

"To the Hank show?"

"No, into the sinkhole."

Scarliotti started the uncontrollable heaving laugh again at this, and the girl reluctantly stroked the shaved side of his head to calm him. At first she barely touched it, but she began to like the moist bristly feel of Scarliotti's wounded head.

Scarliotti woke up and looked out the window and saw a dog and a turtle. The dog appeared to be licking the turtle.

"Ballhoggey wollock dube city, man. Your dog," he said to the girl, "is licking that turtle in its *face*. That turtle can *bite,* man. That dog is, unnaturally *friendly,* man. I don't want to even *go* into salmonella. That turtle can kill your dog from here to Sunday. It dudn' *have* to bite him, man. I *don't* want that turtle to bite your dog, man. On the *tongue* like that. I think I'd start, like, crying. I'd cry like a son of a bitch if we had to get that turtle off your dog's tongue. Your dog's tongue would look like a . . . shoe tongue. It would be blue and red. Your dog would be hollering and tears coming out of *its* eyes. That turtle would be squinting and biting down *hard,* man. I don't want it. I don't.

"You better get your dog, man. We'd have to kill that turtle to get it off. If it didn' cut your dog's tongue off first, man. Shit. Take a bite out of it like cheese. This round scallop space, like. God. *Get your dog,* man. I have an appointment somewhere. What time is it? I think this damn Fruit of the Loom underwear is for shit. You see this guy walking around in his underwear with his kid, going to pee, and then popping out this fresh pair of miniature BVDs for the kid just like his, and they walk down the hall real slow in the same stupid tight pants look like *panties? Get* your dog, man.

"Shit. Fucking turtle. What's it *doing* here, man? I mean, your *dog's* not even supposed— What time is it? *Get* the bastard, will you? I can't move my . . . legs. I don't know when it happened. Last twenty minutes after I dogged you. I'd get him myself. That dog is . . . not trained or what? Did you train him? People shouldn't let their dogs go anarchy, man. Dogs need government. Dogs are senators in their hearts when they're trained. They have, like white hair and deep voices. And do *right.* Your dog is going to get *bit,* man. Get your dog. Please get your dog. This position I'm in, I don't know how I got in it. It dudn' make sense.

"Do you ever think about J.E.B. Stuart? His name wasn't Jeb, it's inititals of J. E. B. He had a orange feather in a white hat and was, like, good. Won. Fast, smart, all that, took no survivors; well, I don't know about that. Kind of kind you want on *your* side, like that. Man. It's hard to talk, say things right. If you don't get your dog I'm going to shoot—you. No, myself. *Claim* your dog out there. The window is dirty as shit. I pay a lot of money for this trailer, you think they'd wash the goddamn window. No, you wouldn't. You *know* they wouldn't wash the goddamn window. I'd shoot the *turtle,* but the window, they wouldn't *fix* it so they wouldn't *wash* it, would they? I'd shoot your fucking *dog* before I'd shoot the turtle. That turtle idn' doing shit but getting licked in the face and *taking* it."

The girl said, "I don't have a dog."

"Well, somebody does," Scarliotti said. *"Some*body sure as hell does."

LETTERS TO WENDY'S

JOE WENDEROTH

October 12, 1996

Like a man who out of anger explodes into a sound he will never know the meaning of, that he will never even hear but will only know in the awkward effects of its being heard—and who then finds himself suddenly in the absence of that sound, having resumed himself as if he could not possibly have contained its violence, its inarticulate force, I come to stand on the other side of my order.

November 3, 1996

Surgeon-light booming. I take a bite. This recent organization of animals, chunks of homelessness dwindling. I take a sip. Gusts of patience—nothing to worry about. I take a bite. Grass finding always a new naive cause. I take a bite. Surgeon-light booming—nothing to worry about. I take a sip. Loud shadow of animals in the causeway, home-gouging. I take a sip, a bite. Guts of patients.

February 8, 1997

Wendy, will you not even poke me? Not even a slow poke? I wonder why you treat me so. Am I a wooden board? Am I to be thought of as a simple wooden board? Come on, just give me a slow poke. I'm not a wooden board, honey. Come on, just poke me like you used to. Just a slow poke. Look into my eyes—are these the eyes of a wooden board?

March 6, 1997

My life is not a story. I'd like to apologize for that. I know what a nuisance it is for you. *I've tried* to make my life into a story—you know I have—but every time I've been returned to the heart of the city in chains. I accept this as the fated role I am to play. I wait here, in chains, for you to pass by. For you to look out of the story and into me, into the way I'm bound, unsheltered, guilty of nothing.

March 20, 1997

If you need someone to hold the fort down, you need someone dead. I'm your man. If I'm not dead, no one is. There's no fort I cannot hold down. It's impossible to convey just how dead I am and how secure the fort would be in my care. Perhaps seeing it evaporate in the care of someone far less dead than myself would make you understand. But then, there is no understanding without the fort.

April 5, 1997

Often I come to Wendy's looking like who'd a' thought it. This is only ever an indication that I am still appropriate, which is to say, still overdetermined by a fascination with the meaty crux. You can call me a scientist if you want to, but if you do, you don't understand how hungry I am. Sometimes I am so hungry I wear a white belt with white pants.

April 19, 1997

It is rare for a baby to be so bad that it is sentenced to be hanged, and even rarer for the sentence to be carried out, and yet, when a baby is hung, what a pleasant surprise it is for the passersby. Even the passerby whose arms and legs are bound is able to inch up close enough to the tiny, swaying, villainous nugget of softness and know, with his bare cheek, the threshold through which real evil sinks away.

July 14, 1997

I will miss this spectacle. Sorely miss. I sorely miss it now. The children writhing on the floor, half-imagining how near they are to being set at ease. Meat induces sleep, they told me when I was a child, but what does sleep induce? Please accept my apology. It was never my intention to be actual.

FIELD EVENTS

RICK BASS

But the young one, the man, as if he were
the son of a neck and a nun: taut and powerfully filled
with muscles and innocence.
                        —RILKE, *"The Fifth Elegy"*

It was summer, and the two brothers had been down on a gravel bar washing their car with river water and sponges when the big man came around the bend, swimming upstream, doing the butterfly stroke. He was pulling a canoe behind him, and it was loaded with darkened cast-iron statues. The brothers, John and Jerry, had hidden behind a rock and watched as the big man leapt free of the water with each sweep of his arms, arching into the air like a fish and then crashing back down into the rapids, lunging his way up the river, with the canoe following him.

The brothers thought they'd hidden before the big man had spotted them—how could he have known they were there?—but he altered his course slightly as he drew closer, until he was swimming straight for the big rock they were hiding behind. When it became apparent he was heading for them, they stepped out from behind the rock, a bit embarrassed at having hidden. It was the Sacandaga River, which ran past the brothers' town, Glens Falls, in northeastern New York.

The brothers were strength men themselves, discus throwers and shot-putters, but even so, they were unprepared for the size of the man as he emerged from the water, dripping and completely naked save for the rope around his waist, which the canoe was tied to.

Jerry, the younger—eighteen that summer—said, "Lose your briefs in the rapids?"

The big man smiled, looked down, and quivered like a dog, shaking the water free one leg at a time, one arm at a time. The brothers had seen big men in the gym before, but they'd never seen anyone like this.

With the canoe still tied around his waist, and the rope still tight as the current tried to sweep the iron-laden canoe downstream, the big man crouched and with a stick drew a map in the sand of where he lived in Vermont, about fifteen miles upstream. The rapids surged against the stationary canoe, crashed water over the bow as it bobbed in place, and the brothers saw the big man tensing against the pull of the river, saw him lean forward to keep from being drawn back in. Scratching in the sand with that stick. Two miles over the state line. An old farmhouse.

Then the man stood, said good-bye, and waded back into the shallows, holding the rope taut in his hands to keep from being dragged in. When he was in up to his knees he dived, angled out toward the center, and once more began breaststroking up the river, turning his head every now and again to look back at the brothers with cold, curious eyes, like those of a raven, or a fish.

The brothers tried to follow, running along the rocky, brushy shore, calling for the big man to stop, but he continued slowly upriver, swimming hard against the crashing, funneled tongue of rapids, lifting up and over them and back down among them, lifting like a giant bat or manta ray. He swam up through a narrow canyon and left them behind.

At home in bed that night, each brother looked up at the ceiling in his room and tried to sleep. Each could feel his heart thrashing around in his chest. The brothers knew that the big man was up to something, something massive.

The wild beating in the brothers' hearts would not stop. They got up and met, as if by plan, in the kitchen for a beer, a sandwich. They ate almost constantly, always trying to build more muscle. Sometimes they acted like twins, thought the same thing at the same time. It was a warm night, past midnight, and when they had finished their snack, they got the tape measure and checked to see if their arms had gotten larger. And because the measurements were unchanged, they each fixed another sandwich, ate them, measured again. No change.

"It's funny how it works," said John. "How it takes such a long time."

"No shit, Sherlock," said Jerry. He slapped his flat belly and yawned.

Neither of them had mentioned the big man in the rapids. All day they'd held it like a secret, cautious of what might happen if they discussed it. Feeling that they might chase him away, that they might make it be as if he had never happened.

They went outside and stood in the middle of the street under a streetlamp and looked around like watchdogs, trying to understand why their hearts were racing.

So young! So young!

They drove an old blue Volkswagen beetle. When the excitement of the night and of their strength and youth was too much, they would pick up the automobile from either end like porters, or pallbearers, and try to carry it around the block, for exercise, without having to stop and set it down and rest. But that night, the brothers' hearts were running too fast just to walk the car. They lay down beneath the trees in the cool grass in their backyard and listened to the wind that blew from the mountains on the other side of the river. Sometimes the brothers would go wake their sisters, Lory and Lindsay, and bring them outside into the night. The four of them would sit under the largest tree and tell stories or plan things.

Their father was named Heck, and their mother, Louella. Heck was the principal of the local school. Lory was thirty-four, a teacher, and beautiful: she was tiny, black-haired, with a quick, high laugh not unlike the outburst of a loon. Despite her smallness, her breasts were overly large, to the point that they were the first thing people noticed about her, and continued noticing about her. She tried always to keep moving when around new people, tried with her loon's laugh and her high-energy, almost manic actress's gestures to shift the focus back to *her,* not her breasts, but it was hard, and tiring. She had long, sweeping eyelashes, but not much of a chin. The reason Lory still lived at home was that she loved her family and simply could not leave. Lindsay was sixteen, but already half a foot taller than Lory. She was red-headed, freckled, and had wide shoulders, and played field hockey; the brothers called her Lindsay the Red.

Lory was not allowed to work at the school where her father was principal, so she taught in a little mountain town called Warrensburg, about thirty miles north. She hated the job. The children had no respect for her, no love; they drank and died in fiery crashes, or were abused by their parents, or got cancer—they had no luck. Lory's last name, her family's name, was Iron, and one night the boys at her school had scratched with knives onto every desktop the words "I fucked Miss Iron." Sometimes the boys touched her from behind when she was walking in the crowded halls.

That night the brothers' hearts beat so wildly, they lay in the grass for a while and then went and got their sisters. Lory was barely able to come out of her sleep but followed the brothers anyway, holding Jerry's hand as if sleepwalking. She sat down with her back against the largest tree and dozed in and out, still exhausted from the school year. Lindsay, though, was wide awake, and sat cross-legged, leaning forward, listening.

"We went down to the river today," John said, plucking at stems of grass, putting them in his mouth and chewing on them for their sweetness, like a cow grazing. Jerry was doing hurdler's stretches, had one leg extended in front of him. There was no moon, only stars through the trees.

"Summer," mumbled Lory in her half sleep. Often she talked in her sleep and had nightmares.

"Who was your first lover?" Jerry asked her, grinning, speaking in a low voice, trying to trick her.

Lindsay covered her sister's ears and whispered, "Lory, no! Wake up! Don't say it!"

The brothers were overprotective of Lory, even though she was the oldest and hadn't had any boyfriends for a long time.

"Michael," Lory mumbled uncomfortably. "No, no, Arthur. No, wait, Richard, William? No—Mack, no, Jerome, Atticus, no, that Caster boy—no, wait . . ."

Slowly Lory opened her eyes, smiling at Jerry. "Got you," she said.

Jerry shrugged, embarrassed. "I just want to protect you."

Lory looked at him with sleepy, narrowed eyes. "Right."

They were silent for a moment, then John said, "We saw this big man today. He was pulling a boat. He was really pulling it." John wanted to say more, but didn't dare. He reached down and plucked a blade of night grass. They sat there in the moon shadows, a family, wide awake while the rest of the town slept.

They waited a week, almost as if they had tired or depleted the big man, and as if they were now letting him gather back his whole self. John and Jerry went to the rapids every day to check on the map in the sand, and when it had finally begun to blur, almost to the point of disappearing, they realized they had to go find him soon, or risk never seeing him again.

Lindsay drove, though she did not yet have her license, and John sat in the front with her and told her the directions, navigating from memory. (To have transcribed the map onto paper, even onto a napkin, would also somehow have run the risk of depleting or diminishing the big man, if he was still out there.) Jerry sat in the backseat, wearing sunglasses like a movie star and sipping a high-protein milk shake. John's strength in the discus was his simple brute power, while Jerry's strength—he was five years younger and sixty pounds lighter—was his speed.

"*Right!*" Jerry cried every time John gave Lindsay the correct instructions. In his mind, Jerry could see the map as clear as anything, and when John gave Lindsay a bad piece of advice—a left turn, say, instead of a right—Jerry would shout out "*Wrong!— Braaapp! Sham-bam-a-LOOM!*"

There were so many turns to the road: up and over hills, across small green valleys, around a lake, and down sun-dappled lanes, as if passing through tunnels—from shade to sun, shade to sun, with wooden bridges clattering beneath them, until Lindsay was sure they were lost. But Jerry, in the backseat, kept smiling, his face content behind the dark glasses, and John was confident, too. The closer they got to the big man, the more they could tell he was out there.

The road had crossed over the border into Vermont, and turned to gravel. It followed a small creek for a stretch, and the brothers wondered if this creek flowed into the Sacandaga, if the big man had swum all the way upstream before turning into this side creek, to make his way home. It looked like the creek he had drawn on his map in the sand.

Blackbirds flew up out of the marsh reeds along either side of them. They could feel him getting closer. There was very much the sense that they were hunting him, that they had to somehow capture him.

Then they saw him in a pasture. A large two-story stone house stood at the end of the pasture, like a castle, with the creek passing by out front, the creek shaded by elm and maple trees, and giant elms that had somehow, in this one small area, avoided or been immune to the century's blight. The pasture was deep with rich green summer hay, and they saw a few cows, Holsteins, grazing there.

Again, the man wasn't wearing anything, and he had one of the cows on his back. He was running through the tall grass with it, leaping sometimes, doing jetés and awkward but heartfelt pirouettes with the sagging cow draped across his wide shoulders. He had thick legs that jiggled as he ran, and he looked happy, as happy as they had ever seen anyone look. The rest of the cattle stood in front of the old house, grazing and watching without much interest.

"Jiminy," said Lindsay.

"Let's get him," said John, the strongest. "Let's wait until he goes to sleep and then tie him up and bring him home."

"We'll teach him to throw the discus," said Jerry.

"If he doesn't want to throw the discus, we'll let him go," said John. "We won't force him to."

"Right," said Jerry.

But force wasn't necessary. John and Jerry went into the field after him, warily, and he stopped spinning and shook hands with them. Lindsay stayed in the car, wanting to look away but unable to; she watched the man's face, watched the cow on his back. The cow had a placid but somehow engaged look on its face, as if it were just beginning to awaken to the realization that it was aloft.

The big man grinned and put the cow back on the ground. He told them that he had never thrown the discus, had never even seen it done, but would like to try, if that was what they wanted him to do. He left them and went into the stone house for a pair of jeans and tennis shoes and a white T-shirt. When he came back out, dressed, he looked even larger.

He was too big to fit into the car—he was as tall as John but thirty pounds heavier, and built of rock-slab muscle—so he rode standing on the back bumper, grinning, with the wind blowing his long, already thinning hair back behind him. The big man's face was young, his skin smooth and tanned.

"My name's A.C.!" he shouted to them as they puttered down the road. Lindsay leaned her head out the window and looked back at him, wanting to make sure he was all right. The little car's engine shuddered and shook beneath him, trying to manage the strain. The back bumper scraped the road.

"I'm Lindsay!" she shouted. "John's driving! Jerry's not!"

Her hair swirled around her, a nest of red. She knew what Lory would say. Her sister thought that all the muscle on her brothers was froufrou, adornment, and unnecessary. Lindsay hoped that Lory would change her mind.

"Lindsay, get back in the car!" John shouted, looking in the rearview mirror. But she couldn't hear him. She was leaning farther out the window, reaching for A.C.'s wrist, and then higher, gripping his thick arm.

"She's mad," Jerry howled, disbelieving. "She's lost her mind."

A.C. grinned and held on to the car's roof, taking the bumps with his legs.

When they drove up to their house, Lory had awakened from her nap and was sitting on the picnic table in her shorts and a T-shirt, drinking from a bottle of red wine. She burst into laughter when she saw them approach with A.C. riding the back bumper as if he had hijacked them.

"Three peas in a pod," she cried. She danced down from the table and out to the driveway to meet him, to shake his hand.

It was as if there were three brothers.

From the kitchen window, Louella watched, horrified.

The huge young man in the front yard was not hers. He might think he was, and everyone else might too, but he wasn't. She stopped drying the dishes and was alarmed at the size of him, standing there among her children, shaking hands, moving around in their midst. She had had one miscarriage, twenty years ago. This man could have been that child, could even have been that comeback soul.

Louella felt the blood draining from her face and thought she was dying. She fell to the kitchen floor in a faint, breaking the coffee cup she was drying.

It was the end of June. Fields and pastures all over the Hudson Valley were green. She had been worrying about Lory's sadness all through the fall and winter, on through the rains and melting snows of spring, and even now, into the ease of green summer.

Louella sat up groggily and adjusted her glasses. When she went outside to meet A.C., she could no longer say for sure whether she knew him or not; there was a moment's hesitancy.

She looked hard into his eyes, dried her hands on her apron, and reached out and shook his big hand. She was swayed by her children's happiness. There was a late-day breeze. A hummingbird dipped at the nectar feeder on the back porch. She let him come into their house.

"We're going to teach A.C. how to throw the discus," said Jerry.

"Thrilling," said Lory.

He had supper with the family, and they all played Monopoly that evening. Louella asked A.C. where he was from and what he did, but he would only smile and say that he was here to throw the discus. He wasn't rude, he simply wouldn't tell her where he was from. It was almost as if he did not know, or did not understand the question.

They played Monopoly until it was time for bed. The brothers took him for a walk through the neighborhood and on into town. They stopped to pick up people's cars occasionally, the three of them lifting together.

There was a statue of Nathan Hale in the town square, and, drunk on the new moon, drunk with his new friends, A.C. waded through the shrubbery, crouched below the statue, and gave the cold metal a bear hug. He began twisting back and forth, pulling the statue from the ground, groaning, squeezing and lifting with his back and legs, his face turning redder and redder, rocking until he finally worked it loose. He stood up with it, sweating, grinning, holding it against his chest as if it were a dance partner, or a dressmaker's dummy.

They walked home after that, taking turns carrying the statue on their backs, and snuck it into Lory's room and stood it in the corner by the door, so that it blocked her exit. It still smelled of fresh earth and crushed flowers. Lory was a sound sleeper, plunging into unconsciousness as an escape at every opportunity, and she never heard them.

Then A.C. went downstairs to the basement and rested, lying on a cot, looking up at the ceiling with his hands behind his head. John and Jerry stayed in the kitchen, drinking beer.

"Do you think it will happen?" Jerry asked.

John was looking out the window at the garden. "I hope so," he said. "I think it would be good for her." He finished his beer. "Maybe we shouldn't think about it, though. It might be wrong."

"Well," said Jerry, sitting down as if to think about it himself, "maybe so."

John was still looking out the window. "But who cares?" he said. He looked at Jerry.

"This guy's okay," said Jerry. "This one's good."

"But do you think he can throw the discus?"

"I don't know," Jerry said. "But I want you to go find some more statues for him. I liked that."

*   *   *

That first night at the Irons' house, A.C. thought about John and Jerry, about how excited he had been to see them walking up to him. He considered how they looked at each other sometimes when they were talking. They always seemed to agree.

Then he thought about John's hair, black and short, and about his heavy beard. And Jerry, he seemed so young with his green eyes. His hair was blond and curly. A.C. liked the way Jerry leaned forward slightly and narrowed his eyes, grinning, when he talked. Jerry seemed excited about almost anything, everything, and excited to be with his older brother, following him down the same path.

Later, A.C. got up from his cot—he'd been sleeping among punching bags and exercise bikes, with dumbbells and barbells scattered about like toys—and went quietly up the stairs, past Lindsay's room, through the kitchen, and into the living room.

He sat down on the couch and looked out the big front window at the moon and clouds as if watching a play. He stayed there for a long time, occasionally dozing off for a few minutes. At around four in the morning he awoke to find Lory standing in front of him, blocking the moon. She was dark, with the moon behind her lighting only the edge of one side of her face. He could see her eyelashes on that one side. She was studying him almost the way Louella had.

"Look," he said, and pointed behind her.

The clouds were moving past the moon in fast-running streams, like tidal currents, eddying, it seemed, all to the same place, all hurrying by as if late to some event.

"What is that statue doing in my room?" Lory asked. She was whispering, and he thought her voice was beautiful. A.C. hoped he could be her friend too, as he'd become a friend of her brothers. He looked at the moon, a mottled disc.

"Do you want to sit down?" he asked. He patted the side of the couch next to him.

Slowly she did, and then, after a few seconds, she leaned into his shoulder and put her head against it. She put both her hands on his arm and held on.

After a while, A.C. lifted her into his lap, holding her in both arms as if she were a small child, and slowly he rocked her. She curled against him as tightly as she could, and he rocked her like that, watching her watch him, until dawn.

When it got light, she reached up and kissed him quickly, touching his face with her hands, and got out of his lap and hurried into the kitchen to fix coffee before anyone else was up. A few minutes later, Louella appeared in the living room, sleepy-eyed, shuffling, wearing a faded blue flannel robe and old slippers, holding the paper. She almost stepped on A.C.'s big feet. She stopped, surprised to see him up so early, and in her living room. He stood up and said, "Good morning," and she smiled in spite of herself.

Around eight o'clock John and Jerry got up, and they chased each other into the kitchen, playing some advanced form of tag. The lighter, faster Jerry stayed just ahead of John, leaping over the coffee table, spinning, tossing a footstool into his path for John to trip over. Lory shrieked, spilled some milk from the carton she was holding, and Louella shouted at them to stop it, tried to look stern, but was made young again by all the motion, and secretly loved it—and A.C., having come meekly in from the living room, stood back and smiled. Louella glanced over at him and saw him smiling, looking at the brothers, and she thought again of how eerie the fit was, of how he seemed to glide into all the right spots them all along—or even stranger, it was as if he were some sort of weight or stone placed on a scale that better balanced them now.

After breakfast—a dozen eggs each, some cantaloupes, a pound of sausage split among them, a gallon of milk, and a couple of plates of pancakes—the brothers went out to their car and tossed all their throwing equipment in it—tape measure, discs, throwing shoes—and they leaned the driver's seat forward so that A.C. could get in the back, but still he wouldn't fit.

He rode standing on the bumper again. They drove to the school, to the high, windy field where they threw. From there it seemed they could see the whole Hudson Valley and the knife-cut through the trees where the river rushed, the Sacandaga melting through the mountains, and on the other side the green walls of the Adirondacks. A.C. looked around at the new town as they drove. He thought about Lory, about how soft and light she'd been in his arms, and of how he'd been frightened by her. Riding on the back of the tiny car reminded him of being in the river, swimming up through the rapids: all that rushing force, relentless, crashing down over and around him, speeding past. Things were going by so fast. He looked around and felt dizzy at the beauty of the town.

There was a ring in the center of the field, a flat, smooth, unpainted circle of cement, and that was where the brothers and A.C. set their things and began to dress. The brothers sat down like bears in the zoo and took their street shoes off. As they laced up their heavy leather throwing shoes, stretching and grasping their toes, they looked out at the wire fence running along the south end of the field, which was the point they tried to reach with their throws.

A.C. put his shoes on, too, the ones they had given him, and stood up. He felt how solid the earth was beneath him. His legs were dense and strong, and he kicked the ground a couple of times with the heavy shoes. A.C. imagined that he could feel the earth shudder when he kicked. He jumped up and down a couple of times, short little hops, just to feel the shudder again.

"I hope you like this," said Jerry, still stretching, twisting his body into further unrecognizable shapes and positions. He was loosening up, his movements fluid, and to A.C. it was exactly like watching the river.

A.C. sat down next to them and tried to do some of the stretches, but it didn't work for him yet. He watched them for half an hour, as the blue air over the mountains and valley waned, turn-

ing to a sweet haze, a slow sort of shimmer that told A.C. it was
June. Jerry was the one he most liked to watch.

Jerry would crouch in the ring, twisted—wound up—with
his eyes closed, his mouth open, and the disc hanging back, hanging low, his knees bent. When he began to spin, it was as if some
magical force were being born, something that no other force on
earth would be able to stop.

He stayed in the small circle, hopping from one foot to the
other, crouched low, but with the hint of rising, and then he was
suddenly at the other end of the small ring, out of room—if he
went over the little wooden curb and into the grass, it would be a
foul—and with no time or space left in which to spin, he shouted,
brought his arm all the way around on the spin, his elbow locking
straight out as he released the disc, and only then did the rest of
his body react, starting with his head; it snapped back and then
forward from the recoil, as if he'd first made the throw and then
had a massive heart attack.

"Wow," said A.C., watching him unwind and recover and
return, surprisingly, to a normal upright human being.

But John and Jerry were watching the disc. It was moving so
fast. There was a heavy, cutting sound when it landed, far short of
the fence, and it skidded a few feet after that and then stopped, as
if it had never been moving.

Jerry threw two more times—they owned only three discs—and
then the three of them, walking like gunslingers, like giants from
another age, went out to get the discs. The brothers talked about
the throws: what Jerry had done right, and what he had done
wrong. His foot position had been a little off on the first throw. He
hadn't kept his head back far enough going into the spin of the
second throw. The third throw had been pretty good; on the
bounce, it had carried to the chain-link fence.

John threw next, and then Jerry again, and then it was John's turn once again. A.C. thought he could do it himself. Certainly that whip-spin dance, skip, hurl, and shout was a thing that was in everyone. It had to be the same way he felt when he picked up a cow and spun through the tall grass, holding it on his shoulders. When it was his turn to throw the discus, he tried to remember that, and stepped into the ring, huffing.

A.C.'s first throw slammed into the center of the head-high fence and shook it. John and Jerry looked at each other, trying not to feel amazed. It was what they had thought from the beginning, after all; it was as if he had always been with them.

But A.C.'s form was spastic. It was wrong, it was nothing. He threw with his arms and shoulders—not with his legs, and not with the twist of his wide back. If he could get the spin down, the dance, he would throw it 300 feet. He would be able to throw it the length of a football field. In the discus, even 230 feet was immortality.

Again, the brothers found themselves feeling that there was a danger of losing him—of having him disappear if they did or said the wrong thing, if they were not true and honest.

But the way he could throw a discus! It was as if their hearts had created him. He was all strength, no finesse. They were sure they could teach him the spin-dance. The amazing thing about a bad spin, as opposed to a good one, is how *ugly* it looks. A good spin excites the spectators, touches them all the way down and through, makes them wish they could do it—or even more, makes them feel as if they *had* done it, somehow. But a bad throw is like watching a devil monster changeling being born into the world; just one more awful thing in a world of too many, and even spectators who do not know much about the sport will turn their heads away, even before the throw is completed, when they see an awkward spin. A.C.'s was, John and Jerry had to admit, the ugliest of the ugly.

His next throw went over the fence. The one after that—

before they realized what was happening, or realized it too late, as it was in the air, climbing, moving faster than any of their throws had ever gone—rose, gliding, and hit the base of the school. There was a *crack!* and the disc exploded into graphite shards. One second it was there, flying and heroic, and then it was nothing, just an echo.

"A hundred and ten bucks," Jerry said, but John cared nothing for the inconvenience it would bring them, being down to two discs, and he danced and whooped, spun around and threw imaginary discs, waved his arms and continued to jump up and down. He danced with Jerry, and then he grabbed A.C.

"If you can learn the steps . . ." John was saying, almost singing. The three men held one another's shoulders and danced and spun across the field like children playing snap-the-whip. John and Jerry had never seen a discus thrown that far in their lives, and A.C., though he had felt nothing special, was happy because his new friends were happy, and he hoped he could make them happy again.

Riding home on the back bumper, the air cooling his summer-damp hair and clothes, he leaned against the car and hugged it like a small child, and watched the town going past in reverse now, headed back to the Irons' house, and he hoped that maybe he could make them happy forever.

The brothers bragged about him when they got home, and everyone listened, and like John and Jerry they were half surprised, but they also felt that it confirmed something, and so that part of them was anything but surprised.

John was dating a schoolteacher named Patty. A shy-eyed Norwegian, she was as tall as he was, with freckles and a slow-spreading smile. A.C. grinned just watching her, and when she saw A.C., she would laugh for no real reason, just a happy laugh. Once when John and Jerry had gone to their rooms to nap, A.C. went outside with Lindsay and Patty to practice field hockey.

A.C. had never played any formal sports and was thrilled to be racing across the lawn, dodging the trees and the women, passing the ball along clumsily but quickly. Patty's laughs, Lindsay's red hair. If only he could live forever with this. He ran and ran, barefoot, back and forth in the large front yard, and they laughed all afternoon.

On the nights when A.C. did not stay with the family, he returned to the old stone house in Vermont. Some days he would swim all the way home, starting upstream at dusk and going on into the night—turning right where the little creek entered the Sacandaga, with fish bumping into his body and jumping around him as if a giant shark had passed through. But other nights he canoed home against the rapids, having loaded boulders into the bottom of the canoe to work his shoulders and arms harder. After he got home, he tied the canoe to the low branch of a willow, leaving it bobbing in the current.

Some nights in the farmhouse, A.C. would tie a rope around his waist and chest, attach the other end of it to one of the rafters, and climb up into the rafters and leap down, swinging like a pirate. He'd hang there, dangling in the darkness. He'd hold his arms and legs out as he spun around and around, and it would feel as if he were sinking, descending, and as if it would never stop.

He would tell no one where he had come from. And he would forget the woman in Colorado, the one he was supposed to have married. Everyone comes from somewhere. Everyone has made mistakes, has caused injuries, even havoc. The woman had killed herself after A.C. left her; she had hanged herself.

This is what it's like, he'd think. This is the difference between being alive and being dead. He'd hang from the rope and spin. This is the only difference, but it's so big.

Sometimes he would sleep all night dangling from the rafters: spinning, a bit frightened, hanging like a question mark, only to awaken each morning as the sun's first light filtered through the dusty east windows. The sound of the creek running past just out front, the creek that led into the river.

There were mornings when Lory was afraid to get up. She thought it was just common depression and that it would pass with time, but some days it seemed too much. She slept as much as she could, which seemed to make it worse and worse. She tried to keep it a secret from her family, but she suspected that her brothers knew, and her mother, too. It was like drowning, like going down in chains. And she felt guilty about the anguish it would cause others.

But her brothers! They anchored her and nourished her, they were like water passing through her gills. If they came down the hall and found her just sitting in the hallway, her head down between her knees, they—John or Jerry, or sometimes both of them—would gently pick her up and carry her outside to the yard, into the sun, and would rub her back and neck. Jerry would pretend to be a masseur with a foreign accent, would crack Lory's knuckles one by one, counting to ten some days in German, others in Spanish or French, mixing the languages to keep her guessing, to make her pay attention. Then he would start on her toes as John continued to knead her neck muscles and her small, strong shoulders.

"Uno, dos, *trey*," Jerry would hiss, wiggling her toes. He'd make up numbers. "Petrocci, zimbosi, bambolini, *crunk!*" he'd mutter, and then, "The little pig, he went to the market. He wanted beef—he wanted roast beef . . ."

He'd keep singing nonsense, keep teasing her until she smiled or laughed, until he had her attention, until he'd pulled her out of that well of sadness and numbness, and he'd shake his finger at her and say, "Pay attention!" She'd smile, back in her family's arms again, and be amazed that Jerry was only eighteen, but knew so much.

They would lie in the grass afterward and look up at the trees, at the way the light came down, and Lory would have the thought, whenever she was happy, that this was the way she really was, the way things could always be, and that that flat, vacant stretch of nothing-feeling was the aberration, not the norm; and she wanted it always to be like that, and still, even at thirty-four, believed that it could be.

When they were sure she was better, one of the brothers would walk to the nearest tree and wrap his arms around it, would grunt and lean hard against it, and then would begin to shake it until leaves began to fall. Lory would laugh and look up as they landed on her face and in her hair, and she would not pull them out of her hair, for they were a gift, and still John or Jerry would keep shaking the tree, as if trying to cover her with the green summer leaves, the explosion of life.

A.C. and the brothers trained every day. When A.C. stayed at the farmhouse, each morning shortly before daylight he would get in his canoe and float all the way to Glens Falls, not ever having to paddle—just ruddering. As if following veins or arteries, he took all the right turns with only a flex of his wrist, a slight change of the paddle's orientation in the water, and he passed beneath dappled maples, flaking sycamores, listening to the cries of river birds and the sounds of summer as he slipped into the town.

Besides hurling the discus outside near the school, the brothers lifted weights in the school's basement and went for long runs on the track. Each had his own goal, and each wanted A.C. to throw the unspeakable 300 feet. It would be a throw so far that the discus would vanish from sight.

No one believed it could be done. Only the brothers believed it. A.C. was not even sure he himself believed it. Sometimes he fell down when entering his spin, trying to emulate their grace, their precision-polished whip-and-spin and the clean release, like a birth, the discus flying wild and free into the world.

In the evenings the whole family would sit around in the den watching *M*A*S*H* or the movie of the week—*Conan the Barbarian* once—their father, Heck, sipping his gin and tonic, fresh-squeezed lime in with the ice, sitting in the big easy chair watching his huge sons sprawled on the rug, with their huge friend lying next to them. Lindsay would sit in the corner, watching only parts of the movie, spending more time watching Lory—and Lory, next to her mother on the couch, would sway a bit to her own internal rhythm, smiling, looking at the TV screen but occasionally at the brothers, and at A.C.

The nights that A.C. stayed over, Lory made sure that he had a pillow and fresh sheets. Making love to him was somehow unimaginable, and also the greatest thought of all; and he had this silly throw to make first, this long throw with the brothers.

Lovemaking was unthinkable—the waist-to-waist kind, anyway. If she gambled on it and lost, she would chase him away from the brothers as well as herself.

The idea was unthinkable. But each night she and A.C. would meet upstairs in the dark, or sit on the couch in the living room, dozing that way, with Lory in his arms, curled up in his lap, her head resting against his wide chest. That was not unimaginable.

A.C. trained all through the summer. Early in the evenings, sometimes the brothers went out looking for statues with him. Their backyard was becoming filled with statues, all of them upright just outside Lory's and Lindsay's windows. A.C. laid them down in the grass at daylight and covered them with tarps, but raised them again near sundown: long-ago generals, riverboat captains, composers, poets.

Louella kept her eye on him, suspecting, and believing in her heart, that he was the soul of her lost son come back in this huge body, come home finally. She did not want him to love Lory—it seemed that already he was too close—but she did not want him to go away, either. Louella watched A.C. carefully, when he could not see she was watching him. What would it have been like to have three sons? What would that third son have been like? She felt both the sweetness and the anguish of it. She could not look away.

*   *   *

He had not been so happy in a long time. He was still throwing clumsily, but the discus was going farther and farther: 250, 255 feet; and then 260.

Each was a world-record throw, but the brothers did not tell A.C. this. They told no one else, either. It was the brothers' plot to not show him off until he was consistently throwing the astonishing 300 feet. Perhaps A.C.'s first public throw of the discus would not only set a world's record; perhaps he'd hurl it so great a distance that no one would believe he was from this earth. Sportswriters and fans would clamor after him, chase him, want to take him away and lock him up and do tests on him, examine him. He would need an escape route, the brothers imagined, a way back to the Sacandaga River, never to be seen or heard from again . . .

The plan got fuzzy at that point. The brothers were not sure how it would go after that, and they had not yet consulted with A.C., but they were thinking that somehow Lory would figure in it.

Certainly they had told no one, not even their mother—especially not her.

A.C. was euphoric as the summer moved on. When he was back at his farmhouse, he often went out to the pasture and lifted a cow and danced around with it as if it were stuffed or inflated. Or in Glens Falls he'd roll the brothers' little Volkswagen gently over on its back, and then he would grab the bumper and begin running in circles with it, spinning it like a top in the deep grass. The muscles in his cheeks tensed and flexed as he spun, showing the most intricate striations. His veins would be visible just beneath his temples. A.C. would grin, and John and Jerry thought it great fun, too, and they'd get on either end and ride the upside-down car like a playground toy as A.C. continued to spin it.

The summer had not softened him; he was still all hard, still all marvelous. Children from the neighborhood would run up and touch him. They felt stronger, afterward.

Lately, on the nights he stayed over at the Irons' house, once everyone else was asleep, A.C. would carry Lory all through the house after she had fallen asleep in his lap. He imagined that he was protecting her. He carried her down all the hallways—past her parents' room, her brothers', past Lindsay's, into the kitchen and out to the garage: it was all safe and quiet. Next he took her into the backyard, among the statues, and then into the street, walking through the neighborhood with her as she slept.

There was a street called Sweet Road that had no houses, only vacant lots, and trees, and night smells. He would lay her down in the dew-wet grass along Sweet Road and touch her robe, an old fuzzy white thing, and the side of her face. The wind would stir her hair, wind coming up out of the valley, wind coming from across the river. He owed the brothers his happiness.

Some nights, far-off heat lightning flickered over the mountains, behind the steep ridges. She slept through it all in the cool grass. He wondered what she was dreaming.

Late in the afternoons, after practice, the brothers walked the mile and a half to the grocery store in town, and along the way they showed A.C. the proper discus steps. Lory and Lindsay followed sometimes, to watch. The brothers demonstrated to A.C., in half crouches and hops, the proper setup for a throw, the proper release, and he tried to learn: the snap forward with the throw, and then the little trail-away spin at the end, unwinding, everything finished.

Jerry brought the chalk and drew dance steps on the sidewalk for the placement of A.C.'s feet so he could move down the sidewalk properly, practicing his throws. Like children playing hopscotch, ducking and twisting, shuffling forward and then pretending to finish the spin with great shouts at the imaginary release of each throw, they moved through the quiet neighborhood, jumping and shouting, throwing their arms at the sky. Dogs barked at them as they went past, and children ran away at first, though soon they learned to follow, once the brothers and the big man had passed, and they would imitate, in the awkward fashion of children, the brothers' and A.C.'s throws.

Lory could see the depression, the not-quite-old part of herself, back behind her—back in June, back in the spring, and behind in winter; back into the cold fall and the previous dry-leaved summer— but she was slipping forward now, away from all that. A.C. took her to his farmhouse and showed her how to hang from the ceiling. He'd rigged the harness so that she could hang suspended and spin.

He had to get over the fear of injuring someone again. Had to hit the fear head-on and shatter it. He had to run a long way to get here. He was ready to hit it head-on. It was worth it, once again. And he wanted her to be brave, too.

"It feels better naked," he said the first time he showed it to her, and so she took her clothes off. Lory closed her eyes and put her arms and legs out and spun in slow circles around and around, and A.C. turned the light off, sat down against the wall, and watched her silhouette against the window, watched her until she fell asleep, and then he took her out of the harness and got in bed with her, where she awoke.

"We won't tell anyone," he said. She was in his arms, warm, alive. It made him dizzy to consider what being alive meant.

"No," she said. "No one will ever find out."

She fell asleep with her lips on his chest. A.C. lay there look- ing at the harness hanging above them, and wondered why he wanted to keep it a secret, why it had to be a secret.

He knew that this was the best way to protect her, and that he loved her.

He stayed awake all through the night, conscious of how he dwarfed her, afraid that if he fell asleep he might turn over and crush her. He rose before daylight, woke her, and they got in the canoe and drifted back to New York State, and were home before dawn. A.C. crept into the basement that first night, and every night thereafter.

Lory had not liked hanging from the ceiling. She didn't know why, only that it had frightened her. She kept the harness with her, kept it hidden in her drawer. She just wanted to love him, was all.

Many evenings the family had grilled corn for dinner, dripping with butter. They sat outside at the picnic table and ate with their hands. Night scents would drift toward them. As darkness fell, they would move into the house and watch the lazy movies, the baseball games of summer, and then they would go to sleep. But Lory and A.C. stayed up later and later as the summer went on, and made love after everyone had gone to bed, and then they would go out on their walk, A.C. still carrying Lory, though now she remained awake.

When she was not too tired—when she did not need to go to bed—they would paddle the canoe upriver to his farmhouse, with Lory sitting behind A.C. and tracing her fingers on his wide back as he paddled. The waves would splash against the bow, wetting them both. They moved up the current slowly, past hilly, night-green pastures with the moon high above or just beyond their reach. Summer haying smells rose from the fields, and they passed wild tiger lilies growing along the shore as they crossed into Vermont. Lory felt weightless and free until it was time to go back.

They lay on the old mattress in the farmhouse, with holes in the roof above them, and through the roof, the stars. No brothers, thought Lory fiercely, clutching A.C. and rolling beneath him, over him, beneath him again; she knew it was like swimming through rapids, or maybe drowning in them. Her brothers protected her and understood her, but A.C. seemed to know what was in the center of her, a place she had believed for a long while to be soft and weak.

It was exciting to believe that perhaps it was strong in there. To begin to believe she did not need protecting. It made his protection of her all the more exciting, all the more delicious— unnecessary, and therefore extravagant, luxurious.

This new hardness and strength in her center.

They sat on the stone wall in front of the farmhouse afterward, some nights, before it was time to leave, and they watched the cattle graze under the moon, listening to the slow, strong, grinding sound of their teeth being worn away as their bodies took nourishment. Lory and A.C. held hands and sat shoulder to shoulder, cold and still naked, and when it was time to go, they carried their clothes in a bundle down to the stream, the dew wetting their ankles, their knees, so that they were like the cattle as they moved through the grass—and they'd paddle home naked, Lory sitting right behind A.C. for warmth against the night.

The brothers continued to train in the daytime, and as the summer ended, there was a haze over the valley below them. They were throwing far over the fence, better than they'd ever thrown in their lives. They were tanned from the long hours of practicing shirtless. The sisters came by with a picnic lunch while the men threw. They laid out an old yellow Amish quilt that had belonged to their mother's mother, with the hexagon patterns on it looking not unlike the throwing ring in which A.C. and the brothers whirled before each heave of the discus. The sisters would lie on the quilt on their stomachs, the sun warm on the backs of their legs. They ate Swiss cheese, strawberries, and apples, drank wine and watched the men throw forever, it seemed, until the sisters grew sleepy in the sun and rolled over and looked up at the big white cumulus clouds that did not seem to be going anywhere. They closed their eyes, felt the sun on their eyelids, and fell hard asleep, their mouths open, their bodies still listening to the faint tremors in the earth each time the discus landed.

A.C. had stopped sleeping altogether. There was simply too much to do.

He and Lory would go for canoe rides out on Lake George, only they would not take paddles with them. Instead, A.C. had

gotten the harness back from Lory, and he slipped that over himself and towed her out into the lake as if going to sea, bare to the
waist, and Lory in her one-piece suit. They were both brown from
the picnics, and with nothing but the great blue water before
them, they appeared to glow red, as if smudged with earth. The
sunlight seemed to focus on them alone, the only two moving, living figures before the expanse of all that water, out on top of all
that water. Their bodies gathered that solitary light so that they
were upright, ruddy planes of flesh, of muscle, dull red in that late
summer light, and with nothing but blue water beyond.

A.C. waded out, pulling the canoe with Lory riding inside,
sitting upright like a shy stranger, a girl met on the first day of
school in September. And then thigh-deep, and then deeper, up to
his chest, his neck—he would take her out into the night.

Once they were on the lake, he would unbuckle the harness
and swim circles around her and then submerge, staying under for
a very long time, Lory thought. She lost track of the time. There
was no way for her to bring him up; she could only wait for him.
She watched the concentric ripples he'd left in the lake's surface
until the water faded to smoothness again. She could feel him
down there, somewhere below her, but the water was flat again,
motionless. She would try to will him back to the surface, as if
raising him with a rope from the bottom of a well, but he'd stay
hidden below her.

For A.C., it was dark and yet so deeply safe at the bottom of
the lake. But then he would kick for the surface, up to the wavering glimmer of where she was, the glimmer becoming an explosion as he surfaced. He found her trying to pretend she wasn't
worried, not even turning her head to look at him.

A.C. would get back into the harness and, like a fish or a
whale, he would begin her on her journey again, taking her around
and around the lake, leaving a small V behind the canoe. Lory
trailed her hand in the water and looked back at the blotted tree

line against the night and the restaurant-speckled shore; or she would look out ahead of her at the other shore, equally distant, where there were no lights at all.

With A.C. so close, tied to the rope, pulling her and the boat through the water as if she were a toy, she wanted to stand up and call out, cupping her hands, "I love you." But she stayed seated and let her hand trail in the coolness of the lake. She was not a good swimmer, but she wanted to get in the water with him. She wanted to strip and dive in and swim out to him. He seemed so at ease that Lory would find herself—watching his wet, water-sliding back in the moonlight, the dark water—believing that he had become a sleek sea animal and was no longer a true human, mortal, capable of mortal things.

Occasionally Lory and A.C. went out to the lake in the late afternoon, and she would take a book. Between pages, as he continued to swim, she looked at the tree line, the shore, all so far away. Sometimes a boat drew near to see if she needed help, but always she waved it away, gave the people in the other boat a cheery, thumbs-up signal. When dusk came, if A.C. had been swimming all afternoon, he would head back to the harbor, side-stroking and looking at her with a slow, lazy smile. But she did not want laziness or slow smiles; she wanted to reach out and hold him.

In the dark harbor he would climb into the boat, slippery and naked, as she removed her own clothes, pulling off the old sea-green sweater she wore over her swimsuit in the chill night air, then removing the yellow swimsuit itself, and then her earrings, placing all of these things in the bow, out of the way, so that there was nothing, only them. She met him, offering herself as if meat to a wet, slippery animal. They would lie in the bottom of the cool green canoe, hold each kiss, and feel the lake pressing from beneath as they pressed back against it, riding the surface of the water. With the water so very nearly lapping at her skin but not quite—separated only by the canoe's thin shell—Lory felt like some sort of sea creature. One or both of her arms would sometimes hang over the edge of the canoe as they made love, would trail or splash in the water, and often she didn't see why they didn't just get it over with, dive into the lake and never come back to the surface.

Later, they would get up and sit on the wicker bench seat in the stern, side by side, and lean against each other, holding hands.

They would sit in the harbor, those cool nights, wet, steaming slightly from their own heat. Other boats rode slowly into the harbor, idling through the darkness back to shore, their lengths and shapes identifiable by the green and yellow running lights that lined their sides for safety, as they passed through the night, going home. At times it seemed as if one of the pleasure boats were coming right at them, and sometimes one of the boats with bright running lights would pass by—so close that they could see the faces of the people inside.

But they were unobserved. They watched the boats pass and let the night breezes dry their hair, dry the lake water from their bodies so that they felt human once more, and of the earth. They would make love again, invisible to all the other passing boats, all of them full of people who could not see what it was like to be in love.

A.C. and Lory would have coffee at a restaurant on the short drive back—five or six miles from home—on a deck beneath an umbrella like tourists, looking out at Highway 9A. Lory drank her coffee slowly, stirring milk and sugar into it, cup after cup, watching the black liquid turn into swirling, muddy shades of brown. A.C.'s weight was up to three hundred pounds now, more muscle than ever, but she would reach over, smiling, look into his eyes, and grip the iron breadth of his thigh and squeeze it, then pat it and say, "How are you doing, fat boy?"

She felt the lake water still inside her, even though they had gone in for a quick cleaning-off swim—A.C. staying right next to her, holding her up in the water with one hand. She felt deliciously wild. They drank coffee for an hour, until their hair was completely dry. Then they drove home, to Louella's dismay and the brothers' looks of happiness, but looks that were somehow a little hurt, a little lost; home to Heck's mild wonderment and interest, looking up from his gin and tonic; home to Lindsay's impatience, for A.C. and Lory would have been gone a long time.

"We're just friends, Mom," Lory would say whenever Louella tried to corner her in the kitchen. "I'm happy, too. See? Look!" She danced, leaped, and kicked her heels together three times, spun around when she landed, then went up on her toes—an odd interpretation of the discus spin that A.C. was trying to learn.

"Well," said Louella, not knowing what to say or do. "Good. I hope so."

One morning when A.C. stayed in Glens Falls, he lifted himself from sleep and moved around the basement, examining the old weights, the rowing machines, the rust-locked exercise bikes, and the motionless death-hang of the patched and battered punching bags. A.C. ran his hand over the weights and looked at the flecks of rust that came off on his hands, and thought how the brothers were outlasting the iron and the steel. He stared at the rust in the palm of his hand and smelled the forever-still air that had always been in the basement, air in which John and Jerry had grown up, spindly kids wrestling and boxing, always fighting things, but being part of a family: eating meals together, going to church, teasing their sisters, growing larger, finding directions and interests, taking aim at things. That same air was still down there, as if in a bottle, and it confused A.C. and made him more sure that he was somehow a part of it, a part he did not know about.

He pictured pushing through the confusion, throwing the discus farther and farther, until one day he did the skip-and-glide perfectly. He would be able to spin around once more after that, twice more, and still look up after the throw in time to see the disc flying. It would make the brothers happy, but perhaps then they would not feel that he was a brother anymore.

He trained harder than ever with them, as if it were the greatest of secrets they were giving him. They put their arms around him, walking back from training. Sometimes they teased him, trying to put his great throws in perspective.

"The circumference of the earth at the equator is more than 24,000 miles," Jerry said nonchalantly, looking at his watch as if to see what time it was, as if he had forgotten an appointment. Lory had put him up to it. She'd given him the numbers to crib on his wrist. "Why, that's over 126,720,000 feet," he'd exclaim.

John looked over at A.C. and said, "How far'd you throw today, A.C.?"

A.C. would toss his head back and laugh a great, happy laugh, the laugh of someone being saved, being thrown a rope and pulled in. He would rather be their brother than anything. He wouldn't do them any harm.

Lory and A.C. took Lindsay canoeing on the Battenkill River, over in Vermont. It was almost fall. School was starting soon. Lory stayed close to A.C., held on to his arm, sometimes with both hands. She worried that the fatigue and subsequent depression would be coming on like a returning army, but she smiled thinly, moved through the cool days and laughed, grinning wider whenever their eyes met. Sometimes A.C. would blush and look away, which made Lory grin harder. She would tickle him, tease him; she knew he was frightened of leaving her. She knew he never would.

They drove through the countryside, past fields lined with crumbling stone walls and Queen Anne's lace, with the old canoe on top of the VW. They let Lindsay drive, like a chauffeur. A.C. and Lory had somehow squeezed into the backseat. Now and then Lindsay looked back at them when they kissed, and a crimson blush came into her face, but mostly it was just shy glances at the mirror, trying to see, as if through a telescope, the pleasure that lay ahead of her.

The road turned to white gravel and dust with a clatter and clinking of pebbles, but Lory and A.C. did not notice. They looked like one huge person wedged into the backseat. Sun flashed through the windshield. It felt good to Lindsay to be driving with the window down, going faster than she ever had. Meadows passed, more Queen Anne's lace, maples, farms, cattle. A.C. reached forward and squeezed the back of Lindsay's neck, startling her, and then began rubbing it. She relaxed, smiled, and leaned her head back. Her red hair on his wrist.

Lindsay drove down the narrow road raising dust, and brilliant goldfinches swept back and forth across the road in front of them, flying out of the cattails, alarmed at the car's speed. Lindsay hit one; it struck the hood and flew straight up above them, sailing back toward the cattails, dead, wings folded, but still a bright yellow color. Lindsay cried, "Oh!" and covered her mouth, because neither A.C. nor Lory had seen it. She was ashamed somehow and wanted to keep it a secret.

They stopped for cheeseburgers and shakes at a shady drive-in, in a small Vermont town whose name they'd never heard of. The drive-in was right by the banks of the river, where they would put the canoe in. The river was wide and shallow, cool and clear, and they sat beneath a great red oak and ate. Lindsay was delighted to be with them, but also she could not shake the oddest feeling. Again, the feeling that there was nothing special, that it had been happening all her life, these canoe trips with A.C. and Lory—and that it could just as easily have been John or Jerry sitting with them under the tree. If anything, Lindsay felt a little hollow somehow, and cheated, as if something were missing, because A.C. had shown up only this summer.

Lindsay had never paddled before. She sat backwards and gripped the paddle wrong, like a baseball bat. And Lory did an amazing thing that her sister never understood: she fell out, twice. It was like falling out of a chair. She hadn't even been drinking. Lindsay shrieked. They had water fights.

Lindsay had baked a cake, and they ate it on a small island.

When the sisters waded into the cold river to pee, A.C. laughed, turned his back, and made noise against the rocks on the shore.

"Lindsay's jealous," Lory said when they came trudging out of the river. Lindsay swung at her but missed, and fell back into the water.

The sun dried them quickly. Several times A.C. got out of the canoe and swam ahead, pulling them by a rope he held in his teeth.

Lory had brought a big jug of wine. They got out and walked up into a meadow and drank from it whenever they became tired of paddling, which was often. At one stop, on the riverbank, Lory ran her fingers through A.C.'s hair. In six years, she would be forty. A crow flew past, low over the river. Farther upstream, they could see trout passing beneath the canoe, could see the bottom of the river, which was deep. Stones lined the river bottom, as if an old road lay beneath them.

On the way home, with A.C. at the wheel, they stopped for more cheeseburgers and had Cokes in the bottle with straws. They kept driving with the windows down. Their faces were not sunburned, but darker.

When A.C., Lory, and Lindsay got home and went into the house, the brothers were immediately happy to see the big man again, as always, but then, like small clouds, something crossed their faces and then vanished again, something unknown, perhaps confused.

The day before school started, Lory and A.C. paddled up to the farmhouse in Vermont. They were both sad, as if one of them were leaving and not ever coming back. Lory thought about another year of school. Tired before it even began, she sat on the stone wall with him, her head on his shoulder. He let her stay that way and did not try to cheer her up with stunts or tricks or feats of strength. The cattle in the field grazed right up to the edge of the stone wall, unafraid of Lory and A.C.

He rubbed the back of Lory's neck, held her close against him. He could be kind and tender, he could be considerate and thoughtful, he could even love her, but she wanted something else. He was afraid of this, and knew he was as common as coal in that respect. He also knew he was afraid of leaving, and of being alone.

A.C. was running out of money, so he took a paper route. He had no car, so he pulled the papers on a huge scraping rickshaw, fitting himself with a harness to pull it. It had no wheels and was really only a crude travois: two long poles with a sheet of plywood nailed to them, and little guardrails so that he could stack the papers high on it.

He delivered papers in the early afternoon. All through the neighborhoods he trotted, grimacing, pulling a half ton of paper slowly up the small hills, and then, like a creature from the heavens, like some cruel-eyed bird, he swooped down the hills, street gravel and rock rattling under the sled. He shouted and tossed papers like mad, glancing back over his shoulder with every throw to be sure that he was staying ahead of the weight of the sled, which was accelerating, trying to run him down. It was funny, and the people who lived at the bottom of a hill learned to listen for him, loved to watch him, to see if one day he might get caught.

But now it was lonely for A.C., with Jerry in his final year at school, playing football, and John coaching. Lindsay was back in school too, and Heck was still the principal. Only Louella stayed at home.

Usually A.C. finished his paper route by late afternoon, and then he would put the sled in the garage and hose himself off in the backyard, his chest red from where the harness had rubbed, his running shorts drenched with sweat. He'd hold the hose over his head and cool down. Louella would watch from the kitchen window, feeling lonely, but she was also cautious, a mother first.

Dripping, A.C. would turn the water off, coil the hose up, and sit at the picnic table silently, his back turned to the kitchen. Like a dog finished with his duties, he would wait until he could see Lory again, see all the siblings. Louella would watch him for a long time. She just couldn't be sure.

When Lory got home from school, riding on a fresh burst of energy at the idea of seeing him again, A.C. would jump up, shake sprays of water from his wet hair, and run to open the door for her. He kissed her delicately, and she would ask, teasing, "How was your day, dear?" Though it was all working out differently from how she had expected, she was fresher and happier than she had ever been.

The children at Lory's school were foul, craven, sunk without hope. She would resurrect one, get a glimmer of interest in one every now and then, but eventually it would all slide back; it had all been false—that faint progress, the improvement in attitude. Sometimes she hit her fist against the lockers after school. The desks with "I fucked Miss Iron" on them were still there, and the eyes of the male teachers were no better, saying the same thing. She was getting older, older, and each year she wondered if this was the year that the last of her youth would go away. It was a gauntlet, but she needed to stay close to Glens Falls. She had to keep going.

It was like traveling upriver at night in the canoe with him, up through the rapids, only it was like being one of the darkened iron statues rather than her live, loving self. It was like night all the time, this job, and in her dreams of it, there was never any sound, no promise, no future. She was in the wrong place, taking the wrong steps, and she knew—she could feel it as strongly as anything—that it took her too far away from him, teaching at Warrensburg each day, a place of darkness.

She was up until midnight every night, grading papers, preparing lesson plans, reading the barely legible scrawled essays of rage—"I wont to kil my sester, i wont to kil my bruthers"—and then she was up again at four or four thirty, rousing herself from the sleepy dream of her life. But A.C. was also up by then, making coffee for her.

When they kissed in the morning she'd be wearing a tattered, dingy robe and her owlish reading glasses. His hands would slide under her robe and find her warm beneath the fuzzy cloth. He wanted nothing else for either of them. There could be no improvement. He knew she wanted more, though, that she wanted to keep going.

They would take a short walk right before she left for school. By the time they got back, John and Jerry would be up. Jerry's clock radio played hard rock. John, with no worries, no responsibilities, sorted through the refrigerator for his carton of milk (biceps drawn on it with a Magic Marker) and got Jerry's carton out (a heart with an arrow through it, and the word "Mom" inside the heart). The brothers stood around and drank, swallowing the milk in long, cold gulps.

Watching A.C. and Lory grow closer was, to Louella, like the pull of winter, or like giving birth. Always, she thought about the one she had lost. Twenty years later, she had been sent a replacement. She wanted to believe that. She had not led a martyr's life, but she had worked hard, and miracles did happen.

It was true, she realized. She could make it be true by wanting it to be true.

She looked out her kitchen window at him, sitting at the picnic table with his back to her, facing the garden, the late-season roses. Sun came through the window, and she could see hummingbirds fly into the backyard, lured by the sweetness of the nectar she had put in the feeders.

Louella watched A.C. look around at the hummingbirds, staring at them for the longest time, like a simple animal. The birds were dancing flecks of color, flashes of shimmering emerald and cobalt. Louella saw a blur of orange in the garden, the cat racing across the yard, up onto the picnic table, then leaping into the air, legs outstretched. She saw the claws, and like a ballplayer the cat caught one of the hummingbirds in midair, came down with it, and tumbled and rolled.

Louella watched as A.C. ran to the cat, squeezed its neck gently, and lifted the limp hummingbird from the cat's mouth. The cat shivered, shook, and ran back into the garden. A.C. set the limp hummingbird down on the picnic table. The other hummingbirds were gone.

Louella went into the backyard. The little bird lay still with its eyes shut, a speck of blood on its throat like a tiny ruby. The glitter of its green back like scales.

"That damn cat," Louella said, but as they watched, the hummingbird began to stir, ruffled its feathers, looked around, and flew away.

Each morning after the others had left, A.C. would sit at the picnic table a bit longer. Then he would come inside and tell Louella that he was going to Vermont for a while. Always, politely, he asked her if she needed anything, or if she cared to go with him for the ride, and always she refused, saying she had things to do. Always, afterward, she wished she had said yes, wondered what it would be like, wondered what his stone farmhouse looked like. But there were boundaries to be maintained; she could not let go and say yes. So A.C. would lift the canoe over his head and walk through the neighborhood, out across the main road and down to the river, leaving her alone.

What A.C. was working on in Vermont was a barn, for throwing the discus during the winter months. He wanted to perfect his throw, to make John and Jerry happy. He had no more money left, so he ripped down abandoned barns, saving even the nails from the old boards. He built his barn in the woods, on the side of the hill behind his farmhouse. It was more like a bowling alley than anything.

He had planned it to be 300 feet long. He climbed high into

the trees to nail on the tall roof that would keep the snow out. There was not enough wood to build sides for the barn; mostly it was like a tent, a long, open-walled shed. He had built up the sides with stones about three feet high to keep the drifts from blowing in. It would be cold, but it would be free of snow.

He cut the trees down with an ax, to build the throwing lane, and then cut them into lengths to be dragged away. He was building a strip of empty space in the heart of the woods; it ran for a hundred yards and then stopped. He kept it a secret from the whole family, and was greatly pleased with its progress as the fall went on.

The air inside the throwing room felt purified, denser somehow. It had the special scents of the woods. He burned all the stumps, leveled the ground with a shovel and hoe, and made a throwing ring out of river stones. The rafters overhead reminded him of the church he'd gone to once with the Irons: the high ceiling, the beams, keeping the hard rains and snows out, protecting them, but also distancing them from what it was they were after.

He would work on the barn all morning, leave in time to get home and do his paper route, and still be back at the house before anyone else got there. Sometimes Louella would be out shopping or doing other errands. He would sit at the picnic table and wait for the sound of Lory's car.

Feathery snow fell on the Hudson highlands on the third of October, a Friday night. They were all walking to the movie theater in the mall, A.C. and Lory holding hands, Lindsay running ahead of them. It was too early for real snow.

The brothers were as full of spirit as they had been all year. It was as if they were fourteen. They danced, did their discus spins in crowded places, ending their imaginary releases with wild shouts that drew some spectators and scared others away, then all three of them spun and whooped—John's and Jerry's spins still more polished than A.C.'s, but A.C.'s impressive also, if for no reason other than his great size. Soon there was a large audience, clapping and cheering as if they were Russian table dancers. (A.C. pictured it being late spring still, or early summer, before he had met them: back when he was still dancing with the cows on his back, a sport he had enjoyed, and which he secretly missed, though the brothers had asked him to stop doing it, saying it would throw his rhythm off. He missed the freedom of it, the lack of borders and rules, but did not want to hurt their feelings, did not want them to know he thought discus throwing was slightly inferior, so he'd done as they said, though still, he missed dancing and whirling with the cattle over his shoulders.)

Lory shrieked and hid her eyes with her hands, embarrassed, and Lindsay blushed her crimson color, but was petrified, unable to move, and she watched them, amazed as always. Lory's fingers were digging into Lindsay's arm; Lindsay smiled bravely through her embarrassment, and was happy for Lory. Everyone around them in the mall kept clapping and stamping their feet, while outside, the first snow came down.

A.C. gave the money from the paper route to Louella and Heck, and as he made more money, he tried to give that to them as well, but they wouldn't hear of it. So he bought things and gave them to Lory. He bought whatever he saw, if he happened to be thinking about her: a kitten, bouquets of flowers, jewelry, an NFL football, a smoked turkey.

She was flattered and excited the first few times he brought something home, but soon became alarmed at the volume of things, and eventually asked him to stop. Then she had to explain to him what she really wanted, what really made her happy, and he was embarrassed, felt a fool for not having realized it before, for having tried to substitute. It was like throwing the discus from his hip rather than with the spin, he realized.

They went out in the canoe again that Saturday night, on Lake George. It was a still night at first, calm and chilly, and the full moon was so bright they could see the shore, even from far out on the water. They could see each other's faces, each other's eyes; it was like some dream-lit daylight, hard and blue and silver, with the sound of waves lapping against the side of their small boat. They were cold, but they undressed anyway. They wanted to get close, as close as they could; they wanted to be all there was in the world, the only thing left.

He covered her with the blanket they had brought, and kept her warm with that and with himself. After making love to her he fell asleep, dreaming, in the warmth of the blanket and the roll of the boat, that he was still in her, that they were still loving, and that they always would be.

"You were smiling," she said when he woke around midnight. She'd been watching him all night. She'd held him, too, sometimes pressing him so tightly against her breast that she was sure he'd wake up, but he had slept on. "What were you smiling about?"

"You," he said sleepily. "I was thinking about you."

It was the right answer. She was so happy.

One weekend, Lory's school had a Halloween dance. A girl had been raped after the dance last year, and several of the teachers' cars had had their tires slashed and their radio antennas snapped. A small fire had been set inside the school and had scorched the walls. Lory was chaperoning this year. She went up there with John and Jerry and A.C., and stayed near them the whole time.

The brothers dwarfed Lory like bodyguards; she was almost hidden whenever she was in their midst. The young thugs and bullies did not attempt to reach out from the crowd and squeeze her breasts, as they sometimes did on dares, and the male teachers, married and unmarried, treated her with respect. The four of them sat in the bleachers and watched the dance, listening to the loud music until midnight. There was no mischief, and they were relieved when it was time to go.

They felt almost guilty, driving home to warmth and love. They rode in silence, thinking their own thoughts, back down to Glens Falls, whose lights they could see below, not twinkling as if with distance but shining steadily, a constant glow, because they were so close.

Geese, heading south late in the year, stragglers. A.C. worked on his barn during the mild sunny days of November. He could feel more snow coming, could feel it the way an animal can. The hair on his arms and legs was getting thicker, the way it had in Colorado in past falls. The barn reminded him of the one that had been out there—the hay barn. That was where she had done it.

The throwing barn was almost finished. It was narrow, so his throws would have to be accurate. There could be no wildness, or he would wreck the place he had built. He would teach himself to throw straight.

He finished the barn in mid-November, as the big flakes arrived, the second snow of the season. Now the snows that came would not go away, not until the end of winter. He brought the brothers up to see the barn, to show them how they could keep training together, how they could keep throwing all through the winter, even with snow banked all around them, and they were delighted.

"This is the best year of my life," Jerry said unexpectedly.

A.C. bought a metal detector, and when throws did not travel perfectly straight—the barn was only thirty feet wide—the brothers and A.C. had to search in the snow, listening for the rapid signal that told them they were getting near. They used old metal discs now, which flew two or three feet farther in the cold air. The brothers ate more than ever, and trained harder.

There was a stone wall at the end of the barn, the 300-foot mark, stacked all the way to the rafters and chinked with mud and sand and grass. A.C. had lodged a discus in it once, had skipped a few of them against its base. Hitting that mark was magical, unimaginable; it required witchcraft, an alteration of reality.

It took the brothers and A.C. about sixty seconds to walk 300 feet. A minute away—and unobtainable, or almost.

Sometimes the throws went too far off into the woods, and the discs were lost for good. Other times, they went too high and crashed through the rafters, like violent cannonballs, cruel iron seeking to destroy.

"Forget it," John would say gruffly whenever A.C. threw outside the barn. They'd hear the snapping, tearing sound of branches being broken and then the *whack!* of the discus striking a tree trunk. John would already be reaching for another disc, though, handing it to him. "Come on, come on, shake it off. Past history. Over and done with. Shake it off."

Past history. No harm done. These were sweet words to A.C. His eyes grew moist. He wanted to believe that. He wanted to make good this time.

As the winter deepened, they set their goals harder and farther. John and Jerry wanted to throw 221 feet, and A.C. wanted to be able to throw 300 feet on any given throw, at will.

And he wanted Lory. He wanted to build fences, to take care, protect. Sometimes while everyone was at school, Louella would decide that she just couldn't keep away any longer. She would challenge herself to be brave, to accept him without really knowing whether he was hers or not. She would ride in the canoe with him up to the barn, to watch him throw. She had come over to his side, and believed in him, and she did that. Louella wanted to know about his past, but A.C. simply wouldn't tell her.

A.C. built a fire for Louella in the barn, and she sat on a stump and sipped coffee while he threw. His spin was getting better. It was an imitation of her sons', she could tell, but it was starting to get some fluidity to it, some life, some creativity. Louella enjoyed watching him train. His clumsiness did not worry her, because she could tell he was working at it and overcoming it. She was even able to smile when the discus soared up through the rafters, letting a sprinkle of snow pour into the barn from above—yet another hole punched through the roof, one more hole of many, the snow sifting down like fine powder.

They were alarming, those wild throws, but she found herself trusting him. Secretly she liked the wild throws: she was fascinated by the strength and force behind them, the utter lack of control. It was like standing at the edge of a volcano, looking down. She moved a little closer to the fire. She was fifty-eight, and was seeing things she'd never seen before, feeling things she'd never felt. Life was still a mystery. He had made her daughter happy again.

"Keep your head back," Louella would caution whenever she saw that his form was too terribly off. "Keep your feet spread. Your feet were too close together." She knew enough about form to tell how it differed from her other sons'.

The whole family came for Thanksgiving: cousins and moved-away aunts, little babies, uncles, and nieces. Everything flowed. A.C. was a good fit; it was as if he'd always been there. Passing the turkey, telling jokes, teasing Lindsay about a boyfriend; laughter and warmth inside the big house.

The roads iced over. There was the sound of studded snow tires outside, and of clanking chains. Football all day on television, and more pie, more cider. Then Thanksgiving passed and they were on into December, the Christmas season, with old black-and-white movies on television late at night and Lory on her holiday break from school. Everyone was home, and he was firmly in their center, her center.

He was in a spin of love and asked her to marry him. "Yes," she said, laughing, remembering last year's sadness and the crazy lost hope of it, never dreaming or knowing that he had been out there, moving toward her.

In her dreams, in the months preceding the wedding, she saw images of summer, of June coming around again. She and her mother stood in a large field, with cattle grazing near the trees. In the field were great boulders and fieldstones left over from another age, a time of glaciers and ice, of great floods.

And in the dream, she and her mother leaned into the boulders, rolling them, moving them out of the field, making the field pure and green. They built a stone wall out of the boulders, all around the field, and some of them were too large to move. Lory gritted her teeth and pushed harder, straining, trying to move them all. Then she would wake up and be by his side, by his warmth, and realize that she had been pushing against him, trying to get him out of bed. That could not be done, and she'd laugh, put her arms around as much of him as she could, and bury her face in him. Then she would get up after a while, unable to return to sleep.

She'd dress, put on her snow boots, go to the garage, and pick up one of the discuses, holding it with both hands, feeling the worn smoothness, the coldness, and the magic of it—magic, Lory believed, because he had touched it. Certain that no one was watching, that no one could ever find out, she would go into the front yard bundled up in woolens and a parka, and under the blue cast of the streetlight she'd crouch and then whirl, spinning around and around, and throw the discus as far as she could, in whatever direction it happened to go. She'd shout, almost roar, and watch it sink into the soft new snow, jumping up and down afterward when she threw well and was pleased with her throw.

Then she would wade out to where she had seen the discus disappear, kneel down, and dig for it with her hands. She'd carry it back to the garage, slip it into the box with the others, and finally she'd be able to sleep, growing warm again in bed with him.

In the spring, before the wedding, after the snows melted and the river began to warm—the river in which A.C. had first seen and swum up to his brothers—he began to swim again, but with Lory this year.

A.C. would fasten a rope to the harness around his chest and tie the other end of it to the bumper of her car before leaping into the river from a high rock and being washed down through the rapids.

Then he would swim upriver until his shoulders ached, until even he was too tired to lift his head, and was nearly drowning. Lory would leap into the car then, start it, and ease up the hill, pulling him like a limp wet rag through the rapids he'd been fighting, farther up the river until he was in the stone-bottomed shallows. She'd park the car, set the emergency brake, jump out, and run back down to get him.

Like a fireman, she'd pull him the rest of the way out of the river, splashing knee-deep in the water, helping him up, putting his arm around her tiny shoulders. Somehow they'd stagger up into the rocks and trees along the shore. He'd lie on his back and gasp, looking up at the sky and the tops of the trees, and smelling the scent of pines. They would lie in the sun, drenched, exhausted, until their clothes were almost dry, and then they would back the car down and do it again.

He liked being saved. He needed her. And she needed him. Closer and closer she'd pull him, reeling in the wet rope, dragging him up on shore, bending over and kissing his wet lips until his eyes fluttered, bringing him back to life every time.

Ben Marcus is the author of *Notable American Women* and *The Age of Wire and String*. His stories have appeared in *Harper's, The Paris Review, McSweeney's, Conjunctions, Tin House,* and elsewhere. The recipient of three Pushcart Prizes, a Whiting Award, and a National Endowment for the Arts grant, he is an Associate Professor in the School of the Arts at Columbia University and lives in New York City.

Acknowledgments

Many writers, editors, and readers offered guidance and insight during the preparation of this book, either directly or through their own innovative work, which exposed me to writers I might not otherwise have known. I would like to thank Ben Metcalf, Rebecca Wolff and the editors at *Fence*, Brian Evenson, Jonathan Lethem, Ryan Bartelmay, Nathalie Schulhofer, Heidi Julavits, George Plimpton, Gordon Lish, Dave Eggers, Binnie Kirshenbaum, David Hyde, Bill Henderson, Rick Moody, Aimee Bender, Matthew Derby, Denise Shannon, Marty Asher, and Robert Coover.